PENGUIN BOOKS

Warrior of Rome III: Lion of the Sun

Praise for the bestselling *Warrior of Rome* series:

'An exceptionally gifted storyteller, drawing on prodigious learning'
Tim Severin, author of the *Viking* trilogy

'The best sort of red-blooded historical fiction – solidly based on a
profound understanding of what it meant to be alive in a particular
time and place' Andrew Taylor, author of *The American Boy*

'Harry Sidebottom's epic tale starts with a chilling assassination
and goes on, and up, from there'
Professor Mary Beard, Chair of Classics, University of Cambridge

'I don't think I've ever experienced antiquity so directly: the
brutality, the directness of expression and feeling, the
deep bonds formed amid unmitigated violence'
Professor David Konstan, Professor of Classics, Brown University

'A well-constructed, well-paced and gripping account' *TLS*

'A vivid, racy and gripping novel . . . from a major scholar who
happens also to be a brilliant master of fiction'
Dr Jas Elsner, Fellow of Archaeology and Classical Art,
University of Oxford

Dr Harry Sidebottom teaches classical history at the University of Oxford, where he is a Fellow of St Benet's Hall and a lecturer at Lincoln College. He has an international reputation as a scholar, having published widely on ancient warfare, classical art and the cultural history of the Roman Empire. Originally from Newmarket in Suffolk, he now lives with his wife and two sons in Woodstock, near Oxford.

Lion of the Sun follows top-five bestsellers *Fire in the East* and *King of Kings* in the epic grand narrative *Warrior of Rome* – a story of empire, of heroes, of treachery, of courage and, most of all, a story of brutal, bloody warfare.

Visit www.harrysidebottom.co.uk for more info.

Warrior of Rome

PART III

Lion of the Sun

DR HARRY SIDEBOTTOM

PENGUIN BOOKS

PENGUIN BOOKS

Published by the Penguin Group
Penguin Books Ltd, 80 Strand, London WC2R ORL, England
Penguin Group (USA), Inc., 375 Hudson Street, New York, New York 10014, USA
Penguin Group (Canada), 90 Eglinton Avenue East, Suite 700, Toronto, Ontario, Canada M4P 2Y3
(a division of Pearson Penguin Canada Inc.)
Penguin Ireland, 25 St Stephen's Green, Dublin 2, Ireland (a division of Penguin Books Ltd)
Penguin Group (Australia), 250 Camberwell Road, Camberwell, Victoria 3124, Australia
(a division of Pearson Australia Group Pty Ltd)
Penguin Books India Pvt Ltd, 11 Community Centre, Panchsheel Park, New Delhi – 110 017, India
Penguin Group (NZ), 67 Apollo Drive, Rosedale, Auckland 0632, New Zealand
(a division of Pearson New Zealand Ltd)
Penguin Books (South Africa) (Pty) Ltd, 24 Sturdee Avenue, Rosebank,
Johannesburg 2196, South Africa

Penguin Books Ltd, Registered Offices: 80 Strand, London WC2R ORL, England

www.penguin.com

First published by Michael Joseph 2010
Published in Penguin Books 2011

1

Copyright © Dr Harry Sidebottom, 2010

The moral right of the author has been asserted

Set in Garamond MT Std 12.5/14.75 pt
Typeset by Palimpsest Book Production Limited, Falkirk, Stirlingshire
Printed in Great Britain by Clays Ltd, St Ives plc

A CIP catalogue record for this book is available from the British Library

ISBN: 978-0-141-03231-3

www.greenpenguin.co.uk

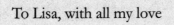
To Lisa, with all my love

Contents

The Roman Empire in AD260–261

.... Provincial borders

1. *ALPES MARITIMAE*
2. *ALPES COTTIAE*
3. *ALPES GRAIAE*

Dvina

Dnepr

Heruli

Goths

arcomanni

Quadi

Vandals

Gepidae

Iazyges

PANNONIA INFERIOR

Mursa

DACIA

Carpi

Black Sea

ARMENIA

rmium

Naisus

MOESIA INFERIOR

Movae

PERSIAN EMPIRE

MOESIA SUPERIOR

Serdica

THRACE

Byzantium

BITHYNIA PONTUS

GALATIA

CAPPADOCIA

Tigris

MACEDONIA

Cyzicus

ASIA

MESOPOTAMIA

EPIRUS

Euphrates

ACHAEA

CILICIA

Antioch

SYRIA COELE

Athens

Palmyra

LYCIA PAMPHYLIA

SYRIA PHONICE

ean

Sea

SYRIA PALESTINA

Alexandria

ARABIA

CRENAICA

EGYPT

Nile

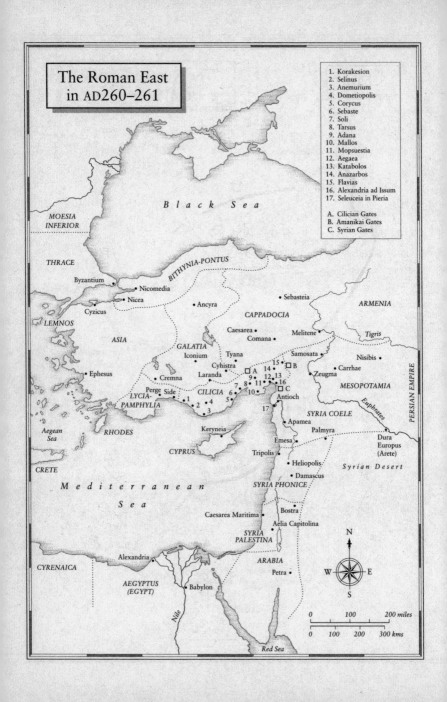

The Roman East in AD260–261

1. Korakesion
2. Selinus
3. Anemurium
4. Dometiopolis
5. Corycus
6. Sebaste
7. Soli
8. Tarsus
9. Adana
10. Mallos
11. Mopsuestia
12. Aegaea
13. Katabolos
14. Anazarbos
15. Flavias
16. Alexandria ad Issum
17. Seleuceia in Pieria

A. Cilician Gates
B. Amanikai Gates
C. Syrian Gates

Black Sea

MOESIA INFERIOR

THRACE

Byzantium
Nicomedia
Nicea
Cyzicus
LEMNOS

BITHYNIA-PONTUS

Sebasteia

Ancyra

CAPPADOCIA

ARMENIA

ASIA

Caesarea
Comana
Melitene

Tigris

Nisibis

GALATIA
Iconium
Tyana

Samosata

Carrhae
Zeugma

Ephesus

Cremna
Cyhistra
Laranda
A 14 15 B
9 12,13 16
7 8 11 C
6 10 Antioch

MESOPOTAMIA

Perge Side
LYCIA-
PAMPHYLIA
1 2 4 3
5
CILICIA

PERSIAN EMPIRE

Euphrates

17

SYRIA COELE

Apamea

Keryneia

Palmyra

Dura
Europus
(Arete)

*Aegean
Sea*

RHODES

CYPRUS

Emesa

Tripolis

Heliopolis

Syrian Desert

CRETE

*Mediterranean
Sea*

Damascus

SYRIA PHONICE

Caesarea Maritima

Bostra

Aelia Capitolina

SYRIA
PALESTINA

ARABIA

N

W — E

S

CYRENAICA

Alexandria

Babylon

AEGYPTUS
(EGYPT)

Petra

0   100   200 miles

0   100   200   300 kms

Nile

Red Sea

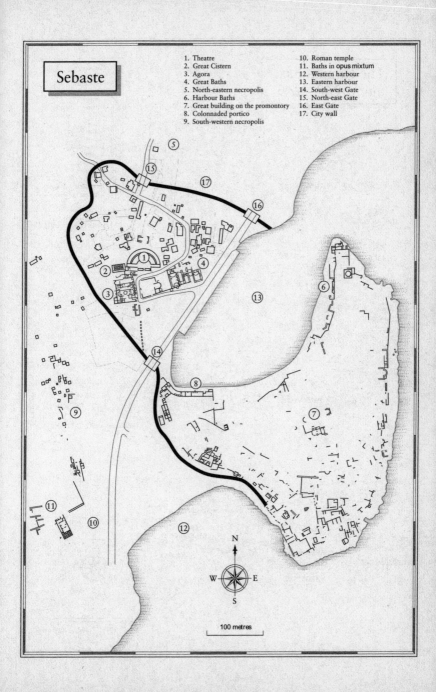

Sebaste

1. Theatre
2. Great Cistern
3. Agora
4. Great Baths
5. North-eastern necropolis
6. Harbour Baths
7. Great building on the promontory
8. Colonnaded portico
9. South-western necropolis
10. Roman temple
11. Baths in opus mixtum
12. Western harbour
13. Eastern harbour
14. South-west Gate
15. North-east Gate
16. East Gate
17. City wall

N
W   E
S

100 metres

Gone is the trust to be placed in oaths; I cannot
understand if the gods you swore by then no
longer rule, or if men live by new standards of
what is right?

Euripides, *Medea*, 490–94

Prologue

The emperor blinked as he stepped out into the bright sunshine. He seemed to wince as the court official called out his full title in Latin. 'Imperator Caesar Publius Licinius Valerianus Augustus, *Pius Felix, Pater Patriae, Germanicus Maximus, Invictus, Restitutor Orbis*'. At a sign, a horse was led forward. Its bridle shone with silver and gold, and its trappings were imperial purple. Needing no prompting, the elderly emperor walked to where the horse waited. As so many times before in the last few days, he got down on one knee, then the other. With a momentary pause, which might be excused in someone his age, he got down on all fours, his elbows in the dust. What seemed an age passed. The horse shifted and exhaled through its lips, the noise loud in the quiet camp. The sun was hot on the emperor's back.

The sound of another man walking towards the horse broke the near-silence. Out of the corner of his eye, the emperor could see two purple boots. Deliberately, the left one was raised and placed on his neck. As many times before, its owner let some of his weight come down through the boot before he spoke.

'This is the truth, not what the Romans depict in their

I

sculptures and paintings,' he declared, then swung himself into the saddle, his weight hard upon his imperial mounting block. 'I am the Mazda-worshipping divine Shapur, King of Kings of Aryans and non-Aryans, of the race of the gods, son of the Mazda-worshipping divine Ardashir, King of Kings of the Aryans, of the race of the gods, grandson of the King Papak, of the house of Sasan; I am the lord of the Aryan nation. You mighty, look on my works and tremble.'

Ballista, the Roman general from beyond the borders in the far north, lay full length in the dust and watched. His reluctant *proskynesis*, or posture of adoration, was enforced by guards and the threat of a beating or worse and echoed by the rest of the Roman high command. Successianus the Praetorian Prefect, Cledonius the *ab Admissionibus*, Camillus the commander of Legio VI Gallicana – everyone of importance who had been with the field army – they were all there. The world had been turned upside down, the whole cosmos was shaken. For the first time, a Roman emperor had been captured by the barbarians. Ballista could feel the outrage and horror of his *commilitiones* as they were forced to witness the humiliation of Valerian – the pious, lucky, invincible emperor of the Romans, the restorer of the world – on his knees and dressed as a slave.

Four days earlier, Valerian had been captured. He had been betrayed by the companion he most trusted, the *Comes Sacrarum Largitionum* Macrianus the Lame. The Count of the Sacred Largess had arranged everything. His younger son, Quietus, had led the aged emperor and his army into a trap and then abandoned them.

Ballista, belly to the ground, furious in his abasement,

thought of the repulsive youth Quietus, by now safely back in the Roman city of Samosata, and he repeated to himself a vow he had made twice before: *One day, maybe not soon, but one day, I will kill you.*

Shapur caracoled his mount, its hooves plunging and stamping dangerously close to the elderly man on the ground. Then the Sassanid King of Kings paced his horse along the line of his own courtiers, noblemen and priests and rode away, laughing.

Slowly, heavily, Valerian began to get to his feet. The butts of spears, freely wielded, encouraged the *Comites Augusti* to do the same.

As he hauled himself up, Ballista looked at the Sassanid courtiers. There, prominent among the priests, was the Persian youth whom Ballista had known as Bagoas when the boy had been his slave. How the wheel of fortune turns. Was the youth smiling at him behind that black beard?

The sight of Bagoas turned Ballista's thoughts to his *familia*. Had his ex-slaves Calgacus, Maximus and Demetrius made it to safety? Were they now also safe in Samosata? Or were they already on the road to Antioch? Antioch, where Ballista's two young sons and wife waited, all unaware. The pain of thinking of them was almost unbearable. Ballista spoke in his heart to the high god of his northern youth: *Allfather, Death-blinder, Deep Hood, Fulfiller of Desire, Woden-born as I am, hear my prayer: I will give whatever is necessary, do whatever it takes, but let me return to them – return to them whatever the cost.*

PART ONE

Captivus

(The East, Spring–Summer AD260)

'What is it like to lose one's native land? Is it a grievous loss?'

Euripides, *Phoenissae*, 387–8

I

Maximus lay motionless watching the Persians. They were in front of and below him, towards the middle of the small upland meadow where three paths came together. They were not above forty paces away. He could see them clearly: in the pale moonlight, men and horses were solid, dark-grey silhouettes. There were twenty-one Sassanid cavalrymen. Maximus had counted them several times.

The Sassanids were confident. They had dismounted and were talking quietly. They were unavoidably in the way. Maximus raised his eyes to check the position of the sickle-shaped, three-night-old moon. There was not much of the night left. With northern Mesopotamia overrun with Persian patrols, Maximus and the others had to be safe behind the walls of Zeugma by dawn. There was no time to retrace their steps or to cast about for another path which ran east–west through the high country. If the Persians did not move on within half an hour, the Romans would have to try and fight their way through. It did not promise well. They were outnumbered three to one. Demetrius had never been much of a one in a fight, and old Calgacus was wounded. Sure, but it did not promise well at all.

Moving slowly, hardly moving his head a fraction, Maximus looked over at Calgacus. The old Caledonian was lying on his left side, favouring his bandaged right arm. His great domed, balding skull blended well with the white rocks. Maximus was fond of Calgacus. They had been together a long time – nineteen years, since Maximus had been bought in as a slave bodyguard to the *familia* of Ballista. Of course, Calgacus had been with Ballista since the latter's childhood among the Angles of Germania. Calgacus was a sound man. Maximus was fond of him, although not as fond as he would be of a good hunting dog.

Maximus studied his companion, the dark lines of his wrinkled forehead and the black pools of his sunken cheeks. Truth be told, Maximus was worried. Sure, Calgacus was tough. But he had seemed old nearly twenty years before. Now he was wounded, and the last four days must have taken it out of the old bastard.

Four days earlier, they had watched Ballista ride out from the trapped army, one of the five *comites* accompanying the emperor Valerian to his ill-fated meeting with the Sassanid King of Kings Shapur. They had done what their *patronus* Ballista had commanded. As the imperial party rode west, they had crossed the perimeter to the south and doubled back behind the eastern slope of the hill. The small group of horsemen – Maximus, Calgacus and Demetrius, Ballista's Greek secretary, along with eight Dalmatian troopers – had made no great distance north when they were challenged by a Sassanid picket. Maximus, the only one who could speak Persian, had shouted out the password, which Ballista had discovered from Quietus, the traitor who had led the Roman army into the trap: *Peroz-Shapur*.

The Sassanids were suspicious. They had been told to let through only one party of Roman horsemen heading north and shouting, 'The victory of Shapur', and one had already passed. Yet they drew back, their dark eyes scowling, their hands on their weapons.

Maximus and the others had ridden on. Not too fast, so as not to look as if they were fleeing; not too slowly as to appear to be flaunting themselves. Against every instinct for self-preservation, they kept to a gentle canter.

Behind them, a lone rider, baggy clothes flapping, horse kicking up puffs of dust, had raced across the plain. He spurred up to the Persian picket. There was gesticulating, shouting. The easterners kicked their boots into the flanks of their horses. They gave tongue to a high, ululating cry. The chase was on.

Pushing hard, Maximus and the others had galloped out of the valley of tears. They did not see Valerian, Ballista and the other *comites* hauled from their mounts and, dusty and bloodied, hustled away into captivity. They had no time to spare a glance for the remainder of the Roman field army of the east, surrounded and hopeless on the hill. They had a large party of Sassanid light cavalry only just over two bowshots behind them. They rode hard to the hills of the north-west.

Darkness had saved them. It seemed an eon coming, then all at once it was there. A dark, dark night; the night before the new moon. Calgacus, whom Ballista had chosen to be in charge, had ordered them to double-back to the south-east. After a time, he had found a place for them to lie up. The land here was rolling hills, sometimes bunching into mountains. On the flank of one of these lay a hollow, deep and wide enough to hide eleven men and horses. There was a small stream nearby. As he rubbed down Pale Horse, the mount that Ballista had entrusted to him, Maximus approved of the Caledonian's choice. His hands working hard, he tried not to think about the grey gelding's owner; once *his* owner, now his *patronus*, the friend he had left behind.

Maximus had been woken the following morning by the sound of goat bells. Despite the many years since he had been taken as a slave out of his native Hibernia and brought to the southlands, goat bells somehow still sounded exotic. Although alien, they were usually reassuring, speaking of a gentle, timeless Mediterranean order. That morning, they had not been. They were drawing closer.

Looking round, Maximus saw that everyone other than old Calgacus was still asleep. The Caledonian was stretched out on the ground, peering over the lip of their hiding place. Maximus had scrambled up next to him and risked a quick look over the top. It was a small flock, no more than twenty head, strung out behind a lead animal. They were coming to the stream to drink. The purposeful tread of the leader would take them right by the hollow, would give the goatherd a perfect view of the fugitives.

Maximus had been surprised when Calgacus gestured for him to go to the far end of the hollow. The goats were close, the tinkling of their bells loud. As Maximus moved past, two or three of the Dalmatians stirred. He motioned them to silence. In position now, he looked back at Calgacus.

Unhurriedly, Calgacus rose to his feet and stepped up over the lip of the hollow. He stood still, hands empty by his sides.

Pulling himself up, Maximus peeked over the top. Through the legs of the animals, he saw the goatherd. He was an elderly man with a huge beard and the air of a patriarch. He was leaning on a staff, calmly regarding Calgacus. The goatherd's untroubled manner suggested that ugly old Caledonians or even daemons popped up out of every other gully he passed.

'Good day, grandfather,' said Calgacus.

For a time the goatherd did not respond. Maximus had begun to wonder if he did not speak Greek. He was wearing baggy eastern-style trousers, but then, everyone in Mesopotamia did.

'Good day, my child,' the local replied at last. Maximus felt an urge to laugh building inside him.

'Is it safe to be out with the goats with the Sassanids all around?'

The goatherd considered Calgacus's question, weighing it up. 'I keep to the higher hills. The goats must drink. If the Persians see me, they may not kill me. What can you do?'

The local had his back almost completely to Maximus. Now the latter saw the point of Calgacus's silent instruction. Quietly, he stood. As Calgacus glanced over, he touched the hilt of his sword. There was a pause before the Caledonian gave a tiny shake of his head.

'May the gods hold their hands over you, grandfather,' said Calgacus.

With due deliberation, the goatherd turned his patriarchal

gaze first on Maximus then back to Calgacus. 'I think they may do already.'

The staff tapped the lead goat on the rump. The herder turned to go. Above the swelling tinkle of bells, he called back, 'May the gods hold their hands over you, my children.'

Maximus stepped over to Calgacus. 'If they catch him, the reptiles will torture him. Not many men could keep a secret under that.'

The old Caledonian shrugged. 'What can you do?'

Maximus laughed. 'How true, *my child*, how true.'

'Shut the fuck up, and take the next watch,' replied Calgacus affably.

They had saddled up at dusk. With the true night came thousands of stars and the thinnest of thin new moons. According to the ways of his people, Maximus made a wish on the new moon, a wish he could never divulge, for certain to do so would spoil its purpose.

Calgacus had led them to the north-west. With two riders out in front, they took it easy. There could not be many miles to the Euphrates. Unless the Sassanids intervened, they would be in Samosata well before dawn.

They had been travelling for some hours, their hopes rising, when, as the malignant gods willed it, the intervention came. A Persian challenge, loud in the night. A cry of alarm, then further shouts in an eastern-sounding language. Calgacus circled his arm, wheeling the tiny column; everyone booted their horses. All around was the rattle of hooves, the ringing of equipment and, from behind, the roar of pursuit.

Maximus had sensed as much as seen the solid black

12

line of an arrow as it shot past him, accelerating ahead into the night. A second later, he had heard the *wisp* of an arrow's passing. Momentarily, he wondered if it was another unseen arrow or the sound of the first. Shrugging this germ of a huge idea out of his mind, he slung his shield over his back. As he rode, it banged painfully into his neck and back. At this short range, an arrow would probably punch clean through its linden boards, but somehow its weight and discomfort made him feel a little better.

They galloped on, over the pale, rolling hills, round dark, upthrust mountains, past gloomy vineyards and orchards, through burnt hamlets and by abandoned farms. They crashed through small, upland streams; their beds stony, the water no more than hoof-high.

It is hard to outride men in fear for their lives. The clamour of pursuit had dropped back, faded to inaudibility beneath the sounds of their own movement. One more rise, and Calgacus signalled a halt. All the men dropped to the ground, taking the weight from their horses' backs.

Maximus looked round, counting. There were too few men in the pale light, just seven of them. Four of the Dalmatian troopers were gone. Had they been killed? Had they been taken? Or had they chosen a different path, either heroically, to lead the Sassanids away, or out of ignorance and terror? Neither Maximus nor anyone else in the party would ever know. They had vanished in the night.

Calgacus had handed his reins to the Greek boy Demetrius and was walking back to the brow of the hill. Hurriedly, Maximus did the same. Keeping low, they gazed back the way they had come.

The Sassanids had not given up. Not much above half a mile to the north, strung out at no great interval, torches flared across the hills.

'Persistent fuckers,' said Maximus.

'Aye,' agreed Calgacus. 'Having lost sight of us, they have thrown out a cordon to sweep the country.'

In silence the two men watched the easterners ride over the hills towards them. The undulating line of torches resembled a great snake coiling sideways, a huge mythical *draco*.

'If they want to stay in touch with each other, they will have to go slowly,' said Maximus. 'It will be fine for us.'

'Maybe,' said Calgacus, 'but if they get close we will try the trick Ballista used the time we were chased before the siege of Arete.'

Memories jumbled into Maximus's thoughts: waiting in a stand of trees down by the river, the smell of mud, a scatter of stones, a desperate fight in a gully.

'When Romulus died,' said Calgacus patiently.

Maximus was grateful for the hint. Although the Hibernian had a high opinion of himself, it did not run to priding himself on his powers of recall. On that occasion, Ballista had tied a lantern to a packhorse. His standard bearer Romulus was to lead the Persians away while the rest of Ballista's men rode to safety. After a time, Romulus was to turn the packhorse loose and make his escape, but something had gone wrong. He must have left it too late. Antigonus had come across Romulus a few days later – or what was left of him – staked out and mutilated. It had not ended well for Antigonus either: not long afterwards, a stone shot by a siege engine had taken his head off. Now,

14

Maximus felt a rush of pity for his companions who had been lost along the way. He steadied himself. As he had sometimes heard Ballista say: *Men die in war. It happens.*

The seven remaining horsemen had pushed south. They rode hard, but not flat out. The stars wheeled and the moon tracked across the sky. There was no need for dangerous tricks with lanterns. Gradually, the lights of the Sassanids had fallen behind. After a time they could be seen no more.

Calgacus had kept them moving, when they could, avoiding the skyline, always aiming south-west. When dawn's rosy fingers showed in the sky, the elderly Caledonian had begun to hunt for a place to lie up. Eventually, when the sun was almost up, he turned aside into an olive grove which ran up the flank of a hill. They had dismounted and pushed through straggly vines and up under the trees.

The dappled sunlight was warm on Maximus's face when Calgacus shook him awake. Unnecessarily, the Caledonian had put his finger to his lips. Silently, Maximus rose and followed him to a space where the gnarled silver-grey trunks were more widely spaced. They looked down to the valley floor.

One thin column of dust followed by a wide, dense one. A solitary rider was being hunted down by at least thirty horsemen. No one in the olive grove spoke. In the randomness of his fear, the hunted man was riding directly towards them.

'The eye of Cronus is on us,' muttered Demetrius. The others said nothing. As the fugitive drew closer, they saw that he wore a light-blue tunic.

'Gods below,' said Maximus, 'it's one of ours.'

The lost Dalmatian trooper was almost in arrow shot when his horse stumbled. The man lost his seat, slid forward down the animal's neck. Trying to regain its balance, the horse plunged. The trooper fell. His momentum made him bounce once, high in the air, then, limbs flailing, he crashed to the ground. He scrabbled to his feet, his pursuers surging all around him.

There was a moment of stillness: the Dalmatian stood, the Sassanids in a ring around him. The trooper's horse ran away to the right. One of the Sassanids followed to catch it.

Slowly, almost apologetically, the trooper drew his sword. He threw it down. The mounted men laughed. One spurred forward. The trooper turned, started to run. A long blade flashed in the sun. There was a scream, a spray of bright blood, and the Dalmatian fell. The Sassanid cantered back into the circle. The wounded man got to his feet again. Another horseman rushed in. Again the flash of a blade. More blood, and again the man went down.

Maximus looked across at Calgacus. The Caledonian shook his head.

After the third pass, the Dalmatian remained on the ground, curled up, his arms covering his head. Their sport spoilt, the Sassanids called out insults, imprecations. Their prey remained down in the reddened dust.

The Sassanid who had gone to the right returned, leading the trooper's horse.

One in the ring of horsemen called an order, and the men unslung their bows. Another word of command and they drew and released. Almost as one, the arrowheads thumped into the Dalmatian's body.

The watchers on the hill had not moved.

A Persian slid from the saddle. Tossing his reins to a companion, he walked over to the corpse. With his boot on the body, he pulled out the arrows. The shaft of one had snapped; the others he handed back to their owners. The riders laughed and joked, teasing each other about their shooting. One carefully tied back his long hair with a bright strip of material.

Maximus became aware of his sword in his hand. He had no memory of unsheathing it. He held it behind his back so that it would not catch the sun. He forced himself to look away, at the others. Their whole attention was on the foot of the hill. They were all willing the enemy to leave.

Finally, when the watchers had thought they could bear no more, when even discovery and doomed violence had seemed better than the agony of waiting, a Persian shouted a word of command. The easterner on foot remounted, and the troop trotted off the way they had come.

Around him, Maximus had heard several men exhale noisily. He realized that he was one of them. 'Bastards,' he said.

Calgacus had not taken his eyes off the Sassanids. 'And would our boys have behaved better?'

Maximus shrugged.

It had not proved easy to sleep having just seen one of their *commilitiones* killed in cold blood, his butchered remains lying in view. Calgacus had moved the men further up the hill. It had done no good. A careless glance through the green leaves still revealed a glimpse of soiled

17

blue tunic. The Greek youth Demetrius had said they should retrieve the man's body, offer him proper burial, at least a coin for the ferryman. Calgacus had overruled him. The Persians might return, they would be suspicious. But, Demetrius had argued, others might be drawn to the sight. Calgacus shrugged: it was the lesser of two evils.

Twilight had found them more than ready to move. Calgacus had outlined the new plan. Since the gods clearly did not care for the idea of them reaching Samosata in the north, they would go west to Zeugma. They would soon come to a broad, high plain, almost twenty miles across, then a range of hills from which the Euphrates would be visible. They could do it in one night. Once in Zeugma, they would be safe. They had passed through the town on the march out. Its walls were sound, manned by the four thousand men of Legio IIII Scythica and another six thousand regulars. Best of all, they were commanded by the ex-consul Valens, and he was no friend of either the Sassanids nor treacherous bastards like Quietus, his brother Macrianus and their scheming father Macrianus the Lame.

Calgacus had been about to give the word to set off when, boots slipping in the powdery soil, Demetrius ran up through the trees. When he reached them, he doubled up, panting like a dog after a run in the hot sun. One of the troopers, a good-looking man, helped him up into the saddle.

'Just a coin, a handful of dust.' Demetrius spoke to Calgacus, his tone defensive. 'I know if the reptiles come it will show that we have been here. But I had to. I could not let his soul wander for ever.'

Calgacus just nodded and gave the word to move out.

It had taken much longer to reach the plain than the Caledonian had suggested. When they did, it seemed to stretch on without end. On and on they had ridden, the stars high above as distant and heartless as the eyes of a triumphant mob. On either side, flat, grey nothingness. The men were bone-tired. They had lived with constant fear for too long. In the face of the plain's immensity, even Maximus had felt his composure slipping, his mind summoning up ghastly imaginings. After a time, it had seemed to him that it was the plain that moved while they stood still. It was like those stories Demetrius told: they were already dead, their sins on earth had been judged. They had been sent to Tartarus and it was their fate to ride this dark plain for ever, never reaching safety, never again seeing the sun.

Yet the grey light of pre-dawn had come all too soon. It revealed the hills in the west, but they were still a way off. All around them lay the emptiness of the plain. There were a few shrubs, the odd wind-bent tree; nothing to hide them. About a mile ahead, stark and incongruous, was a lone building. Anyone with any pretensions to fieldcraft knows not to hide in a solitary building; it is the first place searchers will look. Nevertheless, Calgacus led them straight towards it. There was nowhere else.

The building was a large, rectangular mud-brick barn. It had contained animals and people but now it stood empty. They led their horses in by the one, wide door. Inside, they hoisted a lookout up on to the beams. Some of the tiles were missing; Calgacus pushed out a few more in order to be able to see all around. The elevation increased the depth of his view. The other men rubbed down their horses and searched for food. There was none.

There was a well outside, but there was always the possibility that it might be poisoned. They still had water in their bottles, but they had eaten their last scraps of food the night before. They could cut grass for the horses, but the men would have to go hungry.

Maximus had taken the second watch. He had to shift around the roof to keep an eye on all approaches, and it was just as well: falling asleep would bring with it the risk of a nasty fall. Another of Demetrius's stories floated into the Hibernian's mind. On Circe's island, one of Odysseus's crew had fallen asleep on the roof of the palace. He had tumbled off and broken his neck. Sometimes when Demetrius told the story, the man had been bewitched and turned into a pig. *There* was a thought – roast pork: hot, blistered crackling, the fat running down your chin. Infernal gods, Maximus was hungry.

Somewhat distracted by the demands of his stomach, it had taken Maximus a few moments to take on board what his eyes were seeing. The peasant couple with the donkey, the man riding, the woman walking behind, were quite close by. Maximus dropped down from the beams. He woke Demetrius and gave him a leg-up into the roof. Turning, he found Calgacus on his feet. A word or two of explanation passed between the two men, and they walked outside.

At the sight of the strangers, the peasant stopped his donkey with a word and his wife, her eyes downcast and inattentive, with a stick. His tattooed face registered no surprise. Like the goatherd the other day, thought Maximus, they bred them incurious out here.

'Good day, grandfather,' Calgacus said in Greek.

The peasant replied with a muted flow of words in a language neither of the other men understood. Now they were closer, they could see that it was not tattoos on the man's face but dirt ingrained in every line.

Maximus tried a greeting in Persian. An emotion seemed to run across the peasant's face. It was gone before Maximus was even sure it had been there. Quietly the woman began to sob. The peasant hit her with his stick.

With gestures and broken sentences in a range of languages, Maximus asked if the couple had any food. The man's response, which involved much eloquent waving of hands and minimal grunting of incomprehensible words, was an extended denial. As far as Maximus could make out, riders had come from the east; they had taken all the food, beaten the peasant and his wife. They had done something else, too, taken something, a child. Boy or girl, it would not have gone well for them.

The woman started to weep again. She quietened at the sight of the stick.

Calgacus invited them into the barn. The peasant made it clear that he and his wife would remain outside.

There they sat, hands on their knees, up against the wall of what could well have been their own home. As the sun arced across the sky, they moved around to keep in the shade. At intervals, the woman wept. Depending on how his emotions took him, the peasant would either soothe or threaten her. Maximus spent much of the day watching them, grieving for their naked misery. Even a man of violence such as himself could sometimes see the evil, naked face of the god of war – Mars, Ares, Woden, call him what you will: war is hell.

As the day faded, the men had tacked up, led their horses outside and swung into their saddles. Calgacus led them off to the west. Neither the peasant nor his wife showed any emotion at their departure.

Finally they had reached the hills. Finding an upward path despite the darkness, they took it. As the rocky slopes cut down their vision, they proceeded cautiously, placing two men out on point duty, fifty or more paces in front. And then they had come across the Persians.

Maximus looked away from Calgacus and back down at the enemy. The Sassanids were relaxed, perfectly unaware that they were being observed. They stood around where the three paths met, passing a wineskin back and forth. One of them raised his voice in song:

> '*Dreaming when Dawn's left hand was in the sky*
> *I heard a Voice within the tavern cry,*
> *"Awake my Little ones, and fill the Cup*
> *"Before Life's Liquor in its Cup be dry."*'

The Persians laughed.

That's it, you goat-eyed bastards, thought Maximus, drink up every drop. Before Dawn's left hand is anywhere in the sky, in the next quarter of an hour, if you don't move, we are going to try and kill you – and we want you as drunk as possible when the sharp steel gets close.

Even if they did move, it was quite likely there would be a fight. If the Sassanids took the path to the north, all well and good. If they went west, the Romans might hope to follow and, once out of the hills, somewhere down on the narrow plain before the Euphrates, slip past into

Zeugma. But if the Sassanids rode east, then there was no choice, there must be bloodshed.

One of the dark-grey shadows changed shape: a Persian leapt up into his saddle. He too sang, a voice less mellifluous than that of the first, but with a ring of authority:

> '*And, as the cock crew, those who stood before*
> *The Tavern shouted – "Open then the Door!*
> *"You know how little while we have to stay,*
> *"And, once departed, may return no more."*'

The Sassanids all mounted. They milled, sorting themselves into position.

Maximus, palms slick, held his breath.

The eastern troop clattered off to the north.

Demetrius, as so often, was at the back holding the horses. As well as his own and Calgacus's mounts, he had the reins of the grey gelding Ballista had insisted that Maximus ride. In the near-darkness, every time Pale Horse shifted, stamped a hoof or just breathed loudly, thoughts of the animal's owner crowded, insistent and importuning, into Demetrius's mind. There was pity, a terrible aching pity, for the big blond barbarian who had once owned the young Greek as surely as he had owned the horse. And there was gratitude. Enslavement and his first three years of servitude were things Demetrius preferred not to think about. It had been such a bad time that usually he found it easier to give out, sometimes even to pretend to himself that he had been born into slavery – if you have known nothing else, how can it be that bad? After three years he had been purchased as a secretary to Ballista. The big barbarian had treated him well for nine years. He had given Demetrius no reason to dwell on the old saying 'A slave should not wait for his master's hand.' Finally, four days earlier, on a burnt hillside, surrounded by the remnants of a defeated army, Ballista had given Demetrius the thing he wanted above all others: his freedom.

A noise from further up the path brought Demetrius back to the fearful present. He could see nothing. The narrow upland path was blocked by the remaining four Dalmatian troopers and their horses. The stars and young moon gave little light. Suddenly, there was a rattle of dislodged stones. Fear rose inside him, gripping his throat as he watched the troopers ready their weapons.

'Easy, boys.' Maximus's words were soft. The troopers relaxed. Demetrius sighed with relief.

They mounted up and got moving. They rode across a small meadow where three paths came together. Demetrius balled his fist, thumb between index and forefinger, in a symbolic gesture to avert evil. Crossroads were always bad places; you only had to think of Oedipus encountering his father. A crossroads where three paths converged, and darkness; it was hard to imagine a situation more likely to draw the terrible three-headed goddess Hecate or her dreadful minions up from the underworld.

After they had traversed the meadow, the hills rose up again. In the unearthly light, the white rocks and black shadows rendered the slopes into shattered or crazed mosaics. Demetrius rode just behind Calgacus and Maximus. He felt safer near them. The soft gleam of Pale Horse sent his thoughts back to Ballista. How had it gone for him at the hands of the Persians? The northerner had defied Shapur the King of Kings for months at Arete, had slaughtered thousands of his warriors below the city walls. He had routed a Sassanid army at Circesium – the waters of the Chaboras had run red with eastern blood. Worse, much worse, he had defiled the sacredness of fire, which the Zoroastrian Sassanids worshipped, by burning the corpses of their dead after the battle. It was unlikely things had gone well for him.

Maximus and Calgacus had their heads together and were muttering low. The Hibernian pulled Pale Horse out of line. As he passed, Demetrius smiled over. Maximus made no response; his eyes were far away, as distant as those of a distracted child. The grey horse standing there turned Demetrius's thoughts yet again to Ballista. On that scorched hillside, moments before they had left, Ballista had embraced Maximus, had whispered something in his ear. The Hibernian had promised he would die before he let anyone harm Ballista's two sons. At the memory, Demetrius felt a stab of jealousy. He pushed it away as unworthy. He was not a fighter. He did not have man-killing hands. Of course Ballista would ask his old companion in arms to put his body between the hostile blades and the bodies of his sons. Isangrim had just turned eight and Dernhelm was not yet two; both were beautiful, and both now fatherless.

A flash of movement to his right caught Demetrius's eye. He stared hard. Nothing: just rocks and shadows. He was looking away when he glimpsed it again. Yes, there it was. High up on the slope. About a discus throw away. A movement. Then he saw it clearly: a dark figure, a man on foot moving parallel to them.

Demetrius looked round at his companions. No one else seemed aware of the follower on the hill. Maximus was nowhere in sight. When Demetrius looked back, it took a few moments to spot the shadow again. There he was. Shabby, grey-black clothes, with maybe a hint of red. He flitted from rock to rock. No noise came down from him. With a chill in his heart, Demetrius saw the follower's face was dark, terribly dark. It was black. Grey-eyed Athena watch over us, he mouthed. This was no mortal that stalked them but a daemon or ghost.

Some ghosts were thin, insubstantial wraiths. If you tried to grab them, they slipped through your arms like smoke. Such ghosts were an annoyance, but they could not harm you. The daemon on the hill was not one of them. This ghost was one of the terrible ones. This was an embodied daemon, something terrible and dangerous, something like Lykas, who had slain old and young alike in Temesa; like Polykritos the Aitolian, who after nine months had risen from his tomb to seize his hermaphrodite son and tear him limb from limb, then devoured his body.

Demetrius fought down the rising tide of horrible ghost stories within him. Sometimes wide reading and a retentive memory could be a curse. He peered wildly about. The faces of the others betrayed nothing. Where was Maximus?

Demetrius, urging his mount forward to come alongside Calgacus, gazed again at the thing on the hill. As he did so, it changed shape, dropping to all fours. Swiftly, it ran like a wolf or a dog to the next cover. From out of the darkness, clear even above the noise of the horsemen, came the bray of a donkey. The beast reared up, briefly standing on two legs – looking around, sniffing the air – before slipping to the ground and slithering like a snake behind a rock.

Pallas Athena and all the gods of Olympus hold your hands over us. Demetrius was too scared to pray out loud. This was worse than a daemon. Far, far worse. They were being stalked by a shape-changing *empusa*, one of Hecate's ghastly servants from the underworld. Hecate, the dark goddess, none of whose desires were ever denied by Zeus.

Demetrius had read in Philostratus that the holy man Apollonius of Tyana had once routed an *empusa* with just a shout. Demetrius was too scared to shout. Anyway, would a shout not bring the Sassanids down on them?

The young Greek leant over, almost overbalancing from the saddle in his anxiety. He grabbed Calgacus's arm.

'Quiet, you young fool,' the Caledonian hissed.

Eyes wide, Demetrius gazed, silent but uncomprehending. Why was Calgacus doing nothing? Where was Maximus? Why did these barbarians not do something? Had they no concept of what an *empusa* could do?

As they rode slowly on, Demetrius saw that Calgacus was watching the thing on the hill out of the corner of his eye. The Caledonian was rigid with expectation. His mount tossed its head as it sensed the tension.

Up on the hill, higher up the slope, there was another movement. Another dark shape slipped over the skyline. It crept slowly down towards where the first was hidden.

Could there be two of the creatures? Darkness, fatigue and fear were taking their toll on Demetrius. Gods below, what if the things hunted in packs?

The first dark shape must have heard or sensed something. It suddenly stood and scanned the hillside. Then, quick as a flash, it sprang and raced away to the west. The other figure leapt up in pursuit. Stones slid out from under their feet. Dislodging others, they bounced in showers down towards the path.

Calgacus booted his horse. It clattered down the path. After about fifty paces, the Caledonian brought it skidding to a halt. Belying his age, he threw himself off its back, tugged a couple of javelins from the holster on the saddle and started up the slope to cut off the fugitive.

Seeing the new threat, the fugitive tried to veer back up the incline. It was no good: the second figure was already in position, ready to block any escape in that direction.

Like Celtic hounds, the two pursuers coursed their prey over the stony slope. They turned him this way and that, ever closing.

'Stop or I will run you through,' Calgacus yelled in Greek. His prey raced on. The old Caledonian drew back his arm and cast a mighty throw. The javelin winged over the fugitive's shoulder. A spark flashed as it glanced off a rock.

The fugitive pulled up dead in his tracks. Calgacus grabbed his arms, twisted them behind his back, pushed him down towards the waiting horsemen.

Maximus rejoined the men moments later. 'Fuck, that nearly killed me,' he panted.

Relieved beyond words, Demetrius studied the prisoner. No feast for the eyes, but he was no daemon or *empusa*: he was a small man, face blackened, wearing the pelt of a dark-grey wolf and a cap of weasel skin. He too was breathing heavily.

Quickly and efficiently, Maximus searched the prisoner for weapons. Finding none, he stepped back and kicked the man's legs from under him.

'Don't kill me! Dear gods, please don't kill me!' The man spoke in Latin. It was oddly accented, like something unpractised. He was terrified. He cowered on the ground, teeth chattering.

'Courage,' said Maximus. 'Death is your last worry.'

'I am just a soldier, a Roman like you. Please don't kill me!'

'Name? Rank? Unit?' Maximus snapped out the questions.

'Titus Esuvius, *miles*, Legio IIII Scythica. Don't hurt me.' The words tumbled out.

'You are a deserter.'

'No, no, *Dominus*, a scout. I am a scout.'

'What are you doing out here?'

The prisoner gulped. 'Just trying to get back to Zeugma. Please, take me with you.'

'Where have you come from?' Maximus's questions were relentless.

Again the swallowing, the slight hesitation. 'From the field army. Please, take me with you.'

Maximus glanced at Calgacus, jerked his head. The Caledonian roughly hauled the prisoner to his feet, pinned his arms behind his back. Maximus drew his sword. The blade of the short *gladius* shone in the pale light.

'Time to tell the truth.'

The man sobbed. 'I am. Please believe me. I have a family, don't hurt me.'

'Tell me,' said Maximus, 'have you ever been drawn to eastern religion?' As he spoke, he moved forward and deftly, with one hand, unbuckled the man's belt.

Fear and incomprehension played across the prisoner's face. He shook his head. 'No, never. I don't understand.'

Two tugs and the man's trousers and undergarment were round his knees. 'No interest in, say, the goddess Artargatis? No yearning to take a trip to her temple at Hierapolis?'

Suspicion clouded the man's face. 'No, I . . . no, never.'

'Pity, considering what's going to happen to you.' Maximus reached out and grasped the man's testicles. With the other hand, he showed him the sword. The man whimpered. 'They make a good living, her devotees, the *Galli*. Of course, they castrate themselves. And I think they use a stone blade, flint most likely. But *mutatis mutandis* – if you survive, I'm sure they'll take you in.'

The man was making incoherent begging noises.

'Now, what is it to be? Are you going to tell me the truth, or is it off to Hierapolis for you?'

As if a dam had broken, the words poured out. 'My name really is Titus Esuvius. I was born in Lutetia in Gaul. I was with a cavalry *ala*. We came out east for the campaign of Gordian III. I . . . I did something wrong. I had to desert. Been with the Sassanids for years – married, got a Persian family. The Lord Suren himself ordered me to Zeugma to spy out the defences. What could I do? I had no choice. Please, let me live. I want to see my children again.'

The stream of words was cut off when one of the Dalmatian troopers led his horse up from the rear. 'The reptiles are coming.'

The prisoner wriggled free of Calgacus. He threw himself on his knees. 'Please, leave me here – bound and gagged – I won't tell them anything.'

'No more words.' Maximus's face was set.

Just as the man reached up a hand to grasp Maximus's chin in supplication, the Hibernian's sword swung. A flashing hack caught the prisoner square across the neck. Blood sprayed hot.

'Mount up,' said Calgacus.

Demetrius stood near the corpse with the half-severed neck. Maximus was cleaning his blade on the dead man's wolfskin.

31

'You promised him his life,' the Greek said.

'No, I said death was his last worry.' Maximus swung up on to Pale Horse. 'Is that not so for all of us?'

They were riding flat out, the Sassanids hard on their heels. The thunder of their passing echoed back from the stony slopes on either side. At least it was simple, thought Maximus, just two choices: run or fight. No need to be thinking of clever tricks with decoys, lanterns or anything else. Nowhere to hide and nowhere to go but down the one track: just run or fight.

The track twisted and turned, rose and fell as it graded across the hills. It was narrow, the surface loose and un-even. The hooves of the horses scrabbled as they slid around sharp corners. More than once, riders had to grab the twin front horns of their cavalry saddles to prevent themselves being thrown. A couple of times Demetrius was nearly on the floor. The young Greek was no centaur. This cannot go on, thought Maximus.

'Ease up, Calgacus,' he called. 'The body of the spy will have delayed them. Ease up, or there'll be a fall, probably a pile-up.'

The Caledonian considered then brought his mount down to a fast canter.

Maximus looked up at the sky. The night was rushing on, not much of it left. But they must be getting to the edge of the hills. After that, just a small plain, four or five miles across, and they would be safe behind the walls of Zeugma.

The small figure was standing in the middle of the track as they came round the corner. Maximus and Calgacus pulled hard on their reins, thighs braced firm into the leather and wood of their saddles. They swerved round the obstruction as they drew to a stop. Behind was confusion. Demetrius's mount barged into the back of Pale Horse. Miraculously, no one had ridden down the child.

Maximus scanned the slopes all around. No movement. Nothing. It couldn't be a trap. He swung a leg over Pale Horse's neck and dropped to the ground.

The child was a fine-looking boy, about eight years old. He had a heavy, fine neck ornament. He was crying.

'My mother has gone. She was scared. She said I was too slow. She has gone.'

Maximus held out his arms. The child hesitated for a second. Maximus knew that his battered face, the tip of his nose missing, was unlikely to be reassuring. He scooped the boy up. The child buried his face in the Hibernian's shoulder.

'My father is on the *Boule* of Zeugma. He is a rich man. He will reward you.' The boy chattered in Greek.

'We'd best be moving,' Calgacus said.

Maximus put the boy on Pale Horse then jumped up behind him. They headed off.

They had not gone far when they heard the sounds of pursuit: high, keen cries, the low rumble of many horses. Calgacus pushed the pace. The horses were slow to respond. They were as tired as the men. These four days had taken it out of them all.

From the crest of a rise, Maximus glimpsed the flat, empty greyness of the plain below; it wasn't far ahead. As the track dropped down behind him, a trooper's mount stumbled. In its fatigue, it almost went crashing. If it had, it would have brought others down with it.

This is no good, thought Maximus. If we're out on the

open plain on spent horses, the Persians will run us down as easy as catching mackerel.

The horses were labouring up a straight incline. It ran for about fifty paces. The hill on the left reared up into a small, sheer cliff. Stones fallen from its face were scattered across the track. Near the top of the incline, a sizeable pile narrowed the path to single file.

As good a place as any, thought Maximus. He pulled over, indicated to Calgacus to join him, and waved the others past.

'I think I'll be staying here a while.' Maximus jumped down. He unhooked his shield from the saddle. 'Change horses and take the child.'

Calgacus said nothing. Stiffly, he dismounted, collected his own shield and, while Maximus held the heads of both horses, climbed up on the grey gelding behind the boy.

'You sure?' Calgacus asked.

'Sure.' Maximus looked up at the Caledonian. 'Back before we left the army, I promised Ballista I'd look after his boys. That is on you now.'

'Aye, it is.' Calgacus did not meet Maximus's eyes. His gaze wandered over the face of the cliff.

The noise of the pursuit was clear.

'Say goodbye to Demetrius for me.'

'I will.' Calgacus untied the bowcase and quiver from Pale Horse's saddle. He threw them down to Maximus. 'Keep mine as well.'

The noise of the pursuit swelled.

Calgacus gathered Pale Horse's reins, turned his head and moved on. His eyes still did not meet Maximus's but continued to look here and there over the cliff.

Left alone, Maximus worked swiftly. He led the horse a little way beyond the large pile of fallen stones and, with a strip of leather, hobbled its front legs. He scooped up Calgacus's bow and quiver together with his own. He ran back and took his stand half behind the mound. He drew his sword and put it and his shield in front of him, near to hand on the ground. He propped up the quivers so he could easily reach the arrows, and the spare bow beside them. He selected an arrow, examined the straightness of its shaft, tested its point. Satisfied, he notched it, half drew his bow and sighted down the track.

As he waited, time played strange tricks on Maximus. It slowed down; stopped altogether. Each breath seemed to take an age. The noise of the Sassanids grew louder, but they did not appear. The sounds seemed to fade. Maximus relaxed the bow. He counted his arrows: twenty. He looked at the stars, as unknowable as the hearts of men. They were paling. It was nearly dawn.

The first two Sassanids took him by surprise. They turned the corner side by side, at a good canter. Maximus drew the bow. He aimed at the one to his right, deliberately low, intending to hit the horse. He released. Having grabbed another arrow, he saw the horse was down, its rider rolling in the dust. He shot at the other and missed. He shot again. The arrow buried itself into the horse's chest. The animal somersaulted forward, its rider catapulted over its head. He crunched hard into the stony path.

Another Sassanid had negotiated the first fallen horse. Sword out, he was urging his mount up the incline. Calmly, deliberately, Maximus shot him. The arrow plucked him off his horse's back. The smell of blood strong in its nostrils, equine cries of pain loud in its ears, the horse bolted up past Maximus and away.

The remaining Sassanids at the foot of the incline were at a standstill, unsure how many were against them, uncertain whether to go forward or withdraw. Maximus drew and released again and again. The deadly shafts whistled through the pale-grey light of pre-dawn.

An easterner on foot was rushing at him from the left. Maximus dropped his bow. He crouched to scoop up his sword and his opponent loomed over him. The Sassanid held his sword over his head in a two-handed grip. The long blade started to come down in a great sweep like an axe. Uncoiling, sword out in front, Maximus drove himself forward under the blow. The sharp point of the Hibernian's *gladius* drove into the stomach of the Sassanid. The two men were pressed together. There was a slaughterhouse stench. Maximus pushed the still-gasping easterner away.

The Sassanids drew back out of sight. Under his shield, peering round the stones, Maximus could see two dead horses and two dead men. Nothing else. He counted his remaining arrows: eight. He wondered whether to run for it. Had he bought enough time for the others?

No time now. A rising war cry. The Sassanids were coming again. Maximus put down the shield, sprang to his feet and drew his bow. The Persians thundered into sight. Maximus released. He grabbed another arrow. Working as fast as he could, he poured missiles down into the enemy.

An arrow sliced a hand's breadth past his head. This time, the easterners at the rear were shooting over the heads of the ones in front.

Maximus released again. A Persian horse went down.

He shot once more. He missed. He reached for another arrow. There were none left. He took up sword and shield. There was no stopping them this time.

The Sassanids were almost on him. He could see the flaring nostrils of their mounts, hear the snap of the long streamers they wore. A small stone bounced off his helmet. He glanced up. A shower of stones was falling. Above that, the air was full of rocks.

Maximus turned and ran. Stones and rocks slewed off the ground all around him. One caught him a painful blow on the shoulder. Behind him there was an awful roaring, a grinding.

He had moved beyond the torrent of debris. Maximus stopped and looked back. The track was invisible behind a thick cloud of dust. He stood staring stupidly at it. Beside him, his horse whinnied, struggling against its hobble. Maximus walked over. He found he still had his sword in his hand. He sheathed it. He must have dropped his shield. He calmed the horse, untied its hobble, climbed on its back.

The dust had started to drift away: the track was almost obliterated under the landslide. The Sassanids were gone; either crushed or fled.

A noise above him made Maximus look up at the top of the cliff. An ugly face gingerly peered over the edge. Seeing the Hibernian, it broke into a huge smile.

'Try not to look so surprised. Who did you expect would save someone like you? Surely you don't think the gods love you enough to cause a landslide? I am not really sure *I* do,' said Calgacus. 'And now I have to find my way down again.'

His back to the wall, Ballista could not move. His thighs
were pinned by those of two other men, the tribune Marcus Accius on his left, Camillus of the VI Gallicana on his
right. Ballista could feel the heat coming from their bodies. His own was dripping with sweat. The air was thick
and he was finding it hard to breathe.

Ballista had always feared confined spaces. The subter-
ranean cell was tiny. The majority of the senior officers of
the Roman field army had been pushed into it and there
was barely enough space for them all to sit. Ballista badly
needed to stretch his legs, to check his cut and bloodied
feet, but there was no room.

The *dignitas* of Rome was humbled, the emperor Valerian captured, his entire army dead or surrendered.
Almost all the high command had been herded like slaves
into this stinking prison – almost all: Valerian and his *ab
Admissionibus* Cledonius were not there. They had been
taken elsewhere, to endure further humiliations, to be
gloated over at leisure. And Turpio was not there either.
He was dead. Ballista had taken a last look at his friend as
they left the valley of tears, a last look at his decapitated
head stark on a pike.

From somewhere in the crush of bodies came the voice of the Praetorian Prefect Successianus. 'Discipline, we must keep our discipline. These cock-sucking Sassanid reptiles do not know *disciplina*. Keep our *disciplina* and we can beat them.' Over and over he muttered it. Ballista thought Successianus might be losing his mind. If so, it would be no wonder.

The march south could have robbed any man of his reason. It had been two days of hell. The line of prisoners had been driven along by blows, from whips, the butts of spears and the flats of blades, sometimes the edges. Valerian had been at the head of the line, dressed as a slave, a crown of thorns digging into his aged head. His officers, loaded with chains, followed him. Their boots had been taken and they had stumbled as the sharp rocks tore their feet. Behind them had trudged the long tail of the rank and file.

It had been hot, unbearably hot. Overhead, the sun was merciless. Swirling clouds of dust had blinded them, lodged in their throats, threatened to choke them. They had been terribly thirsty. Once a day they had been driven like cattle to water. Many had not had a chance to drink before they were beaten onwards. Twice, rounds of stale bread were thrown to them. Some had been too far gone to eat; others had fought over these scraps.

Degradation had been added to cruelty. If a man fell out to relieve himself, the Sassanids amused themselves by jeering and throwing stones as he squatted. When a man collapsed, he was beaten to his feet. If he did not rise quickly enough, he was summarily killed.

The ordinary *milites* had suffered worse than the officers.

No residual eastern respect for rank had protected them. If a young soldier's looks, not totally obscured by the dirt and suffering, happened to catch the eye of a guard, he was hauled out of the ranks. Held down, often in full view, he was raped, sometimes repeatedly. After the assault, the victim was left lying in the dirt. Some staggered back to the column; others remained prone in the dirt. Ballista had watched as one, a fresh-faced youth not yet twenty, covered his head and waited to die.

Not long after setting out, they had come upon a dry stream and the march was stopped. Glorious in purple and white raiment, with streamers floating behind, the Sassanid King of Kings had ridden up to inspect the stream. After consultation with some of his courtiers, Shapur had ordered a squad of legionaries to be forced down into the low watercourse. The banks had been ringed with horsemen. The Romans had fallen to their knees, arms out in supplication. It had done no good. To the accompaniment of mocking laughter, the defence-less men were riddled with arrows. An imperious order, a flurry of blows, and the column had been forced to march over the still-bleeding bodies of their comrades.

Towards the end of the first day, they reached Edessa. The white-walled city was still holding out. The ragged line of captives was halted within arrow shot, their abject-ness displayed to the defenders. Near Ballista, a tribune had wept at the tantalizing closeness of safety.

Valerian had been escorted up to the eastern gate. Under duress, the elderly emperor had called for the gov-ernor. When he appeared, Valerian commanded him to surrender the city. High on the battlements, Aurelius

Dasius put his fingers to his lips and blew a kiss. Having performed *proskynesis*, the governor snapped a military salute and wordlessly turned away.

The second day, they had been marched down to Carrhae. Across the flat plain, the city rose like a platform in the distance. Word ran down the column that Carrhae had opened its gates to the Persians.

A few miles short of the city, they were brought to a halt by the temple of Nikal, the bride of Sin. The sanctuary of the moon goddess and her powerful consort was a hive of peaceful activity. Under watchful Persian eyes, local priests scurried around the banks of the sacred lake. Soon a great fire was lit and a holocaust committed. It had been hard to choose which was the more tormenting, the smell of whole animals roasting or the sight of the unattainable clear waters of the lake.

A Sassanid noble had ridden up to the bedraggled Roman officers. Laughing, he had called out in Greek, 'See, we treat you, our honoured guests, like the gods. They too dine on the smoke of sacrifice.'

The ordinary *milites* had been left outside the city walls. The officers were marched under an ornate gateway, through streets where the citizens were encouraged to jeer and throw things, then manhandled into the cramped, airless cell.

'*Disciplina* . . .' In the gloom, the Praetorian Prefect's mutterings ran on. Ballista's legs were seized with cramp. Apologizing to Aurelian, the young Italian prefect wedged in front of him, Ballista painfully flexed them. He was weary to the bone. He wanted to shut his eyes, but he knew that when he opened them again the airless press of bodies and his inability to move would cause a wave of panic that might engulf him. On the march he had been glad enough not to be one of the rank and file, but now he would have given a lot to be with them. At least they had the night air on their faces and the delicious luxury of just a little unrestricted movement.

There was the screech of a drawn bolt, and the door swung open. Two easterners, long swords in hand, scanned the crush.

'Which one of you is Ballista?'

Unwillingly, Ballista raised his hand. This was not a good turn of events. The Roman general who had slaughtered so many easterners at Arete, had defeated a Sassanid army at Circesium and had then in their eyes committed the terrible sacrilege of burning their bodies could expect only harsh hospitality from the King of Kings.

'You come with us.'

It took some time for Ballista to get out of the cell. First he had to get to his feet. This involved levering himself up by using the wall. Then the Roman officers had to clamber on top of one another, all *dignitas* dispelled, to clear a path.

As the door shut, Ballista heard Successianus. '*Disciplina*, keep your *disciplina*,' the Praetorian Prefect repeated.

Fuck you and your Roman *disciplina*, Ballista thought. I was born a warrior of the Angles. We have our own ways of facing down fear. *Allfather, Deep Hood, Death-blinder, Woden-born as I am, do not let me disgrace myself or my forefathers.*

Two guards took Ballista's arms. Two more, weapons drawn, followed. Ballista felt the cuts on the soles of his feet open as he shuffled along. The chains fastened to his ankles threatened to trip him at every step. Movement made the manacles on his wrists and the weight of the chain that linked them hurt like all hell.

He was hustled along corridor after corridor through the palace cellars. At first he tried to memorize every turn. Then he realized he had forgotten the route they had taken in getting to the cell. After that, he concentrated on not giving way to his fear.

The guards opened the door to another cell. They pushed him inside, surprisingly gently. He did not fall full length, merely staggered. The door was shut. The bolts slammed.

Standing still, Ballista took stock. The cell smelled musty but clean. There were no windows, so it was completely dark. Squatting into position for an ungainly crawl, Ballista explored his new prison: about six paces by six, bare earth floor, rough stone walls, nothing movable, nothing that could be used as a weapon.

With a grunt of effort, Ballista settled himself against a wall. He tried to make himself as comfortable as possible, easing the metal away from the abrasions and sores on his wrists and ankles. Now he was alone he missed the companionship of the other officers. At least they had all been in it together.

Ballista was tired. His fatigue was a mine that each of the last two days had dug deeper, the tunnel burrowing away from the light, the air even harder to breathe. He thought of Julia, his wife, of Isangrim and Dernhelm, his two beautiful sons. He imagined their pain when news reached Antioch of the disaster. If he died, would they ever hear of it? Or would he just be gone, his end an empty space their minds would fill with terrible tortures and pain?

Shutting his eyes, Ballista promised himself that if there were a chance – no matter what it took, no matter at what cost to himself – he would get back to them.

The door crashed open and Ballista was temporarily blinded by the light. Two easterners entered and put lamps on the floor. Someone laughed outside. The door shut. Ballista peered up at the two men. The younger, he half recognized. The man was dressed in the garb of a Persian nobleman, his face made up, kohl around his eyes. He exuded a smug air of self-controlled menace. The older wore more outlandish clothes, a jacket with empty, hanging sleeves and a fur cloak, and had strange braids in his hair. Ballista did not know him. The stranger stepped over to Ballista and kicked him. The blow landed on his arms. The man shouted something in a language Ballista had never heard and kicked out again.

'On your feet,' the Sassanid by the door said, in Persian.

Ballista stayed where he was. He peered out from behind his raised arms, trying to look confused, helpless. 'Latin, I only speak Latin.'

The Sassanid moved from the door. He leant down, bringing his face close. He did look very familiar. Smiling unpleasantly, he spoke. 'We have met before. The first time, at Arete, your excellent command of my language tricked me into letting you escape. I vowed there would be a reckoning. The second time, not long ago, your status as an ambassador robbed me of my revenge.'

Ballista remembered now: he was Vardan, son of Nashbad, a captain in the service of the Lord Suren. Wherever you go, old enemies will find you. And Woden knew, Ballista had made enough of them.

As Ballista got up, Vardan grabbed him from behind, pinioning his elbows to his sides. The manacles dug into Ballista's wrists, the chain between them drew tight across his stomach.

'Be assured, northerner, nothing can save you tonight,' Vardan hissed, his breath hot in Ballista's ear. 'We have the whole night. My revenge and pleasure will be sweet as they come together.' Vardan laughed. 'But first . . .'

The other man spat in Ballista's face. He began to shout furiously, the unintelligibility of the words to the northerner making them more frightening. The man spat again. His breath was heavy with spicy food and strong wine. This man was full of hatred, but Ballista had no idea why.

The man stepped back and removed one of his slippers. Screaming what was abuse in any language, he beat Ballista around the head with it. Even though the slipper was light, it hurt. The frenzied attack went on until Vardan said something in the incomprehensible language.

Vardan again whispered in Ballista's ear. 'This is Hamazasp, King of Georgian Iberia. You killed his son at Arete.'

Vardan spoke again. The language must be Georgian. Hamazasp laughed. He began to unbuckle his belt. 'Do not worry, barbarian, you will not have to live with the shame for long.' He smirked. 'Afterwards, we will kill you.'

Ballista threw himself backwards, smashing Vardan into the wall. The Persian wheezed as the impact forced the air out of his lungs. Ballista stamped his left heel down on Vardan's foot, making him howl.

Hamazasp was bent forward, fumbling his trousers up.

Ballista lunged and hooked the chain of his manacles over the Georgian's head. Pulling him close, Ballista drove his right knee up into his crotch.

As Hamazasp doubled up, Ballista freed the chain and spun round, swinging it with him. The hard metal links snapped into Vardan's face. There was a scream, blood sprayed and the Persian staggered sideways.

The door was thrown open. Ballista rushed at the guards. The chains around his ankles tangled in his feet. He crashed forward on all fours. Scrambling, he tried to rise. A savage kick caught him under the chin. His head snapped backwards. There was a blinding flash of light, a roaring sound in his ears.

Something animal makes the body defend itself, even when the mind is dazed. Ballista found he was curled up on the floor, arms trying to shield his head. The kicks were hard, shrewdly aimed. One after another they came, in his kidneys, stomach, mouth, ears. Ballista felt blood pouring from his nose. His mouth was full of shattered tooth fragments. Relentlessly, the beating continued.

'Enough.' Vardan's voice seemed to come from miles away. The kicking stopped.

Ballista lay, muscles twitching, stabs of pain flickering through him. Several men seized him. He was rolled face down. His limbs were stretched out. Hands hauled up his tunic, gripped the waist of his trousers.

'Stop!' A voice new to the room, Persian but distantly familiar.

'This is nothing to do with you priests, Hormizd.'

'The great god Mazda has willed that everything is the concern of his *mobads*.' The voice was controlled but tight with emotion. 'I am sure that neither you, Vardan, nor the King of Georgia would be so unrighteous as to deny that the caste of warriors must abase itself before that of priests.'

There was a charged silence that seemed to indicate unwilling acquiescence.

'Even should you have been led so far astray by Ahriman the Evil One, it would be unwise for a vassal king or an officer in the service of the Lord Suren to ignore the will of the Mazda-worshipping King of Kings.' The voice was growing in command, becoming mellifluous. 'Shapur himself, may his name be praised, has commanded the prisoner called Ballista be brought before him at the first audience of the day, as soon as the pious King of Aryans and non-Aryans has performed the rites that greet the dawn. Now my servants will take charge of the prisoner. You may go.'

Ballista heard the men leave the room, their footfalls and mutterings dwindling down the corridor. Spitting out tiny bits of tooth, painfully, he turned over. A young man with an earnest face and a big beard was bending over him. Ballista ran his tongue over his split lips. Croakily, he spoke.

'Greetings, Bagoas. It has been a long time.'

Ballista lay in the warm waters of the *tepidarium*. It had been agony getting in – the grazes had stung even sharper than the cuts – but now the water was supremely soothing. It was scented with carnations and cloves. Relishing the seclusion of the small private bath, Ballista checked his physical condition. His wrists, ankles and the soles of his feet were badly cut from the march. The rest of his body was covered in bruises and abrasions. He squinted into a small, highly polished metal mirror, which kept steaming up. His right eye was blackened, the left almost closed. His front teeth were broken; some at the back ached abominably. But apart from a stabbing pain in his left side when he moved – probably a cracked rib or two – he did not seem to have any broken bones. He was battered and exhausted yet, if a chance came, he could still run or fight.

A door opened and the young priest entered.

'Thank you, Bagoas . . . sorry – Hormizd.' The Persian youth smiled slightly in acknowledgement of the correction. 'You know,' Ballista continued, 'when you first joined my *familia* in Delos, I thought you were lying when you said that was your original name.'

'The idea had crossed my mind. I had no wish for anyone to know from what family I came before I was captured. Now the time of my servitude is something not spoken of at court. The divine King of Kings has declared that it should be as if it never occurred. It is as unmentionable as those traitors condemned to the Castle of Oblivion.'

'Why did you save me?'

'Such things are an abomination. When I was . . . *with you*, your men Maximus and Calgacus saved me from the same fate.'

'Thank you. But you had already repaid the debt. Maximus told me that you sent our pursuers on the wrong path after the fall of Arete.'

Hormizd smiled, his even teeth very white behind his black beard. 'One who seeks to be a virtuous man does not wait to incur a debt before doing good.'

'I am sure. But now I am in your debt. Although it is

hard to imagine how I could be in a position to repay you.'

'One can never tell what great Mazda holds in store for a man,' Hormizd said seriously. 'Now, let me wash your hair. Talk is more free without servants.'

The young Persian knelt by the bath. His fingers worked carefully around the cuts on Ballista's scalp as he cleaned the northerner's long hair.

'Tell me,' said Ballista after a while, 'why does Vardan hate me?'

'For the loss of his jewelled hair-clip.'

'What?'

'The King of Kings gave it to him. After you tricked Vardan into letting you go outside Arete, it was taken back. I imagine that every time someone dresses Vardan's hair, the hurt rankles.'

Ballista laughed. 'The old Greek Herodotus was right: everywhere, custom is king.'

'Come, let me help you out of the bath. I will call my servants to dry you. There is time for a few hours' sleep before you are taken to the King of Kings.'

'Shapur really wishes to see me?'

'Yes.'

'Why?'

'That is not for me to say.'

It was dark, a warm Mesopotamian spring night. Ballista was taken out on to the top of the citadel of Carrhae. At the eastern end of the terrace, off to one side, stood two iron tripods. Cledonius was sitting on one of them. Ballista was led to the other. He sat down with relief. Even in delicate silk slippers, it hurt to walk. As Ballista waited, he watched the eastern sky slowly pale to an eggshell blue.

The King of Kings came out of the palace and stopped in front of the high golden throne. The entourage that flanked him arranged itself into two divisions. On his left were the priests, on his right the high nobility and his client kings. Among them, Ballista saw, was Valerian. The Roman emperor stood some way from Shapur. The King of Iberia, Hamazasp, was significantly nearer the throne.

The great orb of the sun broke the line of the distant hills. Gracefully, the King of Aryans and non-Aryans sank down until he was full length on the ground, prostrating himself before the newly risen deity. There was complete silence as, from the very tips of his fingers, he blew a kiss. Then he stood up.

A pure white stallion was led before Shapur. High-stepping, its neck arched, the beautiful Nisean went consentingly to its fate. The King of Kings rubbed its nose, whispered into its velvet ears the message it would take then, suddenly, struck the sharp blade deeply into the base of the stallion's neck. With the deftness of long practice, he swiftly pulled the knife out and stepped to one side. A stream of blood as thick as a man's arm spouted out.

The horse stood quite still as its life blood pumped away. Everyone watched. For what seemed a long time, nothing moved, except for the gushing blood and the spreading dark, cloudy pool. Then, without preamble, the horse collapsed.

When the horse was dead and the communion between Shapur and his god complete, all the members of the court, Valerian included, performed *proskynesis*.

Shapur settled himself on the throne. A scribe moused

forward. Giving the impression of keeping low to the ground, he began to read from a book. Although the Persian king's hands toyed with a strung bow, his eyes were attentive. The sound did not carry, but Ballista knew the *dibir* was reading the words spoken by Shapur the night before when he had been drinking.

At length the scribe had finished and was dismissed. Ballista and Cledonius were gestured forward. They got down on their bellies by the carcass of the horse, the smell of its blood strong in their nostrils.

'Rise.' The Sassanid king's jewels and crown glinted in the morning sun. His dark, kohl-lined eyes regarded them.

'*But what is to be done? The will of heaven must be endured.*' Shapur recited the Greek verse with but the slightest hint of an eastern accent. Recognition swam just below the surface of Ballista's thoughts.

'*But how to ask what I want to know without causing you any pain, that is my dilemma. And yet I long to be satisfied.*' Shapur raised his hands in mock-uncertainty.

Cledonius replied. '*No, ask your question; leave no desire unfulfilled. Your wishes are also what my own heart desires, Great King.*' Only the title broke the metre.

Shapur smiled. He pointed his bow at Ballista. 'And does a barbarian from the quarter of the world not to be named by the pious know the works of the troglodyte of Salamis?'

'*A man has to bear the senseless acts of his rulers.*' As Ballista finished the quotation from Euripides, a terrible stillness spread across the terrace.

Shapur clapped his hands, threw his head back and laughed. Quickly, but more quietly, those around him joined in.

'The power of Euripides transcends all.' The courtiers fell abruptly silent as the king spoke. 'Last night, we diverted ourselves with his poetry. Everyone finds what he wishes in it. Truly, there are as many interpretations as readers.' The long line of heads nodded to acknowledge the profundity of the monarch's words.

'Now to affairs of empire.' Shapur still spoke in Greek, but his tone became brisk. 'It was the will of heaven for me to capture in war, to seize with this, my right hand, the emperor of the Romans. Now my prisoner Valerian begs for me to reinstate him on his throne. It is his heart's desire to become my vassal. He wishes to arrange his ransom.'

Out of the corner of his eye, Ballista looked at Valerian. The heavy old face was immobile.

'Valerian assures me that no one has more influence with the crippled servant he left in charge of those troops fortunate enough to have remained in Samosata than the two of you.' Shapur paused. 'As a messenger to Macrianus the Lame, the name of Cledonius was received with pleasure by my ears and those of my court. Who could be more fitting for the task than the faithful doorkeeper, the man who once said come and men came, who said go and they went.' A polite titter at the king's playful words ran through his entourage.

'But many were shocked, no – many were angered at the name of Ballista, the unrighteous man who offered me futile defiance at Arete, who tricked my loyal warrior Garshasp the Lion into defeat at Circesium, who there defiled the purity of fire with the corpses of the slain. Even our majesty was surprised when the *mobads* led by Kirder our high-priest spoke in favour of letting you go.'

52

Ballista glanced at the priests. There were two distinct groups, one ranked around a priest with a long nose and a jutting chin, with Hormizd standing at the shoulder of what must be Kirder the *Herbed*; the other gathered about a figure wearing a sky-blue cloak, yellow-and-green-striped trousers and carrying a long ebony cane. Between the two groups there was a palpable animosity. In every monarch's court there are factions, Ballista thought.

'Yet the arguments put forward by Kirder and the *mobads* were telling,' Shapur continued. 'A man to whom Mazda has not shown his face cannot know the ways of righteousness. How could a barbarian born in the cold quarter of the world where lies the gate of hell discover Mazda?'

Shapur leant forward and closely scrutinized Ballista. 'And it is as Hormizd said: you have one or two of the marks of the Evil One on your face. It is certain that Mazda will not reveal himself to a man with freckles.'

Ballista fought down a suicidal urge to laugh.

'Now, to the question I must ask you,' said Shapur. 'Will you, of your own free will and following the custom of your people, swear a binding oath, a great and terrible oath, to carry out this task and, in success or failure, return to perform *proskynesis* before my throne?'

When Ballista and Cledonius gave their assent, Shapur commanded the things necessary for the ritual to be brought forth. The priests came forward carrying several bowls and two lambs. Ballista wondered what exactly was behind all this. What was Valerian thinking? It would be hard to find two Roman officers more detested by Macrianus the Lame. And what game was the King of Kings playing? Macrianus had betrayed Valerian to Shapur. He was hardly likely to want the old emperor freed and returned to power.

Hormizd handed a heavy knife and one of the lambs to Ballista. The young Persian explained in Greek the form the oath would take and said that Ballista would swear first. The northerner's heart sank at the weight of the words. An oath was an oath. But there was nothing else for it.

Crouching, Ballista pinned the lamb between his thighs. It bleated piteously. With one hand he gently pulled up its chin. With the dagger he cut some tufts from its head. He tossed the tufts in the air. They floated away in the quickening breeze. Lifting his arms to the sky, he began to speak.

'Zeus, be my witness first; the highest, the best of gods! Then the Earth, the Sun, and the Furies who stalk the world below to wreak revenge on the dead who break their oaths – I swear I will carry out my task in good faith. I will travel to Macrianus and spare no effort to arrange the ransom of Valerian, emperor of Rome. I swear, in success or failure, I will return to perform *proskynesis* before the throne of Shapur, the Mazda-beloved King of Aryans and non-Aryans.'

Again Ballista pulled up the lamb's head, roughly this time. He dragged the ruthless blade across its soft throat. The little lamb fell at his feet, dying, gasping away its life breath.

Ballista took a silver bowl in one of his bloodied hands. 'Zeus, god of greatness, god of glory, all you immortals.' He tipped out some of the wine. 'If I break my oath, spill my brains on the ground as this wine spills, my brains and the brains of my sons too.'

IV

Calgacus and the others rode up to the walls of Zeugma late in the morning. It had all taken far longer than they had expected.

After the landslide, the Caledonian and the three cavalry-men had climbed down from where they had levered the rocks from the cliff. Demetrius and the other Dalmatian were where they had left them holding the horses. They had all mounted and waited.

Maximus had walked his horse up to them. The Hibernian was powdered white like a man who has worked a long day on the threshing floor. A cut showed bright red in the dust on his cheek. His face was motionless, drained. He had thanked them, haltingly, in a monotone.

Calgacus had seen the like before. A man who has resigned himself to death is unexpectedly saved but, instead of revelling in the reprieve from execution, in a released-from-gaol euphoria, the man is overcome by his troubles and fears, things he thought he had left behind him. Calgacus was not unduly perturbed. He knew that Maximus's moods changed like the weather in springtime. In no time the Hibernian would be his usual self.

Almost as soon as they set off, Calgacus had noticed a

track leaving their path and running off to the left between a fold in the hills. Not long after, he saw another climbing the slope to the right. As the stars had paled and the sky lightened, track after track appeared.

The sun had risen as they came down from the hills, revealing a broad plain heavily worked by man. It was dotted with barns and farms and, here and there, hamlets, and even small villages. Although some of the buildings had been burned, it had not been done recently. Most showed signs of repair. In all probability, the destruction dated back to the previous Persian invasion, the so-called 'time of troubles', seven years earlier. Stretching away on either side of the path were thick groves of trees, mainly olives and pistachios, vineyards in leaf and corn standing tall even this early in the year.

Calgacus looked over at Maximus. The Hibernian's face still wore the blank thousand-pace stare of a man back from near-death in combat. If Maximus had not realized his stand may have been unnecessary, Calgacus was not going to tell him.

The horses were done in, so Calgacus had ordered the men to dismount. Leading their tired mounts, they had trudged across the plain. The last stage seemed to take for ever. In the distance, on the other side of the Euphrates, was the rounded mound of the citadel of Zeugma. The outlines of the city were clear in the bright spring air: the red roofs of the close-packed houses climbing the slopes, the sharp line of its wall, some type of tree dotted above and, on the very summit, the great temple and the palace. Gradually, they had been able to make out the details, but for a long time it seemed to come no nearer.

Finally, they were only half a mile or so from the city walls. They had reached the outskirts of the eastern necropolis. Calgacus gave the order to remount. They trotted past many types of tomb, bearing many gloomy images in stone. Among the heavily sculpted swags of flowers framing baskets of offerings to the dead and the eagles which the pious hoped would carry their souls to a better place, there were portraits. The men depicted stood, respectable in Hellenic cloak and tunic; the women sat demurely. Children clutched their toys. The paint was flaking from quite a few. Some of the tombs had been broken open and not resealed. Their doors gaped open, the interiors loomed black in the sunshine.

None of it depressed the spirits of the riders. They were almost at safety. The walls of the town were no further away than a goatherd could throw a stick. Calgacus flexed his wounded right arm. He had taken a sword cut in the final fight before they had escaped from the valley of tears. The wound hurt like a bastard. Still, here they were: safety in their grasp and the welcome hope of a fat reward from a grateful town councillor for returning his lost son. Calgacus glanced at the boy, who was fast asleep in the saddle in front of Demetrius. The Caledonian momentarily wondered how the family reunion had gone when the mother had returned without the child. Well, that was their concern. It would be an unfeeling sort of father who did not reward, and reward to the limit of his means or even beyond, a man who brought his son back from a fate that unmans one for ever, or maybe death itself.

Get hold of a decent reward, have a bath, a long sleep,

clean clothes, then off for a drink and a girl. Maximus could always be relied on to sniff out the latter two. But their old companion Castricius, centurion of Legio IIII Scythica, was stationed at Zeugma. He had the inside knowledge. On the march out, he had taken them to a couple of places. The upmarket one on the Apamea side of the river had been horribly expensive. The other, the bar near the military base, had been fine.

Calgacus thought of Castricius in quite a fond way. The centurion had a thin little face, all lines and points, like that of a mythical creature dreamed up to entertain children with its mischievous tricks. But before he had joined the legions Castricius had been condemned to the mines – surely there was a law that stopped ex-slaves enlisting in the legions? – and he had survived. And not only that, he had lived through the fall of Arete. It would be a bad error to mistake Castricius for something harmless that entertained children.

'*Virtus*.' The challenge rang out from the walls. The gates were shut.

Calgacus moved his mount forward. He called up that they did not know the day's password – they were come straight from the field army north of Edessa.

'Identify yourselves,' shouted the guard.

'Marcus Clodius Calgacus.'

'Marcus Clodius Maximus.'

'Marcus Clodius Demetrius.'

Calgacus identified the boy – Antiochus, son of Barlaha, member of the *Boule* of Zeugma – and the four Dalmatian troopers gave their names, rank and unit.

'Wait there,' came the response.

As he waited, Calgacus thought of Marcus Clodius Ballista. When the Angle had given them their freedom, he
had also, in legal terms, given them Roman citizenship.
They, as custom prescribed, had taken both his *praenomen*
and *nomen* as their own. For the rest of their lives,
two-thirds of their names would bind the four men
together.

Calgacus climbed down from the saddle. He pulled
Pale Horse's ears, scratched its nose. Ballista loved the animal and, in an awful moment of clarity, Calgacus felt how
much he loved Ballista. The Caledonian had been little
more than a child himself when he had been taken as a
slave north of the wall. A quick succession of owners –
thank the gods his looks had forestalled any of them
taking too close an interest in him – and he had found
himself in Germania, in the hall of Isangrim, warleader
of the Angles. Ballista had been just four when Isangrim
had instructed Calgacus to serve as his son's manservant.
Ballista had been a rather shy, sensitive child. Calgacus
had watched Ballista as a youth trying to be brave on the
training ground, in the hunting field and, eventually at the
age of fifteen, in the battle line. Calgacus had been there
on the dreadful day when the Roman centurion had ridden up and announced that the emperor Maximinus
Thrax had demanded one of Isangrim's sons as a hostage.
Of course there had been no question that Ballista's elder
brother could go.

Calgacus had watched Ballista face down his misery.
He had ridden at Ballista's side into the alien world of the
Romans. On any reckoning, Ballista had done well in the
service of the *imperium*. Yet Calgacus had always felt sorry

for the young Angle, as surely torn from his people as the Caledonian himself. Whatever was thrown at him, Ballista tried to be brave. And now he was a captive of the Sassanids.

Calgacus buried his face in Pale Horse's flank. If all the miseries of the world had been set before him, it would not have touched him. He was already too full. Soundlessly, he mouthed some prayers to the half-forgotten gods of his childhood, to the gods he had never really believed in.

'Let them in.' The voice of the centurion broke into Calgacus's unhappiness. He straightened up.

The gates swung back. They led their horses in. Moorish auxiliaries, weapons drawn, swarthy faces mistrustful, ringed them. The gates slammed shut.

The centurion stepped down from the wall walk and appraised them closely.

'You are deserters.'

'No,' said Calgacus. 'Our *patronus*, the commander of these Dalmatians, ordered us to leave.' The Caledonian decided to take the initiative. 'If you could direct us to the house of the member of the *Boule* called Barlaha, we will return his son to him.'

'Oh no.' The centurion grinned. 'I can take care of that.'

Beside him, Calgacus felt Maximus stiffen. Calgacus put out a hand to restrain him.

The centurion gestured for the child to come to him. Unaware of the tension, the boy walked over to the officer. Reaching him, he turned and, in formal Attic Greek, thanked his rescuers. The centurion motioned a soldier to lead him away.

Calgacus was not ready to give up yet. 'We must see the governor Valens straightaway. Our *patronus*, Marcus Clodius Ballista, is an *amicus* of his, and we have much information about the Sassanids.'

'Oh, you will see the governor, but not the traitor Valens.' The centurion smiled unpleasantly. 'Valens fled to the west when ordered to report to Samosata. Given the emergency, Macrianus the Elder, as *Comes Sacrarum Largitionum* and the commander of what remains of Valerian's field army, has been forced temporarily to assume *maius imperium* over the whole East. Macrianus has appointed his *amicus*, the noble ex-consul Gaius Calpurnius Piso Frugi, to be governor of Syria Coele.'

Calgacus said nothing.

'I have no doubt that the new governor, Piso Frugi, will want to see you. Especially as I understand that your *patronus*, Marcus Clodius Ballista, led the emperor Valerian into a Persian trap and the barbarian has now justly been declared an enemy of the Roman people.'

The centurion smirked. 'Oh yes, the noble Piso Frugi will want to question you – although probably not until you have spent a few days in the cells under the palace.'

Calgacus remained silent.

'Now give up your weapons.' The centurion was thoroughly enjoying the moment.

Calgacus looked at Maximus and shook his head. Slowly, the Caledonian unsheathed first his sword then his dagger and threw them down in the dust at his feet. The others followed his lead.

At a signal from the centurion, soldiers came forward and efficiently searched the unarmed men. Calgacus winced as his wounded arm was wrenched. Their mounts, Pale Horse among them, were led away.

'All in all, a good morning's work,' the centurion said to his second-in-command.

'Just so, *Dominus*,' replied the *optio*. 'Three freedmen of a *hostis* arrested, four deserters apprehended and, to come, the gratitude of a member of the *Boule* whose son we will return.'

'Take them away.'

The high country north of Edessa going up to the Euphrates and Samosata all looks much the same. But Ballista knew where he was as soon as he saw the lone pike standing stark on the horizon.

They had been riding hard all day. Two or three times, Persian patrols had closed to investigate. They had veered away, no explanation necessary, when they saw the golden ornaments on the bridle of the Sassanid officer's horse. No easterner in his right mind would interfere with a man going about the business of the King of Kings.

Now, the sun was low. Elongated shadows stretched out as they rode up to the crest. Tired and sore, Ballista composed himself in preparation for what he was about to see. It was not chance that the Sassanids had led them this way. Ballista halted his mount and looked up.

Turpio was just recognizable. Birds had pecked out his eyes; some of the flesh on his face was gone. Being impaled on the pike had prevented the scavengers of the earth reaching his head. What remained was barely corrupt. Although it seemed an age, it had only been five days. Ballista looked at his friend.

Don't cry
Over the happy dead
But weep for those who dread
To die.

The Persian officer broke into Ballista's thoughts. 'It was the will of Mazda.' Garshasp was also looking up at the grisly thing on the pike. 'I saw him die. Your friend died well.'

'He never lacked courage. Once, at Arete, he came this close' – Ballista snapped his fingers – 'to killing your king. As you say, the will of the gods.'

'When I was commanded to bring you this way,' Garshasp continued, 'I was told you were not to bury him. I am sorry.'

'Thank you. I would have done, even though the burial rites of Romans like him are not those of my people. We often burn our dead warriors.'

Garshasp grunted. 'Let us move on. It would be best to camp beyond the battlefield.'

Even in shadow, the valley of tears was a horrible sight. The tidal wave of war had swept its debris across its length. Everywhere were strewn discarded, hacked shields, bent and broken swords, the snapped shafts of arrows and, everywhere, the corpses of men and beasts. Here they lay in ones and twos. There, to the right, leading to the isolated hill rising from the floor of the valley, a thick carpet of them, where the Sassanid cavalry had broken Legio VI Gallicana. Another hideous pile on the slopes, where those too wounded to walk had been killed after the surrender.

The horses, unnerved by the scent of death, placed their hooves nervously amidst the carnage. A vulture, too gorged to fly, waddled off a bloated corpse. Some of the dead were more decayed than others. Ballista half remembered Turpio telling him it was all to do with climate and diet; damp westerners rot more quickly than desiccated men from the east.

They rode on after the sun had gone down. Garshasp was evidently as keen as the others to put some distance between them and the dead. Eventually, he called a halt.

Their new status as envoys had brought temporary eastern servants for Ballista and Cledonius. The two Roman officers sat on the ground and watched their horses being groomed and their tents erected. The sharp north wind made the latter tricky; sudden gusts flicked leather sheets aside, coiled guy ropes around limbs.

Cledonius sent away the youth who would have seen to Ballista's dressings. By the guttering torchlight, Cledonius did it himself. The *ab Admissionibus* had been kept by Valerian's side and had thus been spared some of the hardship of the march. Now, his long, thin face was close to the northerner; his hands worked deftly. They talked together softly in Latin.

'Ballista, it is – what? – over twenty years since you came into the *imperium* as a hostage for the good behaviour of your father's tribe – not that it has always curbed the inherent ferocity of you Angles. Anyway, you have spent more than half your life, not just in the *imperium*, but connected to the imperial court, and at times you are as naive as the day you emerged out of your damp northern forests.' Cledonius smiled affectionately. 'Of course Valerian knows that Macrianus loathes us – although I would say rather more you than me. I have never punched one of his sons in the balls.'

'So Valerian wants our embassy to fail?'

Cledonius shook his head in mock-wonder at Ballista's obtuseness. 'That is the general idea. Thanks to you, Valerian knows he was betrayed by Macrianus. But only a few know it. And those now within the *imperium* might find it hard to be believed. So Valerian has created a public spectacle where the lame one must break his oath *to value the safety of the emperor above everything*. At the very least, such despicable lack of loyalty and flagrant disregard of the gods will give a very poor start to Macrianus's campaign if he intends to elevate his odious sons to the throne. At best, it gives Gallienus in the west a just cause for war: revenge on the oath-breaker who betrayed his father, Valerian.'

Ballista thought for a moment. 'Why has Shapur agreed to the embassy?'

'Harder to say.' Cledonius shrugged. 'The King of Kings has not chosen to confide in me. But it seems he is equally well served by our success or failure.'

Now it was Ballista's turn to shrug. Immediately, he wished he had not. It hurt. 'Explain.'

Cledonius waited for a servant, who had come to tell them that their tents were ready, to move out of earshot. 'If, as expected, Macrianus rejects the demand to ransom Valerian, then Shapur has an excellent cause for the war to carry on. But on the other side of the coin, if, by some divine intervention, we get Macrianus to give up what is demanded, then Shapur gets a huge amount of gold and silver and certain other things which make his glory all the greater and, I feel sure, Mazda will guide him to another good and just reason for the fighting to continue.'

'Either way, we end up back on our bellies before the Sassanid throne.' Ballista sounded depressed. 'And then . . .'

'There is a lot of talk around Shapur of using the expertise of the Roman prisoners: building towns, dams, bridges, fortifications. As a trained siege engineer, you might end up doing that. It might not be too bad.'

Having agreed, in the most half-hearted way, Ballista said goodnight to Cledonius and went to his tent. The northerner was very tired.

It was long into the night, possibly around the end of the third watch, when Ballista woke with a feeling of profound dread. The wind had risen. He could hear nothing over its howling and snapping around the tent. It was not the noise that scared him, though, it was the smell: the thick, lanolin smell of waxed canvas.

Although he knew what he would see, a tiny part of Ballista hoped he was wrong. He forced himself to look. He was not mistaken. The faint glow of the torches outside illuminated the figure. It was standing, the tip of its hood touching the roof of the tent. As every time before, it was waiting.

Ballista got a double bridle on his fear. 'Speak,' he commanded.

The figure spoke, a deep, grating sound: 'I will see you again at Aquileia.'

'I will see you then,' Ballista replied.

The figure did not move. Under the hood, its eyes

glittered. It hissed another word: 'Oath-breaker,' then turned and left.

Ballista did not call out for the guards. There was no point. On no previous occasion had anyone else seen the daemon of the emperor Maximinus Thrax.

Twenty-two years before, Ballista had sworn the military oath to Maximinus Thrax. *By Jupiter Optimus Maximus and all the gods, I swear to carry out the emperor's commands, never desert the standards or shirk death, to value the safety of the emperor above everything.* Ballista had not kept the *sacramentum*. Instead, at the siege of Aquileia, he had killed Maximinus Thrax, plunging a stylus into his throat. The other conspirators had beheaded the emperor, desecrated his body. Denying him burial, they had condemned his daemon to walk the earth for eternity.

Ballista had only told four people about the daemon: his wife Julia, bodyguard Maximus, body servant Calgacus and Turpio – and Turpio was dead. Julia, brought up by an Epicurean father, had tried to comfort her husband by rationalizing it. Maximinus only appeared when Ballista was tired, under great stress. It was just a figment of his overheated imagination. Ballista sniffed the air – waxed canvas. He did not think bad dreams left a smell.

It had been four years since the last apparition, the night Arete fell. Never before had the daemon said 'Oath-breaker'. He was a long way from Aquileia, but Ballista knew the daemon's words foretold something bad.

V

Demetrius sat on the hard-packed earth floor, his back against the rough stone wall. It was almost completely dark. There was just one tiny slit of a window, high up. It had admitted little light during the day and, when the sun went down, next to none.

After their arrest, the four Dalmatian troopers had been marched off straight away to the military cantonment. Ballista's three freedmen had been kept waiting at the gate until well past midday. When Maximus asked for food, the centurion had hit him hard across the back with his vine stick.

At long last, they had been ordered to their feet. Under heavy guard, they were led through the squared-off streets to the bridge over the Euphrates which gave the twin towns of Apamea on the eastern bank and Zeugma on the west a reason to exist.

At the bridgehead, the party had been brought to a halt. The approaches, narrowed anyway by bales of merchandise, were completely blocked by a mass of men, camels, mules and horses. Amid a fearful noise, the crush had surged up to the barrier, where a lone *telones* backed by some club-wielding members of the watch attempted to extract the custom dues rightly owed to both the *imperium* and the city. Demetrius wondered whether it had always been like that or if refugees from the east had made things worse.

When the Moorish auxiliaries laid about them, trying to force a way through, initially it had merely exacerbated the situation. Men had cursed, mules brayed, horses lashed out, and some camels had sunk to their knees, roaring. The centurion snapped an order. Swords were unsheathed. The men, if not the animals, in the crush scrambled to get out of the way.

Having told the *telones* and the civic watch to go fuck themselves, the soldiers had marched the prisoners across the pontoon bridge. The river was busy with boats and barges coming downstream from Samosata. Half a dozen big barges, piled high with produce, were moored, waiting for a gap to be opened in the pontoon so they could continue on south.

There had been another pause at a military checkpoint on the western bridgehead. It had been quieter there. The *slop, slop* sound of screws raising water from the river floated up. To one side, Demetrius noticed a massive iron chain coiled with vines and ivy growing through the unrusted links, the remains of the original bridge constructed by the god Dionysus on his way to the east to conquer India.

The formalities conducted, they moved on through what had until recently been a rich residential area. The majority of the houses showed signs of having been burnt. Only some had been repaired, and those hastily. After that, the land rising, they passed a theatre and crossed an *agora*, which brought them to the foot of the citadel. The path up was stepped and ran between dwellings that clung to the vertiginous slope. The tall terraced houses seemed to be built on top of each other and the path between them like the bottom of a ravine.

They entered through a gate in a low, rough wall and climbed on up through an orchard of fruit trees. At length, out of breath, they reached the summit. To their left was the great temple of the Tyche of Zeugma; a statue of the seated goddess could be glimpsed through the open doors. The guards turned them sharply to the right, towards the palace complex. From there they were taken to a side entrance, frogmarched down a flight of steps, along a corridor and unceremoniously pushed into a cell. The door slammed behind them, and they heard bolts being pushed home.

Demetrius had slumped to the floor. From there he watched Maximus and Calgacus carefully inspecting every inch of the gloomy, bare cell. They tried the door, stood on each other's shoulders to check the narrow window, tapped the walls, scraped at the floor. Eventually, frustrated, they hunkered down next to the young Greek. The older men talked in low voices. If they could get out, they would need horses, or they could try to make it to one of the barges waiting at the bridge, hide themselves among the produce, or maybe overpower the boatmen and take their place.

At some point in the afternoon, they heard the bolts drawn back, and the door swung open. Watchful guards covered them with drawn swords as a tray of food was put on the floor. The door was shut again.

There was some stale bread, a few handfuls of raisins and a big pitcher of water. Demetrius and Maximus fell on it. Calgacus used some of his share of the water to wash his wounded arm. When everything had gone, they were still hungry.

When the light faded, Maximus and Calgacus both fell fast asleep. There was no furniture, so they slept on the floor, their heads on their arms.

Demetrius could not sleep. It was not his hunger. Desperate though it was, the prison-stench of unwashed bodies, shit and fear took the edge off it, made him feel nauseous. He envied the calm, natural fatalism of his companions. Gods below, they had travelled so far, come through so much – and for it to come to this. Confined in this filthy cell – if he still lived, could Ballista himself be worse off? And the centurion had said that Ballista was now declared a *hostis*. Falsely accused of having led the old emperor Valerian into the trap that had cost his freedom, Demetrius's *kyrios* was now an outlaw to be killed on sight by any Roman citizen. The true traitor, that scheming bastard Macrianus the Lame, had seized the moment and was now the master of the eastern provinces of the *imperium*. Was there no such thing as divine justice? Did the gods even exist?

Demetrius lay down in the darkness. To steady himself, he turned to philosophy and the teachings of the Stoic masters. Everything that lies outside the inner man is an irrelevance. The things over which we have no choice – illness, bereavement, exile and imprisonment, death itself – all are irrelevant. Throw them aside. When enslaved, Diogenes was a free man. The King of Persia on his gilded

71

throne may be a slave. Iron bars and stone walls cannot make a prison. A little comforted, he fell asleep.

A while later, a gentle pressure behind his left ear brought Demetrius awake. He jerked up. A hand clamped over his mouth. A faint light came from the open door. A figure stood there.

'Come.' The figure spoke in Greek with a heavy eastern accent. 'You come now.'

Maximus removed his hand.

'It could be a trap,' Demetrius whispered.

'Then we will swap one for another.' Maximus grinned.

The figure went in front of them along the corridor and up the steps. He stopped, looked about and led them out. Quickly and quietly, they moved through a maze of alleys until they emerged on the far side of the citadel to that through which they had come in.

The figure stopped again to look and listen, then waved them to follow him down into the orchard. The slope was steep, the soil underfoot crumbling and dry. Slithering and sliding, they went down, grabbing tree trunks to slow their momentum. The pale light of the young moon shone through the branches.

They came to a low wall. Demetrius realized that it must be the one that encircled the citadel. Without a word, the figure climbed it like a lizard. He dropped out of sight down the other side. Maximus and Calgacus followed, the latter protecting his wounded arm as he did so. Now that he was alone, a wave of panic threatened to overwhelm Demetrius. He started to climb. The wall was made of irregular stones. There was no mortar. Even so, Demetrius found it difficult. He grazed his knees, felt a fingernail tear. Lying on the top, he looked down. There was a drop, something over a man's height, on to the roof of the first of the terraced houses. Nervously, he swung himself over, hung for a moment and let go. He landed awkwardly. Hands steadied him.

The figure put a finger to his lips then gestured for them to follow. In single file, Calgacus, then Demetrius, Maximus bringing up the rear, they set off.

At first they went to the right. They were sheltered there, between the wall and the gentle pitch of the roof. Demetrius walked carefully, one hand on the wall, watching where he put his feet, afraid a tile would shift or give way.

They turned left into a ridged dip where the roofs of two houses came together. At the end was another drop, a bit deeper this time. One by one, they turned round, lay down flat, pushed their legs out, wriggled backwards, hung by their hands for a second and let go. The landing site was the apex of a roof.

The figure indicated they were again to go to the right. Demetrius felt his heart shrink. The pitch of this roof was steeper, and it ran down to the black, square opening of an atrium. Slip here, and there was nothing to stop you sliding all the way down, over the edge and out into emptiness; a fall of two storeys to a shattering impact on a concrete *impluvium*. Demetrius imagined his smashed body lying there, his blood staining black the waters of the shallow raintank.

Their mysterious guide climbed down, fingers hooked into the gutter at the top, legs spread wide, and edged crabwise along the horrible slope. Calgacus followed.

Demetrius stared at the gutter. It looked so fragile: his existence would hang by an insubstantial piece of fired clay.

'No choice, boy,' Maximus whispered in his ear. 'Don't look down.'

Fumbling, clumsy with fear, Demetrius lowered himself. He could feel the heat of the day's sun still in the tiles under his body. Tentatively, he began to edge along. *Athene, Artemis, all the gods hold your hands over me.* Inch by inch he crept. *Great Zeus, Hermes, protector of travellers.* His palms were slick with sweat. He crept further. Fear sent little spasms of cramp running through his limbs. His breath was coming fast and shallow. He looked over his shoulder. The tiles went on and on, sickeningly steep, dropping into yawning black nothingness. His muscles locked. He could not move.

Demetrius felt Maximus grip his right wrist, Calgacus his left. The mere touch of the other men made the young Greek feel a little calmer.

'We will guide you,' Calgacus said in his ear. 'One hand at a time. Mine first.'

Demetrius felt the increased pressure on his left wrist. Reluctantly but obediently, he unclenched his fingers and let Calgacus move his hand along. He grasped the next length of guttering. Maximus repeated the procedure with the other hand.

Only once did Demetrius look to his left. The roof stretched away into the distance. A wave of panic rose in him. He fought it down. He kept his eyes on the tiles under his nose. Hand by hand, Maximus and Calgacus helped him along.

Demetrius became aware that Calgacus was shifting his position. A moment later, his boot struck the roof that extended out to form the next side of the atrium. A jerky scramble and the Greek boy was on the ridge, legs either side, in no danger of a fall for the time being.

On the far side of the ridge, a gentler slope ran down to a low wall. They slithered down. Past this was a drop to a stepped lane. No matter, they were safe where they were. In the shelter of the wall, they paused to get their breath back. Somewhere, not far away, a baby was crying. It had not struck Demetrius that the noise they were making could wake those sleeping in the houses below. At any moment, they might raise the alarm. Suddenly, he was eager to be moving again.

Calgacus touched Demetrius's arm. They were off once more, crouching below the level of the parapet wall, using their hands, scurrying like monkeys. This uncomfortable but unthreatening way of moving lasted all too short a time. The wall on the right and the roof on the left were at an end. Demetrius was unhappy to see Calgacus get down on all fours. The Caledonian crawled out on to a free-standing wall.

Great Athene of the Aegis, I can do this, thought Demetrius. On one side, there was a drop to the stepped street, on the other an equally awful fall to a paved court-yard. I can do this. Grey-eyed Athene, I can.

Demetrius inched out. The top of the wall was a couple of feet across. *No reason to fall. Just keep going. No earthly reason to fall.*

He was concentrating so hard on keeping his balance that he almost bumped into Calgacus. The Caledonian had stopped and was manoeuvring himself to lie down full length. Not knowing why, Demetrius did the same.

The noise came from behind. The Greek boy peered anxiously over his right shoulder and down. Two watchmen were walking down the street. They carried lanterns, and each had a club over his shoulder. As they drew nearer, Demetrius could hear one of them talking.

'So the tribune says, "So, Centurion, is that how the men use the camel?" And the centurion says, "No, Tribune, they use it to ride to the nearest brothel."'

The other watchman laughed briefly. 'That joke was old when Cronos was young,' he said. When he was level with Demetrius, he stopped. He held up his lantern and shone it into a small courtyard on the other side of the street. He went in and carefully looked all around a fountain in the middle. *Gods below, he was far too diligent.*

The watchmen moved on. The humourist started up again. 'Do you know the one about the donkey and the murderess?'

'Yes,' replied the other unencouragingly.

Giving the impression that such rebuffs were not uncommon, his companion stopped and put his lantern down on a step. He retied his laces. Retrieving the lantern, he stood up and walked on. Then, without warning, he stopped again. He turned to look back the way they had come. Then he looked up.

'Thieves! There up on the wall!'

Calgacus was up, running fast. Without time for thought, Demetrius was doing the same.

The slope of the roof loomed in front. Scrambling up it, boots slipping on the tiles, Demetrius glanced down.

The first watchman had a bell in his hand. Demetrius saw him pull out the straw which held the clapper in place. Its clanging echoed across the sleeping city.

Their unintroduced guide led the fugitives on. The pitch of the roofs here was gentle. Up and down they went, vaulting over ridges. Fear gave wings to Demetrius's feet. Below, the watchmen were chasing. Somewhere in front, another bell was ringing.

'Alley ahead. No problem to jump.' In the stress, the guide's eastern accent had dropped away.

Demetrius saw Calgacus leap the divide. Demetrius found himself mouthing one of Ballista's sayings – Do not think, just act.

As soon as he took off, the young Greek knew he had mistimed it. Arms flailing, he was dropping too fast. His stomach thumped into the edge of the roof, knocking the wind out of him. He was slipping back. His fingers clasped the corner of a tile. It came loose. He was slipping faster, legs thrashing in the void. Far below, the tile shattered.

Demetrius clung to the final row of tiles. They began to shift. A hand gripped his wrist. Calgacus's face was contorted with effort; Demetrius's weight was dragging the old Caledonian with him.

'Let go,' Demetrius screamed.

Slowly sliding to his doom, Calgacus hung on. Sweat was pouring down his ugly old face.

Another hand grasped Demetrius's other wrist.

'One, two, three, pull!' Together, the guide and Calgacus managed to haul Demetrius up a little.

'One, two, three, pull!' Demetrius's chest was over the lip of the roof. He clawed himself fully over. His saviours yanked him further up. Calgacus was doubled up, holding his injured arm. Maximus landed like a cat behind them.

'This way, quick!' The guide was off again.

Below, the streets and alleys echoed with shouts and the ringing of bells. Here and there shutters were thrown back, light spilling out.

They raced around the opening of an atrium and across an unbroken span of roofs. Temporarily, they were out of sight from the ground.

'Down there.' The guide pointed. 'Stay there until I come back.'

One by one, they dropped into a dark space formed by four converging slopes. The guide's face appeared above them. 'Do not move,' he said. Then he was gone.

A few moments later, there was a cacophony of yells. Demetrius could not resist peeping out. The guide had gone back the way they had come and was now standing over an alley, gazing this way and that, a picture of uncertainty. Then, as if spurred by the shouts from below, he set off. Moving fast, he passed the hiding place and ran off to the south. The sounds of pursuit followed him. With one hand, he swung up over a wall and was gone from sight.

Slumping back down, Demetrius saw that Maximus was tearing strips from the sleeve of his tunic and binding Calgacus's arm. The old Caledonian's eyes were screwed shut. Dark blood was running from his wound.

'Thank you,' Demetrius whispered.

Calgacus opened his eyes. 'Think nothing of it.'

They waited. The sounds of the chase faded. Immobile, they grew cold.

Demetrius wondered what they would do if the guide

did not return. Was the underworld like this? Cold, power-less, an eternity of unfulfilled waiting? One thing was certain: they could not stay here for long. They had to eat soon or else become too weak to flee. Demetrius could not stop shivering.

There was a slight scraping sound and the guide was back. 'Good exercise, yes?' His thick eastern accent had returned. 'Now, you follow. Is easy now.'

True to his word, the rest of the rooftop journey con-sisted of straightforward stages. Only one passage gave Demetrius concern. A beam jutting out from beneath the eaves held two leaning buildings apart. As he wriggled across, Demetrius looked down. An intricate pattern of washing lines ran across the alley. They would do nothing to slow a falling man. The young Greek kept his eyes on the wood in front of him.

At long last, they reached the lowest level of houses. Via an outhouse, they dropped to the ground. Across the street was the inner side of the main city wall. At no great interval, the torches of sentries could be seen up on the walkway. The guide pressed them back into the shadow of the outbuilding. He hissed for them to wait. Calmly, he walked out into the open and around the corner.

This time, the guide returned more quickly. Wasting no words, he indicated that they should follow. He took them towards one of the towers. On the battlements, the torches illuminated a standard bearing the eagle, lion and Capricorn of Legio IIII Scythica. Fortunately, the sentries were all on the other side. Under the tower, low in the wall, was a small postern gate. It was unlocked. The guide led them through and pulled it shut behind them.

Keeping close to the wall, they moved south. Every time a sentry paced above their heads, they froze. Out in the night, a fox barked. They followed the wall as it curved round to the east. Before long, the low, gloomy structures that indicated a necropolis emerged from the darkness on their right. With a wave of his hand, the guide led them away from the wall into the city of the dead. Like ghosts, they flitted between the tombs. He stopped before one that had been cut into the living rock. The door opened easily. Once inside, he closed the door and pulled a curtain across its frame.

Sparks flashed as the guide worked a flint on a steel. He lit a small clay lamp. Their shadows danced grotesquely on the walls. Demetrius looked around. A table and three couches stood in the centre of a large room cut from the rock itself. On the wall opposite the door were relief sculptures of eagles, wicker baskets, swags of flowers. In the other two walls were arched recesses; inside them long, low piles of broken roof tiles. The air was still, with a strong odour of mould and decay.

'You wait here. Your friend will come.' The guide's eastern tones were now thick to the point of parody. 'I go now. You wait.' He indicated for Maximus to shield the lamp and slipped behind the curtain. They heard the door open and close again. They were alone in the house of the dead.

Exhausted, Demetrius sat on one of the couches. With a wince, Calgacus sat beside him. Maximus put the lamp on the table and busied himself. First, he checked for any food that may have been left behind from a funeral feast. There was none. Then he started sorting through one of the mounds of tiles in one of the recesses. He came across with three shards, handily shaped and razor-sharp.

Demetrius gazed at the recess from which Maximus had emerged. In rooting about, he had disturbed the tiles. A hand stuck out from the wall now, yellow-black with decomposition. How could people use these places for sexual assignations, thought Demetrius. He could understand a low-class prostitute maybe, with no place of her own to go. You often saw them hanging around the tombs outside city walls. But others – free men and women? It was unthinkable. No wonder that, in the famous story, the shade of Philinnion left her tomb to visit her lover in her old house.

Maximus pointed to the curtain and the door behind it. In his most serious tone, he said, 'Sure, but you have to ask, just who the fuck was he?'

'No idea,' said Calgacus. 'But he could climb the shite out of a wall, just like a monkey.'

'Do you remember,' said Maximus, 'when we were in Arete, there was a woman that fucked a monkey?'

Demetrius found himself laughing with the others. 'I think you will find,' he said, 'it was just a woman who gave birth to a child that looked like a monkey.'

'And how did that happen?' Maximus sounded indignant, before adding thoughtfully, 'Unless of course she happened to look at a monkey just at the moment love reached its true, destined end.'

A sound from outside stopped their laughter. Men with horses. Several of them, reining in by the door; dismounting.

Quick as lightning, Maximus and Calgacus were either

side of the curtain, the shards of tile to the ready. Maximus blew out the lamp. Unsure what to do, Demetrius rose from the couch. Feeling foolish, he adopted an approximation of the fighting crouch of the others.

There was the sound of the door being opened. The curtain moved slightly as the night air caught it. Demetrius held his breath.

'I am a friend.' The voice from beyond the curtain was pitched low, the Latin words muffled. 'I am coming in alone. Do not attack.'

The curtain was drawn back. Pale moonlight flooded into the tomb. In the opening was the black silhouette of a man. He stepped over the threshold and stopped, his eyes taking their time to adjust. He did not flinch as Maximus noiselessly put the shard to his throat.

'Welcome back from the dead, boys.' As he spoke, the man turned to look at Maximus and the moonlight fell on his face – a strange-looking face, all lines and points.

'Castricius, you little bastard!' Maximus hugged him. Calgacus slapped him on the back. Demetrius shook his hand. The centurion's palm was gritty.

'Shite, I hoped our saviour would turn out to be the *eupatrid* whose son we rescued.' Calgacus shook his head in what seemed genuine sorrow. 'He would have given us a fine reward.'

'And if it had to be you, Castricius,' Maximus joined in, 'there was no need to leave us there so long.'

'And it's lovely to see you too,' said Castricius. 'You are lucky I'm here at all. I only got back tonight from a tour overseeing the quarries up the road at Arulis. Nasty, dirty, dangerous work – by Silvanus, the legionaries hate it –

very tiring. I thought about getting a good night's sleep, maybe rescuing you tomorrow.'

'Certain, I imagine the new governor thinks your life history fits you for the quarries.' Maximus was grinning.

'Quite possibly – Piso is a cunt.' The centurion's voice changed. 'I was very sorry to hear Ballista was taken.'

'He will get back,' said Calgacus. 'Always does.'

'I do not doubt it.' Centurion Castricius became businesslike. 'The last watch of the night is almost over. There are three horses outside, tacked up, weapons to hand, food and water in the saddlebags, even a little money. Which way will you go?'

'Do you think it unwise just to ride down the main road west – Regia and Hagioupolis to Antioch?' Calgacus asked.

Castricius considered for a time. 'Piso will be annoyed you have escaped. Of course, you three are of no importance, and Piso is naturally indolent. But he is desperate to appear competent in the eyes of his Macrianus the Lame. He might be so keen to suck his *dominus*'s cock that he will send a troop of horses down the obvious route.'

'I have a friend in Hierapolis – well, a man I met on the journey out . . .' Demetrius's words trailed off.

'There is no direct road,' said Castricius. 'It must be about forty miles as the crow flies, tough going, but it still might be best to go south.'

Outside, a legionary was holding the horses. In turn, the fugitives thanked Castricius and mounted up.

'One thing,' said Maximus. 'Who was the easterner who led us over the roofs?'

The small centurion laughed. 'That was no local. One

of my boys from Legio IIII – a *scaenicus legionis*. If you had to talk your way out of something, I thought it would be useful to have an actor to help you.'

As they rode away, Demetrius reflected on life's absurdities. Most legions, especially those stationed out in the east, contained a troupe of soldier-actors. It helped pass the time. A *scaenicus legionis* had appeared to save them like the *deus ex machina* he must have so often played.

VI

Ballista was standing in the governor's palace in Samosata. He was watching the Sassanid envoy trying to control himself. Garshasp the Lion might have first won his *cognomen* in some battle in the east, but presumably it had stuck because it suited him. Unusually for a Persian, his hair had a reddish tinge. Long and thick, it invited comparison with a mane. When angry, as he certainly was now, his eyes flashed.

They had been in Samosata for nine days. Finally granted an audience with Macrianus the Lame, they had been left waiting in the basilica for over an hour. If you thought the Sassanid King of Kings the equal of a Roman emperor, the twin eyes of the world, the two lamps in the darkness of mankind, as Ballista had heard Garshasp put it, this was a studied insult.

Ballista himself had relished the delay. Every night that passed took him further away from the nocturnal apparition of the daemon of Maximinus Thrax. Ballista needed recourse to his familiar mantra – *the* daemon *cannot physically harm you, avoid Aquileia and all will be well* – less and less frequently There were other reasons Ballista welcomed the delay. Every day in Roman territory was a day he did not have to return to Sassanid captivity. Here in Samosata he could indulge the fantasy that all he had to do to be reunited with Julia and the boys was call for a horse and set out on the road to Antioch. And he wanted to be far away from the memory of the cell in Carrhae. Rolled face down, limbs stretched out, tunic hauled up; Allfather, that had been close. The assault had shaken the northerner more than he cared to admit.

To break the run of his thoughts, he looked around the basilica. The last time he had been here, there had been plague. It was long gone, but the ends of some of the swags of laurel – their scent considered a preventative of disease – had not been removed. The floor was unswept. If one were planning a coup, as Ballista was convinced Macrianus was, such incidentals might well be overlooked. Valerian's imperial throne had gone from the dais at the end of the long room. Instead, six seats adorned with ivory stood in a row – the *curule* chairs symbolic of high Roman magistracies.

The doors swung open. A herald announced Marcus Fulvius Macrianus, *Comes Sacrarum Largitionum*, *Praefectus Annonae*, holder of *maius imperium* in the *Oriens*. The titles rang out sonorous and impressive: the treasurer of the whole empire, its supply-master, with overriding military authority in its eastern territories.

Click, drag, step. Macrianus advanced down the aisle. Click went his walking stick, his lame foot dragged, and his sound one took a step. He was followed by two more youthful versions of himself. His sons had the same long, straight nose, receding chin and pouchy eyes, but Quietus and Macrianus the Younger walked easily, with a confident swagger.

Behind the family came three more men. All had deserted the setting sun of Valerian in time to rise high in the newly emerging regime. There was the elderly *nobilis* Pomponius Bassus, recently appointed governor of Cappadocia, the senator Maeonius Astyanax, as ever clutching a papyrus roll as evidence of his intellectuality, and, most sinister of all, Censorinus, commander of the *frumentarii*. Emperors came and went, but there was always a feared *Princeps Peregrinorum* like Censorinus in charge of the imperial secret service.

On the dais, Macrianus handed his stick to one of his sons. He pulled a fold of his toga over his head and poured a libation of wine. Raising his hands to the heavens, he said a prayer to the immortal gods of Rome. His tone was imbued with the fervour of true belief. This was a man who had caused untold suffering to his fellow citizens with his persecution of Christians. Few could be more dangerous, more inhumane than an active and shrewd politician guided by burning religious certainty.

Once everyone was settled in their seats, Macrianus the Lame indicated that the embassy should begin.

Garshasp spoke briefly. Avoiding Greek, the diplomatic language of the east, he used his native tongue. Having captured Valerian in battle, Shapur, King of Kings, would now accept a ransom for him. Cledonius and Ballista had been brought here to arrange it. Knowing Persian, Ballista noted that the interpreter filled out the phrases to make them less brusque.

Cledonius took the floor. Having served for many years as *ab Admissionibus* to Valerian, he was well versed in courtly etiquette. His speech was full and round in its

Latin orotundity. He moved seamlessly between high-flown sentiments and hard details.

The words slid off Ballista's mind like rain off a tiled roof. No one expected this embassy to succeed; not Shapur or Valerian, and none of the men in this room. Macrianus the Lame had exercised great ingenuity and foresight in order to betray Valerian to the Persians. The very last thing he would want was the return of the aged emperor. Instead, as Quietus had told Ballista in a moment of fury, Macrianus intended that his sons take the purple. Cledonius's speech ran on. As the historian Tacitus had revealed long ago, the rule of the emperors had created a gulf between words and reality.

Suddenly, with a flourish, Cledonius produced a document from his toga. He began to read. It was a letter from Valerian to his loyal servant Macrianus. It was a direct order to the Count of the Sacred Largess to leave Samosata and come to the emperor in Carrhae.

In the silence that followed Cledonius's rhetorical device, Macrianus rose to his feet. He came to the edge of the dais and leant on his stick.

'Is anyone so insane that he would willingly become a slave and prisoner of war instead of being a free man?' Macrianus shook his head, as if overcome by the folly of it all. 'Furthermore, those who are ordering me to go from here are not my masters. One of them, Shapur, is an enemy. The other, Valerian, is not master of himself, and thus can in no way be our master.'

It was in the open. Macrianus had publicly denied that Valerian was emperor any longer. Although Ballista knew the devious Count of the Sacred Largess had been working towards this for at least a year, he still felt vaguely shocked. The northerner looked around to see how everyone else was taking it. Up on the dais, all heads except one nodded in solemn agreement. Quietus was smiling in exultation. Again, through the main body of the basilica, there seemed much muted approval. Ballista noted that the audience contained a significant percentage of those high-ranked senators who had followed Valerian to the east.

Macrianus pointed to Garshasp. 'You will return to your master tomorrow morning.'

When the translator had finished, the Sassanid warrior turned and, without a word, left the room.

Macrianus gestured with his walking stick. Its silver head of Alexander the Great flashed. 'Cledonius and Ballista, you will remain here to serve the *Res Publica*.'

Cledonius spoke up clearly. 'I will not.' His thin face was a mask. 'I am bound by the *sacramentum* I took to Valerian Augustus and by a specific oath to return to Shapur.'

'And you, Ballista?' Macrianus betrayed no emotion.

'The same.'

The lame man leant on his stick, thinking. 'The *sacramentum* is a personal oath to an emperor,' he said at length. 'When a man ceases to be emperor – he dies or is taken prisoner – the oath ceases. Any oath you made to Shapur was under duress and so is invalid. The gods of Rome would want you to remain and give your service to the *imperium*.'

'Sophistry,' said Cledonius. 'No emperor has ever been held captive by barbarians before. Who is to say Valerian is no longer emperor? In any event, there was no duress when I gave my oath to Shapur. I will return.'

Macrianus pointed at Ballista.

Temptation caressed Ballista. One word. Just one word, and he was safe with his family. Back with Julia. Back with his sons; looking into their huge blue eyes, burying his face in their long hair, inhaling the smell of them.

No – Ballista tried to push temptation away. It clung like a whore on a Massilia dockside. Think of Julia, Isangrim, Dernhelm. No – there would be no safety. The very opposite. One word would bring down the terrible curse in the oath he had sworn to Shapur. If it were just on his own head, he could take it. But not on his sons'. *If I break my oath, spill my brains on the ground as this wine spills, my brains and the brains of my sons too.*

'I return with Cledonius to the emperor.'

'So be it.' Macrianus's face was impossible to read. He tapped his stick for quiet, declared the *consilium* over, intoned another heartfelt prayer and made his way out. Click, drag, step. His supporters jostled as they were forced to keep to his slow pace. Click, drag, step.

Outside, Maeonius Astyanax was waiting. 'Ballista, a word,' he said.

The senator led Ballista round the basilica to a south-facing garden which abutted on to the palace. The path was flanked by statues of Greek intellectuals, arranged alphabetically: A was Aristotle, B, Bion. They stopped by Homer.

'Your wife and sons are well in Antioch.'

'Thank you.' Ballista felt a hollowness in his chest.

Astyanax fiddled with the book roll in his hands and looked up at the marble bust of Homer. He was going to say more.

Ballista waited. He had spoken to Astyanax a few times.

But, beyond the senator's fervent support for Macrianus the Lame, Ballista knew little about him. Julia had once said that rumours linking the two men all involved disgusting impropriety.

Ballista realized he had never really looked at Astyanax before. He was a middle-aged man, with short hair and a short, full beard. His lips were soft and fleshy; his forehead intensely wrinkled. Astyanax twisted the papyrus between his fingers. The man was nervous.

Astyanax looked away from the marble face of the blind poet. His gaze traversed the wall of the palace, as if seeking something to distract him in the diamond-pattern limestone blocks.

At last, glancing at Ballista, then looking away, he began to talk. 'Macrianus genuinely believes he has the mandate of the gods to restore the *Res Publica*.'

'I do not doubt it.' Ballista's voice was neutral.

'The Christians have to die. Their open denial of the gods, their disgusting atheism, turns the immortals against the *imperium*.'

'Quite possibly.'

Astyanax turned and looked Ballista in the eye. 'Valerian had to go. He was old, weak, irresolute. The gods demand a strong hand at the helm.'

Ballista said nothing.

'In this age of iron and rust, we must have an emperor.' There was a wheedling quality to the senator's voice.

'We have one: Gallienus. And a Caesar in his son Saloninus,' Ballista replied.

Astyanax shook his head. 'They are far away on the northern frontier.'

'One of them could travel east.'

Astyanax's fleshy lips twitched. 'They are beset by your barbarian cousins.'

Ballista ignored the gibe. 'Gallienus has a brother and another son in Rome. One of them could assume the purple.'

'Gallienus is a degenerate. There is no reason to think his close relatives any better.'

'Certainly Gallienus likes to drink and he likes to fuck.' Ballista nodded at the papyrus in the other's hands. 'He writes poetry and listens to philosophers too. But I have campaigned with him. He knows how to fight.'

Astyanax dismissed the argument with a wave of his hand. 'Macrianus has all the virtues necessary in a *princeps*. He has self-control, piety, courage, intelligence, far-sightedness.'

'And a crippled leg.' Ballista spoke more harshly than he had intended. 'No man can ascend the throne of the Caesars with a physical deformity.'

'True.' Astyanax smiled. 'That is why Quietus and Macrianus the Younger must take the throne. The sons will be guided by their father.' The treason voiced, Astyanax hurried on. 'The majority of the senate will be with us. They hate Gallienus – his lack of *dignitas*, the way he excludes them from military commands, panders to the common soldiers, promotes illiterate barbarians.'

Ballista was silent for a moment. There was more than some truth in it. 'A senatorial majority does not win a civil war, armies do,' he remarked.

'Quite so. Those who matter in the east – those who hold the armed provinces – are already with us. While you were away, the governor of Cappadocia met an unfortunate end. Exiguus was killed by bandits.' Astyanax raised his eyebrows. '*Latrones* everywhere – dangerous times. Cappadocia is now held for Macrianus by Pomponius Bassus.'

When Ballista did not react, Astyanax carried on. 'Strangely, when he heard the news, Valens, the governor of Syria Coele, fled to the west. He has been replaced by Piso Frugi, another close *amicus* of the Count of the Sacred Largess. Achaeus, governor of Palestine, is with us. A devout persecutor of Christians, he is aware what the times call for. The prefect of Egypt, Aemilianus, is an ambitious man, and the governor of Syria Phoenice, Cornicula, a weak one. They both realize where their advantage lies. Doubtless, the isolated governors of Osrhoene and Arabia will fall into line.'

Astyanax spread his hands wide in a studied oratorical gesture. 'Then there is Sampsigeramus, the king of Emesa. Seven years ago, in the time of troubles, he put a myriad horsemen in the field. The god he serves has told him to pledge his support. As I said, we command all the armed might of the east.'

Ballista laughed. 'Then why do you need me?'

'We are not sure we do. Yet you might be useful. Much of Valerian's field army was drawn from the west. You have served there. They might like a general they know.' Astyanax sighed. 'And, corrupted by Gallienus, they might prefer a general of your *origins*.' There was a wealth of contempt in the last word.

'Then it is unfortunate for you that I am oath-bound to return to Shapur.'

Astyanax turned a bland face to the northerner.

'Macrianus dealt with that in the *consilium*. Anyway, you do not have a reputation for being over-pious. Under you, the persecution of Christians in Ephesus ground to a halt. Your wife's family are Epicureans. Like them, you may think the gods are uninterested in humanity.'

At the mention of Julia, the hollowness in Ballista returned.

Now Astyanax looked pained, his forehead even more wrinkled. 'After Valerian was captured, you were declared a *hostis,* an outlaw to be killed on sight. That order has not yet been rescinded.' He paused. Ballista feared where this was going.

Astyanax resumed, in short, measured sentences. 'Your family is in Antioch, the capital of the province of Syria Coele. The new governor is on his way there from Zeugma. Piso Frugi is a zealous supporter of Macrianus. Some might say overzealous. The wife and children of a *hostis*, a traitor to the *Res Publica*, a traitor to Macrianus – things might not go well for them.'

Ballista could not speak.

Astyanax patted his arm. 'Never take a hasty decision. Sleep on it.'

Dawn came up over the stirring city of Samosata. As every day at this time, the beams were removed and the Edessa gate was swung open. Since the capture of Valerian, the guards had exercised great vigilance. When they were satisfied there were no Sassanids lurking, they waved the *telones* to carry on. The customs official stood back as Ballista and Cledonius led the horses through the gate.

Outside, the two men moved off the road to wait for

Garshasp. Ballista did not want to talk. He studied the motley throng of refugees. Day by day, more arrived from south of the river. Ballista wondered how many of them were Persian infiltrators. It was an obvious move. Certainly, Shapur would have thought of it. Yet the *telones* seemed to be doing nothing but searching them for taxable goods. Perhaps it had not occurred to Macrianus.

Ballista could sense Cledonius's growing impatience to talk. The northerner turned his back and looked at the defences of Samosata. On the other side of the ditch, the wall was tall and thick. Although its facade was a diamond pattern of small blocks, it was smooth enough. But here and there were buttresses. Were they ornamental or did they indicate structural weakness? Either way, they were a bad thing, providing a modicum of cover for attackers. And the town wall was long. It would take an enormous number of men to defend it. Up on its hill, the citadel might be daunting, but the town itself would be difficult to hold.

The horse Ballista was holding tossed its head. He soothed it, bringing his face close to its nostrils, letting it inhale his breath. The automatic gestures did not break Ballista's line of thought. Did Macrianus even intend to try and hold the town? What were the lame one's plans?

Astyanax had outlined the plot in the most favourable light. Yet in some ways it was what he had not said that was most important. Astyanax had not mentioned any western governors as supporters. Presumably, there were none. And he had not talked of the governors of the so-called unarmed provinces of the east. While they commanded no legions, there were small detached troops of soldiers in every province. As well as these *stationarii*, there would be some whole units of auxiliary cavalry and infantry. It seemed that the governors of Asia, Lycia-Pamphylia, Cilicia and the other unarmed eastern provinces had not fallen in behind Macrianus either.

Astyanax had admitted that Virius Lupus, with his one legion in Arabia, and Aurelius Dasius, with the remnants of two in Osrhoene, had yet to commit. His ambiguity concerning the allegiance of Cornicula in Syria Phoenice and Aemilianus in Egypt was also telling. Two more eastern legions not yet secured.

Yet most important of all was what Astyanax had not said about the client rulers. He had made much of the adherence of Sampsigeramus of Emesa but had said nothing about Odenathus, the Lord of Palmyra. In the time of troubles, Odenathus had raised thirty thousand warriors, horse and foot. Ballista had commanded Palmyrenes: Cohors XX Palmyrenorum at Arete and Equites Tertii Catafractarii Palmirenorum at Circesium. They were fine fighters, deadly with a bow, fearsome hand to hand. The oasis city of Palmyra, Tadmor to its inhabitants, lay between Rome and Persia. Now its lord, Odenathus, the Lion of the Sun, held the balance in the east.

Garshasp, his devotions complete, the risen sun worshipped, walked out of Samosata. He shook Ballista's hand. Ballista passed him the reins and gave him a leg-up. The Persian waited.

Cledonius embraced Ballista.

'Are you sure?' There was no accusation in the voice of the *ab Admissionibus*.

'Yes.' Ballista made as if to say more.

'There is no need to explain,' said Cledonius. 'My wife is dead, my son with Gallienus.'

Ballista nodded. He helped Cledonius into the saddle. 'We are playthings of the gods,' said the *ab Admissionibus*. 'They give us harsh choices.'

The two mounted men turned and rode slowly away towards the bridge south. Ballista watched them go.

The words of his oath tormented Ballista: *If I break my oath, spill my brains on the ground as this wine spills, my brains and the brains of my sons too.*

Julia put the papyrus roll down on the desk with the others. She pinched the bridge of her nose between forefinger and thumb. It was hot, even in the shaded part of the atrium. She had chosen this house for their family dwelling in Antioch because the Epiphania district caught whatever breeze there was. This morning, there was none.

She tapped the stylus against her teeth. The deeds of the property just outside Daphne were straightforward enough, but the other was more complicated. Ever since the charcoal burner had died, intestate, two of his relatives had disputed ownership. If Julia wanted the property, there seemed nothing for it but to pay off both. She was not sure why she was so determined to buy it. Certainly you could build a wonderful summer retreat there, high on the southern slopes of Mount Silpius, magnificent views but tucked away, almost impossible to find. Had she not been brought up in a household of the strictest Epicurean philosophy – the gods are far away and have no interest in humanity – she might have thought a deity had put the idea in her mind. Four years earlier, Ballista had narrowly survived an attempt on his life there. Possibly she wanted to buy it as a sort of offering for the return of her absent husband. If so, her philosophical rationality was slipping. Her late father, the stern senator Gaius Julius Volcatius Gallicanus, would not have approved.

Julia signalled for Anthia, the maid attending her, to bring a drink. At least Julia was not one of those Roman women of the old *Res Publica* whose husbands only kissed them to smell if there was wine on their breath. And she was not one of those Greek women still to be found in some cities whose menfolk made them wear the veil in public and locked them in their rooms at night.

Anthia brought the drink, mixing the water and wine as the *domina* liked it. Julia thanked her and sent her away. Sipping the cool liquid, she reflected that it was still a man's world. She would have to get her *tutor* to approve her purchases. Luckily, it was a formality. He was one of her many cousins, far away in Gaul and far more concerned with his fish ponds than anything else. She was lucky too in her husband. Ballista had never had much interest in their domestic arrangements. As soon as they were married, he had handed the household keys and the *cura* of their home to her.

Julia smiled to find herself playing with the iron ring on the third finger of her left hand. When Ballista had given it to her at their betrothal party, she had not loved him. Far from it. Her mother, may the earth lie lightly on her, had been opposed to the match, but her father had talked her round. Julia had dutifully done what her father wished. Although her family was still able to prove the senatorial property qualification, many of their ancestral estates had been confiscated more than half a century before by Septimius Severus, as a result of the family's unwise support for his rival Albinus. Their influence had not recovered. Marcus Clodius Ballista may have been born a barbarian but, nine years ago, he had held equestrian status in Rome, and – her father's winning argument – he had been a close *amicus* of the then reigning emperor Gallus.

If, as Epicurus taught, the ultimate aim of human life was freedom from disturbance, Julia wondered why people got married. *Ataraxia* and marriage did not seem obvious companions. It was not as if Ballista had many more faults than most husbands. To the usual insensitivity, stubbornness, drunkenness and outbursts of violent temper, he added only an ineradicable barbarian naivety. No, it was none of these that unsettled her freedom from disturbance. Since she had come to love him, it was his absences on campaign. One day, he would not return. Julia thought of their sons. Their beautiful, innocent sons. She would never, like the Spartan women of old, tell them to return with their shield or on it.

As Julia picked up her writing block, her new steward appeared. Before he could announce them, three shabby-looking men followed him out into the shade on the far side of the atrium. Julia had time for just a flash of annoyance before she recognized them. Dropping the writing things, she ran around the pool. *Dignitas* forgotten, she threw her arms around the neck of the ugly old man at the front.

'Calgacus.' She kissed him on both cheeks.

'Steady, *Domina*. The servants will talk,' said Maximus. She kissed him too, then turned and embraced Demetrius.

'How did you get here? We had heard nothing.'

Their smiles faded. The three men looked embarrassed. 'We travelled by night, avoiding people. A . . . a friend of Demetrius hid us for a time in Hierapolis. Before that, Castricius got us out of a problem in Zeugma.' Calgacus stopped. He fiddled with the sling on his arm.

'It was as if the underworld had swallowed you.' Julia clapped her hands. 'Now you are back – the gods be praised. Let me look at you. Calgacus, you are injured.'

'It is nothing.' The elderly Caledonian waved his good hand indecisively. '*Domina*, your husband . . .' His voice trailed away.

Maximus also tried to speak and failed.

'*Domina*' – Demetrius took a deep breath and let the words out in a rush – 'your husband is a prisoner of the Sassanids. He ordered us to leave him. There was nothing we could do. I am sorry.'

Julia tipped her head back and laughed. The three men exchanged looks. Women were fragile, their grip on reality weak. Had the news unhinged her?

Wiping her eyes, she shook her head. 'The news has outrun you.' She raised herself on tiptoe and kissed Demetrius on the forehead. 'He is free, back with the Roman field army in Samosata. He has been appointed Prefect of Cavalry.' She laughed again. 'Not only is my husband free, Ballista is now officially a *Vir Perfectissimus*.'

PART TWO

Ubique Pax

(The West, Cisalpine Gaul, south of the city of Mediolanum, Summer AD260)

'O Zeus, what pitiable suffering, what bloody trial approaches
that drives you onward, man of sorrows?'

Euripides, *Orestes*, 332–3

VII

The emperor Gallienus reined in his horse. Its trappings gleamed purple and gold. Well-schooled, it stood quietly, waiting for the ritual to start again.

This time, unexpectedly, a soldier called out from the ranks of the closest unit. 'A coin for a shave, *Dominus*.'

Gallienus smiled and held his hand out to his *a Memoria*. Achilleus placed a coin in the emperor's palm. Gallienus flicked it through the air. 'Good luck.'

'May the gods grant you victory, *Dominus*.'

Another soldier called out. 'Me too, *Imperator*.'

Gallienus slowly studied the man. 'After due consideration, *commilitio*, and with the best will in the world, a face like yours is better hidden by a beard.' The soldier himself joined in the laughter as he caught the coin that was thrown in any case.

Gallienus unlaced his helmet and hung it on one of the rear horns of his saddle. He ran his hand through his sweat-dampened, dyed-blond hair. It was hot on the north Italian plain in the summer.

There could never be complete silence in any unit of the Roman army. There was always the clink of metal on metal, the creak of leather, the occasional cough. When it was as quiet as it was going to get, Gallienus raised himself by the front horns of the saddle and began to make his pre-battle speech yet again.

'We have waited a long time and marched a long way for this day. Finally, we have these barbarians where we want them – on an open field, cut off from the mountains and any hope of safety. There are a lot of them.' Not deigning to look, Gallienus languidly gestured over his shoulder to the south. 'It will do them no good. They will merely get in each other's way. They have no *disciplina*.'

The soldiers banged their spears on their shields.

'These Germans call themselves the Alamanni. They think themselves *All Man*. We know better. They are all *cinaedi*. These hairy bum-boys reached Rome. The eternal city is unwalled. They ran from a rabble of plebs and slaves led by a few delicate old senators.'

Gallienus waited for the laughter to subside. 'The quickest and bravest of them have already crossed the Alps. And you all know what happened to them on the other side. The acting governor of Raetia, with just a handful of regular troops and some local peasants, cut them to pieces.'

'We know it. We know it,' chanted the soldiers in their rough northern accents.

Gallienus raised his voice. 'Today we will free Italy from the barbarians. Today we will free our fellow citizens whom they have cruelly enslaved. Today we will take back the Germans' booty and share it among ourselves. By tonight there will not be a poor man in our army!'

As one, the soldiers roared their approval.

'Are you ready for war?'

'Ready!'

As the third repetition of the ritual response was still ringing out, Gallienus looked at Achilleus and his standard bearer. He winked at the two men and nodded forwards. Then, suddenly grabbing his helmet, he kicked his heels into the flanks of his horse. It leapt ahead, closely pursued by those of the other two.

Behind the emperor, his senatorial entourage was caught unawares. They milled in confusion, their horses bumping into each other as they hastened to follow. The soldiers loved it. As he sped away, Gallienus heard them mocking their social superiors before the unit battle cry boomed forth: '*Io Cantab! Io Cantab!*'

Gallienus turned into a gap between two of the units and galloped north towards where the reserve of Horse Guards and the rest of his entourage waited.

An emperor never travels alone. As they drew near, the emperor indicated his permission for his *a Memoria* Achilleus to draw off to one side, where the other heads of his imperial bureaucracy waited. He smiled at their incongruously civilian aspect. There was Quirinius, the *a Rationibus*, who oversaw his treasury; Palfurius Sura, the *ab Epistulis*, who handled his correspondence; and Hermianus, his *ab Admissionibus*. They were all powerful, important men. The *imperium* could not function without them. But far away from their desks in the imperial chancery, they looked lost.

Holding their horses' heads under the Horse Guards' flag – a red Pegasus on a white banner – the military high command were very different. Three stood out in front: Volusianus, the Italian former trooper, now Praetorian

Prefect; Heraclian, once a Danubian peasant, now the commander of the Equites Singulares; and Aureolus, the one-time Getan shepherd promoted to Prefect of Cavalry. Behind them were the other *protectores* – part bodyguards, part staff officers: three more Danubians – Tacitus, Claudius and Aurelian; two more Italians of plebeian origin – Celer Venerianus and Domitianus; and finally, the Egyptian brothers Theodotus and Camsisoleus, and Memor the African. At the sight of these tough, loyal men, Gallienus's heart lifted.

The emperor dismounted and called for his battle charger. As it was led forward, the senators came up all in a bunch. They radiated hurt dignity. These were the men of Gallienus's father. The emperor Valerian trusted them. He had grown up with several among them; he was one of them. Men like old Felix, who had been consul no less than twenty-three years earlier. He was in his late sixties, but Valerian had trusted him with the defence of Byzantium from the Goths just three years ago. Then there was the yet more elderly and more polyonomous Gaius Julius Aquilius Aspasius Paternus, who had governed Africa in the year of Felix's consulship and had himself held that office at some even more remote date.

For a moment, Gallienus thought he should not have wounded their *dignitas* to get an easy laugh from the soldiers. To be fair, the Goths had not taken Byzantium, and no harm had come to Africa. But the senators' race was run. In the golden age, when the *imperium* was conquering all it surveyed – even in the silver age, when it was easily holding its own – its armies could be commanded by elderly landed amateurs, more at home designing an exotic fishpond than sweating on the march. But this was a new age. A harsh age of iron and rust. It called for a hard, new sort of man. It called for Gallienus's recently formed *protectores*.

Even in an age of iron and rust, the previous year had been a bad one. Late in the campaigning season, when the leaves in the north had already turned, the Alamanni had burst across the border between the headwaters of the Rhine and the Danube. The governor of Raetia had been cut down in battle, his army routed. The Alamanni had swarmed on and crossed the Alps. Unarmed Italy had been at their mercy. Gallienus had cut short his campaign in the far north near the ocean and desperately given chase, just getting over the mountains before the snow shut the passes. As soon as he and his field army had departed, another confederation of Germans, the Franks, had crossed the Rhine. There had not been enough Roman troops to oppose them, or even to chase them.

Thank Hercules, thought Gallienus, that his second son, the Caesar Saloninus, had been safe with Silvanus the *Dux* of the Rhine frontier behind the strong walls of Colonia Agrippinensis. Silvanus was a good man. He would see no harm came to the imperial prince. Gallienus pushed away the thought of his eldest son, the beautiful and dead Valerian the Younger. It had been just two years since the boy had died on the Danube. Foul rumours had sought to implicate Ingenuus the governor of Pannonia. But it could not be. Ingenuus was a sound man, loyal through and through to the imperial house. The gods had willed the darling boy die. It just had to be accepted. Take what comfort you could from philosophy, it just had to be accepted.

Gallienus had not caught up with the Alamanni last autumn. They had wintered in Italy, the Franks in Gaul. The barbarians had scoured the land around their quarters. It had been a cruel winter: iron and rust.

As the gods would have it, this year had started better for the Romans. First, in the spring, news had come to Gallienus at Aquileia that yet another northern barbarian invasion had been thwarted. Thousands of Sarmatian horsemen had crossed the Danube into Pannonia but had been resoundingly defeated by Ingenuus. Then had come messengers telling of the repulse from Rome of the Alamanni. In truth, most of the credit was due to Gallienus's brother Licinius. But, for once, some of the senators had played their part. Men such as the Prefect of the City Saecularis and the Father of the Senate Arellius Fuscus. With a wince that almost hurt him physically, Gallienus recalled reading how, in order to keep morale high, his orders to send his youngest son Marinianus to safety in Sicily had been ignored. The infant prince had been paraded in front of the makeshift army. It was fortunate for Licinius that this news had come in a laurel-adorned letter of victory.

Events had continued to unfold well for the Romans. The Iuthungi and the Semnones, two of the tribes that made up the confederation of the Alamanni, had left the main body and set off early for home. As Gallienus had told the troops, the new acting governor of Raetia had massacred them on the far side of the Alps. Simplicinius Genialis had done well in Raetia. Now it remained for Gallienus to finish the rest of the Alamanni here on the plain before the walls of Mediolanum.

'The barbarians are doing something else.' The old senator Felix sounded personally offended.

Gallienus looked at the enemy. The high-priest of each of the three Alamannic tribes on the field – the Hermunduri, Mattiaci and Bucinobantes – had finished the rites to win the favour of Woden and Thor. The magnificent horses and the prisoners who had been selected lay in their blood, decapitated. As each *sinistus* melded back into the host, he was replaced by a greater number of large figures in wolfskins. Individually, slowly at first, the fur-clad men began to dance. Somewhere among them would be the leader of the expedition, the Alamannic war-leader the Romans called Crocus. Hroc – or Wolfhroc, as his own people knew him, would be dancing and howling, offering his sword to Woden, drawing down the savage, slathering power of the Allfather's beast into his body.

To most Roman eyes, the foreign rites were incomprehensible barbarity; primitive, unchanging, irrational. Apart from those in the ranks with Germanic ancestry, only a few could interpret them. The emperor was one of these few. Gallienus knew he would have understood no more than the majority had it not been for the years in his youth that he was detained at the imperial court as a guarantee of the loyalty of his governor father. There he had been educated with a shy young barbarian hostage from the north. Ballista had opened his eyes to the peoples beyond the frontiers.

Gallienus did not condemn the bloodthirsty rites of the Alamanni. Different gods demanded different things. Only a fool failed to realize that a battlefield was a god-haunted place. How could it be otherwise? Imagine the tedium of immortality. How many years into eternity before one had drunk every wine, sampled every exotic food? Or was one shackled to an unchanging diet of ambrosia, nectar and the smoke of sacrifices? And sex? How many beautiful girls or boys before satiety set in, followed by perverse experimentation then disgust? Think of the boredom of rereading the same books again and again. Imagine the envy of the unattainable emotions of mortals – the sweaty thrill of the unknown, the gripping fear, the true courage in the face of death, the pain of loss. Nowhere were these more sharp than on the field of battle. No wonder the gods came close.

Gallienus could feel his patron god Hercules close by – a crackle in the air, the tightness in his skin, the god-given clarity in his mind. In his battle calm, he surveyed the scene.

The Alamanni were about five hundred paces away. Their infantry was massed in the centre, a solid block of maybe thirty thousand men straddling the Ticinum road. The cavalry, probably in the region of ten thousand horses, were more or less equally divided between each flank.

Gallienus had made his dispositions accordingly. He had about the same number of cavalry. He had stationed four thousand on either wing and kept two thousand back as a reserve. His infantry in the centre were badly outnumbered: just fifteen thousand. But he had arranged a couple of things in their favour. And, above all, he had a plan.

Across the plain, the wolf-dancers had worked themselves into a frenzy. Their howls were being drowned by the start of the massed singing. The various tribes of the

Alamanni sang the deeds of their forefathers. The battle would start soon.

Gallienus got into the saddle and turned to his staff. '*Comites*, it is time to take your posts.'

The emperor had exercised tact. Old Felix and Volusianus were to command the infantry; young Acilius Glabrio and Theodotus to take the cavalry on the left. There was to be one of the senatorial nobility and one *protector* at each division but, for the horsemen of the vital right wing, two *protectores*: Claudius and Aurelian. Gallienus would lead the reserve of Horse Guards himself.

The *comites* mounted up and saluted. 'We will do what is ordered, and at every command we will be ready.'

Felix spoke up, his aged voice querulous. 'Your plan – it is not Roman. It goes against our traditions and our nature. It is better suited to the guile of barbarians – Moors or Parthians.'

To hide his irritation, Gallienus settled his helmet on his head, laced it tight. 'Then it is good we have four *alae* of Moors among our cavalry and one of Parthians.' He paused, then spoke heavily. 'The first tradition of the Romans under arms is obedience to orders.'

Wordlessly, Felix saluted again, and turned his horse's head. The commanders of the divisions rode away.

Across the plain, the standards of the Alamanni were raised. As the barbarian advance began, the discordant songs died. They were replaced by the *barritus*. Low at first, like distant thunder, the German war chant rose from forty thousand throats. The warriors held their shields over their mouths to increase the reverberation. The *barritus* crescendoed to a harsh climax. It faded away then returned – harder, yet more menacing. Again and again, it rolled across the plain, intermittent, petrifying. Fear enters by the ears.

Gallienus knew the *barritus* did more than intimidate. The Germans believed it foretold the outcome of battle. If it sounded strong, they thought they would win. It sounded strong.

From the Roman ranks came a medley of war cries. The northern units gave back the *barritus*. The North Africans, howling and clapping, gave tongue to a faster, higher chant. The easterners wailed an ululating yell.

Gallienus saw that the Alamanni were committed. They came on slowly, the horsemen on the wings keeping pace with the infantry. They were menacingly unified, full of purpose. Fear also enters by the eyes.

There was no need for orders from the emperor. The dice was cast. When the Germans were about four hundred paces away, Volusianus gave the signal for Gallienus's first device to aid his outnumbered infantry. Twang-slide-thump: the quickest of the *ballista* crews shot. In a moment, the others joined in. Twang-slide-thump. The sound of the torsion artillery echoed along the line of Roman infantry. Almost too fast to see, the bolts sped away.

There were only fifteen *ballistae*, but their effect was out of proportion to their number. Here and there, holes appeared in the Alamanni ranks. Warriors were punched backwards. Some were pinned grotesquely to the man behind. Shields and mail coats gave no protection against the inhuman power of the steel-tipped bolts.

Stung, seeing their friends and kinsmen die with no way to exact revenge, the Alamanni infantry came on faster.

The war-leaders quickened their pace. Their retinues surged behind them. Wedges of the best fighters emerged from the straight line – the boars' snouts that would crash home first.

Out on the flanks, the German cavalry shook their bridles and urged their mounts to stay level with the men on foot.

Like a wind moving a field of corn, a tremor ran through the Roman infantry. Across the left and centre of the line arms swung and threw. Thousands of flashes of light arced out in front and fell to earth. Now battle was irrevocable, Volusianus had ordered the caltrops to be deployed.

A caltrop is a horrible thing: three or four vicious spikes emerging from a ball of metal. No matter how it falls, one, needle-sharp, points upwards. Thousands of them now carpeted most of the ground in front of the Roman infantry, waiting to tear through boots and soft flesh. Gallienus's second ploy was in place.

The emperor looked all around the field. He could feel his god beside him. Once a man like Gallienus himself, Hercules' labours for mankind had won him immortality and Olympus. Now, on this dusty plain before the walls of Mediolanum, Hercules held his hands over the emperor. In his god-given clarity of mind, Gallienus judged distances and speed, estimated time. The Alamanni infantry were within two hundred paces. Disciplined volleys of arrows flew out from the rear ranks of the Roman infantry. Individual Germans shot back on the move. Gallienus's reading of the battle told him it was time; he commanded that the prearranged signal be given.

Trumpets rang out, and his personal standard, a purple *draco*, hissed back and forth.

A cheer was heard from each flank. From where they were drawn up, a distance behind the infantry, the Roman cavalry walked forward. At the sight, their German counterparts broke into a cacophony of shouts and charged. Quickly, they drew ahead of their infantry. The Roman *alae* moved to a trot then a canter.

On both wings, the cavalry clashed roughly level with the stationary line of Roman infantry. In a moment, the combatants were intermingled. All order vanished. Squadrons, smaller groups, even individuals charged, wheeled, retreated, then charged again. In both melees hand-to-hand and distance fighting coexisted. Each mounted man sought to press home his attack or seek safety as his courage or circumstance dictated. On the left, Gallienus caught a glimpse of Gaius Acilius Glabrio. The young senator, resplendent in scarlet and gold, was laying about him manfully. Soon, most such details were hidden by plumes of thick dust.

The Alamanni foot were closing. A number of warriors were falling to arrows. A few were still snatched backwards by artillery bolts. The Roman archers and *ballistarii* were doing their best. They could not stop the charge. A few parts of the German line seemed to hang back, but the wedges headed by the war-leaders and their household warriors were moving fast. Long hair flying, these big, well-armed men were a fearsome sight.

The *barritus* had dropped to a low murmur. After their long advance, the Alamanni needed their breath. Stationary, the Romans continued to bellow out their war cries.

Gallienus peered through the dust at the cavalry melees. On the left, Acilius Glabrio and Theodotus seemed to be holding their own. At least the swirling dust cloud had not moved appreciably. The right was a different story. The troopers under Aurelian and Claudius appeared unusually reluctant to stay at close quarters. They were giving ground, being driven back behind the Roman infantry line. Gallienus was pleased.

Javelins flew from both sides, just as the infantry of the Alamanni centre and right reached the caltrops. Running close together, pushed on by those behind, some Germans could not avoid the terrible spikes. Others were too distracted by the incoming missiles to notice the menace underfoot until they felt the searing pain. Warriors fell, shrieking. Battle-mad, their comrades ran over them.

The Alamanni crashed into the Roman line. The din hit Gallienus like a blow. There was one huge noise, louder than a temple collapsing, composed of a myriad smaller noises: shield on shield, steel on wood, men shouting, men screaming.

The momentum of the boars' snouts was driving them into the Roman line. Blades and spearheads flashed. Arrows whistled overhead. Men jabbed, hacked, pushed, shouted. Sharp steel bit into flesh. Men fell. The ground ran slippery with blood and spilt intestines. Men lost their footing. They were trampled in the horror by friend and foe alike.

The Roman line looked painfully thin. At the rear, junior officers shouted, threatened, cajoled. They physically pushed men back into line. They beat men with the flats of their swords, yelling for them to give their all.

From somewhere – *disciplina*? The hand of a god? Hercules himself? – the Romans found the strength to resist. Digging their heels in the ground, bending their knees, calling out to each other, they pushed their shields into the backs of those in front. The line held. The German wedges were halted.

Except for one out on the Roman right, where there had been no caltrops. Tipped by a gigantic warrior, his sword slicing intricate patterns, the one boar's snout edged forward.

Gallienus snapped orders. One unit of his cavalry reserve cantered forward. The men dismounted. Leaving one in five to hold the horses, the armoured troopers added their weight to the threatened point. Four hundred fresh men made the difference. Here too the line held. For the moment.

Blinking from the dust, Gallienus took stock. The cavalry on the left were still holding out but, on the right, the Romans were losing ground fast. A clear gap had opened between this cavalry action and the infantry combat. The feigned retreat had worked. It was time.

There were only fifteen hundred horsemen still in his reserve. Gallienus was not worried. His plan was working. It was time.

Gallienus unsheathed his sword. His palm was wet. His heart was pounding. It was not fear. There was nothing to fear. The god was with him. Like Antony long ago in Alexandria, he would know if Hercules left him. The emperor signalled the advance.

They set off at a walk. With disciplined ease, they changed formation on the move. What emerged would have impressed anyone. Two solid wedges of armoured men on armoured horses. The smaller, some five hundred men, was led by Aureolus, and rode under the red Pegasus on white banner of the Horse Guards. The larger, some thousand men, followed the imperial purple *draco*. At their apex was the emperor himself.

Without waiting for an order from the emperor, Aureolus angled his horsemen towards the cavalry melee on the right wing. Gallienus approved. The *protectores* should show initiative, and none more so than the *protector* appointed Prefect of Cavalry. The emperor watched as Aureolus quickened the pace. The big horses went from a trot to a gentle canter. They moved easily, making little of the weight of man and armour on their backs. A noble cloud of dust rose behind them.

Gallienus led his men towards the gap between the central infantry fight and the mounted one on the right. He kept to a slow walk, fighting down an urge to hurry. He needed to keep his troop together.

A previously unseen ditch appeared in front of Gallienus. Manoeuvring on a battlefield, there was always something. A ditch, a line of vines, a dry-stone wall – an unexpected obstacle always appeared.

The ditch was not too deep, its bottom dry. Gallienus leant back, letting his mount pick its way down, then forward as they climbed out. A few paces across on the far bank, he pulled up, giving the men behind him a chance to sort themselves out.

Gallienus looked to his right. The Pegasus banner streaming above them, Aureolus's troopers were forging into the confused melee. The men under Claudius and

Aurelian seemed to have taken heart and were also pressing the enemy. One or two of the Alamanni had had enough. They were spurring their mounts away south across the plain. On that part of the battlefield the tide had turned.

To Gallienus's left, things were not going so well. In the man-made gloom, the thin, thin line of Roman infantry was being forced back. In places it had buckled dangerously. It could not be long before it broke. Now there was no time to lose, no time to fuss over parade-ground cohesion.

Gallienus kicked on, quickly coming to a near flat-out gallop. His men followed. The hooves of a thousand horses rattled on the hard ground as they surged past the cavalry fight on their right. Gallienus led them in a sweeping curve to the left that brought them to about two hundred paces behind the left rear of the German foot.

Now! Strike now! I am with you. The god whispered urgently in Gallienus's heart. No! Not yet. Not like this. Not with the troopers strung out like the trail of a meteor. Hercules had always been hasty. Too hasty when he had sacked sacred Delphi. Too hasty when he had hurled his guest Iphitus to his death from the highest tower in Tiryns. Gallienus, the emperor, who suspected that, one day, he would be a god, stood up to the god who had once been mortal. There was only one throw of the dice. This charge had to break the heart of the enemy, had to rout their infantry beyond recall. Gallienus could feel Hercules' barely suppressed anger, but also his acquiescence. The god still held his hands over the emperor.

Gently, Gallienus brought his mount to a standstill. Horses snorting and stamping, weapons and armour ringing, officers shouting, the troop reined in and got itself back into order.

The warriors in the rear ranks of the Alamanni infantry were more than aware of Gallienus's men. They looked over their shoulders, pointed, gesticulated. Some turned to face the new threat. Others shouted to their war-leaders. If any of the latter heard, caught up in the business of staying alive at the front of the fight, there was nothing they could do.

'Now!' Gallienus spoke as much to his god as to the men behind him. The *bucinatores* blew the charge. The brassy notes sliced through the din of battle. The now close-ordered arrowhead of armoured horsemen set off. The purple *draco* writhed and snapped over them as they picked up the pace. The ground seemed to tremble beneath them.

A cavalry charge against infantry was a bluff. It was not so much that, once launched, it was almost impossible to stop, it was more that it surrendered the outcome to the other side. Horses do not run into solid objects. A line of men, shoulder to shoulder, two, three or more deep, was a solid object. One or two horses might be goaded or maddened enough to crash into it, but not several hundred of them. Unless the infantry ran, or at least were scared enough to flinch away, for gaps to open in their formation, the horses would pull up short. The magnificent charge would end up as a chaotic stationary mass; horses wheeling and plunging, riders thrown.

At least, thought Gallienus, as the Horse Guard thundered on, we do not have to cross our own caltrops to get at the nearest enemy. Not to have the right of the Roman infantry line throw caltrops had been a last-moment decision. Memor had pointed it out. The African *protector* would go far.

The rear ranks of the Alamanni began to swarm like a disturbed wasps' nest. Some warriors who had turned to face the new menace were hefting their shields, standing firm, but others were trying to edge back into the illusory safety of their comrades. A handful had lost their nerve altogether; small groups and lone men were running away to the south-east. Gallienus felt the blood pounding in his head, sensed Hercules beside him. This was going to work.

The emperor aimed at a hole in the line. His charger bowled over an isolated German. The warrior tumbled to the ground, then vanished behind, under the hooves of the Roman cavalry.

A big warrior aimed a cut at Gallienus. The emperor caught the blow on his blade. He rolled his wrist, forcing his opponent's sword wide. He slashed downwards, but missed.

The *protectores* were trying to catch up and cover their emperor, but Gallienus surged ahead. Sunshine flashing on his blade, he swung left and right. He felt no fear. The god had covered him in his lionskin. The pelt of the Nemean lion was proof against iron, bronze, stone. There was no need for fear.

Three mounted Alamanni appeared out of nowhere, one ahead, one on either side, murder in their eyes. Heraclian, the commander of the Equites Singulares, drove his horse between the emperor and the German to his right. A blow caught him on the helmet. The *protector* was knocked forward on to his horse's neck. The German drew back his arm for the killing blow. Ignoring the other two enemy, Gallienus leant far out of his saddle, putting all his weight behind the blow. As the impact ran up his arm, Gallienus saw the warrior's helmet buckle. The blood sprayed hot up his arm, into his face.

With god-granted time, Gallienus regained his seat, blocked the slash of the warrior on his left. The German's bearded face twisted in agony as Camsisoleus drove his sword through the mail between his shoulderblades.

The third of the Alamanni had vanished. The immediate threat gone, his *protectores* around him, Gallienus looked about. Everything had changed. Where there had been battle, now there was rout. Where there had been fighting, now there was only killing. The Alamanni were broken; a mob of individuals fleeing for their lives.

'Horse Guards stay with me,' Gallienus shouted.

The Germans seldom employed a reserve, but Gallienus knew that many a battle had been lost by an overconfident pursuit. The *protectores* got most of the cavalrymen who followed the emperor back in hand. No one and nothing was going to snatch this victory away from Gallienus.

'*Imperator! Imperator!*' Fierce faces roared out the traditional acclamation. In the levity of victory, men clasped Gallienus's hand, thumped him on the back. '*Imperator! Imperator!*'

Volusianus rode up: 'I give you joy of your victory, *Dominus*.' Gallienus smiled and shook the veteran's hand.

Aurelian galloped up: 'Claudius is chasing their horsemen on our flank. He will keep our boys in order.' More hugs and handshakes.

Theodotus came to report from the left: 'Acilius Glabrio

has hared off after them, but I have a couple of hundred troopers held back.' Yet more rejoicing.

Gallienus felt the exhilaration begin to drain out of him. He heard soft music on the air. The god was leaving. Not for ever, merely withdrawing. Hercules would return to stand with the emperor again. Gallienus looked at his sword. It was slick with blood, right up to the eagle pommel. He sheathed it anyway. Someone else would clean it later. Gallienus noticed his hands were shaking.

Flanked by two of the *protectores*, a mounted man was led forward. Dressed in travelling clothes stained with sweat, neither very old nor young, the man was familiar to Gallienus, but he could not place him at once. At odds with the surrounding relaxed discipline of success, the man snapped a formal salute. He dismounted and performed *proskynesis* full length in the dirt. When he got up, Gallienus recognized him.

'Valens, you are a long way from the east.' As he spoke, Gallienus realized something had gone terribly wrong. The governor of Syria Coele should not be here.

'*Dominus* . . .' Valens stopped.

Gallienus could feel the tension mounting inside him.

Valens took a deep breath and let the words out. '*Dominus*, the Augustus Valerian has been defeated. I am sorry to tell you your father is a prisoner of the Persians.'

A ripple of silence spread outward. In the distance, shouts, screams, snatches of songs, the sounds of victory. Here the silence of shock. In the emptiness, half-formed thoughts raced through Gallienus's mind. *Father . . . too old, too infirm for this. Hercules help me. What should I say? What would an emperor say? What would a Roman of the old republic say?* The phrase came fully formed.

'I knew my father was mortal.'

Grim-faced, the officers nodded. The phrase had been good. It had the right *gravitas*. Gallienus gathered himself.

'How stands the *imperium*?'

Relieved, Valens spoke a little more normally. 'Carrhae and Nisibis have gone over to the Sassanids. The people of Carrhae opened their gates. At Nisibis, they say a thunderbolt split the walls.' Valens shrugged. 'Whatever, Edessa still held when I left. Shapur had not advanced further.' Valens still looked on edge.

'Who was captured with my father?'

'It is thought some ten thousand men. Many of the high command: Successianus the Praetorian Prefect, Cledonius the *ab Admissionibus*, Ballista . . .'

'No!' Aurelian shouted out. Red-faced, he punched his saddle. His horse flinched.

Gallienus remembered the close friendship between Aurelian and the young northerner. 'We will all have lost *amici*.'

'*Dominus*,' Valens continued, 'there is more.'

'Speak.'

'When the news reached the Danube, Ingenuus had your portraits and those of your father and son torn from the standards. His men have invested him with the purple.'

A babble of voices rose up in indignation. Gallienus held up his hand for quiet. Valens had not finished.

'On the Euphrates, Macrianus the Lame has taken command of what remains of the field army. He has claimed *maius imperium* over the east. He has had Exiguus, the governor of Cappadocia, killed. He is appointing his own men to commands. When I fled Syria, it was openly said he would put his sons, Macrianus the Younger and Quietus, on the throne.'

Treachery, revolt, civil war – would it never end? A time of iron and rust. This was not a moment to show weakness. Gallienus knew he had to be decisive.

'When we have killed and enslaved the last of these Alamanni, we will send troops to the Caesar Saloninus on the Rhine. He has good, loyal men around him. Silvanus and Postumus will help him hunt down the Franks in Gaul. We ourselves will march without delay against Ingenuus. When his head is on a pike, we can deal with the cripple in the east.'

Gallienus forced himself to smile. 'The *imperium* was not won without bitter strife. It will not be held by the faint-hearted. No one has defeated us. We will triumph over these rebels as we have triumphed over these Alamanni.' The emperor raised his voice, made it ring. 'Today we won a heroic victory. Tonight we will hold a heroic feast. We will distribute the booty and then drink until the sun is back in the sky, until the wine peeps through our scars.'

As the *protectores* and others close enough to hear his words cheered, Gallienus's thoughts flew to the east. Shapur at the head of the Sassanid horde. Macrianus the Lame commanding the Roman forces. And between them, holding the balance, was Odenathus, the Lord of Palmyra. The man they called the Lion of the Sun.

PART THREE

Vir Perfectissimus

(The East, Summer–Autumn AD260)

'You know well that you have not kept your oaths to me.'

Euripides, *Medea*, 495

VIII

Hidden in the unlit colonnade, Ballista waited. It was the last hours of the night, some time after the start of the fourth watch. Away from the palace to the south, across the open space of the citadel, he could make out furtive figures in the darkened temple of the Tyche of Zeugma. Without Ballista consciously directing it, his right hand moved: first to the dagger on his right hip, freeing it an inch or so from its sheath and snapping it back, then to the sword hanging on his left, drawing it a couple of inches and pushing it home again, finally to the healing stone tied to the scabbard. What was going to happen was all bad. But he had no choice but to play his part.

At last he heard them moving up the hill; a confused murmur of voices, the rattle of weapons, no attempt at concealment. As the first of them came through the gate, the torches they carried flickered through the leaves of the fruit trees. Snatches of boisterous, rough voices reached Ballista. The men emerged from the orchard fully armed for war – helmets, mail shirts, shields and weapons. But the column was in no order. The soldiers walked with friends from their units, talking in loose groups. The centurions present led some of them off to left and right. In no time at all, the palace was surrounded.

There goes all hope of escape, thought Ballista. His mind had been running on slipping away on the far side of the citadel; down through the trees, over the low wall, across the roofs, saddling Pale Horse and riding west, following the route Castricius's man had shown Calgacus and the others. Of course it had been an idle thought. Even if he reached Antioch, how would he get Julia and the boys away? Come to that, what welcome would Gallienus give him in the west? He remembered entertaining a similar idea before the siege of Arete. Childish fantasies. It was time he put such things aside. Still, it was good of Castricius to have reunited him with Pale Horse and his own weapons. He touched the healing stone again.

The ring of armed men around the palace began to chant.

'Come out! Show yourselves! Quietus and Macrianus, come out! You cannot hide from the soldiers!'

Nothing happened. The soldiers clashed their weapons on their shields. Their chants became impatient. Flasks of drink passed from hand to hand. One or two whistled, called out obscenities.

This cannot go on for long, thought Ballista.

A rectangle of orange light sprang out from the palace as a door opened.

'Come out! Come out!'

Quietus and Macrianus the Younger stepped out. There was tension in their movements, none of the usual arrogant swagger.

Macrianus the Younger raised his right arm in an

oratorical pose. The noise from the soldiers gradually fell away. Torches hissed in the night air.

'Soldiers of Rome, what is the meaning of this? Have you forgotten your *disciplina*? Return to your quarters.'

'Never! Never!' The men roared back.

Now Quietus came forward. His arms were stretched out in entreaty. 'Remember our youth, our blameless lives. Have pity on our father's grey hairs. Do not put us in this danger. We have not asked for this. We have done nothing to deserve it.'

A few soldiers laughed. Then, as if at an order, they all began a rhythmic chant:

'Quietus *imperator*, Augustus free from all guilt, may the gods keep you. Macrianus *imperator*, Augustus free from all guilt, may the gods keep you.'

Over and over, the words were chanted. Quietus and Macrianus the Younger made half-hearted gestures of unwillingness.

From the gloom, Ballista listened and watched. He had heard that, in some Scythian tribes, a man's ritual reluctance to rule was overcome by pelting him with mud. It seemed a custom the Romans could adopt with profit.

A new chant boomed out. 'The good faith of the soldiers, happiness!' Louder and louder it was repeated. '*Fidei militum feliciter! Fidei militum feliciter!*'

Slowly, Macrianus the Lame made his way out of the palace to stand between his sons. He raised his walking stick. The silver head of Alexander glinted. The soldiers instantly stopped chanting. The father gestured Quietus to speak.

'Fellow soldiers, it is a heavy burden you wish to place

on our shoulders. *Commilitiones*, you know that neither my brother nor myself has sought this honour. Yet the gods know our love for the *Res Publica*.'

Quietus paused, as if in deep thought – the effect slightly spoilt by the half-smile on his weak mouth.

'*Commilitiones*, we hear your command. The soldiers of Rome are the sword and shield of the *imperium*, the embodiment of our ancient *virtus*. But to be Augustus is not just to be a military commander. Our minds would be easier, our burden less heavy, if we knew that the senate and people also called us to the purple.'

As Quietus finished, lights blazed out from the temple behind the soldiers. Through its open doors Ballista could see a group of civilians gathered around the statue of the Tyche of Zeugma. The ring of soldiers opened to let them pass.

Maeonius Astyanax, toga-clad and backed by other senators, halted before the candidates for the throne. In the torchlight, his eyes were like pebbles under water.

'Too long the ship of state has drifted, no firm hand on the rudder. Valerian was old and ineffectual. Now he is gone, may the gods have mercy on him. His son, Gallienus, lies sunk in luxury and debauchery. Shunning the senate house, the forum and the army camp, he disports himself with pimps and prostitutes, actors and barbarians. Fit only to be dragged with a hook, he brings disgrace and disaster. The throne of the Caesars calls for vigorous young men of courage and decency. The senate calls for Titus Fulvius Iunius Quietus and Titus Fulvius Iunius Macrianus. Take the purple. Each of you: trust us, trust yourself!'

The senators took up the call: '*Crede nobis, crede tibi; crede nobis, crede tibi.*'

At the twenty-fifth repetition, another group of civilians came forth from the temple. The man at their head looked overawed. He was sweating heavily.

'I am Barlaha, son of Antiochus, a member of the *Boule* of this city.'

Some of the soldiers, well refreshed with wine, sniggered. Barlaha stumbled on.

'Rome has made one city of the civilized world. She has given all who dwell in the *imperium* citizenship. All the citizens of Rome speak through us, the *Boule* of Zeugma, when we call Quietus and Macrianus to the throne.'

The two young men inclined their heads in acceptance.

'The immortal gods grant long life to Augustus Quietus, long life to Augustus Macrianus. Happy are we in your *imperium*, happy the *Res Publica*.'

Like a well-trained chorus, the audience chanted.

Two small groups of soldiers encircled Quietus and Macrianus. A flat, oval infantry shield was placed on the ground before each brother. They stood on them. The soldiers bent down and carefully, if with a certain unsteadiness, lifted the shields and raised Quietus and Macrianus to the heavens.

Macrianus the Younger, wobbling just a little, waved and made a fair show of imperial *dignitas*. Quietus, pouchy little eyes darting here and there, could contain himself no longer. Now and then clutching at the top of a soldier's head for balance, he giggled in open exultation.

Once the two young men were safely back on terra firma, their father embraced them and spoke.

'This has been so sudden, so unexpected, the hands of the gods must be behind it. Man must always bow to the dictates of the divine. But it has been so sudden that the necessary regalia is not prepared.' The old man produced two ropes of gold, glittering with jewels. 'These were your late mother's necklaces; for now, use them as diadems.'

Quietus held up his hand. 'Thank you, Father, but no; such a female adornment would not be right. There will be nothing womanly about our reign,' he simpered.

A couple of cavalrymen approached. 'Use these gilded horse trappings, *Domini*.'

This time it was Macrianus the Younger who demurred. 'Many thanks, *commilitiones*, but what has been worn by a beast would impair the *dignitas* of an Augustus.'

There was an awkward pause. A centurion hissed, 'Now, you fools.' Two standard bearers shuffled up. They removed the gold collars from their necks. Evidently overcome by the occasion – or by alcohol – they had forgotten their lines. The new emperors snatched the offerings and placed them on their own heads.

Servants swarmed out. Two purple cloaks were produced and draped around the shoulders of Quietus and Macrianus. In front of each was placed a low altar on which burned the sacred fire of an emperor. Behind them, men ran about fixing imperial symbols to the front of the palace: eagles, the shield of four virtues, wreaths, bay leaves for victory, oak leaves for saving citizens' lives.

All of this rather gave the lie to the 'impromptu' nature of the events, thought Ballista. He would not be able to remain lurking in anonymity behind a column for long.

His own unwanted part in these ghastly theatrics was fast approaching. He fiddled with his sword.

It was Quietus who made the expected formal speech of acceptance.

'*Commilitiones*, senators, citizens of Rome, it is with humility that we accede to your demand and take the *imperium*. Our joint reign will be marked by courage, clemency, justice and piety.' He gestured at the golden shield now being hammered to the wall behind him on which '*Virtus*', '*Clementia*', '*Iustitia*' and '*Pietas*' were inscribed.

'It is gratifying to us that the senate, people and soldiers unanimously call us to the throne,' continued Quietus. 'All shall benefit. The senate shall return to its ancient *dignitas*. Our *consilium* shall be open to senators. The senate house will be purged of informers. Senators will be free of unjust condemnations and confiscations of their estates. The great military commands will again be open to men of the senatorial order.'

The senators at least cheered this with enthusiasm.

'To the people, their ancient *libertas* will return. We decree that ten days of games will be held, starting as soon as gladiators and animals can be gathered.'

The town councillors of Zeugma, as the only representatives of the people on hand, made suitably grateful noises.

'Fitting reward must be given to the loyalty of the soldiers – two gold pieces to every man with the standards. But to those of our *commilitiones* present, to those through whom the gods brought us to the throne, much more is due.'

Quietus had his audience now.

'The majority of the Praetorian Guard was lost with Valerian. All those here will be enrolled in the reformed unit, and accrue the resulting increases in pay.'

The men cheered. Shouts of 'Rich soldier' broke out. Quietus gestured for silence. He was ignored until his father joined in.

'And a donative – five gold pieces and a pound of silver per man,' Quietus continued.

The shouts returned, much louder, swelling into unison: '*Dives miles! Dives miles!*'

Again Macrianus the Lame had to calm the throng.

Quietus resumed. 'A new guard needs a new commander. A man of loyalty. As our new Praetorian Prefect, it is right that Maeonius Astyanax should be first to take the *sacramentum* in our reign.'

Chin high, short beard jutting, Astyanax stepped up and took the military oath:

'By Jupiter Optimus Maximus and all the gods, I swear to carry out the emperors' commands, never desert the standards or shirk death, to value the safety of the emperors above everything.'

Ballista listened to the words with misery. He had broken the *sacramentum* he had made to Maximinus Thrax and earned himself the undying hatred of that emperor's daemon. He had broken his oath to Valerian. Now he was about to take another *sacramentum*, one he had no intention of keeping. But all this was nothing. It was breaking the oath to Shapur that plagued him: *Spill my brains on the ground . . . my brains and the brains of my sons too.*

Next up was Gaius Calpurnius Piso Frugi, the new governor of Syria Coele. He was followed by the other two governors present, Annius Cornicula of Syria Phoenice and Achaeus of Palestine. Then it was the turn of Ballista, the *Vir Perfectissimus*, Prefect of Cavalry, as he was announced.

As Ballista stepped out, most of the soldiers cheered perfunctorily, but one group showed real enthusiasm. The eagle, lion and Capricorn on their shields showed them to be from Legio IIII Scythica. They must have been part of the detachment that fought under Ballista at Circesium. The distinctive angular face and huge hooked nose of one of the legionaries confirmed it – Ahala, Aharna, his name was something like that. His was not a face you would easily forget. Ballista waved.

Having mouthed the words of the oath in a daze, Ballista found himself part of the new emperors' entourage. He watched as everyone else took the *sacramentum*; those of importance as individuals, others in groups. The ceremony was far from over. When the oath-taking was done, they would process down to the main army camp and tour selected temples in the town before climbing the hill again for dedications in the temple of the Tyche of Zeugma and an audience in the palace.

Ballista supposed the ceremony had been well enough planned. Certainly Astyanax had devoted much effort to it; even trawling through old acts of the senate to select exactly right 'spontaneous' acclamations. Holding it at night had added some drama. Allowing only those soldiers already selected for the Praetorian Guards had been sensible. The unexpectedly generous donative had generated genuine excitement. Ballista could see the point of the theatricals with the diadems. It was meant to show that the new emperors had the *dignitas* of the *imperium* at heart, were close to their soldiers and could stand up to their father. Of course it was all nonsense.

Although the ceremony was passing off well, the same

could not be said for the realities of the bid for power. Admittedly, all Roman provinces east of the Aegean had come over, including the initially uncertain military ones of Egypt, Arabia, Osrhoene and Syria Phoenice. But no governor in the west had declared for the sons of Macrianus, despite the sending of urgent letters accompanied by large bribes. And there was no possibility of winning over the vital Danubian armies now Ingenuus was leading his own revolt.

Far worse than all this, the Persians were on the move. Bypassing Edessa, they had crossed the Euphrates and taken Samosata. Macrianus the Lame had adopted what he called a strategy of containment. In the face of the Persian advance, Samosata had been hurriedly abandoned. The twenty thousand Roman troops there had been divided. Ten thousand had rushed south to Zeugma with the emperors-to-be. Five thousand had been sent north to reinforce the governor of Cappadocia, Pomponius Bassus. The final five thousand had been ordered to Doliche to block the road west. Ballista saw the latter as the problem. Unsupported, they had no chance of preventing Shapur riding west to Cilicia and beyond, should he wish.

Of course, there was another problem looming in the east. The Lion of the Sun. Still no word had come back from Odenathus. No one knew what the Lord of Palmyra would do. Would he join the revolt? Would he remain loyal to Gallienus? Was it possible he would throw in his lot with the Persians? Only a couple of months before, Ballista had been there when Odenathus had sent envoys to Shapur. They had been rejected, but events had moved fast, and a second approach might yield a very different outcome.

And then there were the gods. Macrianus the Lame had consulted widely among the oracles of the east. The responses were far from uniformly favourable. At the shrine of Aphrodite Aphacitis in the mountains between Byblos and Heliopolis was a sacred lake. If the offerings thrown in were accepted by the goddess, they sank, light and heavy alike. If rejected, they did not. The gifts of Macrianus – silk and linen, gold and silver – all had floated. The oracle of Apollo Sarpedon at Seleuceia in Cilicia had been similarly robust. When the envoys of Macrianus had asked about the success of the uprising, the god gave a reply that no amount of sophistry could make favourable:

Leave my temple, guileful baleful ones,
Who cause pain to the glorious race of gods.

Since breaking his oath to Shapur, the gods were much on Ballista's mind. Were all the gods the same? If not, could his northern gods protect his sons from the southern gods of the Greeks and Romans? And even were they able to, would they wish to? Somehow, he doubted it. But he prayed anyway: *Allfather, Hooded One, Death-blinder . . .*

The bad news had reached Zeugma six days before. The Persians had marched from Samosata. With no warning, they had appeared before the walls of Doliche to the north-west of Zeugma. Outnumbered, the Roman force of five thousand stationed there could do nothing but watch them sweep on to the west. The following day, an exhausted scout had ridden into Zeugma with the further news that the enemy were taking the road up into the

Amanus mountains, heading for the Amanikai Gates. Once through that undefended mountain pass, Shapur's force, variously estimated at fifteen, thirty and fifty thousand men, would have the rich territory of Cilicia Pedias and the unarmed provinces of Asia Minor at its mercy.

Having predicted just these events won Ballista no commendation. Summoned before the new emperors, the northerner was brusquely ordered to take five thousand cavalry, ride west and defend Antioch. The Syrian Gates, the southern pass back over the Amanus range, must be held at all cost. Similarly, Seleuceia in Pieria, the port of Antioch, had to be defended in case the Persians commandeered ships along the Cilician coast.

It had taken Ballista some effort and considerable patience to explain to the unmilitary father of the young emperors that, to hold ground, one needed infantry. Eventually he had been given permission to replace one thousand of the cavalry with mounted infantry. He was to requisition a thousand horses and mount on them any legionaries he could find from Legio IIII Scythica who admitted any hint of equine experience. His old companion Castricius was to accompany him.

The journey had been hard. It was July, blazingly hot in Syria, so they had left at dusk. They had reined in after a couple of miles to check girths and tack. Then they had ridden on until nearly noon the next day. Some sixteen hours in the saddle, with just a brief halt every hour to drink and four longer ones to give their mounts some respite from the weight on their backs. They were eating up the ground, but it was tough on man and beast.

Three days of this and they had reached the village of

Gindaros. From there, still keeping to this regime, Castricius had taken half the force on towards Antioch and Seleuceia. Ballista had rested his men overnight in the village. He would need daylight for the last stretch of his march, crossing the swampy and roadless plain to the north of the Lake of Antioch.

Now, finally, they were in an unprepossessing village called Pagrae at the foot of the Amanus range. Their blistering pace had had an effect. Of the two thousand cavalry, half bowmen, half spear-armed, some two hundred had dropped out. Unsurprisingly, things were much worse with the mounted legionaries. Only about three hundred of the complement of five hundred remained. Ballista wondered how many men Castricius would still have with him when he reached the coast. The centurion had faced another two days' travel when he rode out of Gindaros. Still, Ballista had instructed him to gather any troops he could find in Antioch.

It was early evening. The men were looking to their horses, settling in. They would spend at least some of the night here, gathering their strength. They would need it, but there would be no such luxury for Ballista.

The village headman had provided information. It was about five miles to the narrows of the Syrian Gates, the road good but demanding. He had also recommended a guide; a wiry goatherd. Having asked for volunteers, Ballista had selected two scouts from the cavalry. On his instructions, the *exploratores* had discarded all armour and weapons except their sword belts, tied scarves around their heads and put on dark cloaks. They had bound their horses' hooves to muffle the noise of their approach.

Reluctantly swapping Pale Horse for a black gelding, Ballista had done the same.

Having eaten, relieved himself and handed over command to one of the prefects of cavalry, a Syrian with the impeccably Roman name of Servius, Ballista could see no reason to delay. He gave the order. They rode out of the village and took the road up into the mountains.

It was a dark night. The wind from the east was pushing black clouds across the stars. Possibly it would rain later, one of those sudden torrential summer thunderstorms. Initially the incline was gentle, the hills wide-spaced, but soon the slopes reared up and came close. Beside Ballista, the goatherd on his pony did not talk. The *exploratores* behind were quiet also. An owl hooted, and another replied. Once, something sent a scatter of stones rattling down the slope to their right. Apart from that, there was just the creak of leather and the deadened sound of the horses' footfall.

When the ascent became steep, Ballista spelled the horses, the men swinging down to walk for a time before getting back up. With the repetitive landscape and their fatigue, time soon lost meaning. There was nothing but the road and scrub-covered rocks all around.

Possibly, this would all go well. Ballista would find the defile of the Syrian Gates empty. They could wait peacefully in the pass while one of the *exploratores* galloped back to tell Servius to rouse out the men and bring them up.

Ballista regretted not writing a note for Castricius to give to Julia as he passed through Antioch. But it would have delayed the centurion, and he did not dare to entrust it to anyone else. The imperial spies were never more active than at a time of insurrection. Censorinus, the feared head of the *frumentarii*, had long been close to Macrianus the Lame. He would have his men prying into everything. Beyond a formal note saying that he was safe, Ballista had not written to Julia since his return, since the breaking of his oath.

The goatherd's outstretched arm startled Ballista. Unnecessarily indicating silence, the man mimed that they should dismount. Having handed his reins to one of the *exploratores*, Ballista took stock. The mountain walls had come closer on either side. The road ran up straight for another hundred or so paces then turned to the right. The goatherd put his mouth to Ballista's ear. He smelled rank, like one of his animals. The Syrian Gates were ahead, around the bend.

Alone and on foot, Ballista set off. There was no cover beyond a few fallen rocks at the sides of the path. He walked on the balls of his feet, feeling for loose stones before he put his weight down. He stayed close to the right mountain wall. Moving inconspicuously at night was not a problem for him. Following the custom of his people, as a youth he had gone to learn warcraft in the tribe of his maternal uncle. He had been lucky his mother came from the Harii. They were feared night-fighters.

When he reached the turning, Ballista remained motionless for a time, stilling his breathing, listening hard. Nothing. He sniffed the air. Nothing. He listened some more. When there was still nothing, he crouched down, carefully arranging his belt over his back so that his scabbard lay between his shoulderblades, the hilt of his sword just behind his head. Looking back the way he had come, he half noticed the dark shape of his companions. That was of no interest. When the shadow of one of the clouds came in from the east, he looked round the corner.

The low, smouldering fire was unexpected: bright red in the night. Ballista did not look directly at it. Keeping his eyes on his hands and feet, he crawled to a fallen rock and lay behind it.

Closing one eye to keep his night vision, Ballista studied the scene. The road ran about one hundred and fifty paces to the fire. It grew increasingly narrow. The rock walls were jagged; at the fire, no more than fifty paces apart.

There was a campfire burning in the Syrian Gates. The wind was from the east. That was why Ballista had not smelled it. He could see the silhouette of what looked like a small cart. Other smaller, dark shapes indicated men by the fire. A group was spending the night there. But who were they? It could be an innocent caravan. But it could be a Sassanid war party.

For a long time, Ballista lay silent, hoping to hear what language the men by the fire spoke. Now and then, he heard a murmur of conversation, but they were talking low, and the wind was against him. There was nothing for it: he would have to get closer.

Waiting for the clouds, using the movement of their shadows, Ballista crawled nearer. It was slow, painful going. His hands were cut, knees grazed. The last twenty-five to thirty paces, there was no cover. Ballista stretched out behind a rock little bigger than his head. The cloud cover had increased, but every time it cleared he felt horribly exposed. Suddenly, from beyond the camp, a horse called.

From behind him, clear on the freshening breeze, came an answering neigh from one of the Roman horses.

There were voices from the fire now: 'Did you hear that?' 'What?' 'Listen!' They were Persians.

Outlined by the glow, two men stood up.

'We should go and look.'

'Not me. Who knows what daemons lurk in these hills at night?'

A third man spoke. His voice conveyed authority: he must be some form of officer. 'If it was not misfortune enough to be sat on this bleak mountain missing all the pleasure the others are enjoying in Iskanderun – but to be stuck with a man who sees a Roman behind every rock, and another who fears *devs* everywhere. Sit down. Let the night pass quietly.'

The men sat.

If he had not been so well trained, Ballista would have sighed with relief.

It was mid-morning the following day when Ballista returned to the Syrian Gates. Time plays tricks. His crawl back to the others had seemed to take for ever; the ride to Pagrae passed in moments. He had given orders and fallen into a heavy sleep for a couple of hours.

The troops had been roused well before dawn. Having been tormented by mosquitoes, few complained.

Ballista had called a *consilium* of officers, down to the rank of *optio*. He had made sure everyone knew the order of march and his tactical plan, such as it was. They were to explain it to the men under them and see that all had a good breakfast.

Food was important. Ballista knew the Persians ate only a light breakfast but took lunch earlier than westerners. If his timing was right, his men would be well fed, the Sassanids hungry. It was not much of an advantage to build on. This was a battle that would be decided by the *disciplina* and sheer fighting quality of the Romans; above all, that of the legionaries.

The march up had been glorious. In daylight, the Amanus range had revealed its beauty. The men had climbed upwards in the shadow of pine and wild olives, between banks of lavender and myrtle. In every shelf of soil, every crevice where a tree could thrust its roots, was a mass of vegetation. The view, looking backwards, at times took in the whole plain, with the lake of Antioch glittering in the centre and the valley of the Orontes off to the south.

They had marched on foot, quickly, but with no attempt at concealment. There was no chance of surprising the Sassanids. A column of over two thousand armed men cannot but make a lot of noise, but their numbers would only be sufficient if the Persians had not had time to summon reinforcements.

As they halted near the summit, the wind picked up. Big, dark stormclouds again rolled in from the east. Strong gusts tugged at Ballista as he made a final check that everything was in order.

At the front were the saddlesore, aching legionaries; a block fifty wide and six deep, close-packed. Behind them were five hundred dismounted horse archers, in loose order. The rest, nine hundred spear-armed and four hundred bowmen, again all on foot, were stationed as a reserve a few hundred paces back, where the space was wider.

'Remember, boys, they are just a bunch of easterners. They hate fighting on foot, and they get frightened close to the steel.' Ballista had to bellow to compete with the wind. Even so, he was not sure how many even of the legionaries could hear him. 'Get through the arrows and we will kill them. Remember they carry their wealth on their persons. But no looting until the order. Keep your places. Look after your brothers.'

The legionaries clashed swords on shields.

'Are you ready for war?'

'Ready!'

When the third response echoed from the rocks, Ballista took his place in the front rank. His right hand freed his dagger a little then snapped it back, drew his sword an inch or two then rammed it back, and finally touched the healing stone on the scabbard. His personal pre-battle drill done, he took up the borrowed oval shield, and told the *bucinatores* to sound the advance.

As they trudged the last fifty paces to the turning, Ballista wondered how this would turn out. He had no idea how many Persians they were facing. The vital snatch of conversation he had overheard the night before suggested that the majority of the enemy force was down in the western plain, sacking Iskanderun, as the Persians seemed to call the town of Alexandria ad Issum. But, as he did not know how many easterners there were in total, it meant next to nothing. Again, he did not know what, if any, obstructions or defences they might have placed in the defile. All he had seen was a fire, a handful of men and a cart. It would all fall out as the gods willed it. One thing was certain. It would be unwise for a man who had broken an oath to the Persian king to let himself be taken prisoner. Ballista thought of the cell in Carrhae, thought of what had nearly happened there. No, he was not going to be taken alive.

The men of Legio IIII Scythica jogged round the corner and into range of the eastern bows. They heard yelled Persian orders. The sky darkened.

'*Testudo!*' Ballista's was not the only voice shouting. He crouched and held his shield out in front of him. The man behind slammed his shield down on the top edge of Ballista's, covering the northerner's head. The noise was repeated from behind as the shields of each rank in turn slammed home, overlapping like tiles on a roof.

Seconds later came the arrows, thumping into wood, dinging off metal bosses, skittering off the road. Ballista felt the shield above him bang down on to his helmet as an arrow struck. Somewhere, a man screamed. Nearby, a man swore fluently. Another was praying.

'Bind and advance.'

Ballista grabbed the back of the mail shirt of the man to his right, gripped it in his fist. He felt his own tighten as the man to his left did the same. Half turned to the right, taking short steps, crabwise, the left foot always first, they advanced.

'Left, left, left,' they muttered, getting into rhythm, the momentum mounting.

Another volley of arrows whistled down. More men screamed, cursed. More men were praying, calling out encouragement.

'Only officers will speak! This is not a fucking *symposium*!'

It was hot and close in the *testudo*; a strong smell of sweat and unwashed men. Ballista peeked out of the gap between the top of his shield and the overlapping one to the right. The air was full of missiles. A line of men. Incongruous in the centre, a four-wheeled cart. A long way to go. At least a hundred paces.

The arrows fell like rain. The Persians were shooting at will.

A cheer spread through the *testudo*. The Roman bowmen were round the corner. They were shooting back. Now the Sassanids could try the bitter luck of war.

Above all the noise – the impact of arrows, the hard breathing, the rattle of equipment, the intermittent howls of pain – there was a rumble of thunder.

Ballista risked another look around his shield. Getting there: about sixty paces to go. But something struck him as odd. There were fewer missiles in the air. A commotion in the centre of the Sassanid line. Warriors pushing the cart forward.

'Halt!'

Surprised, but obedient to orders, the legionaries bumped into each other as they came to a sudden stop.

The easterners had let go of the cart. It was beginning to gather speed down the incline.

'Legio IIII, lie down. Cover yourselves with your shields. Pass the word back to the archers to stay on their feet and spread out.'

In a confused, uncertain scramble, the men around Ballista got to the ground.

'Face down. Shields over your backs.'

Ballista had no time to explain or check that his

instructions were carried out. The cart was moving faster. He dropped down, nose an inch or so from the road, grit under his elbows, shield braced above his head.

The terrible rumbling and squealing grew louder as cart and the inevitable collision drew near. The trick had worked for Alexander the Great. Arrian's *Anabasis*, Ballista thought. That was where he had read about it.

There was an awful sound of splintering wood, agonized screams. A moment's silence, then a sickening crash.

'On your feet. Close ranks.'

Alexander's ploy had not worked so well for Ballista. At the front, men were down where the wheels had hit them. The cart must have been airborne for a time. But it had not cleared the unit. There was a mangled mess of broken bodies and shattered woodwork where it had landed, towards the rear. The sound of low sobbing could be heard.

'On your feet! Close ranks.' The legionaries, eyes wild with shock, were slow to move. 'Close ranks!' Ballista took stock as the men shuffled to obey. The incoming arrows had dropped away as the Persians watched. Still about sixty paces to go: further than he would have liked. But the legionaries were in no state to reform the *testudo*. It had to be now.

'Ready for war?' Ballista roared at the darkening sky.

'Ready!' Each time, the routine response was bolder, more angry. After the third, Ballista ordered the charge.

As they set off, swords drawn, the arrow storm recommenced.

The road was steep here. Within a few paces, Ballista felt the muscles in his legs complain. His chest began to burn as he dragged in air. Another peal of thunder.

Splinters flew hideously close to Ballista's eyes. He felt a sharp stab of pain, blood hot on his cheek. The wicked barbed point was near his face. An arrow had punched half through his shield. He snapped the shaft. Kept moving.

The Sassanid now facing Ballista was coming forward. He was a big man, scale-armoured, eyes hidden by his helmet. The long sword blade hissed through the air as the easterner aimed a mighty two-handed overhead blow. Ballista punched upwards with the boss of his shield. The impact almost forced Ballista to his knees. Instinctively, he drove upwards, thrusting his sword. The point slipped off the armour. The two men were locked together. Ballista cracked the pommel of his sword on to the back of the Sassanid's helmet. The man grunted.

There was a deafening crack of thunder.

In the press of bodies, neither of the men could wield their blades. The Sassanid tried to bite Ballista's face. Horrified, the northerner twisted back. The man's beard scratched his cheek. Ballista dropped his sword. Its wrist strap dug into his flesh, the weight hard on his arm. He grabbed the plume on the Sassanid's helmet; dragged his head back with a convulsive lunge, and Ballista headbutted his opponent. The metal ridge of the northerner's helmet connected with the bridge of the man's nose. Both their faces were running in blood. The crush of bodies pressed further.

A vivid flash of lightning illuminated the hellish scene.

The Sassanid had freed his sword arm. Overhand, he was sliding the tip of the steel over the rim of Ballista's shield. Arms pinioned, the northerner struggled desperately. If only Maximus were here. The Sassanid set himself to thrust down into Ballista's throat. He spat blood, broken fragments of teeth.

There was a surge of pressure from behind Ballista. Driven backwards, the Sassanid adjusted the angle of his sword. His mouth opened. More blood, pouring into his black beard. The sword fell from his hand. He looked down at the Roman blade driven into his armpit. His body went into spasm, became limp.

'Gratius, *Dominus*.' The legionary withdrew his sword. The corpse of the Sassanid fell underfoot.

'I will remember,' said Ballista.

A space had opened up. The Persians were giving ground. Another boom of thunder, and the rain began. It fell in heavy curtains. Ballista could feel it beating on his back. It was driving into the faces of the enemy.

'One more step,' yelled Ballista. He launched himself forward.

Ballista did not know if anyone was with him. His boots slipped in the water. No arrows came at him. The rain had soaked the bowstrings.

The Sassanid in front of Ballista looked around, hesitated, then turned and ran. Another flash of lightning lit the gloom. All the easterners were running through the rain.

Ballista laughed to be alive. If the gods wanted vengeance on the oath-breaker, they were biding their time.

Julia finished inspecting the house in the Epiphania district of Antioch. Everything was in order. She dismissed the maids. It was important that a house was in order when the *dominus* returned. It was especially important in one with senatorial connections. She went and sat in a wicker chair on the shady side of the atrium.

It was hot, but the regular afternoon breeze was blowing up the Orontes valley. The wind moved the material on the loom propped against the wall. Julia looked at its two vertical timbers, shed race, weights and cross bars with something close to loathing. Its presence was necessary in a well-run household. Yet she liked it about as well as an Armenian tigress liked a cage. For women, the loom had always been there. Penelope in the *Odyssey*, weaving by day and unravelling by night, holding off the suitors while she waited, in the hope that her philandering husband might return. The character displayed an unpleasant mixture of passivity and cunning in the story, Julia thought. Maybe it had been necessary for a wife to weave in the primitive and poor heroic age at the dawn of time, but wealth had rendered the loom redundant for many women. The Roman *imperium* had added a new level of hypocrisy to the image: Livia, the wife of the first emperor, in a houseful of servants, sitting at the loom playing the dutiful matron of old, in between procuring young virgins for her husband to deflower. Nothing annoyed Julia more than those male doctors who claimed that such work was good for the delicate health of a woman.

Julia mastered her impatience. Ballista would not care or notice if the wretched loom was there or not. She did not know why she bothered. In the two months since he had escaped from Persian captivity, he had sent just two notes, both brief and impersonal. She knew as well as anyone the danger of the *frumentarii* intercepting a letter, but he could have sent something more intimate with a trusted friend. That little pleb he put such faith in, Castricius, had been in Antioch.

Yesterday, the second formal note had come: standard enquiries after her health and that of the children, then much of the public duties of a Prefect of Cavalry and *Vir Perfectissimus*. The Sassanids had made no further attempt on the Syrian Gates. Nor had they commandeered ships. Neither Seleuceia nor Antioch presently was in danger. The Sassanids had marched to the north to plunder Cilicia. Ballista was ordered to raise ships and men to pursue them. He would return to the house today at noon.

Except he had not. Three hours after the lunch things had been cleared away, a grubby little legionary by the name of Gratius had arrived. With an impertinent air, he had said that the Prefect of Cavalry had been summoned to the palace down on the island; there was no way of telling how long the emperors' *consilium* would last; war was a weighty matter.

Julia had dismissed him coldly. 'War was a weighty matter.' Indeed. *Let war be the care of men*, as Hector had told Andromache. Men – what fools they were. *I would rather stand three times in the front of battle than endure childbirth*, as a heroine in a tragedy had said. Both lines had been written by men, but the tragedian had been nearer the truth than Homer had. Julia thought of her childhood friend Metella, dead giving birth before she reached sixteen. If men bore children, it would put an end to their puerile glorification of war. How could the dangers of war compare with those of childbirth?

Now she was waiting. As always when he returned, Ballista would want sex – he was like an animal marking its territory. At least he was not a womanizer, did not bother the maids. Not like poor Cornelia's husband. He was a complete *ancillariolus*. Their house was almost unendurable with its endless tears and recriminations. Julia had always found Ballista's fidelity flattering, but strange. It was part of his barbarian upbringing, like his jealousy. There had been more than one terrible scene at dinner parties when he had thought that she was flirting. She did not want to be a Messalina, but his jealousy was stifling. It was un-Roman.

'*Domina*,' the porter announced, 'Marcus Clodius Ballista, *Vir Perfectissimus*, has returned.'

Julia stood and walked around the pool to greet her husband. Ballista smiled. His front teeth were chipped. He looked tired and careworn.

'*Dominus*.' Julia's senatorial family had not encouraged

public displays of affection between wife and husband. Julia kept her eyes modestly down.

'*Domina.*' Ballista leant down. She raised her face and he kissed her on the lips.

Julia told the porter to summon the children. The silence stretched as they waited. She looked down again. The wind rippled the surface of the pool, making the fishes, dolphin and octopus in the mosaic at the bottom seem to swim.

A cry of pleasure, and Isangrim ran out. The eight-year-old hurled himself at his father. Julia felt a twinge of irritation. In a senatorial home, it was not just the wife who should behave with decorum. A son should greet his father solemnly, call him *Dominus*.

Ballista scooped up the boy, burying his face in his neck. They talked low together.

Julia noticed the new scars on Ballista's wrists and forearms. She had always liked his forearms. There was something different, attractive, about a man's forearms.

A high-pitched squeal. Dernhelm, not yet two, was being carried by old Calgacus. They were followed by Maximus and Demetrius. Setting his eldest son on his feet, Ballista took Dernhelm in his arms. Again he buried his face in his child's neck, inhaling the smell of him.

Having handed Dernhelm to Julia, and with Isangrim still clinging to his waist, Ballista embraced each of his freedmen in turn.

'Welcome home, *Kyrios*,' said Demetrius. The other two were less formal.

'Like a counterfeit coin, I knew you would return,' said Calgacus.

'So far,' replied Ballista.

'We must celebrate, have a drink,' beamed Maximus.

Before Ballista could reply, Julia cut in. 'It is time Isangrim was at his lessons, and Dernhelm must sleep.'

The three freedmen took the hint. Soon husband and wife were alone again.

Julia put her hand on Ballista's forearm. She led him through to the private *cubiculum* towards the rear of the house. The shutters were half closed, the covers on the couch drawn back. Man and wife made love, urgently, briefly.

Afterwards, they lay drinking and talking. They were naked. Julia knew that, after the wedding night, a respectable wife never showed herself naked to her husband. That was the behaviour of a whore. But she knew it pleased Ballista, excited him.

Julia traced the fresh scars on his wrists and ankles. 'You had a bad time with the Persians.'

'The boys look well.' He made no effort to hide the fact he was changing the subject.

'Mmm.' Julia kissed his chest, his stomach. She did something no respectable Roman wife should ever do. The very wickedness of her behaviour excited her. They made love again, more slowly this time.

'How long will you be in Antioch?'

'Two days. Then as long as it takes to find ships in Seleuceia. I can requisition a house there. You should come down, bring the boys. We will have a little time until I have to sail north after the Sassanids.'

Julia watched him fiddle with his wine cup, felt his desire to be gone. Men, from what her friends said, were all the same. The act of love would last longer if left to women: all night, if men were made that way.

'Go on,' she smiled. 'Go and find your friends. It is a long time since they have had a chance to drink with you.'

There was a hollowness to Ballista's grin. 'Edessa, a couple of months ago. The festival of the *Maiuma*. At the end of the night, someone tried to kill me.'

After he had gone, Julia put on a robe. She called for a maid. Ignoring Anthia's complicit smile, she asked for her bath to be made ready. He was trying to hide it, but there was something preying on her husband's mind. She had a couple of days. She would discover what it was.

Demetrius stood on the prow of Ballista's flagship. Since the fleet had left Seleucia in pursuit of the Persians, things had not gone well. Demetrius looked at the port of Aegeae.

All sacked cities are the same: in each, the kicked-in doors and smoke-blackened buildings; the ransacked houses and defiled temples; the muted sounds where there had been terrible noise; the splayed and huddled corpses; the smell of burning, excrement and corruption.

Yet each is different. There is always some specific thing that catches the observer's eye, moves his heart to fresh pity: a treasured heirloom smashed in the street; an old woman sobbing noiselessly; a child wandering alone. Those who say compassion is blunted by repetition are wrong.

Demetrius stood on the ship looking at the city of Aegeae.

For in my heart and soul I also know this well:
the day will come when sacred Troy must die,
Priam must die and all his people with him . . .
That is nothing, nothing beside your agony
when some brazen Argive hales you off in tears,
wrenching away your day of light and freedom!

The lines of Homer – Hector's all too prescient words to his wife – came unbidden into Demetrius's thoughts. Human happiness is very fragile. One day, a prosperous, peaceful town; the next, a stinking ruin. One day, a happy, free youth; the next, a slave at the whim of a capricious and brutal master.

Demetrius had seen too much horror in the last few days. Ballista's ships had followed the Persians around the bay of Issus. Alexandria ad Issum, Katabolos and now the port of Aegeae – all had been sacked.

There had been no way Demetrius could avoid the horror. At each town, his duties as *accensus* required him to accompany Ballista. Ashore, the *kyrios*'s dark mood had worsened. But Ballista was diligent. He interviewed survivors. He investigated which supplies, public and private, had been taken, attempting to estimate enemy numbers. Here at Aegeae, he had even studied the horse droppings on the road to the interior taken by the Sassanids as they rode out of the sacked city.

Demetrius did not think he would do well in the sack of a town. In the noise, confusion and fear, he doubted he would make the right decisions. Would he run or hide? In either case, where? Would he follow the crowd, hoping for some safety in numbers, or slink off alone, praying to be overlooked? Would his courage fail him altogether? Would he drop to his knees in the pose of a suppliant, trusting in his looks to spare his life? And if they did, at what cost? His first years of slavery had taught him all about degradation.

Demetrius returned his thoughts to the present. Ballista's *consilium* was not going well; as expected, his plans were not being well received.

'No, we will not pursue the Sassanids inland. We are outnumbered. They have at least fifteen thousand cavalry. We have five thousand infantry and the crews of twenty warships. The Sassanids have taken the road to Mopouestia. The open plains of Cilicia Pedias are ideal for horsemen. They would surround us and shoot us down at their pleasure.'

The assembled officers, some forty men, down to the rank of *pilus prior* and including the centurions commanding the warships, listened in unconvinced silence. They wanted revenge. However, Ballista's second-in-command, Ragonius Clarus, the legate appointed by Macrianus the Elder, nodded sagely.

Ballista continued. 'We will adopt the strategy used by Fabius Cunctator to defeat Hannibal. We will wait. The prefect Demosthenes will take a composite unit of five hundred spearmen and archers to hold the Cilician Gates. Apparently, they command the only road north over the Taurus mountains viable for a large force of cavalry. The warships can take Demosthenes' men to Tarsus – there will just be space if the marines temporarily transfer to the transport ships. From Tarsus, Demosthenes will force-march north to the Gates.

'The warships will rendezvous with the rest of us at

Soli. There we will plan with Voconius Zeno, the governor of Cilicia, to guard the narrow coastal path west to Cilicia Tracheia.

'If the Syrian Gates to the south-east are still held, and the emperors have taken my advice and blocked the Amanikai Gates to the north-east, the Persians will effectively be trapped in the lowlands of Cilicia Pedias. Then we watch and wait for opportunities. With our fleet, we can come and go as we please. Sooner or later, the Persian horde will split up to plunder or we will catch them at some other disadvantage.'

This was Ballista at his best, thought Demetrius. The *kyrios* was putting aside his personal troubles and fears to plan meticulously, to do what needed to be done. Yet the officers still seemed unhappy.

Ragonius Clarus interjected in patrician tones. 'An admirable strategy – time-hallowed and in keeping with the ways of our Roman ancestors. Thus Cunctator vanquished the Punic evil of Hannibal, Crassus destroyed the servile menace of Spartacus. Our noble young emperors will approve.'

Everyone knew that Clarus had been foisted on Ballista to report to Macrianus the Lame. His words elicited no enthusiasm from the military men.

'We will do what is ordered, and at every command we will be ready.'

Ballista declared the *consilium* over and, with his *familia*, retired to his cabin at the stern of the *trireme*.

'Sure, but it must be a joy to know our noble young emperors will approve of your thinking,' said Maximus.

'Joy unbounded,' Ballista replied flatly. Obviously he

was not in the mood for joking. Since his return from captivity, he seldom had been.

'A drink?' Calgacus suggested.

'No, thank you. I think I will rest.'

As the freedmen filed out, Ballista called Demetrius back.

The young *accensus* watched as his *kyrios* looked at the lists and plans piled on the desk. Distractedly, Ballista picked one or two up, moved some others about. A few moments of this, and Ballista stopped. He went over to his bed, retrieved a papyrus roll that lay on the covers and sat down.

'Demetrius, you are a Hellene. Are these Cilicians Hellenes?'

Over the years, Demetrius had got used to the abruptness of Ballista's conversational openings when he had something on his mind. The point usually became clear after a time.

'They like to think they are,' Demetrius replied. 'In terms of descent, most of the cities of Cilicia claim a founder from the ancient Hellenic past. The claims of some of the *poleis* are plausible. Hesiod and Herodotus tell of Amphilochus, the seer who fought at the siege of Troy, journeying here. He is said to have founded Mallos. The town of Mopouestia is named after another seer, Mopsus. But other claims are most unlikely. The citizens of Tarsus themselves are unsure who founded their town: one of the Hellenes – Perseus, Heracles or Triptolemus – or an oriental called Sandan. Zephyrion openly admits it was the creation of the Assyrian king Sardanapallus.'

When Demetrius stopped, Ballista nodded for him to go on.

'In terms of culture, it is true they pay almost exagger-ated respect to Hellenic *paideia*. Chrysippus the Stoic was from Soli. The two men called Athenodorus, the one who lived with Cato and the one who was Julius Caesar's teacher, were both from Tarsus. There are several schools of phi-losophy and rhetoric in Cilicia. But those who attain distinction tend to travel away, and few men of the highest attainments ever come here from abroad. I think there is something suspect about the Cilician nature which under-mines their *paideia*. In quite recent times, the two sophists from Cilicia who became famous under the emperors, Antiochus and Philagrus, each had a violent temper. The latter would get so angry he could not declaim. Once, in a fit of anger, he went so far as to utter a barbarism.'

Ballista smiled ruefully, and used the papyrus roll with which he was fiddling to indicate to Demetrius to continue.

'It is not just the *pepaideumenoi* – all the inhabitants have a reputation for being hot-tempered, unwilling to submit to anyone being placed over them. As a province, they often try to prosecute their governors before the emperor. Among themselves, the cities quarrel incessantly. Only the *Pax Romana* – the boots above their heads – stops them resorting to open violence, if not war.'

Ballista had stopped playing with the papyrus. He looked thoughtful. 'If they are not truly Hellenic but part oriental, and they are unhappy with Roman rule, might some of them side with the Persians? Or might the hatred of one city for another induce it to go over to Shapur?'

Now Demetrius smiled. 'I am sure any of their cities would point out the weak place in their neighbour's wall rather than be sacked themselves. But a Sassanid monarch is more alien to them than a true Hellene or a Roman.'

'Then why do they not fight?' Ballista was thinking aloud. 'Admittedly, Alexandria was taken by surprise, but at Katabolos they fled the walls, and here at Aegeae it appears traitors opened the gates.'

'There may be two reasons, *Kyrios*,' Demetrius replied. 'You remember how at Antioch, a few years ago in the time of troubles, some of the poor, encouraged by a man called Mariades, betrayed the city to the Persians? It might be much the same in Cilicia. Here in the cities of the plain, the poor are oppressed. They hate the rich, and the feeling is reciprocated. Many years ago the great philosopher Dio of Prusa endeavoured to persuade those who controlled Tarsus to give citizenship to the poor they call the linen workers. Eventually they got the title, but by all accounts they remain as downtrodden as ever.'

All air of distraction had vanished from Ballista. 'That may explain the treachery at Aegeae, but not the cowardice at Katabolos.'

'The plains of Cilicia Pedias are soft and fertile.' Demetrius, like his *kyrios*, could come at things from an angle. 'Wheat, sesame, dates, figs, vines – all grow in abundance. The streets of the towns groan with the sound of wagons laden with fruit and vegetables. A soft place breeds soft men,' Demetrius concluded in Herodotean mode.

Ballista nodded. 'True, they are unaccustomed to fighting.'

'No, *Kyrios*, it is much worse than that: they snort.'

'They what?'

'Snort.' Demetrius waved his hands about, palms up. 'You know, they *snort*.'

As Ballista clearly did not know, Demetrius, using one finger, adjusted his hair with elaborate care.

In the face of Ballista's continuing non-comprehension, Demetrius tried a more obvious tactic. He bent slightly forward, looked over his shoulder and made a sudden noise halfway between a man snoring and the squeal of a stuck pig.

'Ah,' Ballista laughed, 'that sort of snort.'

This was embarrassing. Demetrius knew that his *kyrios*, like Calgacus and Maximus, was aware of the ways he found his physical pleasure. But, apart from some occasional, oblique teasing, it was not something mentioned within the *familia*.

Straightening up hurriedly, Demetrius rushed on. 'It is not just the men, the women do it too.'

Ballista was still laughing.

'They are all totally without restraint. Luxury, improper jests, insolence; they give more thought to their fine linen than to wisdom. Here in Aegeae, in the very temple of Asclepius, the holy man Apollonius of Tyana met a one-eyed Cilician –'

'Thank you, Demetrius,' said Ballista.

Although his run of thoughts had been broken, Demetrius continued his flustered diatribe. 'Of course, that is just those from the lush lands of Cilicia Pedias. The hill men of Cilicia Tracheia are very different. All brigands and pirates. All killers.'

Ballista held up his hand. 'Thank you.' The laughter had gone from his eyes. 'I think I will read now.' Ballista swung his legs up on to the bed and unrolled the papyrus to find his place.

As he made to leave, Demetrius risked a glance at what Ballista was reading. It was Euripides, the *Medea*, the tragedy in which Jason breaks his oath to Medea and she, without losing the favour of the gods, kills their innocent sons. It was hard to think of worse reading for a man in Ballista's position.

X

Ballista stood at the top of the small stone theatre in the town of Sebaste. He had not chosen the location solely to wrongfoot the man he was to meet, although that would not be unwelcome. In every port at which the fleet had moored since it sailed west from Aegeae, Ballista had sought out a good vantage point from which to assess the town's defences.

The heart of the city of Sebaste was spread out below him. The island, as it was called, although clearly it had never been other than a promontory, stuck out into the sea like the blade of an axe. The south-western harbour was only partly sheltered. It lay outside the walls and was little more than a beach on which longshore fishermen drew up their boats. To the north-east, the island curved back, nearly meeting the shoreline. The main harbour here was almost completely enclosed. Ballista had noted it was silting up with the prevailing current from the east.

The island was walled. A chain which could be lowered and raised stretched across the north-eastern harbour mouth to the first tower of the land walls. These ran away to Ballista's left, out of sight. He knew they encircled the mainland extension of the town, including the theatre where he stood and the civic centre, public baths and *agora* below him. The walls did not look as if they had undergone any work for a number of years but still seemed essentially sound. Some high ground overlooked the landward walls. On all the roads into Sebaste, a jumble of suburban villas and tombs screened the approaches. There was no artillery. Despite all this, the town was basically defendable. There was no internal source of fresh water, and the aqueduct could be cut, but there were plenty of cisterns. The granaries contained food for several weeks. All in all, there was no pressing reason why the citizens of Sebaste should not hold out when the Persians reached the port.

Yet Ballista was not hopeful. Since he had left Aegeae, the Persians had taken Mopouestia, Mallos, Adana and the provincial capital, Tarsus. A despatch boat had just brought him the news that a detachment of about three thousand had now pressed ahead and seized Zephyrion. As far as he could ascertain, there had been no real reason any of these cities should have fallen either. Zephyrion was not much over forty miles away.

Things were not going well. Admittedly, when the warships had rejoined him, they had brought Ballista the news that Demosthenes and his five hundred men had marched north from Tarsus before the Persians had arrived. With luck, the Cilician Gates were now garrisoned. But everything else was bad.

Dropping anchor at Soli for his rendezvous with the governor of Cilicia, Ballista had been disappointed. Voconius Zeno was not there. He had fled west, leaving behind a letter in which he denounced Quietus and Macrianus the Younger as rebels and accused their father Macrianus the Lame of being the chorus master behind them. Zeno said he had gone to join the legitimate ruler Gallienus. With several nice turns of phrase, the departing governor had encouraged all other officials likewise to hasten to throw themselves on the *clementia* of the true emperor. Ballista had thought, sourly, if only it were that simple – if only his wife and sons were not in Antioch, effectively held as hostages by the rebels.

In any case, Zeno had gone, and now Ballista had to deal with this man Trebellianus here at Sebaste. He had been suggested by Macrianus's man Ragonius Clarus. 'Yes, Trebellianus is a local, from Cilicia Tracheia. But we must never hold a man's origins against him. And, with Trebellianus, it could well prove most useful in dealing with some of the wilder elements in the rough country. Trebellianus is a man of honour, wealth and influence. Right at the beginning, he wrote pledging his support to Macrianus the Younger and Quietus. He stands high in the regard of the young emperors, and Macrianus the Elder himself will have no qualms if Trebellianus were to be appointed acting governor of Cilicia. Rather the reverse – who knows what form his disappointment might take?'

It was a *suggestion* that Ballista could not ignore. But even the briefest and most superficial investigation – by Demetrius in the houses of the councillors of Sebaste and by Maximus and Calgacus in the bars of the waterfront – had revealed much to bring disquiet. Not least that Trebellianus was commonly referred to as 'the Archpirate'. Given the nature of the inhabitants of Cilicia

Tracheia, it was little surprise that the title was most often given with respect.

'Here they come,' said Maximus.

Ballista saw the small party leaving the gate from the island. They had expected Ballista would see them there, in the old royal palace. Now they had to toil across town up to the theatre. But as far as Ballista was concerned, if they were put out, it was no bad thing.

As he waited, Ballista regarded his fleet, moored in the main harbour. They were all there except the seven little war galleys, which were shuttling back and forth monitoring the enemy force at Zephyrion. The quays were crowded: twenty-five transport vessels, ten big *triremes* and the other three little *liburnians* not at sea. The sword of Damocles may have been hanging by a thread over the heads of the citizens of Sebaste, but those who ran the bars, brothels and baths down by the port had never had a more profitable time, with a fleet and four and a half thousand soldiers to service.

Ragonius Clarus entered the theatre. He was followed by a big man in a toga. He in turn was followed by two tall men wearing what looked like goatskin cloaks. It was a mild summer day, but their choice of clothing was strange. In single file, they began to climb the stairs.

Ballista sat down on the top row of seats. The man in the toga must be Trebellianus. He was a powerful-looking individual in middle age, broad-shouldered, with a shock of black hair; restrainedly good-looking. The two trailing him were younger. They had the same black hair but looked thinner and hungrier. Both wore swords at their hip.

As they reached the top, Ragonius Clarus stepped aside.

The other three passed him and halted. They said nothing. None of them was blowing after the steep climb. Together, they exuded menace. Ballista felt Demetrius, standing to his left, shrink back. Maximus, on his right, drew himself up to his full, not over-tall height. Calgacus and Castricius remained lounging a little way off. Ballista wondered what impression he and his followers must convey.

Unexpectedly, the northerner found himself thinking how many men these three Cilicians had killed. Come to that – how many men had he himself killed? And then there were those killed by Maximus, Calgacus and Castricius. That must make a legion of souls, flitting and shrieking across the dark meadows of Hades.

'Gaius Terentius Trebellianus?' Ballista pronounced it as a question.

'Yes.' He had a soft, pleasant speaking voice.

'You have brought bodyguards.'

'Not at all.' Trebellianus's smile went nowhere near his eyes. 'These are my young friends Palfuerius and Lydius.'

'It is illegal for a civilian to carry arms in the *imperium*.'

'Not if the weapons are necessary for a man's profession, are inherited, or are carried for self-defence.' Trebellianus's smooth cheeks had the sheen of good living.

Ballista nodded. It was so. The Arch-pirate knew the law.

'I am told you have influence with the people of Cilicia Tracheia.'

'Some of my fellow citizens are kind enough to come to me for advice.'

One of the young men smirked. Ballista ignored him. 'On what subjects do you advise them?'

Trebellianus gestured to the mountains. 'Our country is a poor one. What little livelihood we have comes from the humble goat. In summer he must go to the high pastures. In winter he comes down to the coastal lowlands. Moving many animals and men up and down, across other people's land, through different communities, always involves difficulties. I make these difficulties go away. I help my friends.'

And what do you do to those who are not your friends, wondered Ballista. 'And your friends, what do they do for you?'

A smooth smile crossed Trebellianus's face. 'They are good enough to show me honour.'

'What town is your *patria*?'

'My family estates are up country around Germanicopolis. I have been fortunate enough to acquire others on the coast at Korakesion and Charadna.'

So, Ballista thought, your lands lie at either end of the trail, and your armed toughs escort the herds up and down. Your 'influence' rests on violence and intimidation. He remembered his friend Iarhai at the desert city of Arete. Trebellianus was a small-scale version of that caravan protector. A strong man provides 'protection', and those he protects give him 'gifts'. And just as Iarhai had rivals at Arete, so would Trebellianus here in Cilicia Tracheia. The gods knew what misfortunes would be heading their way now that Macrianus the Lame had decided that this Arch-pirate was to become a senior official with the weight of the *imperium* behind him.

Ballista held out his hand and Demetrius placed an ivory and gold codicil in it. Standing, Ballista passed the imperial codicil to the Cilician. 'Gaius Terentius Trebellianus, you are hereby appointed acting governor of the province of Cilicia.'

'We will do what is ordered, and at every command we will be ready.' The answer came back blandly.

'Your first task, in the face of which nothing else matters, must be to block the coast road to the west. I take it you can call on armed men?'

Trebellianus did not speak, but inclined his head.

Ballista went on, 'I have collected what detached troops were to be found in the ports between Aegeae and here. These *stationarii* only amount to just over three hundred, but they are at your command. The *eirenarch* I have left in each town, along with his armed men of the watch. These officers and their *diogmitai* are locals. They should fight to defend their homes, but may well desert if we attempt to move them somewhere else. Where do you propose to close the road to the Persians?'

'Korakesion.' The answer came without hesitation.

'A long way to the west.'

'Indeed, and it will leave my own estates at Charadna at the mercy of the Sassanids. But, at Korakesion, the mountains come down to the sea, and the town itself is fortified by nature as well as by man.'

Ballista was more than suspicious that some private motive was behind the choice. Korakesion was at the western extremity of the province. Perhaps Trebellianus was sacrificing some of his own estates in the knowledge that his rivals would suffer worse. But there was nothing to be done. The Cilician knew the country. Macrianus the Lame wanted him as governor.

'So be it,' Ballista said, as if he had the power to decide. 'I am going to base the fleet and army on Cyprus, at the port of Kyreneia. The *liburnians* will keep me in communication. You will submit written reports of all your actions.'

Again Trebellianus wordlessly inclined his head.

'I am afraid I cannot spare you any transport ships. You will have to march the *stationarii* from here.'

Trebellianus smiled his smooth smile. 'Forewarned by Ragonius Clarus, I took the liberty of requisitioning some merchant ships at Corycus. We can sail from there.'

Ballista kept his face expressionless. 'So be it. I will not detain you further.'

Trebellianus sketched a salute. He and his young followers, both of them smirking now, turned and set off down the steps.

Took the liberty . . . requisitioning ships. Ballista was fuming. Come what may, the owners would never see them again.

Ragonius Clarus was mouthing some platitudes. Ballista was too angry to pretend to listen. How much suffering would he spare this province if he just killed Trebellianus now? A word to Maximus and Castricius. He could do it with his own hand. And those two evil-eyed goatboys. Nothing here could stop him. The troops would not care. They would follow Ballista, not Ragonius Clarus. Nothing to stop him – except what would happen to Julia and the boys at the hands of Macrianus and his repulsive sons in Antioch?

Ballista drew a big breath and calmed himself. What were these Cilicians to him anyway? And if he killed Trebellianus, it would only leave a space for his equally murderous rivals to fight over. Fuck them all.

Mind you, The Allfather willing, one day it would be good to send Trebellianus to meet Charon. *And* that sniggering pair of young strong-arm boys. Palfuerius and Lydius. Which was which? Fuck it, they could cross the Styx together.

Julia sat in the seating reserved for respectable matrons. It was pleasant in the great theatre of Antioch, with the afternoon breeze blowing up the Orontes valley. She felt more relaxed than she had for a long time. Macrianus the Lame and Quietus had taken the army south to Emesa in an attempt to overawe Odenathus of Palmyra and secure his allegiance. Since the arrival at Antioch of the new imperial court, Julia had largely kept to her house. But when Quietus chose to visit, it was impossible to refuse entry to a man who, however unworthily, wore the purple. It was not as if she could not deal with his oily innuendoes. And while Macrianus the Elder needed the services of Ballista, Quietus was too scared of his father to attempt force. But his presence was deeply unwelcome.

It was a pity Quietus did not follow the example of his brother, Macrianus the Younger, and remain in the palace indulging a passion for making small wooden toys. Imagine, a grown man, an emperor, indulging in such a childish pastime, doing the menial work of a slave or paid pleb. It was less harmful, but almost more demeaning than Nero singing or Commodus fighting as a gladiator.

Imagine a man such as Ballista fiddling with glue and little saws. As she framed the thought, suddenly she found she could imagine it all too easily. Men never really grew up. Not that her husband would be enjoying any such fripperies in his present mood. Before he sailed, Julia had discovered what was troubling Ballista: the ridiculous oath he had made to Shapur; the fear that breaking it endangered their sons. He had not lost the superstitions of the dark forests of his childhood. Part of him would always remain a barbarian.

The actors reappeared on stage. It was a domestic mime, and Julia was enjoying it. The wife was running rings around her old miser of a husband. Julia had checked the programme before bringing her boys. Nothing too untoward. Nothing like the striptease of the *Floralia* or the naked whores of the *Maiuma*. The husband and wife who ran the troupe had a reputation for a more moral sort of mime.

Isangrim was bored. Julia fished in the purse tied to her girdle and gave some coins to the *custos* who attended her. The elderly manservant shuffled off to buy a sweet for Isangrim and something suitable for two-year-old Dernhelm. For once, Julia was in such a good mood that being saddled with the *custos* and two maids – the minimum that custom dictated should accompany a married woman of her status in public – did not bother her. A sticky treat would cheer Isangrim up, and the next mime was about the bandit Selurus, the Son of Etna. Apart from Tillorobus, the terror of Mysia and Mount Ida, there was no legendary outlaw the boy liked more. The hiding in a cave, the daring escapes, the cunning disguises and tricking of the centurion, even the poignant death scene – all captivated him.

The old woman on the stage stopped mid-line. She pointed to the rear of the seats.

'Am I dreaming, or are the Persians here?'

Heads began to turn. First one or two, then everyone looked back. There was muttering, then shouts of consternation, screams. Dark figures could be seen on the roofs of the houses towards Mount Silpius. With a terrible whistling, the first flight of arrows rained down. More screams, accompanied by yells of pain. Pandemonium.

Julia scooped up Dernhelm, grabbed Isangrim by the hand. 'Come,' she said.

The two maids stared, open-mouthed.

'Come,' Julia shouted again.

The maids sat on in moronic immobility. Stupid girls.

Julia set off. The nearest entrance was only a few paces away. Some of the audience sat, stunned. Others, as if woken from sleep, were getting to their feet. The more acute were scrambling over the seats already. More arrows sliced through the air.

The stairwell was full of terrified people. They tore down the steps. Isangrim stumbled. As he started to fall, Julia felt his hand slipping through hers. Go down now and he would be trampled. With unrecognizable strength, she gripped his damp fingers, hauled him to his feet.

'Run, boy.' Her fear for him made her snap at him.

At the bottom of the stairs they ran into the backs of a stationary knot of people. More bodies thumped in behind them. In a moment everyone was crushed together. The pressure was increasing. Up on her shoulders, Dernhelm was all right. But Isangrim was in trouble. She was finding it hard to breathe. All matronly restraint gone, she braced her legs, arched her back, pushed out with her free elbow; anything to make a space. Isangrim, arms wrapped around her waist, looked up with huge, frightened eyes.

She went to speak, to reassure. The pressure surged. The words were cut off. Her face was pressed into the tunic of the man in front.

They were moving. Gripping her children, Julia prayed. Like the liquid when a stopper is taken out of a flask, the crowd burst free of the doorway. Julia felt something soft under her sandals. A woman, bloodied on the threshold.

For a while they went with the crowd: down the street, away from Mount Silpius, away from the Sassanids. An eddy in the mob carried them to the far side of the street. Julia pulled Isangrim into the shelter of a porch. Putting Dernhelm down, she hugged her sons to her. There was an angry red weal where she had grasped Isangrim's wrist. She kissed them both. She was crying. They were not.

More and more people were streaming past, down towards the river, down towards the potential safety of the palace on the island and its remaining garrison. Julia had to think. Not the palace. The mob would block the bridges. Not the island. Home. She must get her sons home. Julia looked out. There was a sidestreet to the left, about thirty paces away. Hoisting Dernhelm back on her shoulder, taking a firm grip of Isangrim's hand, she set off again.

Around the corner it was quieter. Julia knew the Epiphania district like the back of her hand. Instinctively turning left or right, she began to cross it. Within a few streets, they were in a different world. All was peace. Citizens strolled, hawkers called out their wares, pack animals plodded. Thrown by the normality of it all, Julia stopped. In a portico, she set Dernhelm down, tried to get her breath back, make sense of what was happening.

A sharp cry. A thunder of hooves. More cries, then screams. Three Persian horsemen were spurring down the street. Bows in hand, they were shooting at anyone who took their fancy. They were laughing.

Sweeping up the children, Julia pushed them to the back of the portico. Bundling them close together, she covered them with her body. The noise of the hooves grew louder. Her face buried in the boys' hair, Julia waited for an arrow to rip into her back.

The horsemen passed. Julia looked up. The Persians had gone. A few steps away, a bread-seller was on his knees, curled around the arrow in his guts. Not sparing him another glance, Julia got the boys and ran on.

Between its two pillars of imported marble, the door to their house was open. The porter must have fled. The news must be all through the town by now. The street was completely empty. Julia put Dernhelm down. Together they stepped over the mosaic of the improbably endowed hunchback. As if even a superstitious fool could think that would avert evil. Inside, it was dark. The door to the porter's lodge was open, too. They set off down the long corridor.

Behind them, someone stepped out of the lodge. Julia whirled round. A Sassanid. His drawn sword was wet. Dernhelm wailed. The Sassanid raised his weapon to silence the child. Julia stepped in front of him. The Sassanid altered his aim to cut her down. She knew what she had to do – what Helen had done to get Menelaus to spare her life.

With trembling fingers, she tore at her clothes, pulling her *stola* open, her tunic down, letting her breasts spill free.

The man grinned. With a hand at her throat, he slammed her against the wall.

'Run, take your brother, hide,' Julia said quietly to Isangrim, who was out of sight behind the man.

The man released her neck. He sheathed his sword. With both hands, he grabbed her breasts. He fondled them roughly, grunting something in his language. One hand still pulling at her nipples, with the other he fumbled with his belt, pushed his trousers down.

Julia reached up to let her hair down, working the long hairpin free. The man was slobbering on her breasts. He stank: a feral reek of unwashed male lust. His hand hauled her tunic up over her thighs. He lurched back, screaming.

Isangrim's miniature sword was embedded in the man's left leg. The Sassanid doubled up, gripping the hilt. As he pulled it free, he screamed again. And Julia plunged the hairpin into the side of his throat.

The man was on his knees in a spreading pool of blood. His fingers clutched the end of the hairpin. Julia slid away from him along the wall. She held out her hand. Isangrim led his brother to her.

Harsh noises echoed around the atrium. Towards the back of the house, things – expensive things – were being smashed in the family's rooms. To the left, a group of Sassanids had gathered behind the columns. They were laughing and joking but intent on what they were doing – drinking. And there was a servant girl in their midst – suffering what her mistress had just escaped.

With her children, Julia slipped into a door to the right leading to the servants' quarters. Little to loot there. Apart from rape, little reason for the Sassanids to be there. Gods below, gods above, by all the gods, let them not be there. Diligent in her *cura* of the household, Julia knew every twist and turn of the rabbit warren of tiny cells and confusing corridors. Flitting through dark corners and in the shadows of the walls, she led the boys to the stables at the right of the house.

The tack room was locked. Julia struggled to get the keys from her girdle, find the right one. Shutting the door behind them, she locked and bolted it. Intended to prevent pilfering, it would not stand for long under a determined assault. But it was something.

Telling the children to stay where they were, Julia grabbed a saddle and bridle and went through to the stables. Thank the gods she had often gone hunting with her husband. Few of her friends could ride, let alone saddle a horse. She selected her favourite bay gelding; it was quiet, unflappable. Her breath was still coming in gasps, but the mechanical work of her hands calmed her a little. She realized her clothes were torn, her breasts still half exposed. She started to make herself decent, then stopped, annoyed with herself.

The horse ready, girths double-checked, she went back to the tack room. Isangrim was holding Dernhelm's hand, talking softly to him. The little boy had been crying again. No time now; she would comfort him later.

There was plenty of stuff to choose from. Ballista had always been a keen huntsman. Stripping off her clothes, Julia tugged on a man's pair of trousers and tunic. All too big, but she held them in place with her own girdle; the keys and purse jingled as she struggled to fasten it. Finally, she pulled on the smallest pair of riding boots she could find. She was ready. As she collected the children, her eye fell on the neatly arrayed hunting weapons, polished and softly gleaming on the wall. Dismissing the idea of taking a boar spear or bow and quiver, she slung a sword belt over her shoulder. Then, as an afterthought, she handed one to Isangrim. The miniature sword had no great intrinsic value, but it had been one of his treasures. His father had given it to him when he came back from Ephesus last year. Dear gods, even in his barbarian homeland Ballista had not had to kill a man until he was fifteen.

Julia helped Isangrim on to the horse, then put Dernhelm up in front of him. She unbolted the outer gate. Outside, the street was empty. She heard distant sounds of uproar, their direction uncertain. Using the mounting block, she got into the saddle.

Where to go? Out of the city, but then where? To Daphne? In the time of troubles, Shapur had spared the suburb after a sign from the god. There was no telling if such superstition would hold him back this time. So possibly not to her estate at Daphne. Maybe the other place. But first get out of the city.

Julia set off towards the postern gate in the south-east. As they crossed the affluent Rhodion district the streets became wider and steeper, the houses more impressive. The sun was getting low. She had no idea how much time had elapsed since she had left the theatre.

The broad streets were eerily deserted, the mansions shuttered. Now and then, she glimpsed individuals or small groups, who scurried away at the sight of someone on horseback.

Julia turned a corner – and there stood more Persians,

six or seven warriors. They were inspecting their loot at the gate of a large property. Their horses were tethered nearby.

For a few heartbeats, the Persians did nothing. Then three of them stepped out into the street. Julia kicked her heels into the flanks of the gelding. It leapt forward. One of the easterners lunged for its bridle. She urged the horse on. The Persian missed his hold. The horse's shoulder sent him spinning.

Julia looked back. All the Persians were running for their mounts. Holding the children with one arm, Julia hauled the animal round the next corner.

She had a small start. But the horse was burdened with her and the children. Soon the sounds of pursuit swelled behind. She forced herself to think. Two blocks to the south was her friend Sulpicia's house. There was a small alley at the back, its entrance overgrown. She kicked on.

Her pursuers were close but not in sight when she reached the alley. Ducking low, she forced the gelding through the overhanging branches.

From the street came the rattle of hooves. Three, four horsemen rode past. Hushing the children, she waited. The sounds dwindled. She turned her mount. Outside, more noise. Another two Persians clattered by. Again she waited, heart pounding, hands slick on the reins. No sound. Nothing. She urged the horse out into the wide, empty street.

The shadows were lengthening. She was near the gate now. One final turn and there it was. And in front of it three more Persians on horseback.

Confidently the warriors walked their animals towards her. The easterners were smiling broadly.

Julia ran her hand along her girdle – the keys, her purse – to the belt hanging from her shoulder and the hilt of the sword. The Sassanids were not going to take her or her children alive.

XI

Ballista walked out on to the battlements of the north-east tower of the fort guarding the harbour of Kyreneia on the island of Cyprus, where he had taken the fleet and army. The wind was strong, blustery. Standards snapped and hissed, metal fittings clicked against their wooden shafts. He had summoned his *consilium* to meet up here to catch the breeze. Down below, inside the fort, it was stiflingly hot.

With much voluble swearing, Maximus and Calgacus set down the table. *Did he realize how fucking heavy it was; how difficult to get up the fucking stairs?* Demetrius spread out and weighted down the maps.

Ballista leant back against the crenellations and looked around. To the west, a mist was forming over the mountains. In August, it was unlikely to presage rain. There was a dark line on the horizon to the north. It looked like land. It was not. The mainland was some sixty or seventy miles north of Cyprus. But behind or under that dark cloud were the Persians, ranging at will, ravaging unopposed the coast of Cilicia. Turning, Ballista saw a bright little war galley coming from the east. It was rowing into the wind. There was quite a swell running. The gaudy *liburnian* was in a hurry. It was not one of Ballista's – all his ships had been painted an inconspicuous blue-grey. Most of them crowded the small, half-moon harbour in the lee of the fort.

Ragonius Clarus cleared his throat and announced that the members of the *consilium* were all present. The fighting top of the tower was quite spacious, although not designed to accommodate a meeting of over forty Roman officers.

Ballista thanked the legate and, raising his voice against the wind, began the telling of how the war went.

'*Commilitiones*, as I am sure you know, the Sassanid forces have split in two. The smaller part, the three thousand or so that had taken Zephyrion before we left the mainland, have pressed far to the west. Those places that have offered anything other than token resistance, they have bypassed. But, even so, they have sacked' – he pointed at the *periplous* showing the coast of Cilicia Tracheia unrolled on the table – 'Sebaste, Corycus, Calendris and Anemurium. On the last report, they were before the walls of Selinus.'

There was a murmur of surprise. Selinus was a very long way west.

'The main force, estimated at about twelve thousand and led by the King of Kings, Shapur himself, has ridden back east into Cilicia Pedias. They have sacked Augustopolis, Anazarbos, Kastabala, Neronias.' One by one, Ballista tapped the places off on the itinerary map of Cilicia Pedias spread on the table. 'They were last heard of at Flavias.'

The muttering was louder this time, as the scale of the depredations registered. 'Unprecedented disaster'; 'Slaughtered citizens'; 'Insult to the *imperium*'; 'Something must be done'; 'The barbarian *superbia* of Shapur must be humbled'; 'Sail with the evening offshore breeze'; 'Teach the eastern reptiles how to fight.'

Ballista looked away as he let them run on. The commander of the bright little *liburnian* was in a tearing hurry. His left-hand oars were almost shaving the headland that sheltered the harbour from the east.

'*Dominus.*' The voice demanding attention belonged to Marcus Aurelius Rutilus, the prefect of a unit of Thracian auxiliaries. He was a big man, with a square head and an obviously broken nose. The bright-red hair that had given him his *cognomen* probably indicated Celtic or Germanic ancestors.

Ballista gave Rutilus permission to address the *consilium*.

'*Dominus, commilitiones*, the news is not good. But given our strategy, it was to be expected. The Persians remain trapped in Cilicia. Trebellianus still blocks the coast road to the west at Korakesion. Demosthenes still holds the Cilician Gates through the Taurus mountains to the north, and imperial forces occupy both the Amanikai Gates and the Syrian Gates through the Amanus range to the east.'

There was something about Rutilus that reminded Ballista of his old friend Mamurra. It could be just the shape of his head. But maybe there was something more – the same intelligence and unusual self-possession in a man risen from the ranks. That poor bastard Mamurra. Ballista had left him to die in a siege tunnel at Arete in Syria. It had been that or let the Persians swarm in and take the town, kill everyone. But Ballista did not like to think about having given the order that had collapsed the entrance to the tunnel and entombed his friend – may the earth lie lightly on him.

'And now the Persians have divided their forces, as the prefect Marcus Clodius Ballista said they would.'

Clever bastard, thought Ballista. Quicker than Mamurra. You will repay watching. Was it possible Rutilus was a *frumentarius*? Usually those who spied on the emperor's own subjects were of lower rank. But you could never be sure.

Ragonius Clarus, with only the barest nod in Ballista's direction to ask for permission to speak, launched into a repetition of the substance of Rutilus's words interleaved with a eulogy on the wisdom of 'our beloved, noble young emperors' for designing this so very successful strategy.

Down below Ballista, the *liburnian* skimmed past the rocks of the western breakwater and bumped to a halt against a jetty. A man sprang off the ship and ran pell-mell towards the shore.

'Quite so,' Ballista interrupted as Clarus was settling into an extended discussion of the foresight of Quietus and Macrianus the Younger. 'Unexpected *providentia* in ones so young – could not have put it better myself, Legate.'

Although one or two of the officers grinned, Clarus forced himself to smile.

'Rutilus and Ragonius Clarus are right,' Ballista continued. 'The Sassanids at Selinus are in a poor position. Trebellianus at Korakesion blocks them to the west. It would not be easy for a force of cavalry to withdraw into the Taurus mountains to the north. We will land to their east at Charadros. With luck, they will be trapped. There are only about three thousand of them. Shapur and his men are far away. We have four and a half thousand infantry. The narrow coast road should favour us.'

There was a commotion at the rear of the *consilium*. An

officer pushed to the front. Red-faced, out of breath, it was the man from the *liburnian*. This messenger did not bring good news.

'*Dominus*, Antioch the Great has fallen.'

Amid the general shout of horror, Ballista was silent. There was a terrible hollowness in his chest.

'My sons? My wife?' Ballista asked quietly.

The officer looked down. 'They are gone.'

'Gone?'

'They have not been seen since. The Sassanids killed many. Took no prisoners. Many of the bodies are burnt . . . gone.'

Maximus was watching Ballista. He had been for days, almost unsleeping. He had watched Ballista throughout – his silence during the night of frantic preparations for sailing, sitting alone at the prow of the ship for the two days it took them to cross to Seleuceia, disembarking at the smoking port, riding to Antioch, tearing through the streets to the house, finding the pool of dried blood on the mosaic just over the threshold, and by it the discarded miniature sword.

Four days in which Ballista had eaten and drunk next to nothing, had not washed, shaved or slept. Four days in which Ballista had hardly spoken.

Now, the stench of burning and corruption in his nostrils, Maximus watched his friend leaning against one of the columns by the door of the ransacked house, waiting for news. Any news.

Withdrawn in his grief, Ballista had effectively relinquished command. The senatorial legate Ragonius Clarus was incapable. Some of the junior officers, Castricius and Rutilus to the fore, had taken charge. The troops had secured the walls, sent out patrols. Work parties were dealing with the bodies. Selected men were searching among them for Ballista's wife and children. Calgacus and Demetrius were scouring the city for witnesses.

Having sacked Antioch, the Persians had turned on the great city's port of Seleuceia. Then they had left the city and ridden north, possibly to retrace their steps to the obscure, unguarded pass south of the Amanikai Gates by which they had come, possibly to take the small garrison of the Syrian Gates from behind. Macrianus the Younger had escaped the palace, hustled to safety by a unit of the Equites Singulares. He had been taken towards the army of his father and brother, now belatedly rushing north from Emesa. All of this Ballista neither knew nor cared about. Maximus did not care either.

There was a rattle of hooves and Calgacus and Demetrius returned. On foot between them was an old, dishevelled man.

'The *custos*. He was at the theatre with them.' Calgacus pushed him forward.

The old man started talking. 'The *kyria* had sent me for sweets. For the boys. The reptiles came out of nowhere. It was chaos. I could not get back to them.'

For a time Ballista looked at him, seemingly uncomprehending. Then he fished in the purse at his belt. He took out a coin and passed it over.

The old man took it.

'In your mouth.' Ballista's tone was flat.

The *custos* did not move.

'Put it in your mouth,' Ballista said, 'to pay the ferryman.' Ballista hefted the miniature sword.

The old man fell to his knees. Pleading, he clasped Ballista's thighs.

'Too late.' Ballista aimed the blow.

Maximus caught Ballista's arm. Quick as a flash, the Hibernian's hand was knocked away. The tip of his friend's blade was at Maximus's throat.

'Ballista, it is me. Killing the old man will not help.'

The sword clattered to the ground. Ballista sank down. Both hands clawing in the soot and filth, he poured it over his head, fouled his face. Black ashes settled on his tunic.

Maximus shoved the old man out of sight.

Overpowered by loss, Ballista sprawled in the dirt. 'A man who has killed his father is sewn in a sack . . . a dog, snake, monkey and cock for company . . . all drown together. What punishment for a man who by his perjury has killed his sons?'

'*Dominus*,' said Maximus, 'this is not you.'

'What punishment for him? Something worse? Nothing special? Just an old-style Roman death – tied to the stake and beaten to death?'

Then Maximus, raising his voice at Ballista's rambling, 'Marcus Clodius Ballista, stop! This is not you. This is fucking unseemly shit.'

Ballista seemed surprised. He gazed at the sky. 'Gentle breezes, a benign zephyr – most unseemly shit. No rain, wind, thunder and fire. Unseemly. The sky should fall, drench our temples, drown our priests, drown the *Galloi*, drown every cock.' He made a sound a little like laughter. 'Drown every monkey, snake and dog. Drown every man, woman and child. A second flood, with no boat for Deucalion and the good and deserving. Drown every god. Cut them down. Ragnarok – the death of gods and men. The sun swallowed by the wolf Skoll. The stars vanish from the sky.'

Maximus bent to get the miniature sword.

'Leave it!' Ballista snatched it up.

'*Kyrios*' – Demetrius spoke quietly – 'it is not your fault.'

On all fours, Ballista scurried over the threshold like an animal. He crouched on the blood-stained mosaic of the deformed dwarf. The blade in his fist flickered this way and that.

Maximus made to go to him. Calgacus's hand held him back.

Ballista's voice came from a faraway place. 'At Arete, my friend Iarhai told me his nightmare. Under the dark poplars he crosses the Styx, and there waiting for him on the fields of Tartarus by the ocean stream are the "kindly ones", and behind them every person he had killed. An eternity of retribution.'

He took a deep breath and turned from Greek to his native language. 'Now I can cross the icy river Gjoll, pass the gates of Hel, come to Nastrond, the shore of corpses. A different destination, the same fate. The faces of the dead, all turned to me. So many – the newly dead, the green and rotting, those more bone than flesh, those I remember – Maximinus Thrax, Mamurra – those I have forgotten, but at the front my own dear boys.'

Abruptly he reverted to Greek: mangled phrases of poetry. 'Set on me those maidens with gory eyes and snaky hair, with their dog-faces and gorgon-eyes, those priest-esses of the dead, goddesses of terror – spare my boys.'

'That way madness lies,' said Maximus. 'Shun it. No more of that.'

'Not for long.' Ballista pulled the front of his tunic taut, slit it open. With his left hand he guided the point of the little sword to just the right place under his ribs.

Maximus was measuring the distance when Calgacus crossed in front of him. The old Caledonian knelt by Ballista. He drew his sword.

'That is my job.'

From his knees, Ballista looked up dully.

'My job,' Calgacus repeated. He tapped his blade on the mosaic. 'You remember. In your father's hall, after the centurion came for you, it was one of the things your father told us. My final duty to you. Then myself.'

Ballista lowered his own blade. No one relaxed.

'Do it,' Ballista said.

Calgacus carried on tapping the metal on the little coloured stones.

'Everything has been taken from you.' Calgacus spoke quietly. 'But before you go, you owe them one thing.'

Ballista did not respond.

'Vengeance. You are a killer, born, bred, trained. Now use it.'

Ballista gave no reaction.

'You have man-killing hands, a gift for death. Rest, eat, collect yourself – give them vengeance.'

Ballista was still. Then, almost quicker than Maximus could follow, he struck. Once, twice, three times.

The tesserae shattered. The hunchback dwarf was eyeless, its genitals mutilated.

Calgacus nodded slowly.

191

Again Ballista spoke in Greek verse, a different metre, this time perfect:

> '*Done is done.*
> *Despite my anguish I will beat it down,*
> *the fury mounting inside me, down by force.*
> *But now I will go and meet that murderer head on,*
> *that Hector who destroyed the dearest life I know.*
> *For my own death, I'll meet it freely – whenever Zeus*
> *And the other deathless gods would like to bring it on!'*

Calgacus stood at the prow of the *trireme* with Ballista. The sea was calm. The great warship lay on its oars. The sun had not yet burnt off the early morning mist. Around them, the rest of the fleet faded into the greyness. To the north, behind the mist, was the port of Soli.

It was thirteen days since they had left Antioch, eleven since they had sailed from Seleuceia. Again they had tracked the enemy, around the Gulf of Issus and along the Hollows of Cilicia. The Sassanid force that had raided Antioch had crossed the Syrian Gates, overwhelming its small garrison from the rear. Across the Amanus range they had reunited with their main body and together plundered the city of Rhosus. Then they had ridden through the devastated plain of Cilicia to the coastal city of Soli. This morning they would assault its walls. The Romans were well acquainted with their plans. Calgacus had been horrified at the ingenuity with which Ballista had tortured the Sassanid stragglers, appalled at the cold-eyed lack of emotion – or was it controlled pleasure? – with which he had finally despatched them.

Calgacus cast a sly glance at Ballista. The boy was far from right. Ballista stood, unnaturally immobile, staring ahead into the mist. He had had one of the armourers make him a new helmet. The broad nasal covered most of his face, and on either side was a curled metal ram's horn. Calgacus had not felt he could ask him why. No one had. Not even the bumptious Hibernian Maximus.

Calgacus was worried – more than worried, he had an ill-defined sense of foreboding and, worse, a strong sense of guilt. Dissuading Ballista from suicide, Calgacus had not spoken the whole truth. Ballista had never been a born killer. Some men are, Maximus for one. Maybe Calgacus was himself. But not Ballista. He had been a gentle child, sensitive. Left to his own devices, he might have become a farmer, been happy tending his flocks, or maybe a bard; he had always spouted poetry. There had been no hope of that, not for the son of Isangrim, the warleader of the Angles, trained by his uncle among the fierce Harii then hauled off into the *imperium*. Ballista had been shaped into a killer but, until now, it had never come completely easily to him. Never before had Calgacus seen him torture and kill in cold blood – or at least never take pleasure in it. Calgacus was worried – to keep the boy alive he had pushed him further down the path.

'There!' Maximus was pointing. Out of the thinning mist a *liburnian* was racing out towards them. At its prow a marine was holding a red cloak above his head.

Ballista came back from wherever he had been. He shouted, 'Full ahead.'

The rowing master gave the count. 'One, two, three, strike.' Almost as one, the oars bit the water. The *trireme* shivered like an animal waking then gathered way. By the third stroke, the ship was accelerating smoothly, the water running fast down her sides. All around, the fleet was getting underway.

Under the enclosing helm, Ballista was speaking softly. Calgacus, next to him, had to strain his ears to catch the words. 'Come what may come. What advantage in living? No fatherland, no house, no refuge.' More gloomy Greek poetry. The boy was in a very bad way.

Yet, bad way or no, Ballista could still set out a fine plan. The Persians had two main advantages: there were more of them, and they had horses. With luck, Ballista's plan might negate both. When the Romans landed, most of the Persians would be committed to the assault on Soli's walls. Under Rutilus, the ten little *liburnians*, just fifteen soldiers on each, would rush the camp. In their lazy *superbia*, the easterners had neglected to build a palisade or even set a proper guard. If they wanted their possessions, including their vast booty from Cilicia, the Persians would have to give up their superior mobility and fight hand to hand. The gods willing, many would have left their horses in the camp. The men with Ballista would form the initial line of battle just outside the camp. He had crammed fifty soldiers on to the decks of each of the *triremes*. These five hundred men, in only one rank, would have to hold until Castricius could get the four thousand or so reinforcements on the transport ships up in support. Even now the latter were wallowing behind, men labouring at enormous sweeps to propel the fat roundships to the shore.

The mist was lifting fast. Through the last wisps, the shore came into view. Off to the left were the walls of Soli

– ringed by a mass of tiny dark figures; just to the right, the huge, sprawling array of tents, pavilions and horse-lines that formed the camp. In the far distance rose the snow-capped Taurus mountains. It was a beautiful summer morning.

Trumpets rang out from the Persians around the city, shrill cries of alarm carried across the water from the encampment. It would take time for the Persians to disengage from the assault and form up to face this new threat.

With a shudder that threw men off their feet, the *trireme* grounded on the shelving beach. Boarding ladders splashed down.

In a moment Ballista had descended the first one. Calgacus rushed to follow.

As he leapt down, Calgacus lost his footing. He went down on his hands and knees into the shallow water. A boot caught him in the back. He came up spitting, blinking salt from his eyes. Ballista was away – pounding up the beach. Calgacus scrambled to his feet and ran after him.

It was hard to run on the sand in full armour carrying a heavy shield. The muscles in Calgacus's legs screamed, his chest burned. He was far too old for this shit. He ploughed on.

Soon there was harder ground under his boots. Shutting out the pain, he closed his mind to everything but running.

Ballista had stopped. Calgacus pulled up – doubled over, retching dry and painful. Ballista was looking around, arms waving the line into place. Maximus had taken station on Ballista's right shoulder, the last man in the line. Demetrius, dressed for all the world as a soldier in a comedy, was at his left. Gently, Calgacus pulled Demetrius behind his *kyrios* and took his place. Every man in the line would have to stand firm. There was no point in letting the young Greek get himself or all of them killed. The new standard bearer, Gratius, was on Calgacus's left.

Calgacus looked out to sea. The transports were still some way out. Snaking down to the waves, just five hundred men of Legio IIII Scythica would have to face the anger of the Persian horde, and face it alone for some time.

'Here they come.'

The first Persians were closing, a cloud of mounted archers. Through the dust they raised, Calgacus could see a solid mass of armoured cavalry forming up. The gods had not been willing: all the easterners in sight were on horseback.

About fifty paces away, the leading Persians wheeled their mounts, loosed their bows.

The legionaries tucked their chins into their chests, hunkering down behind their big shields. Arrows thumped into leather and wood, sliced past.

'Ignore them – they are nothing,' Ballista roared.

'Girls' spindles,' a legionary shouted. 'Come here, darlings, and I will give you a good fucking.'

Soldiers laughed. Calgacus grinned sourly. Something Ballista had once said floated at the edges of his thoughts. Is this what it was to be a man? True male grace under pressure?

Calgacus leant back, looked at the shore. The transports were nearly there. He squinted round his shield at the enemy. The archers were withdrawing. The Sassanid knights, the dreaded *clibanarii*, were ready. The pitifully thin line with Ballista would somehow have to survive one charge.

A thunder of drums. The heavy cavalry walked forward. A dark phalanx, impossible to see how deep.

Hercules' hairy arse, this was not going to be pleasant.

When the Persians' individual armour – mail, plate, gaudy surcoats, steel visors – could be made out, at about five hundred paces, they moved to a trot. The banners above their heads – lilac, red, yellow – were bright in the sun.

Trumpets rang out from the *clibanarii*. They began to canter. Now the banners jerked this way and that. The horses seemed to rock back and forth as they exerted themselves under the weight of man and metal.

They came on. Calgacus looked at the sea. The Roman re-inforcements were splashing ashore. Too late for the initial shock. But enough of that. 'Eyes front, hold the line,' he found himself shouting.

Horribly quickly, the Persians came on. The noise was like a wave crashing on a shingle beach, louder and louder.

'*Stand for your brothers. Hold the line.*' Legionaries called encouragement to themselves and their *contubernales*. Many prayed to their favoured deities: '*Let me live, great god, and I will give . . .*'

Calgacus drew his sword, thrust it out beyond his shield. He dug his heels in the ground. The very air seemed to be shaking.

Gratius, next to Calgacus, was trembling. Out of the corner of his eye, Calgacus saw the urine run on Gratius's legs. It happened. And not just to cowards. The man was still in place.

The Sassanids came on – a wall of steel, inhuman,

filling the world with their coming. Wicked spear points gleamed.

One hundred paces, seventy, fifty – dear gods, let this be over – thirty – they will scatter us like chaff. Calgacus ground his teeth.

About the distance a boy could throw a stone, the first horses refused the immobile wall of shields, digging in their feet, swerving, colliding. Men fought to stay in the saddle, sliding up their horses' necks. Losing their grip, some riders crashed, tumbling to the ground, lost under the hooves.

Ten paces from the Roman line, a confusion of stationary horses. Milling, backing, heads tossing, stamping, they bumped and bored into each other.

'Charge!' Ballista was running forward. He was yelling something. It sounded like, '*Nasu! Nasu!*'

Ballista's long sword arced. It smashed into a horse's rear leg just above the hock. Tendons severed, the animal collapsed backwards, throwing its rider. Two quick steps and, almost casually, Ballista finished the man on the ground. The northerner's blade swung again, this time slicing off a horse's muzzle. Blood sprayed. Maddened by pain, the animal leapt forward. It crashed into another. Both went down in a tangle of limbs.

A Sassanid thrust at Ballista. Sidestepping, Ballista punched the tip of his weapon through the beast's armour and deep into its chest. It stood for a moment, pink froth at its nostrils, chest heaving, suffocating. It too went down, its rider tumbling in front of Calgacus. Chop – immediately the Persian's helmet cracked under Calgacus's blade.

Ballista was gone, into the mass of the enemy. Neither Calgacus or Maximus could keep up with him. Fucking fool, thought Calgacus. Never get in the midst of panicking horses. You will get trodden, knocked down, crushed, trampled.

Calgacus saw Ballista duck clean under a horse. As he came up the other side, large coils of pinky-grey intestines slithered from the animal's sliced belly. It tried to run, slipped on its own guts, went down.

Some god had to be holding his hands over Ballista. Calgacus watched him move with the grace of a dancer, untouched through the thundering chaos, sword flashing, quick as a snake. Men and horses were screaming. There was blood everywhere.

Calgacus took a blow on his shield, ducked, pushed forward. Over the hellish din, he could hear Ballista: '*Nasu! Nasu!*'

Some of the Sassanids were fighting; more were sawing on their reins, trying to turn, get free from the chaos.

'*Nasu! Nasu!*' – oddly it seemed that some of the Persians were taking up Ballista's chant. '*Nasu! Nasu!*' – they fought to get away from the huge, grim figure in the horned helmet.

Behind the tumult, pushing against the tide of retreating easterners, and astride the most splendid horse, a tall figure in purple and white, a high golden crown on his head. The King of Kings gesticulated. His mouth was open, shouting, but the words vanished into the uproar. Calgacus could see, near Shapur, the aged figure of the captive Roman emperor Valerian.

Ballista had been standing, hands down, a still centre in

the eye of the storm. Now he recognized Shapur. He hurled his shield away and leapt forward, howling.

Shapur saw Ballista coming. The King of Kings drew his sword, kicked his mount forward.

A big Sassanid warrior put himself in front of the king. He swung at Ballista. The northerner ducked. The blade glanced off Ballista's helmet.

Shapur's nobles swarmed around their monarch. They grabbed his reins, turning his horse's head. The beloved of Mazda roared orders. For once they were disobeyed. The nobles closed ranks, their gorgeous silks surrounding the king.

Try as he might, Calgacus could not get to Ballista. Horses, men, friend and foe got in the way. Maximus also was caught up in the melee.

Ballista's sword sang – desperate to be past the big Persian warrior and at Shapur. In a berserk fury, Ballista hacked his sword deep into the back of the neck of the Persian's horse. The steel edge cut through the armour, severing the ligament. As the horse went down, the warrior jumped free. He landed on his feet.

The great war standard of the house of Sasan was moving away. Shapur was being forcibly led to safety. Valerian was being dragged after him.

The big Persian warrior cut at Ballista's left thigh. The northerner caught the blow on his blade, pirouetted like a dancer and sank his own sword into the man's left shoulder. The warrior staggered. Dropping his sword, his right hand automatically went to the wound. He swayed in agony. He did not fall.

Overhead, Ballista brought his weapon down on to the

man's other shoulder. Metal buckled, and gave. The man sank to his knees. In a flurry of blows, Ballista finished him.

'*Nasu! Nasu!*' Ballista cried at the fluttering Drafsh-i-Kavyan, the battle standard of the Sassanids, and the retreating Persian king. They were gone too far. Like an animal savaging its prey, Ballista chopped again and again at the corpse at his feet.

Calgacus reached him. Ballista continued his gory work of mutilation. The Persian's head was nearly severed, his reddish hair spread in the dirt.

'Stop, boy,' Calgacus said.

Ballista continued the butchery, dismembered the body.

'Leave him. It is over.'

Ballista stopped. He looked down at the dead Persian.

'Garshasp the Lion,' Ballista said, and drove the tip of his blade into the man's chest. He left it there, quivering.

Blood ran in every crevice of Ballista's armour, clotted in the links of his mail coat. It dripped from his dented helmet, his unshaven face.

Ballista was in a place where Calgacus could not follow.

'*Nasu! Nasu!*' Ballista screamed at the sky.

Calgacus remembered: Nasu was the Persian daemon of death.

XII

'And this,' Rutilus said to Ballista, 'is the pavilion of the King of Kings.'

'*Kyrios*,' Demetrius interrupted, 'Ragonius Clarus wishes to see you. He says it is most urgent – for the good of the *Res Publica*. He has been waiting for hours, since the Persians ran.'

Ballista did not look round. 'Let him wait.'

No one was quite sure why the Persians had run. Despite their disarray, everyone had expected them to canter out of range, rally and charge again. Centurions and *optiones* had shouted themselves hoarse getting the legionaries back to the standards, getting the reinforcements into position. When the line was re-set – this time eight deep and with a comforting barrier of dead and injured horses in front – they had been surprised that the Persians were a distant smudge of dust. The only easterners left were dead or too maimed to hobble to safety. The latter were soon dead as well.

Panic can spread through an army in seconds. Certainly some credit had to go to an opportune sally into the Persian rear from the town. This had been led by the *eirenarch* of Soli – a man called Perilaus. Demetrius thought, if ever in the history of mankind, let alone of the *imperium*, there was a case of a brigand turned estate guard, it was Perilaus. He had to be either a close ally of Trebellianus or, more likely, one of his deadliest enemies.

Yet Demetrius knew Perilaus was not the real reason for the Persian rout. Demetrius had been there. He had stood in the battle line. True, that was all he had done – stand in the battle line. When Ballista, Calgacus and the others had run forward, Demetrius had taken just a couple of steps after them. He had his sword out. His intentions were good. But there had seemed no way into the maelstrom of horses and men. Everywhere flailing, falling horses, terrible, sharp weapons. Demetrius had not fought, but he had seen and he had heard everything that mattered: Ballista, miraculously unscathed, sword swinging, screaming from under his helmet – '*Nasu, Nasu.*' Demetrius had witnessed the fear of the daemon of death spread through the Sassanid warriors. He had seen Shapur, the proud King of Kings, hustled away.

If ever a man had won a battle single-handed, it was Ballista today. But had Ballista been alone? Demetrius seriously thought that his beloved *kyrios* had been possessed – Nasu, the daemon of death.

Demetrius followed the others into the cool, purple shade of the royal tent. A long corridor later, they emerged into a cavernous room. Wherever they looked were bowls, pitchers, tubs and caskets, all exquisitely worked. The chamber itself breathed a marvellous scent of incense and spices. Couches and tables were laid for a banquet. At the far end was an ornate throne. Before it was a low altar on which burned a sacred Zoroastrian flame.

Ballista spoke, to no one in particular. 'This, it seems, is what it is to be a king.'

The northerner, his face still largely hidden under the blood-spattered helmet, looked around. He picked up a big pitcher of wine, took a drink. Then he carried it to the altar. Slowly he poured the wine over it. A cloud of steam rose as the sacred fire hissed and died.

This was too much for Demetrius. 'When a man who takes a city includes in the general destruction temples of the high gods . . .'

A laugh came from under Ballista's grim helmet. He finished the quotation from Euripides: 'He is a fool; his destruction follows him close.' Ballista laughed again, strangely carefree. 'I know it all too well, boy.'

At the sacrilege, two eunuchs, who had been hovering quietly behind the throne, started wailing.

Ballista went over to them. His hand went to his sword. It was not there. He had left it embedded in the corpse of Garshasp. Ballista drew Isangrim's miniature sword from his other hip. He killed both the eunuchs.

'Never cared for their sort in the north.'

From behind the hangings at the rear of the room came a terrible high keening.

Rutilus smiled. If, like Demetrius, he had been shocked by the killing, he had recovered quickly. 'To the victor the spoils.' He whisked back the curtain. The wailing redoubled.

'Heaven on earth,' said Maximus. 'Sure, a man could die happy.'

Wherever they looked now were girls. Tall, short; thin, rounded; dark and blond. All beautiful.

'The concubines of the King of Kings,' said Rutilus, having to raise his voice. 'About four hundred of them. At least one for every day of the year.'

Calgacus joined Maximus, crowding behind Rutilus and Ballista. Demetrius hung back. All five men were silent.

The noise dropped to some stifled sobs. The girls got down and performed *proskynesis* to the tall, red-haired man.

Rutilus laughed and pointed to Ballista. Hurriedly, the girls realigned themselves.

'It makes no difference,' said Ballista. 'Give them to the troops. Then kill them.'

Some must have understood Greek. The wailing redoubled.

'*Kyrios*' – Demetrius had to shout – 'this is not you. This is wrong.'

Ballista did not respond.

'*Kyrios*' – Demetrius pushed in front of him – 'you cannot kill defenceless women. They are slaves. They did not kill the *kyria* or your boys.'

'No,' said Ballista, 'I killed my sons. I took an oath. Like Jason, I broke it. Like Jason, the gods took the lives of the oath-breaker's darling sons. Soon they will take mine.'

'*Kyrios*,' said Demetrius, 'your mind is wandering, confused by grief. Medea lied. Jason took no oath. Your oath was taken under duress. It has no meaning.'

Ballista took off his helmet. His hair was matted, his face streaked with dirt and dried blood. He gazed far away, lost in thought.

'When Medea accused Jason of perjury, he did not

deny it. In my case there is no woman, no lie. I took the oath. Of my own free will.' Again he seemed far away. 'Free will,' he murmured.

Suddenly Ballista snapped out of it. 'Rutilus, go and tell Ragonius Clarus I will see him soon. Wait for my order.'

If Rutilus was surprised, he hid it. He saluted and left.

When he had gone, Ballista started to talk fast. 'I am perjured three times over. I broke the *sacramentum* I took to Maximinus Thrax, and the one to Valerian. I broke the terrible oath to Shapur. One more broken oath makes no difference. I never really intended to keep the one to Macrianus's sons – *value their safety above everything*, indeed.' Ballista's voice had something of its old tone. 'Demetrius, pass me your writing things.'

Busily, Ballista dashed off a few lines. He handed the stylus and block back to Demetrius. He pulled the ring with his seal off his finger and gave that to Demetrius as well.

Confused, the young Greek gazed at the seal – Cupid winding a siege engine.

'Go to the ships, find the *Concordia*; her *trierarch* Priscus owes me a favour from long ago – you may remember him. That is an order for him to transport you to the west. Go to Gallienus. The ring should get you an audience. Tell him how things stand in the east. Tell him I would never have served the pretenders if their father had not held my family hostage.'

Ballista swung round to Maximus and Calgacus. 'You two, find a sack or something. Fill it with gold for the boy.'

As the other two rummaged around, Demetrius tried to find words. '*Kyrios*, if I can go, so can you. We all can.'

Ballista shook his head.

'*Kyrios*, as your family are . . . now they are gone, Macrianus has no hold over you.'

Ballista smiled ruefully. 'I am what the Romans call *devotus*, dedicated to the infernal powers, to death. I will stay here – take what vengeance I can on the Sassanids, before the gods strike me down.'

Demetrius was crying. '*Kyrios* – Calgacus, Maximus, you love these men. Let them come with me.'

Ballista looked at Calgacus.

The old Caledonian stopped stuffing precious trinkets into a pillowcase. 'I swore an oath to your father, the northern oath. If you fall on a battlefield, I will not leave it. I did outside Edessa, to protect your boys. I will not do so again. Fuck that.'

'Maximus?'

'I take it you have forgotten you saved my life in Africa all those years ago and me somehow never getting round to returning the favour.' The Hibernian grinned. 'And sure, you are a strange man – trying to tear me from all these lovely girls.'

Ballista took the bundle of booty from Calgacus and gave it to Demetrius. He hugged the boy, kissed him on the forehead. 'Go now. And do not worry, the men must have the girls, but they will not be killed.'

Tears streaming down his face, Demetrius embraced the other two. He stopped at the curtain, looking back.

'Go now.'

Demetrius left.

'What now?' Maximus asked.

'Now who is the strange one?' said Ballista. 'All these

girls. Pick a couple for yourselves, more if you want, and take the rest out to the troops.'

Maximus, using his best Persian, ordered the terrified concubines to get moving.

'Wait,' said Ballista. He also spoke in Persian to the girls. 'Which of you is the favourite of the King of Kings?'

None of them answered, but several pairs of eyes slid to one tall, statuesque girl.

'You stay. The rest out.' Ballista turned to Maximus and Calgacus. 'And do not come back until I call you.'

Back in the tent, Maximus was looking at the girl. No one else was. Ragonius Clarus, Rutilus and Calgacus were all looking at Ballista, and he was looking at the drink in his hand.

The girl, huddled on the floor by the throne, was crying, painful, dry sobs. Gods below, she is a concubine. What had the fucker done to her? Unpleasant thoughts crept up on Maximus. So much for Ballista's ridiculous superstition of fidelity – fuck another woman and get a *theta* after his name on the military roll next time in combat. Julia was dead. But it was not that. The fool was putting up one finger to the gods. It was the same as putting out the fire on the altar – *fuck you, come and get me.*

'*Dominus*,' Calgacus was using his courtly voice, 'the *Legatus et Vir Clarissimus*, Gaius Ragonius Clarus, accompanied by the *Praefectus et Vir Egregius*, Marcus Aurelius Rutilus.'

Ballista looked up with no evident interest.

Unfortunately for Ragonius Clarus, he had just caught sight of the two slaughtered eunuchs at the rear of the room. He stared open-mouthed, horrified, like Demetrius after the killing.

Maximus hoped the young Greek would be on his way by now. It would all be fine. The *trierarch* Priscus of the *Concordia* had been promoted to that position five years ago by Ballista. The ship's home port was Ravenna. Its crew were westerners. They would be glad to go home.

So Demetrius's journey should be fine, but his arrival was another matter. How exactly would the emperor Gallienus respond to what the pretty-boy Greek had to say to him? *Dominus, I am the* accensus *to the traitor Ballista, and thus privy to all his secrets. He is very sorry he left your father to rot in Persia and that he is now leading the armies of your sworn enemies. He was forced into it. Now his family are dead, he has no intention of returning to the fold but intends to kill Persians until he is dropped by a stray arrow.*

And then there was the Maximinus Thrax problem. Most of, if not all, the other twelve conspirators were dead. They had all had good reason to keep quiet. Ballista had told only four people of his role in killing that emperor. There was Maximus himself and Calgacus; the other two, Julia and Turpio, were dead. Recently, in his ravings, Ballista had spoken of it twice in front of Demetrius. Unlike the others, the boy had not been sworn to secrecy. He would not want to tell, but he was not tough. Even his pleasures were womanish. Under pressure, he would talk. It was not that Gallienus was likely to have any fondness for the memory of the long-dead tyrant, but a track record of killing emperors was unlikely to endear anyone to the man on the throne of the Caesars. It would seem a nasty precedent.

'You wanted to see me.' Ballista spoke conversationally, apparently unaware of the oddity of the scene: a northern barbarian in a stained tunic sitting on the throne of the King of Kings, bits of armour scattered around, a sobbing, half-naked girl, and two dead eunuchs in a pool of blood.

'Indeed.' Clarus tried to rally himself. 'Yes, indeed.' He cleared his throat, as if about to address the senate or recite a poem.

Well, well, thought Maximus, *you are scared of my boy. And so you fucking should be, especially as he is now.*

Clarus produced an ivory and gold codicil. He glanced at Rutilus for reassurance. The big red-headed officer nodded.

Shame, thought Maximus, *I rather liked you, Ginger. But you are obviously a cunt like the rest of Macrianus's boys.*

'Marcus Clodius Ballista,' intoned Clarus, 'I give you joy of your victory.'

Ballista took a drink.

'In recognition of your success,' Clarus ploughed on, 'our noble emperors show you the great honour of appointing you joint Praetorian Prefect with Maeonius Astyanax. Henceforth your status is raised from *Vir Perfectissimus* to that of *Vir Eminentissimus*.'

Ballista raised his glass almost mockingly.

'With your new *dignitas* come new *mandata*.' Clarus seemed about to pass the codicil to Ballista then thought better of it. 'Some three thousand of the Sassanids have fled west towards Sebaste. You are to take the entire fleet and a thousand infantry and prevent these reptiles effecting a union with the Sassanid force which we understand is returning via the hills from Selinus in the west.'

Ballista made no comment.

'The emperors have shown me the honour,' Clarus continued, 'of appointing me to your old post of Prefect of Cavalry. I am to assume command of the remaining troops here at Soli. Once joined by five thousand cavalry making their way from Syria, I am to march north after the bulk of Shapur's horde. While the enemy still has some nine thousand horsemen, the gods willing, Demosthenes will hold the Cilician Gates against them, and I will bring them to battle on the plains south of the Taurus mountains.'

Oh fucking great, thought Maximus. *Clarus gets an equivalent force to fight Shapur, while we get just a thousand men and a few marines to take on three thousand reptiles at Sebaste, maybe six thousand if the ones from Selinus join with them before we do. Fucking great. Just as well Ballista has decided he is* devotus.

'Soli today, Sebaste next; it is all the same to me,' said Ballista. 'Maybe we should all have a drink. Roxanne?'

As the girl, sniffing once or twice, got up and busied herself, Maximus looked at the luxury all around in the inner sanctum of the King of Kings. It took him a while to realize why it bothered him. The only man he knew that had seen it before was old Turpio. And look how it had ended for him. Defying the fates, Maximus picked up a discarded necklace and hung it around his neck.

XIII

The headland of Sebaste was low but solid in the dark night. The little boat rode the gentle swell. Ballista had commandeered the fishing smack from Soli. They had sailed down to Sebaste at last light and started their fishing. Ballista worked it with the old fisherman. They used a dragnet with floats here. The boat was square-rigged, nothing too different from the fishing boats of Ballista's childhood.

Maximus, Calgacus and two marines huddled in the bottom of the boat. Sounds can carry a long way over water at night, so they did not complain.

Ballista had watched the Great Bear circle and pale. It had been a long night, but soon it would be over. He yawned, stretched and gazed up at the eastern sky. No sign of it lightening yet.

It was the old man who first saw the signal. Tapping Ballista's arm, he pointed to the shore. There it was. A solitary beacon to the east of Sebaste, on the road from Soli. The first part of Ballista's plan had worked. The land forces, even though only an inadequate thousand men, were in position.

Ballista unshuttered and hoisted the lantern. As the old

man hurriedly pulled in his nets, Ballista scanned the dark sea to the south. Nothing. No sign that the second, crucial element of his plan was in place. He could not wait. There was no time.

With the old man at the steering oar, Ballista brought the sail round. It was far too early for the morning breeze from the sea, but the hint of the prevailing westerly should bring them in to the beach west of Sebaste.

As the low headland slid past to their right, the old man talked inaudibly to himself. Mastering an urge to look south, Ballista stared at the sky. Now there was a faint but definite pink tinge above the black outline of the town. Maximus started to get up. With a hand on his friend's arm, Ballista indicated it was too soon.

Sudden and clear a trumpet rang out from the town. Before its echo had faded, it was answered by others. Torches flared along the wall. Some of them were moving. One or two shouts floated across the water. The Sassanids were aware of the Roman troops to the east. So far so good – providing the dark-painted ships of the fleet, their oars muffled, were gliding in out of sight behind the fishing boat. Ballista did not think what would happen if it were not so. In many ways, he did not care. Soon there would be more blood for the ghosts.

> *For those whom fate has cursed*
> *Music itself sings but one note –*
> *Unending miseries, torment and wrong!*

A word of warning from the old man, and he ran the boat up on to the beach.

Ballista swung himself over the side. He landed knee-deep in the water. Maximus passed him his sword belt. Ballista buckled it on. Then he pulled the floppy cap from his belt. Scooping his long hair under it, he crammed it over his brows.

Maximus was beside him, fiddling with his own eastern cap. Calgacus and the two marines jumped out of the boat. While they readied themselves, Ballista and Maximus pushed the boat off. The old man just waved as he unshipped the oars.

Ballista pulled Isangrim's little blade on his right hip an inch or two out of its sheath, snapped it back, drew the big sword on his left a little, pushed it back, touched the healing stone tied to the scabbard. He was glad Calgacus had retrieved his sword from the body of Garshasp. At moments like this, Ballista was painfully aware that, much of the time, he was not thinking clearly.

> *My heart would burst,*
> *My sick head beats and burns,*
> *Till passion pleads to ease its pain.*

Ballista checked the others.

'Time to go.'

The sand crunched under their boots. The town wall was black off to the right. The west gate was hidden in shadow. It was, Ballista thought, a good job they had been here before and knew the layout. The noise from the town seemed to have faded.

A couple of trees grew in front of the gate. The land smelled hot away from the sea. The heavy doors were shut. Ballista looked back at the sea. Was there a line of white – not a wave – out there?

Ballista unsheathed his sword. With the pommel he beat loudly on the gate.

'Open the gate,' he called in Persian. 'Open the gate. The country is alive with Romans.'

From inside came a babble of talk.

'Open.' Ballista beat on the gate again. 'I am Vardan, son of Nashbad. I have an order from Shapur.'

A bonneted head popped up over the battlements.

'Open the gate now,' roared Ballista. 'The man who delays the command of the King of Kings will suffer.'

The head disappeared.

A few moments later there was a scraping sound – the gate opened.

Ballista pushed past the first Persian. There were two more inside. He killed one with a thrust to the stomach, the second with a blow to the back of the neck. Maximus was sawing his blade into the throat of the first one. It had all taken about four seconds.

'Calgacus, take the marines and get up on the wall walk. Maximus, you stay with me.'

Ballista took stock. He had hoped there might be something, say a cart or some barrels, anything really, to wedge the gate open. There was nothing obvious. Still, it should not be for long.

'Maximus, help me drag the bodies to block the gates.'

No sooner had they finished than figures appeared in the street.

'Shut the gate,' a voice shouted.

'We cannot – orders,' Ballista replied in Persian.

The men walked up. There were four of them.

'Shut the gate, now.'

Ballista waited until they were close then stabbed the leader in the guts. Maximus cut down another. The two remaining Sassanids went for their swords. Their yells were cut short before their blades were free of their scabbards.

'They will be all over us now, like a cheap toga,' Maximus grunted as he helped pull the fresh corpses to add to the obstruction in the gateway.

'Not for long,' said Ballista, searching through the dead for things of use. 'You could have left with Demetrius.'

'Yes, I could have.'

The two men equipped themselves with small Persian shields, bows and arrows. Maximus added a helmet. Ballista did not. Better no helmet than an ill-fitting one that might slip down over your eyes, impede your movement. There was no time to take any armour.

As Maximus ran up to the wall walk, his arms full of bows, quivers and shields for the others, Ballista studied the town. The sun was not up yet, but it was quite light. To the right was another gate leading to the peninsula. It was open. Through it could be seen a curved portico stretching along the south-west of the enclosed main harbour. Ahead the street ran straight, becoming the north-western dock of the harbour. Off to the left, the theatre rose above the exercise ground of the gymnasium.

The streets were deserted. Down by the empty docks a cat stalked a pigeon. A confused noise came from the east, beyond the far walls. Inside the town all was deathly quiet. Sebaste had fallen twice, first to the Sassanid force that had gone on to Selinus, now to these easterners who had escaped west from the battle of Soli. Those inhabitants who had not fled or been killed would be hiding. It was not surprising there were no civilians, but it was wonderful there were no Persians. Ballista's plan had worked. Seeing just a meagre thousand Roman soldiers advancing from the east, the Persians must have issued out to confront them.

Maximus came back down the steps. He was blowing hard.

'You are out of condition,' Ballista muttered. 'Your wind has gone.'

Before Maximus could answer, an arrow whipped between them. Hunched down, shields up, they stepped back into the shelter of the gateway. More arrows came from under the arch of the gate to the peninsula. They snicked off the stonework.

'Fuck,' said Maximus. 'They did not all fall for it then. Fuck a vestal.'

'Nicely put,' Ballista replied. He peeked out from behind the gate then jerked his head back as three or four arrows sliced towards him. One missed his ear by an inch or so. 'Fuck, indeed.'

'Unless there are enough of them to rush us, we are safe enough here until the boys from the fleet come,' Maximus said.

There was the sound of running feet.

'Fuck,' said Maximus.

Without a word, both men stepped out, drawing their bows. At least half a dozen Persians were coming. Ballista and Maximus released. They dropped the bows, drew their swords. Only one Persian had fallen. More were issuing from the peninsula.

They heard the twang of bows above their heads. The arrows of Calgacus and the marines dropped another easterner. Not enough. The charge did not falter.

The Sassanids were on them. At the last moment, Ballista sidestepped the first one. Too close to use his sword, he stuck his arm out. The straight-arm tackle caught the Persian under the chin. The man's legs shot out from under him. He crashed on to his back, armour clattering on the roadway.

The next Sassanid thrust towards Ballista's middle. The northerner blocked it with his blade, forcing his enemy's weapon wide. He kicked the man's kneecap. Howling, the Sassanid doubled up. Ballista jumped back.

For a moment, the men on the ground impeded the others. To Ballista's left, out of his vision, steel was ringing. Maximus was not down yet.

Two Persians came for Ballista. They stepped carefully, swords ready. They knew what they were about. There were more behind them.

There was no berserk madness upon Ballista this morning, no battle calm. Instead, nothing but cold, sinking fear. His devotion to death had left him. This could only end one way.

The Sassanids struck. Ballista parried one blow, took the other on his shield. The light buckler splintered. One Sassanid aimed high, the other scythed his blade low at Ballista's shins. Somehow the northerner ducked one blade, got the shield in the way of the second. A big chunk flew out of the light shield. It was useless. Ballista threw the thing into the face of the opponent to his left. He thrust at the easterner to his right. The man stepped back out of range.

The Sassanids pressed forward. Shieldless, Ballista relied on his years of training, the memory in his muscle. He acted without conscious thought. His blade weaved fast. Sparks flew. But he could not keep them out for long. Blow by blow, step by step, he was driven back.

Ballista's right heel felt the wall behind him. Nowhere to go. Time nearly up. He was half aware of other easterners jostling behind his opponents. If there was an afterlife – Valhalla, whatever – he would soon be with his boys.

The Persians closed for the kill. One jabbed at his face, one his groin. Ballista chopped down at the lower blade. Instinctively, eyes shut, he jerked his head to one side. Splinters of limestone cut his cheek. There was a sharp pain in his left thigh.

The momentum of the Sassanids had driven them against Ballista. He could smell their sweat, the spicy food on their breath.

The one to his left gasped. His body twisted, fell back. Without thought, Ballista rammed the fingers of his left hand into the other's face, clawing at his eyes. The man swayed back, then reeled. Calgacus's ugly face appeared. The Caledonian drove his blade into the Persian's chest.

Pandemonium. The Sassanids were running back the way they had come. Ballista looked wildly around. There was Maximus. *Allfather, Death-blinder, Deep Hood, they were alive.* More figures were crowding into the gateway from outside.

Ballista caught his breath. The cut to his leg stung, but

it looked superficial. All around, Romans were finishing off the Sassanids on the ground.

'Thank you,' Ballista said.

'Hercules' big hairy arse, I thought it was too late that time. I thought you were fucked.' Calgacus smiled a horrible smile.

'Me too.' Ballista laughed. He had to pull himself together. The job was not yet half done.

'You' – Ballista pointed at an *optio* – 'take the first thirty marines through the gate. Follow the Sassanids. Secure the gate to the citadel. If you can, work through and clear the peninsula.'

The *optio* shouted. The marines jostled and pushed. More were crowding in from outside.

Ballista stepped out from the gate to the more open space in the street. He had to take charge. This could easily degenerate into chaos.

'Everyone but the detailed marines, stay where you are.' Some of the confusion stilled.

'Officers, to me,' Ballista shouted. 'Where the fuck is Rutilus?'

'Here, *Dominus*.' The tall redhead calmly stepped out of the throng.

Ragonius Clarus had insisted Ballista have Rutilus as his second-in-command. It was the emperors' explicit wish. Ballista had not wanted him, but there was no denying he was a competent officer.

'Rutilus, you know the plan. Take the main body of marines straight down this road past the docks. Seize the gate at the far end. Draw your men up in line outside – two deep, open order.'

With a minimum of fuss, Rutilus got on with it. The marines, nearly three hundred and fifty of them, began to rattle past.

The *trierarch* elevated to Ballista's deputy for the next part of the plan appeared. What was his name? Ballista was about to ask Demetrius, then he remembered the boy had gone. He hoped he was all right.

'*Trierarch*, are your men ready?'

The *trierarch* shrugged. 'As ready as they will ever be.'

Ballista had armed around a thousand rowers with a mixture of captured Persian weapons and antique arms from the temples of Soli. The *trierarch*, like all his kind a long-service centurion, had little but contempt for his men's fighting abilities. Unfortunately enough, Ballista thought he was probably right. Still, if it all worked, they might not actually have to fight.

The last of the marines passed.

'Time to go,' said Ballista. With Maximus, Calgacus and the *trierarch* flanking him and Gratius carrying his personal white *draco* behind, Ballista set off.

At first they followed the retreating backs of the marines. Then Ballista led them into a sideroad to the left. Now he quickened the pace to a jog.

It was hard going. The street twisted, twice turning back on itself. Past the theatre it began to climb steeply. Ballista's wounded leg hurt. It was getting harder to get his breath.

About five hundred yards of this, and they reached the north-eastern gate out on to the main road to Soli. The whole way, they had not seen a single Persian.

Emerging from under the archway, Ballista realized the

sun was up. Still low, it cast long shadows but illuminated the scene. The yellow-green slopes of the mountain rose to the left. The sparkling sea lay to the right. And between, about half a mile ahead, the battle.

Perfectly to plan, Castricius had arrayed his thousand infantry from the necropolis on the lower slopes to fill the four hundred or so yards down to the shore.

The Persians, their backs to Ballista, wheeled in front of Castricius's position. Arrows flew, but the rough going and the innumerable tombs badly hindered their evolutions.

Away to Ballista's right, Rutilus's marines were already mainly in line.

Ballista roared orders, waved and gesticulated. The rag-tag mob of armed rowers started off to link with the marines.

The Persians had seen the threat to their rear. Officers, bright figures in silk flashing steel, rode here and there, regrouping the horsemen. They knew they were in a trap. It remained to be seen if they would realize how weak one side of the trap was.

Ballista looked at his men. Rutilus's marines, in reasonable order, filled about half the space. In the other half the rowers, although clumped up, were in some approximation of a line.

'Signal the advance. Slow walk. Keep together.'

The line shuffled forward. From the start, some of the rowers were hanging back. Their part of the line bowed.

Ahead, Sassanid banners waved, trumpets called. The Persians – there must still be nearly three thousand of them, formed into a deep phalanx.

Allfather, Grey Beard, Fulfiller of Desire. The Persians

were facing Castricius's men. The deep boom of a Sassanid war drum sounded. The horsemen accelerated away from Ballista. They charged Castricius's line.

Through the fresh dust, Ballista could not see clearly what was happening. A roar like a thousand trees being felled at once echoed back from the mountain slopes.

Most of the Sassanids had come to a halt. But in one place they still moved forward. From the flanks, others began to funnel after them.

All the horsemen stopped. The gap that had opened in Castricius's line must have clogged with men and horses. It would not have taken much – maybe just one horse going down in the rough terrain.

Panic gripped the Sassanids. Like animals before a forest fire, individuals darted this way and that, seeking an unattainable safety. Some must have broken through. But for those left, there was no way out. What remained was not fighting but slaughter.

Ballista sat with his back to the tomb. He was in the shade and facing the mountains, away from the killing field. The Sassanid custom of carrying much of their wealth on their person probably put an edge on the Romans despoiling the enemy corpses, but they would have done it anyway.

The battle won, Ballista had ordered Rutilus to keep a couple of hundred marines in hand to secure the town and Castricius to hold back about the same number of legionaries on the road. That the Sassanids who had escaped would rally and launch a surprise attack was highly unlikely. The *liburnian* galleys had tracked them up the coast. About three miles to the north-east, the Sassanids had turned off inland. But better safe than sorry.

Ballista shifted his position. The blank wall of well-dressed stone soared above him to a cloudless blue sky. A lot of money had gone into these tombs, which were built like affluent houses. The citizen of Sebaste who could afford one of them would have a townhouse and a residence in the country. Every time they rode from one to the other, they would pass this third house, the one in which they would spend eternity. Ballista wondered what they would feel. A warm glow of reassurance? Their social standing would transcend death. Did they fondly imagine they would gaze out from their final resting place and watch their sons ride past?

It was hard to say. Certainly Greeks and Romans, at least some of them, believed in ghosts. But their afterlife, except for a lucky few who made it to the Isles of the Blessed, consisted of flitting and shrieking like bats in the dark halls of Tartarus. Perhaps they would hope to return, their shades more substantial, when blood offerings were made.

Inexorably, Ballista's thoughts turned back to where he did not want them to go, to the fight at the gate. He had not wanted to die, he had wanted to live. So much for his being *devotus*. True, his thoughts had not been worked out. There had been no understanding of why. But something had changed. He had desperately wanted to live.

Perhaps, too late for his family, the curse had been lifted. He had sworn to return to the throne of Shapur. In the sacked camp outside Soli, he had returned. No, this was shallow sophistry of the worst sort. When he took that terrible oath, it had been in the thoughts of neither gods nor man that he should return bloodied, to defile the sacred fire, kill his defenceless servants and take Shapur's favourite concubine over the ornate throne of the house of Sasan.

He had been maddened then. Now he felt sanity returning. Now, almost against his conscious wishes, he wanted to live. Was this disloyalty to Julia and his darling boys? He would harrow hell to bring them back. But that could not happen. Should he persist as *devotus* – take what revenge he could then, falling, join them?

But would they be reunited? Julia's Epicureanism precluded an afterlife – all returned to quiet and sleep. And what of Isangrim and Dernhelm? What did eternity hold for innocent children? He had always half entertained the hope that, in the natural way, dying before them, the Allfather would accept him into gold-bright Valhalla. There, having proved his courage day on day in the fight in the courtyard, having shown his good companionship night on night in the feasting in the hall, he would intercede with the Hooded One. His boys would be allowed to pass through the western door and join him under the roof of shields. Woden's power and longevity aside, the Allfather was a northern chieftain. He understood love and grief. He had lost his son Balder. At the end of time, at Ragnarok, the Hooded One himself would die, torn by the jaws of Fenrir the wolf.

Perhaps I am still mad, thought Ballista. *Perhaps my grief and the terrible things I have done for revenge have corroded, deformed my soul.* And he had done terrible things. He thought of the teaching of Aesop. Man is born with two wallets tied round his neck. The one at his front contains the sins and crimes of other people – easy to take out and examine.

The one on your back, open to everyone except yourself, holds your own – hard to see, painful to think about.

The approach of Maximus broke into Ballista's thoughts. With the Hibernian was a tall, thin young man wearing a goatskin cloak. It was one of Trebellianus's dagger-boys, Palfuerius or Lydius – Ballista had no idea which.

'*Ave*, Prefect.' The youth did not wait for permission to speak. 'I have good news from the governor of Cilicia.' His pronunciation of Greek was atrocious. 'Those Persians who *evaded* you' – the stress sounded deliberately offensive – 'have been captured by Gaius Terentius Trebellianus. The *Vir Egregius* suggests that you might like to see how we deal with poisonous reptiles here in Cilicia Tracheia.'

'Where?'

'They are at the town of Kanytelis – for the moment.'

The young Cilician gestured for Ballista to accompany him right away.

Ballista did not move. 'You can guide us, when we are ready.'

Calgacus jerked his thumb and, after holding Ballista's gaze a moment too long, Trebellianus's man moved out of earshot.

Good job for you, goat-boy, that something of my self-control has returned, thought Ballista. *If you had turned up a few days ago, things might have been rather different, even if your* patronus *is Trebellianus. Now there is a dangerous man; not sitting quiet in Korakesion but roaming the hills miles to the east.*

'It might be a trap,' said Maximus.

'Trebellianus may be a brigand in a toga, but he is unlikely to have deserted to the Sassanids.'

'But he is a brigand,' Maximus persisted. 'We should at

least arm ourselves.' He pointed to the pile of their equipment, which, far too late, had been brought up from the *triremes*.

'You are right,' Ballista conceded. 'And get Castricius to find about twenty legionaries who can ride. There are plenty of Persian horses about. We might do with the company.'

The road meandered up the coast. To the left were the bare, banded rocks of the foothills; a thickish scatter of scrub and little patches of cultivatable soil, terraces cut with heartbreaking labour. To the right was the lovely blue of the sea.

Seeing the small party of horsemen, one of the *liburnians* rowed close to the shore. Three more were further out. Recognizing Ballista's white *draco* standard and the big figure in the distinctive horned helmet under it, the little galley sheered away.

As they turned inland, the road became worse. Bare and dusty, it zigzagged wildly as it took on the climb. On either side of the narrow track were jagged, piled rocks and sharp thorns. Nothing apart from a goat could move there, certainly not a man on horseback. The true Cilicia Tracheia began the moment you left the coast road.

Soon Ballista ordered the men to dismount and lead the horses. Loose stones scrunched under boots and hooves. The sun was near its zenith. It was incredibly hot. Occasionally the path would dip, only to resume its strength-sapping climb. All around was a wilderness of rocks. The crests in the distance were hazed with heat.

A long black snake slithered across the road in front of them. They waited for it to pass. Beside him, Ballista heard Maximus muttering – prayers or threats. Pity the poor

Persians who had come this way: an early-morning alarm, no breakfast for man nor horse, a desperate battle, the enemy at their rear, cutting a way clear, then this hellish climb – forcing their spent mounts forward, fear riding hard at their backs. At the end of this they would have surrendered to anyone, let alone a gang of Trebellianus's murderous highlanders.

At last they were there. Mounting up, they rode through another city of the dead. This necropolis was far less elaborate than the ones at Sebaste, fewer expensive house or temple tombs, mainly undecorated sarcophagi. The three miles or so they had covered from the sea made all the difference to the wealth of a community.

The noise came to them as they entered the city of the living, the ugliest noise in the world – a mob baying for blood. The mob was at the foot of a tall tower. On horseback Ballista could see over their heads. Surrounded, huddled and cowed were a few hundred Sassanids on foot. Amidst them, one or two still stood proud. Ballista recognized a slim figure in a lilac tunic: a Persian noble – Demetrius could have told him the man's name.

'*Ave*, Marcus Clodius Ballista, I am honoured you could come.' The mob quietened as Trebellianus called out. He stood on the battlements of the tower – lord of all he surveyed.

Now the Persians had seen Ballista in his ram-horned helmet. A murmur ran through the prisoners: '*Nasu, Nasu.*' They seemed no more frightened; if anything, more resigned.

'Come close,' Trebellianus urged. 'See the men of Cilicia Tracheia take their revenge.'

At a sign from their governor, a group of armed toughs dragged ten Persians out of the mass. Prodding them with the points of javelins, they forced them beyond the tower. Two of the Persians fell to their knees, arms behind their backs in supplication. One was kicked and jabbed back on to his feet. The other threw himself full length in the dirt and was finished where he lay. His companions were made to lift the corpse.

Ballista and his group moved after them. Then they saw what awaited the eastern prisoners.

The earth disappeared. There was a huge hole. Roughly oval, it had to be sixty, seventy paces across, fifty deep. Its sides were raw pinkish-white rock. There were vertical streaks of white, stalactites at the bottom where it caverned out. And now there were darker streaks and splashes.

'Behold,' called Trebellianus, 'the place of blood.'

The Sassanids were forced over the edge. Their screams were cut short as they smashed into the side wall, went tumbling, broken, to the floor.

'You have to stop this.' Maximus was speaking in his native Celtic tongue. Apart from Ballista, only Calgacus could understand.

Another ten were being herded forward.

Ballista looked over the edge. At the bottom, in the pile, one or two of the bodies were faintly moving. He could see an arm or a leg shifting in agony.

The next batch was forced over the edge. Some way down the rock, Ballista saw a relief sculpture, a family group in Greek dress, the father and mother seated, the grown children standing. All held a hand to their chin in uniform thoughtfulness as the shrieking men fell past.

'Trebellianus,' called Ballista, 'that Persian there.' He pointed. 'I need to question him.'

Up on the tower, Trebellianus nodded.

The Sassanid was hauled before Ballista. There were tigers or some other big cats embroidered on his torn tunic. Ballista had seen him before, more than once. Demetrius undoubtedly could have named him straightaway.

'We were promised our lives if we surrendered.' Behind the dust-stained beard, the young man addressed Ballista in Persian, his face angry and desperate.

'You were fools to trust these Cilicians,' Ballista replied in Persian. 'You have killed and raped their kin.'

The Sassanid made a gesture of contempt. 'You are no better than them. The superstitious among my men think you are *Nasu*. But you are no daemon of death. I know you – from Arete, from your surrender outside Edessa. I saw you swear an oath in Carrhae. You are Ballista – the oath-breaker.'

'I swore to return to the throne of Shapur. At Soli, I did.'

'Just twisted words – you Romans lie and cheat as soon as you can crawl.'

'And everyone knows Persians never lie. It is against your religion. Yet your priests flay men alive, pour boiling oil in their eyes.'

The Sassanid spat. 'And your men here are far less cruel.'

'I know you now,' said Ballista. 'You are Valash, son of the King of Kings, the joy of Shapur.'

The Sassanid sneered. 'And like your kind, you see a way of making a profit. You think my father will pay a ransom for me.'

'I am sure he would. But I am not going to ask him for one. Although you killed my friend Turpio, left his severed head on a pike, I am going to return you to your father for nothing. Pick six of your men. They can go with you.'

The Persian looked horrified. 'How can I make such a choice?'

'War is a harsh teacher. Make the choice, or they will all die.'

Once it was explained to him, Trebellianus acceded to this turn of events with outward good grace, but the throng of Cilicians were not so politic. They were clearly unhappy.

As the selected Persians were bundled towards them, Maximus again spoke softly in his native language. 'This is wrong. You cannot leave the other fuckers to this mob. I thought you were back to your old self.'

'Maybe I am.' Ballista's face was set, impassive. 'But, as I told the Persian, war is a harsh teacher. These Cilicians outnumber us – twenty to one or more. They will follow Trebellianus, not me.'

Maximus looked round then nodded reluctantly.

'Anyway, even if we could save all the Persians, we do not have troops to guard them all. And there are another three thousand of the bastards still to fight to the west at Corycus.'

XIV

About three miles down the coast west from Sebaste was the town of Corycus. The most notable thing about it was the island lying offshore. It shared a name with other islets: Crambusa, the dry or parched one. It was indeed waterless, small – no more than two hundred paces by one hundred – and the majority of its shore was rocky. But when the mainland was in enemy hands, its utility to a fleet was immense.

Ballista's flotilla had sailed down from Sebaste the day before. Arriving, the ships had made a martial display close in to the walls of Corycus – nine *triremes*, ten *liburnians* and twenty transport vessels. The latter, to aid the bellicose impression, had been tricked out with military standards, and their decks had been covered with marines seconded from the warships. With luck, the Persians in the town would not realize the roundships were empty except for food and water but would think them packed with troops.

Now, in full sight of the city, the ships were moored off Crambusa. The bare islet gave the rowers of the warships a chance to get away from their cramped benches, to stretch their legs, to cook, eat and sleep ashore. Admittedly, if a storm got up, the fleet would have to run for shelter, either east to Sebaste or west to the delta of the Calycadnus river. But the summer weather looked set fair.

Indeed it was a beautiful night. High, benign clouds, backlit by the full moon. The sea was calm as a millpond, silvered by the moonlight. The ships, black silhouettes, rode easily at anchor.

Ballista stood at the prow of the *Lupa*, the *trireme* that carried his standard. He gazed up at the sky. The clouds moving across the face of the moon made it look infinitely distant. In the face of such immensity, mankind seemed very small. It was the trick of most consolations to emphasize the so-called smallness of grief against the enormity of something else. Ballista thought with repugnance of Sulpicius Rufus's famous letter on the death of Cicero's daughter. Do not be profoundly affected by your private sorrow when men like us have lost everything we value: our honourable name, *patria*, *dignitas*, all our honours. Cicero had written back saying it had helped. How could even the narrow-minded leaders of a failing oligarchy have thought in such disgusting terms?

Much better Plutarch's consolation to his wife. Despite the tiresome repetition of the necessity of self-control, despite peddling the evident untruth that giving way to grief was as bad as giving way to pleasure, between all the philosophic platitudes, there was the true grief of a father for his lost child: the most delightful thing in the world to embrace, to see, to hear.

Time is a great healer. Every one of them said it. All the great minds – Plutarch, Seneca, all the rest – reduced to the soothing of a nursemaid: *there, there, time will make it better*. And the sad thing was, it was partly true.

Ballista *was* beginning to feel a little better. Julia and his sons were no longer in his thoughts all the time. Now he woke with just an unfocused sense of something wrong, before the loss of his wife and boys filled his mind. Here and there in the day, he did not think of them at all. Then he remembered, and felt guilty of neglect.

At least he was not raving any more. His thoughts were no longer a seething, incoherent riot of pain, revenge and Euripidean tragedy. At Sebaste, Ballista had shaved, bathed, had his hair cut. Old Plutarch had written something along the lines of looking after the externals helping the inner man. Ballista wondered if it was possible to feel any emotion that was not filtered through the thoughts of others. Did the things one had read or heard just give words to one's feelings, or did they shape them, twist them into different forms? Whatever, did it make the emotion less real?

Behind Ballista came a stage cough. Calgacus had the Persian prince, Valash, with him. So far it could not be said that the King of King's son seemed over-grateful for having his life spared. Perhaps, Ballista thought uncharitably, it had also occurred to the joy of Shapur that being returned to his father, with or without ransom, might not prove to be all that easy. Or it could just be that he did not trust the man his troops – his troops who now lay massacred at the bottom of a chasm called the place of blood – had thought the daemon of death.

'The Persians in Corycus are commanded by a *framadar* called Zik Zabrigan,' Ballista said in Persian. 'His position is untenable. In the morning we will go and talk to him.'

Valash smiled in a superior way. 'Now I see why you were keen to save me. You think I will help you persuade Zik Zabrigan to surrender. I will not.'

'You mistake me.' Ballista was not going to admit that he would have rescued all Valash's men if he had felt able. 'I do not give a fuck if you talk to him or not. And I do not give a fuck if his men lay down their arms or they all die.'

Valash glowered silently.

'But I thought,' Ballista continued, 'you might prefer them not to fall into the hands of Trebellianus and his rough Cilicians.'

Valash made the sign to avert the evil eye. 'You may not be Nasu, but you are a lover of the lie, a true follower of Drug. One day Mazda will deliver you again into the hands of the righteous.'

Ballista was too tired, not physically but emotionally, to have the energy to be angry.

Maximus stepped out of the shadows and did it for him. 'You owe him your life. If you have any honour, you should keep a civil tongue in your head.'

The tall, thin figure swung round, reaching for the long sword that was not on his hip. The sons of the house of Sasan were not reminded of their honour by others, never by non-Aryans. Valash mastered himself. 'You are right.' He turned back to Ballista. 'Although I did not ask you, I owe you a debt.' With an innate grace he performed *proskynesis:* a small, elegant bow, fingers brushing his lips. 'But I will not seek to persuade *framadar* Zik Zabrigan to surrender. I know your transports contain no soldiers. I will not lie to him.'

Ballista smiled. 'To ride, shoot the bow and avoid the lie.'

Valash nodded gravely. 'Just so.'

In the morning, there was a slight choppy swell running from the west, nothing bad, but enough to make the ships fret at their anchors. Ballista had them all move into the shelter of Crambusa, as far as that was possible. Orders were given that no more than one-third of the rowers from each ship, one bank of a *trireme*, were to be disembarked on the islet at any one time.

Ballista and his *comites* spent the time looking over at the hills to the north-east of Corycus. Nothing moved on the scrub-covered slopes. The coast road was empty. A lone cormorant worked a patch of water. As he watched the long-necked bird, Ballista noticed the lack of gulls. Back home in the north, the air would have been thick with them, wheeling and screaming around the fleet.

Back home. Now Julia and the boys were dead there was nothing to stop him returning to Germania. Except, of course, when it became known, a messenger would come from the *imperium* demanding his father hand him over. And his father, the good of his people always coming first, would have to agree. The cost of non-compliance would be too high – the end of subsidies, the strong likelihood of a Roman-sponsored revolt – failing that, even armed intervention by the legions.

Anyway, what would Ballista find in the north? It was twenty-two years since he had left. Much would have changed. Would he still be welcome in the halls of the Angles? It was unlikely that his half-brother, Morcar, his father's heir, would be overjoyed to see him. And Ballista knew that he himself had changed. Twenty-two years in the *imperium*, five years of high command. He was now Marcus Clodius Ballista, *Vir Ementissimus*, Praetorian Prefect, no longer Dernhelm, son of Isangrim. Maybe the smoke in the halls, the parochial concerns, would stifle him. The *imperium* changed everything it touched.

'There.' Maximus pointed.

Around the headland, about three hundred paces from the town walls, were the standards. Below them, a line of legionaries. Castricius, dependable as ever, had come.

'Time to go.'

The *Lupa* won her anchor. Oars dipped as one, its ram sliced through the swell. Spray flicked back into Ballista's face.

There was no artillery in Corycus. The *trierarch* had his orders to take them right into the western harbour. Beyond the mole, the water was nearly still. The great galley came to a halt about a stone's throw from the dock.

A short wait, and a tall standard appeared: an abstract shape in red, a little like a sword, on a yellow cloth. Below it stood a man in steel and silk, with long black hair.

'I am Marcus Clodius Ballista, Praetorian Prefect. Draw me a bath and prepare me a meal. I have come to offer terms of surrender to the *framadar* Zik Zabrigan.'

'Fuck you, and your terms,' the Persian on the wall jeered. 'Oath-breaker. You will not wash or eat here, you arse-fucking cunt.'

Things were thrown from the wall. Ballista and the men on the prow ducked behind their shields. The missiles fell short. Some splashed in the water; others exploded on the dock. Clouds of white powder puffed up: flour, or salt.

'You have your answer,' Zik Zabrigan shouted.

The *Lupa* backed water, turned and left.

'Arse-fucking cunt,' said Maximus.

'Anatomically interesting, but certainly inventive,' conceded Ballista.

'Sure, but they were quick to reach a good judgement.'

Calgacus ushered Valash forward.

'Joy of Shapur,' said Ballista, 'we need your explanation.'

Unlike the others, the Persian was not laughing. 'Vulgar abuse. Unseemly in the mouth of a *framadar* but to be expected at a siege.'

'No, I meant the other thing – the bags of white powder.'

Still Valash did not smile. 'Salt. They condemn you as a perjurer. Persians swear on salt.'

'The oath I took to Shapur was in the Greek fashion.'

'They are Persians. They will assume you took the oath in the form they know. As your Herodotus said: everywhere, custom is king.'

'Just so,' said Ballista.

As the sun arced up across the sky, they took to waiting again. This time, their attention was on the hills directly behind Corycus.

Over his shoulder, Ballista heard Calgacus telling Maximus an unlikely story: 'When Archelaos of Cappadocia ruled Corycus, he had a beautiful daughter.'

'Did she have big tits?'

'Huge – anyway, there was a prophecy that she would

be bitten by a snake and die. Now, worry almost drove the king out of his mind. So he built her a palace on this islet of Crambusa – not a snake in sight. Safe as you like.'

'Sure, she must have been lonely – a hot-blooded girl, all alone, in need of company.'

'Certainly. Now one of her admirers – a far better-looking, better-set-up man than you – sent her a present, a basket of fruit from the orchards below Mount Taurus. But hidden among the apricots was an asp.'

'Fuck you, and your stories. I am not in the least scared of snakes. Never have been. And, anyway, we are not on the island.'

The two men bickered on amiably.

When the sun was at its zenith, the hills shimmered with heat, and the white, limestone walls of Corycus were almost painful to look at. When it was time to eat, Ballista gave an order for Hippothous the Cilician to join them.

As they had left Sebaste, an insignificant fishing boat had smuggled Hippothous out to them. He had been desperate to avoid Trebellianus and, it seemed, with good reason. Hippothous, on his own account, was one of the leading men of the upland town of Dometiopolis. His story, if true, was alarming. When those Persians now in Corycus had ventured inland, he claimed, they had been guided by Lydius, one of Trebellianus's boys. They had passed by Germanicopolis, leaving Trebellianus's home-town untouched, and had fallen instead on Dometiopolis.

Hippothous was sandy-haired, more refined than the average rough Cilician. Yet Ballista had no doubt he was cut from the same cloth as Trebellianus. All these men were trying to turn the calamity to their own advantage.

'You have claimed that the Persians handed some of your fellow citizens over to Lydius,' said Ballista.

A look of distaste passed over Hippothous's face. 'Handed them over, and then watched, laughing, as the Cilicians carried out their disgusting sacrifices. They hang the victims, men and beasts, in a tree. They cast javelins at them. If they hit, the god Ares accepts the sacrifice.'

'And if they miss?'

'They get a second throw.'

'I take it you do not agree with your countrymen's religious practices.'

'Oh no,' said Hippothous. 'I am not Cilician by birth. Mine has been a long and tragic path. I was born in Perinthus, the noble city close by Byzantium. My father was on the *Boule*. When I was young, I fell desperately in love. Hyperanthes was nearly my age. Stripped for wrestling in the gymnasium, he was like a god. And his eyes – no sidelong glances or fearsome looks, no trace of villainy or dissembling.'

As they ate, Hippothous told them a tale of love, lust, subterfuge, murder, flight, shipwreck, loss and exile – a tale worthy of a Greek romance.

'Probably from a fucking Greek romance,' muttered Calgacus.

'Do you think Trebellianus will come?' Ballista asked.

'Oh yes,' said Hippothous. 'These Persians are witnesses to his treachery. He will want them dead.'

An hour or so after lunch, the *trierarch* called them. From the prow of the *Lupa*, they looked at the hills. Through the heat haze, the thin woods above Corycus seemed to be moving. Trebellianus and his men had come.

'Let us go and talk with Zik Zabrigan again.'

This time, the *framadar* offered no physically implausible abuse. Totally cut off by land and sea, aware that the main Persian army was far away, defeated and in retreat, he had to accept the game was up. Although suspicious, his attitude, as they stood between their forces on the seaward end of the mole, was reasonable.

'Lay down your arms, give up your booty and any prisoners, surrender yourselves into my hands and, despite your outrages, your lives will be spared.' Ballista sounded implacable.

'Spared for what?'

'I will give you better terms than are customary. The emperor Alexander Severus settled Persian prisoners as farmers in Phrygia. But your men do not strike me as suited for a bucolic life. If they will swear the *sacramentum*, they will be enrolled into the Roman army. They will be split up into different units, but I will give you my word they will not be called upon to fight against their own people.'

Given Ballista's record, it was quite commendable of the *framadar* to accede with no hesitation. The salt was produced, hands clasped, the right words spoken.

Up on the tower above the docks, the tension was getting to Ballista. So far, things had been reasonably smooth, but the hand-over was tricky. There were many things that could go wrong. Ordered to remain outside the town, Trebellianus had protested civilly enough, his men more truculently. At any moment they might swarm forward to get at the Persians, maybe even sack the town itself.

Ballista had hurried Castricius's soldiers up on to the

walls. The legionaries were under military discipline, but they had no love of the Persians and civilians were always a tempting target. Estate guards could turn brigand; in fact they often did.

And then there were the problems posed by the Persians themselves. The easterners had been very reluctant to be parted from their horses. Now they were far from keen to be herded aboard the six big transports. They had no knowledge of the places to which they were being sent. One thousand of them were bound for Egypt – the Roman garrison there was large enough to keep a check on them. The others, in four units of five hundred, were to be shipped to Cyprus, Rhodes, Lesbos and Lemnos. They could be effectively contained on the islands. There were religious objections also. Magi were forbidden to travel by water. A solution had been found for the five priests in the Persian ranks. The root cause was the prohibition on Magi soiling water with human waste: they had been issued with big *amphorae* with stoppers. How they disposed of the contents at their destination was their own concern.

Some of Trebellianus's Cilicians had advanced down the hill. They were shouting, demanding admittance, hammering on the gate with the pommels of their swords. If more followed, it could be serious.

'*Dominus*, a *liburnian* has come from Antioch. There is a messenger.'

'Not now, Calgacus.'

'Yes, now. You need to hear him now.' The old Caledonian was grinning like an idiot.

Maximus shouldered Calgacus aside. Inexplicably, the Hibernian was crying.

'Ballista – your boys – Julia – they are alive – in Antioch.'

Julia looked away across the atrium. From the corridor to the main door came the tap, tap, tapping of the mosaicist replacing the horrible image of the deformed dwarf which someone had defaced. Julia was not sure why she felt put out. It was not Ballista's reaction when reunited with his sons. Even a senator of the old *Res Publica* would have broken down and cried, would have gone first to them.

Surely it was not the children. Admittedly, Isangrim had continually interrupted her account of their escape. But the boy was rightly proud of his behaviour, above all of stabbing the Sassanid with his miniature sword. Carefully schooled by her, he had not mentioned her torn clothing. And it was not Dernhelm repeating words at random, squeaking intermittently with pleasure. However, she did have to admit to a flash of irritation when Isangrim pre-empted her telling of her ingenious ploy of scattering the gold from her purse to distract their pursuers by the postern gate. Ballista had made that worse, smiling and saying it was clever of her to remember his doing the same with his gold mural crown at the riot in the hippodrome the other year. Men, they always had to take the credit for themselves.

No, it was not the children. It was something about Ballista. He looked haunted, or maybe merely hangdog. No, not really either of those. It was more that he was distant, strange. He had even seemed reluctant to give Isangrim his little sword back.

Julia listened as Ballista finished his tale of what had happened to him and the armies. Like married men often do, he spoke to her through their children. She knew it gave him licence to edit the story.

So he had put the Persian prince and his companions ashore somewhere south of Tarsus. He had given them horses, arms, money and a letter of safe conduct. No, he did not know if they had made it, but it was quite likely. Shapur had forced the Cilician Gates. The Roman force under Ragonius Clarus had given up its pursuit almost before it had begun. North of the Taurus mountains, Tyana had been the first of many cities taken by the Persians. A group of them had split off to sack Cybistra, Barata, Laranda and Iconium. The main body of men under Shapur had gone on to seize Caesarea Masaca – a heroic defence by the retreating Demosthenes had come to nothing in the face of treachery. From there they had ridden to Comana. The two groups reunited at Sebasteia; the Persians had marched south. As they rode by the governor of Cappadocia, Pomponius Bassus had not stirred from behind the walls of Melitene. The governor of Osrhoene, Aurelius Dasius, had shown more spirit. But then, the King of Kings was said to have bribed him and his men to let them pass Edessa, back into the safety of Mesopotamia.

'It may not be as safe as Shapur thinks,' interjected Julia. 'Rumour has it that since you defeated the King of Kings, revolts have broken out in the east of the Sassanid empire, around the Caspian Sea and beyond. And, closer to home, Odenathus has marched north from Palmyra to oppose Shapur in Mesopotamia.'

Ballista looked up sharply. 'So the Lion of the Sun has finally declared for Macrianus and Quietus?'

'No,' said Julia. 'He has declared for Rome against Persia. But not for any emperor. Did you know the Sassanid still has Valerian with him?'

Yes, Ballista had seen the pathetic figure of the captive emperor at the battle of Soli.

'If Odenathus defeats Shapur, frees Valerian, or captures him . . .' She did not finish the sentence. There was no need. If he held Valerian, the Lion of the Sun could deal as an equal – more than an equal – with Macrianus's sons or Gallienus.

'My old friend Mamurra never trusted Odenathus.' Thinking out loud, Ballista had retreated into his distance.

Julia very much wanted to be alone with her husband. Imperiously, she dismissed the others and led him to their bedchamber.

Physically, he was fine, but even as they made love, his mind seemed somehow elsewhere. She decided to approach this indirectly.

'Where is Demetrius?'

For a time he was silent. 'I have a new secretary; a Greek called Hippothous. I sent Demetrius away. To the west.'

Again Ballista fell silent.

She waited.

'It was a bad time.'

She regarded him calmly. Of course it had been a bad time. You do not win two battles against the Sassanids at a *symposium*. He had thought his family slaughtered.

'It is over now,' she said.

'Is it? The oath I made to Shapur?' His voice was flat:

> *'Not to your face, no fear, not to any miscreant's*
> *Will Justice strike the fatal blow; but soft*
> *And slow of tread, she will, in her own season,*
> *Stalking the wicked, seize them unawares.'*

'Euripides,' Julia said.

'I have been reading a lot of him; often his *Medea*. It is confused in my mind.' Again, he recited quietly: '*Soft and slow of tread . . . The sins of the parents on the children, the gods turn.*'

Julia remained silent.

'Jason and me – both oath-breakers. Why were his sons killed and not mine? Or is the divine vengeance delayed? "Soft and slow . . ."' Ballista's voice trailed off.

'The gods do not exist.' Julia's voice was crisp, decisive. 'Even if they do, they are far away, and have no interest in mankind. They do not care.'

She paused for Ballista to respond. He did not.

'Even if they were real and did care, punishing the children of the wicked would be more ludicrous than a doctor administering medicine to the son of a sick man.'

Ballista appeared to be only half listening. 'There is the proverb: *the mills of the gods are slow in grinding, but grind fine.*'

Stubborn and superstitious as her barbarian husband could be, Julia had never seen him quite so given over to morbid, god-haunted introspection. 'Nonsense,' she snapped. 'Even if the gods existed and troubled themselves with the affairs of men, there would be no

246

punishment on you or your children – because you have done nothing wrong. Jason was forced into his oath to Medea. If he had not taken it, she would not have helped him and he would not have won the golden fleece. You were forced into your oath to Shapur. If you had not taken it, you would have shared the fate of Turpio. Oaths under duress count for nothing.'

At last, Ballista seemed to have come back from wherever he had been. 'Then why did Jason's sons die?'

'Medea killed them because he abandoned her.' Julia smiled. 'There is a lesson there.'

Ballista also smiled, if grimly. Then he leant over and spoke close to her ear. 'I took another oath, a voluntary one to myself. Should I keep it?'

Despite herself Julia felt apprehensive. 'What?'

'To kill Quietus.'

Julia was very still, thinking hard. At length, she spoke. 'Yes. You will think yourself less of a man if you do not. And it may be the only route to safety.'

Ballista nodded.

'But,' whispered Julia, 'it will not be easy. You must wait your time.'

Again Ballista nodded.

'And, Quietus alone is not enough. You must kill the entire family.'

PART FOUR

Conservator Pietatis

(The West, the Alps, the city of Cularo,
Autumn, AD260)

'For those whom fate has cursed
Music itself sings but one note –
Unending miseries, torment and wrong.'
Euripides, *Women of Troy*, 120–21

XV

When the heavy hangings were drawn briefly back, it let a chill blast of wind from the mountains into the council house at Cularo. The lamps and the sacred fire guttered. The air smelled of autumn. The campaign season was almost over. Soon the army must retreat back through the Alps to Italy or be trapped when the first snows blocked the passes. The emperor Gallienus had to accept that his revenge must wait until next spring – at least until next spring.

The two men who had entered stood, letting their eyes grow used to the bright lights. One was Hermianus, the *ab Admissionibus*. The other was a messenger from the Danube. The latter carried a small but heavy leather sack. Knowing what was in the sack, Gallienus supposed he should be pleased. But he was not.

Sat on the high throne, Gallienus tried to lighten his mood by enumerating what had gone well this year. In distant Africa, the revolt of Celsus had been crushed. The pretender was dead. So were his backers, Vibius Passienus, the governor of the province of Africa, and Fabius Pomponianus, the *Dux* of the Libyan frontier. It was good that the governors of Mauretania and Numidia, Cornelius

Octavianus and Decianus, had stood firm. But it had been close to genius on the part of Gallienus's female cousin to take those Franks, some of the Bavares who had crossed from Spain and been defeated by Decianus, and enlist them to destroy the uprising. At a stroke, and only at the cost of some land confiscated from Celsus, a dangerous band of barbarian raiders had been converted into a significant military asset. She had done well. At the idea of his family, a horrible thought tried to swim up into Gallienus's mind. He forced it down, pushed on with the good things.

On the Danube, the revolt of Ingenuus had also been crushed. In that case, by Gallienus himself. There had been a glorious victory outside Mursa, another triumph for the *comitatus*, the emperor's new mobile cavalry force, another success for the tactic of feigned retreat. Let old-school senators grumble that it was un-Roman. They were wrong. It was ideal for cavalry. The Romans had always adapted the useful methods of their enemies.

Of course, as soon as Gallienus and his *comitatus* had left for the west, there had been another revolt. But the messenger now approaching the throne had the final proof that Regalianus, the governor of Pannonia Inferior, had shared the fate of Ingenuus.

The Danube frontier was solid again. Untrammelled by over-rigid adherence to Roman tradition, Gallienus had opened negotiations with Attalus, king of the Marcomanni. Now, in exchange for some land in the province of Pannonia Superior, that fierce German ruler protected the peaceful cities and fields from his hairy kinsmen further north. And there was Pippa. To cement the treaty,

Attalus had given his daughter to Gallienus. A German only took one wife, unless he was important and it was necessary to take more than one. Who could be more important than the emperor of Rome? In Pippa's eyes, she was his second wife; in Roman terms, she was a concubine. But what a concubine. Gallienus let his thoughts run over her body – tall, well built; she was blonde, too – one of his favourite types. A virgin when she had arrived, once broken in she could not have turned out keener on what the old emperor Domitian had called 'bed-wrestling'. Pippa, Gallienus's sweet barbarian Pippara, was just how he liked them. Once the duties in this council house were concluded, Gallienus could enjoy an afternoon of pleasure. Sex and drink always took his mind off things.

The messenger was getting up from performing *proskynesis*. Gallienus indicated for him to show what he had brought.

The man put the sack down on the floor, fumbled with its tight lashings. A foul smell emerged.

Standing, the messenger pulled the head out by the hair. Blackened, wide-eyed, lips drawn back from its teeth by the onset of decay, it looked like an image of Medusa. Regalianus, senator of Rome, descendant of the old Kings of Dacia – that was the end of him.

Gallienus regarded the loathsome thing dispassionately. He wondered if head-hunting was a native tradition of the Roxolani, the Sarmatian barbarians he had set on Regalianus. They were nomads, eaters of flesh, drinkers of milk. He remembered that they let their women ride to battle with them. But he was not sure about the taking of heads. Possibly one of the officers he had seconded to them, Camsisoleus or Celer Venerianus, had informed them of the correct Roman protocol for the corpses of men who had dared to assume the purple and then lost.

The living emperor stared at the dead pretender. What to do with the head? Send it to Rome – a pungent message to any senators entertaining thoughts of treason? Put it on a pike here to encourage the army?

'*Sic transit gloria mundi.*' Gallienus's voice was level. 'Take it away, and give it proper burial.'

Still holding it by the hair, the messenger shuffled away backwards. The *ab Admissionibus* Hermianus ushered him out.

Gallienus could see no reason to waste time in a futile show of open discussion. The senators present might expect it, but neither the high military commanders nor the heads of the imperial bureaux would be put out.

'*Comites,*' Gallienus began, 'winter is almost upon us. The punishment of the renegades and murderers in Gaul must wait until next year.' He forced himself to smile. 'The *Res Publica* must survive a winter without Atrebatic cloaks.'

There was polite if sycophantic laughter.

'In two days, the *comitatus* will break camp and re-cross the Alps to winter quarters in northern Italy around Mediolanum. Let everyone see to his duties and make it so.'

As one, the members of the *consilium* saluted. 'We will do what is ordered, and at every command we will be ready.'

As he processed out into the autumnal streets, dark thoughts surged into Gallienus's mind. It was not Regalianus's severed head he wanted but that of Postumus. He had trusted the governor of Lower Germany. Postumus had won a minor victory over a band of Franks returning from Spain. Silvanus, the *Dux* of all the *limes* along the Rhine, had justly demanded Postumus hand over the booty. Instead Postumus had used it to bribe the men under his command. Legio XXX Ulpia Victrix had acclaimed Postumus emperor.

Gallienus would have let Postumus live. *Clementia* was natural to him. He had sent a laconic message from Italy which left a way open: '*What are you doing? Behave! Do you seek battle?*' The sanctimonious insolence of the reply – 'Do not come north across the Alps, do not put me in a position of fighting Roman citizens' – had infuriated Gallienus. Yet Gallienus had tried again – 'Let it be settled by single combat.' Postumus's answer had been even more galling:

I am not a gladiator, nor have I ever been one; rather I have served those provinces which you ordered me to save. I was elected emperor by the Gauls; and I am content to rule those who chose me of their free will. I will help them according to the best of my counsel and capacity.

The snide implications and the self-righteous tone were maddening. But all Postumus's words palled into nothing beside his actions – his hideous, hideous actions.

Postumus had marched on Colonia Agrippinensis, where Silvanus watched over Gallienus's young son, the Caesar Saloninus. The evil Batavian bastard Postumus had invested the city. Food had run short. Scared, over-awed by threats, the cowardly citizens had bargained for their safety. They had secured it – at a price. Silvanus and Saloninus had been handed over in chains. Saloninus, Gallienus's golden, beautiful boy, was killed out of hand with his guardian. What terrors must have gone through his young mind before the sword fell?

Gallienus had vowed to Hercules that Postumus would die – Postumus, his family, friends, every soldier in Legio XXX, and every man, woman and child in the town of Colonia Agrippinensis.

Gallienus had thought that Hercules had listened. The war of retribution had begun well. It had been late to start a campaign, but they had crossed the Alps before the traitors knew they were coming. And then, another betrayal. Genialis, the faithless acting governor of Raetia, had declared for Postumus. He threatened their rear. With the *comitatus* away to the west over the Alps, there was nothing to stop Genialis crossing the mountains and invading Italy from the north. Gallienus had been forced to halt at Cularo. Now he would have to retire to Mediolanum. Next year, he would have his vengeance.

But would it be next year? In the east, Macrianus the Lame had prospered. From the Aegean to Egypt, every Roman province had acknowledged his sons, Quietus and Macrianus the Younger, as emperors. Next year, the old cripple Macrianus must make his play for Rome. Much of his field army was composed of detachments from the armies of the west. They would demand to return home, force his hand.

Thanks to the successes of Ballista in Cilicia and Odenathus in Mesopotamia, the Sassanids would be quiet next year. There was unrest in the eastern reaches of the

Persian empire. By the Caspian Sea, the Cadusii and the Mardi were said to be in open revolt. Macrianus would march west and Gallienus would have to postpone his revenge on Postumus to meet him.

Only one man could stop Macrianus marching in the spring: Odenathus. The Lord of Palmyra had fought the Persians, but he returned ambiguous answers to Gallienus's smuggled letters. He had yet to declare for his rightful emperor or the young pretenders in the east. So much rested on the enigmatic Lion of the Sun.

Gallienus thought of his old friend Ballista. He had listened to the Angle's secretary, Demetrius. He had not harmed the young Greek. There was no advantage in it, and the boy was handsome. Demetrius was to remain at court. Gallienus's spies had informed him of the reappearance in Antioch of Ballista's wife and sons. His old friend was trapped again in the service of Macrianus. Gallienus felt no ill will towards Ballista, but the northerner could not be allowed to lead Macrianus's army to the west. He was too good a general. It was not a problem. All it would take was for one of the *frumentarii* under Rufinus, Gallienus's new *Princeps Peregrinorum*, to speak to one of those serving under Censorinus, the spymaster his father had been so misguided to trust. Hand over a report of Demetrius's words along with Ballista's ring, with its image of Cupid winding a siege engine, and Macrianus would do the rest.

Gallienus felt sorry for Ballista, but politics was politics. Anyway, Ballista's sons had returned, as if from the dead. Saloninus was not coming back. Poor, poor lost Saloninus. *Conservator Pietatis* – one of the coin types those in charge of the mint had shown him. What a cruel irony. Publius Licinius Egnatius Gallienus, emperor of Rome, the preserver of piety – unable to avenge his murdered son, unable to rescue his elderly father.

They were nearing the biggest house in Cularo. It had been voluntarily offered as imperial accommodation. No matter how enforced the offer, the owner would have some explaining to do this winter, after the *comitatus* had left and men retook the town in the name of Postumus.

The sharp wind fretted at the wreaths of bay and oak leaves which marked the emperor's residence. As ever, there was a crowd waiting outside. Among them, Gallienus recognized the bearded figure of Plotinus the Platonist philosopher. The emperor told Voconius Zeno, his recently appointed *a Studiis*, to detain the lover of wisdom. In normal times, Gallienus liked Plotinus's company well enough; in Rome, he and his wife Salonina had enjoyed his conversation. But these were not normal times. This afternoon, Gallienus required other consolations, not those of philosophy.

PART FIVE

Capax Imperii

(The East, Winter AD260–Summer AD261)

'The ways of the gods are slow, but in the end their power is shown.'

Euripides, *Ion*, 1615

XVI

Up on the dais in the palace in Antioch, the chief men of the imperial entourage were in place. The two youthful emperors, Macrianus the Younger and Quietus, were enthroned. To their left, their father, Macrianus the Lame, sat on a *curule* chair nearly as high and nearly as elaborate as the thrones. There were no other chairs. Beyond the father was the spymaster Censorinus, backed by the imperial secretaries. To the right of the emperors stood Maeonius Astyanax, the senior Praetorian Prefect; Ragonius Clarus, the Prefect of Cavalry; and, on the end, as the other Praetorian Prefect, Ballista.

A gust of rain rattled against the windows of the great apse. Outside, it was a cold and grey midwinter morning in Antioch. *I am getting soft*, thought Ballista: *back home in Germania this could pass for mild spring weather. Where Calgacus comes from, this is probably a balmy summer's day.*

The *ab Admissionibus* drew back the hangings at the far end of the big room. Blinking a little in the many lights, the governors who supported the Macriani entered: Piso of Syria Coele, Cornicula of Syria Phoenice, Pomponius Bassus of Cappadocia, Achaeus of Palestine, Virius Lupus of Arabia, Mussius Aemilianus of Egypt, Theodorus of

Cyprus and Trebellianus of Cilicia. With them was Sampsigeramus, the client king of Emesa.

Nine powerful men, but it was interesting who was not there: no governors west of Cilicia – above all, not Maximillianus of Asia; and from the east, no Aurelius Dasius of Osrhoene nor, most crucial of all, Odenathus Lord of Palmyra. Certainly all except the Lion of the Sun had sent excuses: illness, bandits or barbarian raiders. It could mean a great deal, or nothing. Politics in the *imperium*, when the stakes were as high as this, never admitted an easy reading.

The next wave of the *consilium* was ushered in – some forty senators, headed by the ex-consul Fabius Labeo, the *nobilis* Astyrius and a relative of the Macriani called Cornelius Macer. It was impressive. Admittedly, long ago, more had fled east to join Mark Antony in his doomed campaign against Octavian. Yet the *imperium* was now divided three ways between Gallienus, Postumus and the sons of Macrianus. To assemble so far from Rome about one in twelve of all senators was impressive.

The final group was shown in – a huge throng of equestrians, almost all junior military officers: prefects, tribunes and the like. Among them, the bright-red hair of tall Rutilus stood out. Ballista also caught sight of the pointy face of Castricius. The latter winked. He had come a long way since being a slave in the mines.

At a sign from the *ab Admissionibus*, the members of the *consilium* performed *proskynesis*. As he got up, Ballista saw that Macrianus the Elder had merely leant a little forward and blown a kiss. The lesser form of adoration could be put down to his age and incapacity, but it could be interpreted as something very different.

When the *comites* were back on their feet, the senators looked around, trying not to give evidence of their surprise and displeasure at the lack of seats. Ballista could see what the regime was attempting: trying to mark the emperors out yet more from their most powerful subjects, to enhance even further their dignity. But it was a potentially dangerous ploy. All too easily it could smack of arrogance, or even oriental despotism. A real emperor could sit cross-legged on the ground eating porridge with his legionaries and not lose *dignitas*.

Laboriously, Macrianus the Elder hauled himself to his feet. Leaning on his walking stick, he pulled a fold of his toga over his head. In a firm voice, he prayed for all the immortal gods, all the natural gods of Rome, to guide their deliberations, hold their hands over the emperors and their *consilium*. The flame burned blue-green as he sprinkled a pinch of incense over the sacred fire.

Regaining his seat, Macrianus indicated that Maeonius Astyanax should hold the floor. The senior Praetorian Prefect cleared his throat. The air was thick with incense and perfume, although it did not quite cover the bitter reek of burning which still lingered from the Persian sack.

'Most noble emperors, members of the *consilium*, I bring good news.' Astyanax paused. The lights made deep shadows in the lines on his forehead and under his fleshy mouth. His face was inscrutable.

'Only a short time now stands between the degenerate tyrant Gallienus and his death. He fritters away what little is left with prostitutes and pimps, barbarians and buffoons – dressed as a girl, submitting as a girl, mocking the *dignitas* of the throne and the *maiestas* of the Roman people.'

Ballista knew that Astyanax, revelling in his orotundity, could keep this up for hours. Some of the usual phrases of invective floated through his thoughts – 'more unnatural than Nero', 'crueller than Domitian', 'more perverse than Heliogabalus'; 'incest and magic'; 'the profligate', 'the coward', 'the enemy of men and gods'. Rain beat on the windows.

'Now the forces of righteous retribution are ready to march.' Astyanax's words brought Ballista's attention back. 'The minor troubles of a few days ago are a thing of the past. It was nothing more than the almost commendable over-eagerness of a handful of troops from the west to free their *contubernales* and families from the perverted lusts of the tyrant.'

Which, Ballista thought, was a good way of describing a serious mutiny – one only defused by a large donative of cash to the mutineers and a complete capitulation to their demands: yes, the western troops could begin their march home as soon as it was spring, some even sooner.

'Here in the east all is secure. The cities of Carrhae and Nisibis, recovered from the Sassanids by Odenathus, have been handed over to the governor of Osrhoene. Setting them in order, of course, accounts for the absence of Aurelius Dasius from this gathering today.'

It might, thought Ballista.

'I have received a letter from Odenathus himself.' Astyanax produced a piece of papyrus from his scabbard. It neatly reminded his listeners that he, with Ragonius Clarus and Ballista, was one of the three men allowed to go armed in the presence of the emperors.

'The Lord of Palmyra will take the war to the Persians.

He has the Sassanids on the defensive. The Lion of the Sun intends no less than to sack Shapur's capital of Ctesiphon. He expresses his complete confidence that the gods will settle the rule of Rome on those they favour.'

Astyanax flourished the letter before returning it to his scabbard. Ballista saw no more than that there was writing on it. He would not have been surprised had it been blank.

'In view of Odenathus's signal loyalty to Rome, our noble emperors have sent him magnificent presents from among the property justly confiscated from the atheist Christians.'

A large bribe, thought Ballista, *tortured out of the adherents of a supposedly peace-loving sect in response to a wonderfully ambiguous message.* The northerner made sure his face was immobile.

With a grandiloquent gesture, Astyanax turned to the emperors. '*Domini*, the east is secure. Give the word and we will follow you to Rome to free the *imperium* from the cruel tyranny of Gallienus. Just give the word.'

In the murmur of approval, Ballista saw Macrianus nod to one of his sons.

Macrianus the Younger held up his sceptre for silence. 'We thank the *Vir Ementissimus* Maeonius Astyanax. We hear the wishes of our *comites*. We hear the prayers of those oppressed in Europe and Africa. In the spring, as soon as the campaigning season opens, we will march to the west.'

Now he had all their attention.

'I myself, accompanied by my father, the Prefect of Cavalry Ragonius Clarus and the *Princeps Peregrinorum* Calpurnius Censorinus, will lead a force of thirty thousand picked men. Those who will serve as legates we will announce later.'

There was an intensity of gaze among the members of the *consilium*. Whatever they really thought of the young emperors, all the *comites* knew that it was on expeditions like this that serious advancement could be secured, a glittering career made.

'In advance of the main expedition, Gaius Calpurnius Piso Frugi, the governor of Syria Coele, will lead fifteen thousand men to secure first a crossing into Europe at Byzantium, then the provinces of Thrace and Achaea. Again, those who will serve as legates will be announced later.'

Macrianus the Younger looked up at the thick cedar beams supporting the high roof. 'We bow to the will of the immortal gods, put our lives in their hands. They will not fail to support us. The tyrant Gallienus has rescinded the persecution of the Christians. The natural, powerful gods of Rome will not suffer those who deny them to go unpunished. Jupiter Optimus Maximus, all the gods, they will hold their hands over us.'

The young Augustus relapsed into the immobility and distant stare the Romans thought fitting in an emperor. Ballista wondered how much of it was well-schooled play-acting. Was he just mouthing the words, or did the younger Macrianus share his father's terrible certainty about the divine?

Out of the corner of his eye, Ballista saw a movement. It was the walking stick of Macrianus the Elder. Its silver top, with its bust of Alexander the Great, nudged towards Quietus.

As the young emperor prepared to speak, Ballista studied him. Quietus had the features of his family. Since his accession, Macrianus the Younger had acquired a simulacrum of maturity, but Quietus had not. The pouchy eyes, receding chin, the long, straight nose . . . all still carried the look of a spoilt, petulant and vindictive youth.

'*Comites* –' Quietus began in too high a register. He coughed, looked annoyed and started again. '*Comites*, when our brother and father march, we will remain in Antioch, governing the east. The Praetorian Prefects, Maeonius Astyanax and Ballista, will advise us. As Piso Frugi heads the advance to the west, his province of Syria Coele will be governed by our most loyal subject Fabius Labeo.'

The boy paused for the elderly ex-consul to express his thanks.

'As we have heard from Maeonius Astyanax,' Quietus continued, 'in general, the east stands secure. But the duties of a ruler never end. The governor of Palestine, Achaeus, informs us that his province, always an unruly one, is suffering a plague of bandits. These evil-doers must be eradicated. To this end, we order our Praetorian Prefect Ballista, even in the depths of winter, to descend on them with fire and sword. He will take a thousand men, infantry and cavalry, and he will put an end to these brigands. He will rout them out – and their sons too, that they may not grow up to follow the example of their fathers. Not one will be left alive.' Quietus looked at Ballista. He seemed to be relishing in advance the suffering of innocents.

'We will do what is ordered, and at every command we will be ready,' Ballista intoned. Allfather, he hated this.

A half-smile played across Quietus's face. 'To put at rest the mind of the *Vir Ementissimus*, given the unfortunate events when he was last away, we are happy to extend our protection to his family. Ballista's wife and sons will reside with us, here in the palace.'

Ballista had no choice. As he expressed his thanks, he felt a deep foreboding. Allfather, let Julia and his boys be all right while he was away, let nothing bad happen to them.

Quietus could not prevent a high-pitched giggle.

One day, you little bastard, thought Ballista, *maybe not soon, but one day*.

Ballista had marched his men down from Antioch to Caesarea Maritima in the province of Syria Palestina. It had been fine. On their left, the mountains of Lebanon, in the bright mornings their cedars often shrouded in fine mists. To their right, red sandhills and, beyond them, the sea, flashing violet, blue, black in the winter sun. They had passed through the famous cities of ancient Phoenicia: Tripolis, Berytus, Sidon and Tyre. They had negotiated the outcrop known as the Ladder of Tyre, where the road overhung precipices of naked white rock. Once they had rounded Mount Carmel, the coast road had been covered in a drift of millions of shells. White, brown, purple, they cracked and rattled under the horses' hooves and the boots of the men.

Throughout the journey, the noise of the sea was in their ears. The surf was magnificent, rolling in great billows, breaking then forming again. The weather had held fair, but it was obvious the shore was a cruel one. Ballista counted eight ships wrecked; some still almost intact, others little more than discoloured lines in the sand. Maximus, of course, counted fourteen. The new secretary Hippothous claimed to have seen no fewer than twenty.

Caesarea Maritima, the city built by King Herod, was a fine place. Ballista had been busy there: endless sessions with the governor Achaeus, his legates – including the stony-faced senator Astyrius – and other officers to plan operations to scour the land of bandits. It had soon become clear why Achaeus needed aid. Several districts were overrun: Samaria, Galilee, Judea itself. Detachments to the emperors' field armies had cut the governor's command to the bone. There were no more than two thousand men with the eagle of Legio X Fretensis at Aelia Capitolina, and just a thousand with that of Legio VI Ferrata at Caporcotani. The number of auxiliary units had been slashed. There were only two *alae* of cavalry and six cohorts of infantry: nominally four thousand men, but these likewise were under strength. They were spread thin throughout the province.

The troops of Ballista would act as a strike column in Galilee. It was a large area for their very limited force. The northerner had led down a *vexillatio* of five hundred drawn from Legio III Gallica commanded by an amiable centurion called Lerus, and a wing of Dalmatian cavalry of the same number under the big red-headed prefect Rutilus.

The mission was important. It was no fool's errand. Yet Ballista was unhappy to have left Julia and his sons behind in the palace. He prayed they would be all right. He did not trust Quietus.

His worries aside, the stay at Caesarea would have been

pleasant – certainly the palace on the headland by the sea was more than comfortable, and Ballista usually enjoyed throwing himself into military planning – but for the personality of the governor. Not only was Achaeus a close *amicus* of Macrianus the Elder, he was also a bore and a bigot. A Praetorian Prefect Ballista may be, but the rules of society demanded that he frequently accept the governor's hospitality and, at least outwardly, give some small sign of enjoyment. And then he had to campaign with him. Ballista had reclined through meal after meal as Achaeus dilated on his favourite topic: the iniquities of the Jews he ruled.

'I tell you, they are far more pernicious even than the disgusting Christians. Those superstitious fools, when they are not shouting "I am a Christian and I want to die," they at least keep repeating, like the cawing of so many trained crows, "Thou shalt not kill; Thou shalt not kill." If the god of the Jews had mentioned the latter to them, the circumcised ones were not listening. Three massive uprisings under the emperors Nero, Trajan and Hadrian. Continuous trouble the rest of the time. A nightmare to govern, like living with a stepmother. The Jews hate mankind. As the saying goes, they would not show a non-Jew the way or give him a drink of water. More likely, they would cut his throat. They're always fighting. When they're not persecuting good citizens who worship the natural gods or attacking the Christians and the Samaritans, they turn on each other. Do you know, I asked the emperor Valerian why we did not deal with them once and for all? Do you know what he said? "They may be mad, but unlike the Christians, their madness is ancestral." Addled old fool, thank the gods he has gone. When I mentioned it to the father of the noble emperors set over us now, may the gods preserve them, I got far more sense. "One enemy at a time," Macrianus said. "The Christians first, then the Jews.'"

Every evening, when the eating was done, when Ballista could have been enjoying his wine while listening to the roar of the surf on the harbour walls, the boom of more distant breakers, Achaeus told stories that only a child or a Greek geographer could believe: 'Everyone knows what they used to do before the divine Titus destroyed their temple. They would catch a Greek, hold him prisoner, fatten him up, then kill and eat him. They are probably still at it, up in the hills of Galilee under their so-called patriarchs.'

Red-faced, Achaeus would warm to his topic: 'Do you know why they will not eat pigs? No, I will tell you. Because they worship them! Do you know they will not eat hares either? Why? Because hares look like miniature donkeys, and they worship donkeys too!' On and on the calumnies rolled, by turns vile and ludicrous, drowning out the clean roar of the sea.

After fifteen days, Ballista had been glad to get away from the odious governor. But he wished the weather had not finally broken. It had been merely overcast when they set out from Caesarea three days earlier. The first night had been spent in the echoing near-emptiness of the legionary fortress of Legio VI at Caporcotani, the second in the town of Sepphoris. They had waited there a day. At dusk the force had divided and marched out as the rain began to fall. Their target was a village called Arbela which was overrun with bandits. It was to be a pincer attack at first light. The legionaries from III Gallica under Lerus were to march to the Sea of Tiberias and approach the village from the east. Ballista and Rutilus, with the Dalmatian troopers, were to come in from the west. Ballista suspected that Lerus and his men had drawn the better lot. It was as well the cavalrymen had left their mounts at Sepphoris: Ballista was glad Pale Horse was safe in a stable. The hill path was hard going for men on foot. And it was cold, very cold.

Winter had come with a vengeance. In the dark, the wind tore down the rocky Galilean hills. It tugged at the olive trees and dwarf oaks. It gusted rain. *The weather would choose tonight to turn*, Ballista thought sourly.

The wind had veered straight into their faces. The men marched hunched over, heads down and turned away, trying to find some shelter from the blasts.

Not long after midnight, the rain had stopped. Soon after, the first watch fires glittered on the hills. The bandits of Arbela knew they were coming. Ballista was unsurprised. As far as he had gathered, the Jews had no love of the Roman occupiers. Caesarea had a large Jewish population, and Sepphoris was a Jewish town. It was no wonder the brigands had been forewarned. One man's bandit was another's freedom fighter. Ballista set his shoulders. There was nothing to be done but press on.

Ballista trudged behind the native guides. The strap of the shield slung over his back dug painfully into his left shoulder. The sword belt over his right was only a little less painful. He did nothing to shift the weights. Any movement would expose part of him to the wind. Allfather, it was cold.

'*Dominus.*' Maximus's voice broke into Ballista's discomfort. 'I cannot see Calgacus. The old bastard must have dropped back.'

Reluctantly, Ballista looked around. It was a dark night. He could not see far, but Maximus was right. Raising his voice over the keening wind, Ballista told Rutilus to take command and keep going; the standard bearer Gratius and secretary Hippothous were to carry on with the troops.

Ballista and Maximus stepped off the path. Slowly the soldiers passed, like mourners in a procession, only quieter.

Calgacus was near the rear of the column. He was staggering slightly. Ballista and Maximus fell in on either side. The Caledonian did not appear to notice.

'Calgacus,' Ballista called.

The old man did not respond. Swaying slightly, he carried on walking.

Calgacus stumbled, almost fell. They caught his arms.

'I'm fine. Leave me alone.' Calgacus's speech was slurred.

'Halt – that is an order.'

Calgacus stopped. He started to fall. Maximus grabbed him.

'Halt the column,' Ballista shouted to the nearest trooper. 'Pass the order up the line.'

The backs of the nearest troops stopped moving. They stood bent over like beasts of burden.

Ballista and Maximus manoeuvred Calgacus to the side of the track, lowered him to lean against the trunk of a tree.

'I am fine. Get the fuck off me.' Calgacus's words were thick, like those of a drunk. He shut his eyes and groaned.

Now they had stopped, Ballista could feel the muscles in his own legs twitching, trying to cramp.

'*Dominus*.' It was a Dalmatian trooper. '*Dominus*, the rest of them, they have gone.'

Ballista peered into the night. His eyes streamed from the wind. The soldier was right. Six troopers and an empty path. Fuck. Someone had not heard the command over the noise of the marching and the wind. Or someone had been too far sunk in cold misery to understand what had been said. Fuck.

Ballista stood, wondering what to do. The wind plucked at his cloak. There were four watch fires visible on higher ground around them. Nine men left behind, one of them incapacitated. They were cut off, surrounded.

Ballista crouched down, gazed into Calgacus's face. It was very pale in the darkness. The old man was shivering violently. That was good – he was not yet in the last stages of dying from exposure.

'How goes it, old man?'

Calgacus smiled. 'Fine.' Drowsily, he shut his eyes.

Ballista slapped his face. 'Wake up, you old bastard.'

Calgacus opened his eyes. They were not properly focused.

Ballista hugged the old man close. He spoke fiercely into his ear. 'Go to sleep and you will die. And you are not going to die on me.'

Calgacus nodded.

Ballista got to his feet. The nearest fire was not far. There was no other way.

'You four' – Ballista pointed – 'huddle round him, give him your body warmth. You two, keep watch each way down the track, keep moving, try and keep warm. Maximus and I will get fire.'

They got ready. At Maximus's suggestion, they left their shields. A brigand may have a shield, but not a big circular army one. Now their silhouettes would not give them away.

'You remember Pigeon Island?' Maximus asked. It was getting on for two years ago, but to Ballista it seemed half a lifetime ago. On a little island south of Ephesus, the two of them had carried out a similar raid to snatch fire from a Borani watch camp in order to burn the barbarians' longboat. 'Sure, but this will be fun too.'

'You are a very strange man,' said Ballista.

They set off up the hill. Initially, Ballista led them away from the nearest fire. They needed to come up on it from downwind. There was no necessity for extreme caution. The howling wind should cover the noise of their approach, but they moved carefully anyway, a few steps apart, as if patrolling. The concentration needed took their minds off the cold.

Time largely loses meaning when you are climbing a dark, windswept hill with part of your mind on what will happen at the end of the climb. The wind sighed through the trees, branches creaked, stones turned under foot and mud tugged at their boots. It started raining again.

When they grew close, they slowed. About thirty paces away, they stopped behind a dwarf oak. Wiping the rain out of their eyes, they peered around the gnarled, slick trunk. Now the cold returned. Maximus passed Ballista some air-dried meat. He chewed it without thinking; it prevented his teeth chattering.

They could see two guards. They threw elongated, shifting shadows as they paced about, stamping their feet. There were other, indistinct, shapes huddled in blankets by the fire.

Ballista would have liked to observe longer, but there was no time. He touched Maximus's shoulder. They clasped hands.

Stepping out from behind the oak, they walked forward. No point in running, risking a fall, until they were seen.

The man Ballista was after was unobservant. The northerner ran the last few paces anyway. His sword swung. The man started to turn. The blade caught him on the jawline. He screamed wordlessly. Retrieving the weapon, Ballista finished him with a powerful blow to the back of the neck.

Another man was rising from his blanket. Three quick steps, two chopping blows, and he sank down again. Ballista moved on. The next one had risen to his feet and was struggling to free his weapon. Ballista drove the steel into his stomach.

Turning, scanning for threats, all Ballista saw was Maximus finishing off a man on the ground. Seven dead. All over in a matter of moments.

A branch cracked up the hill. Dark shapes were moving through the trees; five, six, maybe more. Fuck. Surprise was on their side. Ballista and Maximus moved a little apart.

The first one tore downhill at Ballista, sword out in front. At the last moment, Ballista brought his blade down and across, driving his opponent's weapon out to the right. Ballista dropped his left shoulder, braced himself.

The man crashed into him. Using the impact, Ballista shrugged him off to the right.

Straightening, Ballista parried the next one's sword to the left. He brought his elbow hard up into the man's nose. As the man staggered back, Ballista cracked the pommel of his sword down into his face. He fell back, howling.

A quick step to the right, and Ballista arced his blade down at the first opponent, now scrambling to his feet. It bit into something. No time to check. Ballista spun round. A third bandit lunged. Ballista leapt backwards, arms up, arching his body. Sparks flashed as the blade scraped along the mail covering Ballista's chest. He and his opponent were wedged together, face to face.

They struggled, feet slipping, too close to use their weapons. Ballista was aware of the second attacker getting up from the ground. The man Ballista was grappling with tried to bite his nose. Ballista twisted away. The teeth tore at his cheek. The blood felt hot. The fingers of the man's left hand were clawing for Ballista's eyes. The northerner slammed the heel of his right boot down on the man's instep. His grip slackened. Ballista broke free, with his left hand drew the dagger from his right hip, stabbed it hard into the man's crotch.

The last attacker on his feet began to back away. Ballista moved carefully towards him. The man turned and ran. Ballista was after him. The man lost his footing in the mud. He sprawled forward. Ballista was on him, driving the point of his blade down into his back.

Ballista got up quickly. No sound of steel on steel. No fighting. Some low sobbing and a high-pitched wailing. A few paces off, a dark figure moved, a bit shorter than Ballista. The blur of its sword glinted in the firelight as it chopped down again and again. Of course Maximus was fine.

Ballista walked back to his two injured opponents down on the ground. Bracing his boots in the mud, he killed both of them. There was no point in keeping them alive. He did not speak their language, could not interrogate them. He was not in the mood to try.

Ballista retrieved his dagger from the dead man's crotch. He wiped its blade and that of his sword, sheathed them.

'Sure, but you cannot say that was not fun.' Maximus was beaming.

'You really are a heartless, violent bastard.' But Ballista could feel the post-battle euphoria seeping through him. He was alive, unhurt. He had done well, not let himself down, nor anyone else. Yes, in a horrible way, Maximus was right: Ballista had enjoyed it.

'Do you think there will be any more of them along?' asked Maximus.

'No idea. But it would be a bugger trying to light a fire down on that track on a night like this. Go and get the troopers to carry the miserable old bastard up here.'

Maximus turned to go.

'And hoot like an owl when you come back, to make sure I do not kill you.'

'As if you could.'

'As if I could,' said Ballista.

It rained on and off all night, but no more brigands appeared out of the darkness. Ballista and his men built up the fire. Sheltering him with their cloaks, they changed Calgacus out of his wet things, massaged him with some oil they had heated, put him in the driest clothes that could be found in the soldiers' packs. They gave him something hot to drink and drank some themselves. The old Caledonian complained a lot – an impressive range of obscenities in a variety of languages. He would be all right.

The morning came up fine; there were just the retreating, tattered remnants of the storm clouds. They went back down to the track and followed it without incident up to Arbela. The village was spectacularly sited on the edge of a cliff. Both units of troops were waiting.

Rutilus made his report. There had been a half-hearted attack just before his column had reached the village. Two troopers had been wounded, neither seriously. Only one dead bandit had been left behind. They had stormed into Arbela at first light. It was deserted. Miraculously, after a lengthy night march, Lerus's legionaries had arrived within half an hour.

'The mission was compromised from the start,' said Ballista. 'No wonder they had all disappeared.'

Rutilus smiled. 'Some of them have not gone very far.'

The tall prefect led Ballista to the edge of the cliff. The view was incredible. Down to the right, the northern end of Lake Tiberias was spread out, shining blue under the winter sun. Straight ahead, far away in the distance, was the snow-capped summit of Mount Hermon. It must have been fifty miles or more away.

On top of the cliff, the wind buffeted them. Ballista looked down. There was a sheer drop of two, three hundred feet of jagged grey rock. Below that, a gentler incline of about the same height. The lower slope had some green cover. A few pale-grey paths graded up it to the foot of the rockface. The tiny figures of Roman soldiers moved down at the bottom of it.

'There are caves in the cliff,' said Rutilus. 'Some of the brigands have taken refuge in them. We cannot get at them from below. The paths are too steep and narrow. A child could tip stones down and sweep our men off.'

Ballista looked at the cliff, the slope, the valley below, and the opposite cliffs. The latter were too far away – nothing of use there. He turned and regarded the clifftop: the few bent trees, the village of well-built houses, a synagogue at one end.

'We could starve them out,' suggested Rutilus. 'Although,' he added, 'we do not know how well they are provisioned.'

'No,' said Ballista. 'Sitting here doing nothing seems weak. If we show weakness, every bandit in Galilee will be on us.'

They stood, gazing down at the pitted rocks, the dry bits of vegetation that offered no safe handholds. Suddenly Ballista laughed. Rutilus looked inquiringly at him.

'The village – tear it down, have the men collect all the timber, anything of a decent length. Have you sent for the horses? Good. When they come, send men down to the town of Tiberias on the lake. It is a port of sorts. There must be ropes and chains there. Collect all of them. And gearing oil and pitch, get a lot of pitch. Also send men back to Caporcotani. Collect bows from the arsenal in the legionary fortress. Not many, about forty or fifty. And a mobile forge – Legio VI should have more than one.'

'We will do what is ordered, and at every command we will be ready.'

'We are going to build two or three cranes up here on the top of the cliff. We will lower bowmen down in cages. They will burn the brigands out with fire arrows.'

Now Rutilus laughed. '*Dominus*, that is brilliant.'

'Yes, it is. Unfortunately, it is not my idea. A client king of Rome had trouble with bandits – it must have been here or nearby. Josephus in his *History of the Jewish War* tells us what he did. You see, a man who reads history is often prepared.'

It took eight days for the preparations to be complete. In the end, available materials dictated that only one crane was built. None of the soldiers was in a hurry to volunteer – it was amazing how few of them admitted any skill with a bow – until Ballista announced that the men in the cage would get a cash incentive comparable to that given to those in a storming party at a siege.

Ballista had never suffered from a fear of heights. That was just as well. The cage rocked horribly as it was swung out over the void. The rockwall looked sharp and unforgiving. The valley was a long way down.

Not a sound came from the well-oiled winches, but inevitably the timber creaked and the ropes seemed to hum with tension as the cage began its jerky descent. Once, a gust of wind threatened to smash the flimsy wooden cage against the cliff face. Ballista clung grimly to the bars. The five soldiers with him cursed or prayed as the mood took them.

Ballista glanced down at the vertiginous drop. Ant-like figures were scurrying up the paths. With luck, the brigands in the caves would be too distracted by the soldiers arriving from above like a *deus ex machina* to interfere with the ones below.

The mouth of the first cave was a rough black oval in the pink-grey rocks. It was too dark to see far inside. Ballista half-saw movement. He ordered his men to shoot. Moving cautiously, they handed round the one guttering torch and lit the pitch-soaked rags tied around their arrow-heads. A word of command and the missiles streaked away. Before the thin, oily trails of smoke had dissipated, there were screams from the cave.

'Surrender,' Ballista yelled in Greek. 'Any old men, women, children will be spared.'

There was no answer. Ballista tried again in Latin. Still no answer. He indicated for another volley. He glanced down. The ascending troops still had a very long way to climb. Looking back, he noticed a faint glow in the cave. Something in there must be alight.

A figure emerged from the depths of the cave. Ballista indicated to his archers not to shoot. The man – in middle age, smartly dressed – looked contemptuously across at the soldiers. He had a drawn sword in his hand.

'Lay down your weapon,' Ballista shouted in Greek. 'Give yourselves up. Women, children, the elderly – all will be spared.'

The man actually laughed. 'Is nowhere safe from you Romans – not even the humblest village, the most remote cave?' He spoke in educated Greek. 'Even your own writers admit that you create a desert and call it peace.'

The incongruity of it struck Ballista – he was dangling

halfway down a cliff and a Jewish brigand was quoting Tacitus to him in perfect Attic Greek.

'Show yourself a man,' Ballista called. 'Give yourself up and save your loved ones.'

'I will show you I am a man.' He turned and shouted back into the cave in a language Ballista did not know – presumably Hebrew or Aramaic.

A woman came out, leading a boy, no more than ten. The man took the boy's hand. The woman fell to her knees, alternately clutching at the boy and the man's knees. Sobbing, she implored him in the language he had used.

The man spoke brusquely to her, waved her away. Reluctantly, she shuffled backwards.

The man ruffled the boy's hair. He talked tenderly to him. Then he seized the boy's chin, yanked it back. The sword flashed. It is not easy to cut someone's throat. The boy tried to wrench free. The man had to saw the blade across his neck repeatedly. Blood soaked the child, the man's arm. The boy writhed and then slumped. The man pitched the pathetic corpse out into the abyss. It fell, thumping into the cruel rocks.

Ballista and the soldiers stared in silent horror. This Jew was like no bandit they had ever encountered.

Once more the man shouted into the cave. He was answered by wailing. He shouted again, angrily.

The fire in the cave must have spread. This time, as the woman led out another, younger child, they were backlit by a hellish orange glow.

Ballista whispered to the soldier next to him: 'Shoot him.'

The man tried to force his wife away. She clung on. He tore her hands from the child. Still gripping her wrists, he swung her around, her sandals off the ground. One push and she was gone. The scream was cut off when she first hit the cliff.

Next to Ballista, the archer waited to get a clear shot.

The little boy – too young to understand – wobbled on immature legs. Allfather, he could only be two – the same age as Dernhelm. The father reached for him.

Intent on his murderous defiance, the man did not see the arrow coming. As he straightened up, it hit him square in the chest. He was pitched backwards, hands clutching at the fletching protruding from his body.

Ballista yelled up to the crew of the crane, some fifty foot above his head. 'Take us in!'

For long moments nothing happened. The child teetered, terribly near the drop. The fire burned in the cave. The cage jerked as the pulleys bit. It swung towards the cave mouth.

Ballista climbed up on the rail. He waited, judging the moment. He did not look down. A couple of paces away, he jumped.

The wind was knocked out of Ballista as his stomach hit the lip of the cave. His weight, that of his armour, began to pull him backwards. His fingers tore at the rocky ground, feet scrabbling a shower of stones. The child shied away from him – the little feet inches from oblivion.

Ballista hauled himself up, lunged across the cave mouth, grabbed the boy around the waist.

The wooden cage bumped against the rockface. The

soldiers leapt out. Drawing their swords, they went into the cave.

'Only the men,' Ballista shouted. 'Only the men.' He hugged the wailing child.

XVII

Julia was standing by a window in the imperial palace on the island at Antioch. It was nearing the end of a gentle spring night. The stars were not yet paling, but soon the eastern sky would start to lighten.

It was the night before the *ides* of May. It should have been more than warm enough to leave the windows open, yet there was a chill to the breeze blowing down the Orontes. Julia could feel it drying the sweat on her body.

She was tired. She took a last look around. The moonlight rendered the room almost two-dimensional, tried to make it unreal. But she knew it would always have a terrible reality in her memories. She would never be able to forget this night before the *ides* of May.

As quietly as she could, Julia crossed the room and slipped through the door. Outside, expensive lamps in niches gave a soft light. She ignored an imperial *a Cubiculo*. She blushed as she felt the chamberlain's eyes on her, sensed his prurient interest. Some way down the corridor, beyond the guards, Anthia, her maid, was asleep on a divan.

Pulling her veil over her head, trying to walk as if it was a normal night, as if nothing was out of the ordinary, Julia passed the Praetorian guards. She could feel their eyes on her too. Had the sounds travelled this far?

Anthia woke at once. 'Is everything all right?'

How could anything be all right after what had happened? 'Yes,' she said. 'It is time to go.'

The imperial palace was a labyrinth of passages. At this hour of the morning, they were largely deserted. Having been forced to live there with her *familia* for months, Julia knew the way without thinking. The two women walked in silence.

Could she have stopped it? Could anything have stopped it? Myths were full of gods and goddesses intervening at the last moment to save girls and nymphs from other deities. A few miles from here stood the very laurel tree that Daphne had been transformed into a moment before Apollo would have had her. But the gods do not exist. Anyway, even in the myths, they seemed only to save young virgins.

There were stories that did not involve any gods. Greek girls drowned themselves in rivers, stern Roman patriarchs cut down their own daughters, but neither situation applied to her. Her father was dead, and she had been trapped in a heavily guarded first-floor dining room with adjoining bedroom. And the threat had been to her children. Dead, she could not have protected them.

She had tried to talk to him, to reason with him. Quietus's father needed her husband to command their forces; Quietus himself needed Ballista to oversee the troops in the east, for his own safety. The odious young man, his hands pawing, had shrugged her arguments aside. His father would triumph in the west. The *imperium* reunited, any need for Ballista was gone. She should think of her future, of her children's future. She and they would need a protector when Ballista was dead. They needed protection now – an emperor's will was law.

Trying to fend off his hands, she had persevered. What if Macrianus did not win? The advance expedition to the west under Piso had gone completely wrong. First Piso had withdrawn to Thessaly, where he had declared himself emperor, then he had been killed by Valens, the governor of Achaea, who was loyal to Gallienus. What if Macrianus did not come back?

Quietus had just giggled. There was, he had said, a sculpture in Cilicia set up by the great Assyrian king Sardanapallus. It represented the fingers of the right hand snapping. The inscription on it read: 'Eat, drink, fuck; everything else is not worth this.'

For a moment Quietus had looked serious. Yes, if his father failed, it would be the end – the end of all things. Yet just as old Sardanapallus had taught how to live, so he showed how to die. He would gather all the things that had given him pleasure. The silks and jewels, the spices and inlaid furniture, he would have them heaped up. The women he had enjoyed and the horses he had ridden would be sacrificed on the pyre. Then, from a high place, he would throw himself into the conflagration.

Julia saw that Quietus was not joking. She was sure he was mad.

As he pulled her off the dining couch and led her to the room next door, he recited poetry:

'For I too am dust, though I have reigned over great Nineveh. Mine are all the food that I have eaten, and my wild indulgences and the sex that I have enjoyed; but those numerous blessings have been left behind.'

Should she have fought him? She had pushed him away from her face when he tried to force her to do something no decent Roman matron should do. He had slapped her hard and asked in a hiss if she would like him to order some Praetorians to come in and hold her down. There was a full *contubernium* of ten men on duty tonight; he was sure they would all like to take turns with her when he had finished. She had done what he wanted. Her reluctance seemed to increase Quietus's pleasure in the act.

She had asked him to put out the lamps. Quietus had laughed: even the most respectable Roman matron lets the lights burn so her husband can admire her on their first night. Surely she would not deny her emperor, her *dominus*, the pleasure of gazing at the shrine where he was worshipping? A shrine defiled by a barbarian, but now being reconquered for Rome.

Julia tried to push the physical from her mind. What should she do now? Of course, early Rome provided a stern *exemplum* – did it not always? Raped by one of the sons of Tarquinius Superbus, the noble Lucretia had killed herself. Why? She herself had said that only her body was defiled, her soul was not guilty. Her husband and her father had agreed; guilt fell not on the victim but on the rapist; the mind sins, not the body. It had made no difference. Lucretia was her own harshest judge. She absolved herself from guilt, but not from punishment. In the future, no unchaste woman would live, thanks to the precedent of Lucretia.

Julia had not tried to kill herself before being raped, and she had no intention of following the precedent of Lucretia now. Julia had submitted to protect her children. She was not going to stop protecting them now. She would just have to carry on as if nothing had happened.

Could she keep it quiet? Rhea, raped by a river-god, had killed herself in case her blush betrayed her to the mob as an adulteress. Ridiculous, thought Julia. It showed the weakness of Rhea, that she let her body betray her by blushing. And it indicated her stupidity – first to equate a woman who had been raped with an adulteress, and then to care what the unwashed plebs thought.

But what about Ballista? He would go mad – literally, mad – if he found out. Was he likely to? The slaves and freedmen of the imperial bedchamber would know. Ballista was highly unlikely to be talking to them. The story might spread amongst the Praetorians, if the two in the corridor had recognized her or one of the imperial servants named her in their hearing. That was far more dangerous; Ballista was one of their commanders. There was nothing she could do about that.

A sickening thought hit Julia. After abducting and raping their wives, the emperor Caligula used to enjoy an over-dinner discussion of their performance with their husbands. Might Quietus gloat in the same way? At first, before he had resorted to threats, when it was still oily seduction, he had tried to encourage her by saying that no one need know – it would be their secret. How much faith could be put in that?

When summoned to the dinner party, Julia had taken only one maid with her. Anthia was loyal. She would not talk. They could slip back into their own apartment. The rest of her household need not know.

Another sickening thought broke over Julia like a wave. *Was she in some way to blame?* Why had she taken only one maid? Had she been expecting it? Had she been already limiting the witnesses, or almost inciting the rape by her lack of care?

Of course it was not her own fault. She dismissed the disgusting idea with the ingrained self-control of her senatorial background. She had feared what might happen from the moment she had been ordered to dwell in the imperial palace while her husband was away. She had not shared her fears with Ballista. His barbarian nature would have driven him to spontaneous and disastrous actions. Daughters of the senatorial nobility of Rome did not give way to emotions; the icy self-control did not slip.

And when at last it was over, when Quietus put out the lamps and straight away fell asleep, why had she merely got dressed in the dark and left? Quietus had been lying on his back, naked, exhausted and defenceless. There must have been something that could have been used as a weapon somewhere in the room. He was unconscious. Why had she not tried to kill him?

Of course she knew the reason: she would have been caught and executed. The children would have lost her, possibly suffered themselves. Even as she framed the thoughts, she knew they were not the real reasons. She had been too shocked and scared to act. She had behaved exactly as a Roman man would expect a woman to behave. Unlike at the fall of Antioch, she had been weak, timorous, irresolute. Her behaviour disgusted her. Her disgust encompassed the world. This world created by men, this *imperium*, was an unfair world.

They were now at the side door, the one that led straight to Julia's private rooms. Anthia was waiting, clearly expecting her to say something. No words came. At last Julia spoke: 'I am no Lucretia. I must protect my children. Tell no one. This must be our secret.'

The waves, driven by the continual south-westerly, crashed and boomed against the harbour defences of Sebaste, the name given to the port area of Caesarea Maritima. Calgacus had walked the southern breakwater, followed it when it dog-legged to the north, all the way to the big light-house at the end. High on the battlements, the late-spring sun was warm on his shoulders. Calgacus remembered the bitter cold of that night back in the winter when he had nearly died on a Galilean hillside. Gods, but it was good to be warm and alive; a free man with time on his hands. He looked around.

To his left, out to sea, the lines of white-topped water rolled in relentlessly. One after another, they thundered against the rocks at the foot of the mole. The spray flew high, jewelled in the sunshine. They were powerful, these waves, but there was no malice in them. They might kill you, but only in an absence of mind. Unlike a winter storm, they would mean nothing by it.

To the Caledonian's right, the port was busy. Out in the roadstead, three big merchantmen were being taken in tow by open rowing boats. The first of them was already being drawn into the narrow, north-facing harbour mouth between the *pharos* where Calgacus stood and the harbour master's house at the tip of the other breakwater. Inside, another six or seven large roundships were tied to the several jetties. There were many more small coasting vessels or local fishing boats at rest or moving. Away in the innermost basin, an imperial *trireme* was moored.

It was good the port was busy. According to local reckoning, the sailing season began eleven days before the *ides* of March, the day marked by the two festivals of the birthday of the Tyche of Caesarea and the coming to the water of the goddess Isis to bless the sailors. That day had long passed. Now, just ten days before the *kalends* of June, even the most cautious would have to admit that the time when the seas could be sailed with some safety was fast approaching. It was good the port was busy, for, with the *imperium* divided into three, attacked on every frontier, and with civil war between the forces of Gallienus and those of Macrianus being fought out in the Balkans, nothing was certain.

Calgacus supposed he should be doing something, but there was no great urgency. Ballista, Maximus and the troops were away on their final mission in Syria Palestina. This task had no particular target, being no more than an armed march through Galilee as a show of strength. No opposition was expected. It was not so much that all the previous missions throughout the winter and spring, and the many they had killed, had destroyed the opposition as the fact the locals knew they were leaving. Why attack a dangerous enemy who is about to withdraw anyway?

The whole thing seemed futile to Calgacus. The Jews were united in their hostility to Roman rule. The Jewish brigands or rebels – how was one to tell them apart? – if they did not want to fight, they just merged back into the population. It was quite clear that no Jewish patriarch would hand over to the Romans even the most blood-stained murderer. The whole thing was a complete kick of the arse to nothing.

In two or three days, the expedition would return. Calgacus and the new secretary Hippothous had been left behind to put their affairs in Caesarea in order. Apart from a couple of minor things, they had done so. As soon as he was back, Ballista wanted to be free to march north, to Antioch and his family. Calgacus knew Ballista was worried about his *familia* living in the imperial palace.

Calgacus wondered what kind of reception they could look forward to in general. Macrianus father and son were in the west. Quietus, the only member of the imperial house in Antioch, particularly hated Ballista. Throughout his campaign in Galilee, Ballista had continuously ignored one detail of his imperial *mandata*. He had always spared the male children – only selling them into slavery, rather than killing them.

Soft-hearted, Ballista had always been soft-hearted, ever since he was a child, thought Calgacus. Still, it was part of his *humanitas*. That hard-to-define quality – it was part of what made Calgacus love him and, very strangely, it seemed to be part of what made rough, violent men follow him.

Calgacus was pleased that Ballista had taken the small Jewish boy he had rescued from the cave at Arbela into his household. Simon-bar-Joshua, he was called. Simon was a good-natured boy. Ballista had bought a young Jewess to look after him. Calgacus was pleased with that too. There was something about the way Rebecca moved, something about the look in her eye, that made you think what she would do for a man she liked. Calgacus felt a familiar stirring. But it was not at all the right moment. It was not yet noon. Almost all the brothels would still be shut. The one he liked, out by the north harbour, very reasonably priced, would certainly not be open.

To break his run of thoughts, Calgacus looked around, taking in the whole city. Caesarea Maritima: the dream of the old Jewish king Herod, the one they called the Great. Ballista had told Calgacus about Herod. A right murderous bastard he had been. Killed his relatives at the drop of a handkerchief. Put several of his sons to the sword at the merest whisper of suspicion. But he had been a political survivor. Having left it almost too late to abandon Mark Antony, he had spent the rest of his life cultivating the favour of his conqueror, the first emperor Augustus. Herod had called this new town Caesarea. Its port district was Sebaste, the Greek for 'Augustus'. The lighthouse above Calgacus's head was named after one of Augustus's stepsons, Drusus. Out beyond the harbour mouth, on two huge concrete bases rising from the seabed, six fine columns supported larger-than-life statues of Augustus and five of his close family. Inland, dominating the town and the harbour on its enormous manmade podium, was Herod's temple to the goddess Roma and the god Augustus. Its red-tiled roof and white columns were visible miles out to sea: no one could miss that.

All those ostentatious proofs of loyalty had kept Herod on his throne. But they had not shielded the Jewish client king from the sharp tongue of the first Roman emperor: 'I would rather be Herod's pig than his son.'

Calgacus decided to walk back along the quayside. Sometimes it was pleasant to walk unarmed through a peaceful crowd. It made a change, gave a teasing glimpse of how life might be different. Calgacus had no weapons on him, except the small knife at his belt – and, of course, the one always hidden in his right boot. He pulled his broad-brimmed travelling hat down on his head to keep off the sun. He whistled, tuneless but cheerful.

It was quite busy down on the waterfront. Bales, barrels, sacks and amphorae were dotted about as stevedores loaded produce from inland farms and unloaded more exotic goods from further afield. As you walked, you had to keep an eye out for the dockers in their leather harnesses hauling vessels into the right berths by sheer physical strength. Here and there at the back of the quay stood a few girls. They were of an age, not all that attractive. It was the cheaper end of the market; they were waiting for sailors for whom the voyage had been long. Such urgent needs would be taken care of standing in the inadequate privacy of one of the empty warehouses. All in all, there was more than enough to keep the *telones* busy. Whores paid taxes like merchants and everyone else.

It was the empty warehouses that got Calgacus thinking. Some were boarded up because they were clearly unsafe. In places, the whole edifice of the breakwater had shifted, tilting outwards, cracking the quayside, weakening the roofs and walls of the buildings. In other places, the warehouses had been shut because the berths in front of them had silted up so much that big seagoing ships could not tie up there. But others had no such physical reasons to be closed. Only a fall in trade could account for it.

When you looked, there were many more mooring places than there were boats.

As he strolled along, Calgacus found himself smiling. If Ballista were here, the boy would be busy calculating the best way to repair the breakwater, dredge the harbour, how much it would all cost. Calgacus, on the other hand, did not give a fuck. He liked looking at ships, but the people of Caesarea Maritima were nothing to him. As far as he was concerned, they could all go to Hades; fuck them.

As he walked past the inner basin, Calgacus saw a crowd at the top of the steps to the temple of Roma and Augustus. The sun on his back and the sight of the girls on the dockside, even though they were not that good-looking, had rekindled his urge. It would be an extravagance to have a girl at midday just on a whim. He would definitely want one tonight, and to pay for two in a day was too much. For distraction, he climbed the steps to see what was happening.

A military awards ceremony was taking place. The governor Achaeus sat on a *curule* chair in front of the temple. He was backed by his *consilium*, including the miserable-faced senator Astyrius. The governor himself was beaming. Presumably, handing out awards and promotions to those who had done well in the campaign against his Jewish subjects was congenial to him.

Off to one side, smiling in the sunshine, stood a crowd of those who had already received their awards. Calgacus thought it typical, in this as in almost everything in Rome: what you got was as much determined by who you were as what you had done. In the *imperium*, the social order had to be seen to be maintained.

First, towards the bottom of the steps, were those of lower rank. They proudly sported different awards: *phalerae*, the metal discs attached to their chest armour; torques around their necks; and *armillae* on their wrists. Above them stood a smaller group, with decorations available to all ranks. These men wore crowns on their heads; of oak leaf if they had saved another citizen's life, of gold for other acts of conspicuous courage. At the top, nearest to the governor and the military standards, were those of the rank of centurion or higher. Most of them grasped the ornamental spears in precious metals deemed suitable awards for brave officers. Just two wore the *Corona Muralis*, the mural crown. Few officers were first over the wall of an enemy position; fewer still lived to receive the crown with its golden walls. Ballista has one of those, thought Calgacus.

The ceremony had moved on from awards to promotions. Calgacus leant against a column to watch. Strangely, on a cloudless spring day, the stone was wet to the touch. Drops of condensation like tears ran down the fluted shaft of the column.

The herald announced the first promotion. A vacancy having arisen in Legio X Fretensis, according to the order of seniority, the *optio* Marcus Aurelius Marinus was to be awarded the rank of centurion. His years of distinguished service, good birth and adequate means fitted him for the duty.

A well-built, soldierly figure, Marinus stepped forward.

Up on the tribunal, Achaeus was all ready to hand over the vine-switch, symbol of the rank of centurion.

Just as Marinus came before the governor, unexpectedly, another man emerged from the ranks.

'*Dominus*,' he called up the steps. Everyone was silent at this interruption.

'By old-established laws, Marinus is debarred from holding rank in the Roman army. He is a Christian. He will not sacrifice to the emperors. By order of seniority, the post of centurion belongs to me.'

For a moment, Achaeus looked bewildered, then he laughed. 'This is not *Saturnalia*, soldier. Not a time for joking.'

Calgacus noticed that Marinus was standing stock-still.

'*Dominus*, I am not joking,' the soldier persisted. 'Marinus is a Christian. He joined the disgusting sect years ago. Ask him yourself.'

Still half-smiling, wishing to brush this off as a piece of ill-timed foolery, Achaeus turned to Marinus. There was something about the unnatural stillness of the *optio* that made the governor pause.

'Is . . . is it true?'

Marinus's jaw started working. He seemed to be reciting something under his breath. He drew a big, slightly ragged breath.

'I am a Christian.'

There was a collective gasp from the audience. A buzz of conversation flew up.

'Silence!' The herald had to bellow. 'Silence!'

'I am a Christian,' Marinus said again, a little louder.

'Nonsense,' said Achaeus. The governor still looked puzzled. 'Do not be ridiculous. How can you be? Soldiers have to worship the standards and the imperial portraits at least once a year.'

'I have sinned. God will be my judge.'

'You have a distinguished war record. Christians do not kill.'

'I have sinned. God will be my judge.' Marinus repeated the phrase as if drugged.

Achaeus looked flustered. This scandal, treasonous and divisive, was not at all what he wanted for this ceremony.

'Marinus, you are not well. You have been through a hard campaign – the constant threat of death, terrible privations, constant bad weather. You are not in your right mind. I grant you three hours to reconsider. Sit and reflect quietly. Talk to men of sense.'

Marinus did not reply.

'You are not under arrest. No one is to harass or detain you. Return here in three hours with a better answer.'

Mechanically, Marinus saluted, turned, marched down the steps and pushed into the crowd of onlookers.

Calgacus moved after him.

Marinus had turned into the *agora*. It was crowded. At first Calgacus could not see him. The Caledonian did nothing precipitous, nothing that would draw attention. He just strolled on, looking this way and that – a man from out of town, travelling hat on head, taking in the sights.

An eddy in the people, and there was Marinus. The *optio* was with another man: older, bearded, a civilian. The newcomer was leading Marinus by the hand, talking to him, low and earnest.

Calgacus followed. They crossed the breadth of the *agora*. They negotiated the many stalls selling various goods. They walked by the imposing facades of the temples of Apollo and Demeter, the shrines of Isis and Serapis, the sanctuaries of Tiberius and Hadrian.

The older man led Marinus out to the north-east. The centre of town was set out in regular, Hippodamian blocks. It was easy for Calgacus to trail them inconspicuously. He thought maybe he should become a *frumentarius*.

After they had been walking some time, they came to the Caporcotani Gate, which led to the Great Plain and the hills of Galilee beyond. Calgacus wondered if Marinus was going to make a run for it. But as soon as they had passed under the gate, the civilian led him off to the right into the suburbs.

Outside Herod's wall, there was no street plan. Lanes and alleys twisted and turned. Calgacus had to keep closer, but he had no great problems staying both in touch and unnoticed.

Marinus and his companion came to an unremarkable door. They knocked and were admitted by a burly-looking man. Calgacus waited at the street corner. This was a poorish suburb. The buildings were mainly low, a bit shabby. The walls of the amphitheatre loomed over the area. Calgacus smiled. If he was right and this was a Christian meeting place, the authorities would not have to drag them far to meet their fate.

Calgacus walked to the door and knocked.

'Yes?' The burly man looked wary.

'I am a Christian,' said Calgacus.

The man just looked at him.

'From out of town,' added Calgacus. 'From Ephesus, just docked.'

Still the man said nothing.

'Appian, son of Aristides, who bore witness during the persecution under Valerian, told me where to find you.' It was a shot in the dark that the man would have heard of the most renowned of the Christians, whom Ballista had killed while they were in Ephesus. Calgacus had no idea if Appian was likely to have known the location of the Christians' meeting place in Caesarea. At any moment he might be needing the knife in his boot, be testing the limits of the sect's pacifism.

The man nodded, pulled back the door. 'The Lord be with you, brother. How can we help?'

'And with your spirit,' said Calgacus, pulling off his hat. 'Nothing too much, just a chance to pray in peace.'

'Come in the love of God. Please take a place at the rear. Our pious bishop Theotecnus is at the altar counselling one of our brothers in the time of his trial.'

Calgacus did as he was told. He had seen and heard Christians pray. They used different styles. But some knelt and kept their heads down. That seemed to fit the bill. From under his brows, he had a good view.

The man he now knew was the Christians' archpriest was standing in front of the altar facing the soldier. The priest leant across and drew aside Marinus's military cloak. He pointed to the sword. Turning, he picked up a book – not a papyrus roll, but a new-style codex. He placed it on the altar in front of Marinus.

'Choose,' said Theotecnus.

With no hesitation, Marinus stretched out his hand and grasped the book.

'Hold fast then,' said Theotecnus. 'Hold fast to God. May you obtain what you have chosen, inspired by him. Go in peace.'

The Christians embraced, and Marinus left.

Possibly a little too quickly afterwards, Calgacus followed. The man on the door gave him an odd look but did not try to stop him. Maybe he put it down to the visitor's prurient desire to see what happened to the martyr-to-be.

Calgacus caught sight of Marinus reentering the town at the Caporcotani Gate. The *optio*, looking neither left nor right, went to a house in the north of Caesarea, near where the aqueducts enter. He stayed inside for some time. Calgacus assumed it was Marinus's lodgings. He waited outside. It was no hardship. It was a nice day.

Eventually Marinus came out and set off south-west. He walked purposefully. His mind on his fate, the love of God or some such, he was easy for Calgacus to shadow. As they got near the *agora*, people began to point, whisper to each other and openly follow. Indeed, quite a throng trailed Marinus as he reached the steps to the temple of Roma and Augustus.

Marinus stopped. The crowd milled, taking care not to get too close to the prodigy who was both a soldier and a confessed Christian.

'Marcus Aurelius Marinus,' a herald roared. 'Your time of grace is over. Present yourself to the tribunal.'

With no outward fear, Marinus stepped forward.

You had to hand it to these Christian bastards, thought Calgacus. It was impressive. It could turn the heads of some of the plebs.

On his *curule* chair, the governor was not smiling now. Behind him, Astyrius and the other members of his *consilium* were equally stony-faced.

Calgacus would not have been alone in noting that, this time, Marinus did not salute. The Caledonian knew why.

Back in the church, Marinus had made his choice: Christian, not soldier.

'Marcus Aurelius Marinus, our magnanimity has given you time to come to your senses.' Achaeus's voice was cold. 'What do you say?'

'I am a Christian.'

'So be it,' snapped Achaeus. He waved some guards forward. They seized Marinus. They stripped him of his sword belt, his cloak, his boots, anything which denoted him as a soldier.

'You will be taken to the south necropolis. You will be beheaded. No one is to give you burial. Your corpse will lie by the road for the dogs to eat.'

Marinus betrayed no emotion.

'There is no reason for delay,' Achaeus announced. 'Take him away.'

Calgacus did not need to exercise any caution in following this time. A centurion and ten legionaries, the condemned man's *commilitiones*, escorted Marinus. Behind them came about thirty civilians – those who especially disliked Christians or particularly enjoyed a public execution, or maybe just had nothing better to do.

Calgacus did not go all the way. He turned off to the right and entered the empty theatre by the city walls. Once he had climbed to the top of the seating, he had a good view over the rear wall.

Sure enough, the centurion halted his men just beyond the town walls, as soon as they reached the first tombs of the necropolis. With a minimum of fuss, a blindfold was put on Marinus.

By the side of the road, the Christian knelt down. He

leant forward to expose the back of his neck. The blade of a sword glittered in the spring sunshine. The *spatha* descended. It was not a good strike. Blood everywhere, but the neck was not severed. Marinus was pitched full length. He was writhing. The executioner had to steady him with a boot on his back and a firm grip on his hair. Four, five times, the *spatha* chopped down until the head came away.

The soldiers left him lying by the side of the road. Without a backwards glance, they marched off into town. Some of the civilians remained standing there for a while, but soon Marinus's remains were unattended.

High up in the theatre, Calgacus made himself as comfortable as he could and settled down to wait. The night after Ballista had killed Appian in Ephesus, someone, presumably Christians, had come and stolen the body – well, seemingly, torn it apart and taken bits of it. Calgacus thought it was worth keeping an eye on what was left of Marinus.

Travellers came and went on the Ascalon road. In wagons, on donkeys, mules, horses, on foot, they passed, usually in groups, occasionally on their own. Some stopped to look at the fresh corpse, the blood already draining into the dirt, but most did not.

The waiting did not bother Calgacus – he could happily do nothing for hours on end – but he was getting very hungry. Tonight, despite the cost, he would treat himself to a really good meal before a girl – maybe that new Greek girl Chloe: she had a look in her eye, made him laugh.

The sun began to sink towards the sea. The western sky was a blaze of purples, blues and reds. The travellers had gone from the road. If nothing happened before dark, Calgacus would have to go down and creep closer.

All that was to be heard was the sound of the surf. It might have lulled Calgacus had his hunger not been so sharp. He was getting ready to move when the file of men appeared from the town.

At their head was a tall figure. From within the folds of his cloak could be seen a flash of shimmering white toga and, amazingly, a broad purple stripe. The man was a senator. It was Astyrius, and he was trailed by four servants.

They reached the dead man. At Astyrius's gesture, the servants spread a magnificent, costly robe on the ground by the remains. Astyrius reverently picked up Marinus's gory head and placed it on the robe. The servants lifted the body to join it.

The robe was carefully folded. Astyrius himself helped shoulder the burden. The illegal cortege moved off, cross-country to the east.

Well, well, thought Calgacus, who would have thought it? As he walked stiffly down the steps, he wondered if his were the only eyes that had been watching. 'Christians to the lion,' he thought.

XVIII

Macrianus the Elder, *Comes Sacrarum Largitionum et Praefectus Annonae*, holder of *maius imperium*, father of the Augusti, washed the blood off his hands. A servant took away the golden bowl; another handed him a towel. They may well be on campaign, somewhere in the wilds between Thrace and Illyricum, but standards had to be maintained.

The sacrifices had told Macrianus nothing. The entrails had been hard to read, ambiguous. Surely the gods would not abandon him now? He had never yet done anything without consulting them, checking they approved. All his life had been devoted to doing their work. Not even the most malevolent could deny he had been zealous in persecuting the atheist Christians. And had he not sworn to all the natural gods – in his heart, not just with his lips – that when he had done with the followers of the crucified Jew he would turn on and eradicate the Jews themselves? Let the godless emigrate beyond the frontiers, for if they remained they would die.

Yes, Macrianus had laboured long on behalf of the *Pax Deorum*, the relationship between man and gods that had always sustained the *imperium* of the Romans. Dangerous choices had been faced, difficult decisions made. But he had been well rewarded, as his piety deserved. His rise from obscurity to riches and power, the elevation of his sons to the throne – both clearly made manifest the favour of the gods.

Macrianus knew he had done nothing but good, had done nothing wrong. True, his conscience initially had been troubled by the idea of removing Valerian. But the old emperor had been too hesitant. He had stood in the way of the work of the gods. Even so, it had been a relief to Macrianus when he received the explicit approval of Jupiter Optimus Maximus in a dream.

The opaque entrails meant nothing. The gods would not abandon Macrianus now, not in the middle of a campaign against the godless tyrant Gallienus. As soon as news of Valerian's capture had reached Gallienus, even while his aged father was being dragged around Cilicia, Gallienus had rescinded the edict against the Christians. It was said he had gone so far as to give them back their unholy meeting places and burial grounds. There was no chance the gods could favour such a man over Macrianus and his sons.

But if the signs from the heavens were mixed, they were not more so than those on earth. The advance expedition to the west led by Macrianus's old friend Piso Frugi had been a disaster. First, in the backwater of Thessaly, of all places, had come Piso's usurpation – what evil daemon could have prompted the fool to that? – then his death at the hands of Valens, Gallienus's governor of Achaea. The situation had somewhat recovered. The troops under Valens, a bunch of auxiliaries as headstrong and unreliable as all soldiers were these days, had mutinied. They had proclaimed Valens emperor. The unwanted eminence had lasted only a short time. *Frumentarii* sent by Macrianus's loyal *Princeps Peregrinorum* Censorinus had abruptly ended the ephemeral reign.

Not everything had gone wrong in the aftermath of the Pisonian debacle. Byzantium had remained loyal to the regime and it afforded the Macriani father and son and their main army a safe crossing from Asia.

As they advanced west into Europe, the mixed blessings had continued. It was a disappointment that Valentinus, the acting governor of both Moesia Superior and Inferior, had kept the provinces in the faction of Gallienus. But to balance that, the four legions stationed in the provinces of Pannonia Superior and Inferior had declared for Macrianus and Quietus. Macrianus the Elder was quite aware that this had not been prompted by love for his sons. The Pannonian legionaries were still smarting at the defeat and deaths of their candidates for the purple – Ingenuus and Regalianus – by the forces of Gallienus. They would have probably followed a trained monkey against Gallienus. Still, it gave an impression of momentum, and it was a useful addition to the expedition. When the Macriani reached Serdica, they found two large *vexillationes* from Legiones I and II Adiutrix had marched down to join them. There had been scenes of celebration as these newcomers mingled with smaller *vexillationes* from all four Pannonian legions who were already serving with the army. The four thousand newcomers roughly replaced those lost to sickness, straggling and desertion on the long march from Antioch.

The events of the day before struck Macrianus as

ambiguous at best. A couple of hours' march west out of Serdica, and the enemy cavalry had appeared. It was light cavalry, and there were a lot of them; mainly Dalmatians, but also quite a few Moors, with their distinctive long, braided hair. They had surrounded the marching column, driven in the cavalry outriders. They had not killed all they could. They had ridden close, up and down the line, calling on their opponents to return to the oaths they had once sworn to the rightful emperor Gallienus. None of the marching men had gone over. Instead they had bellowed out a flow of obscenities, mainly directed at Gallienus's relationships with the barbarian girl Pippa and the philosopher Plotinus. They shouted that he defiled his mouth playing the Phoenician to the former, and all his body acting as a wife to the latter.

The military men, the Prefect of Cavalry Ragonius Clarus well to the fore, had put a positive interpretation on it all. A cavalry skirmish signified nothing. Macrianus's riders had been caught unaware, but not one soldier had left the ranks. Morale remained as high as ever.

Macrianus acknowledged he was not a military man. He always learnt what he could about any units under his command, but he was not at home in the field. Yet, even so, he was concerned at the ease with which the cavalry had given way. He half regretted leaving Ballista with Quietus – may the gods hold their hands over the boy; unlike so many, the barbarian spoke his mind. Ragonius Clarus and Censorinus had combined to allay Macrianus's apprehensions. After dark yesterday, the *Princeps Peregrinorum* had announced that he would go through the camp and gauge the mood of the men before going beyond the palisade and sounding out the loyalty of the enemy pickets. If anyone was considering desertion, it was likely to be the enemy. He had promised to take care, as much care as Dolon had taken in the *Iliad*. Macrianus had wondered at the inappositeness of the reference. Censorinus had not been seen since.

As the butchers dragged away the carcases of the sacrifices, Macrianus took up his walking stick and slowly made his way to where the imperial standards hung limp in the early morning air. His son Macrianus the Younger sat straight and true on a magnificent black charger. The boy had come on well since his elevation to the throne. He wore the purple and the radiate crown as if born to them. There was a nobility to his aquiline nose and high brow, a hint of hard service to the *Res Publica* in the slight bags under the eyes. If he chose occasionally to relax from the cares of empire by making small wooden toys, there had been many emperors with far more damaging pastimes.

A quiet gelding was led out. Macrianus's lame leg made riding a trial. Stoically, he let himself be helped into the saddle. Once there, he reached out and briefly gripped his son's hand. Ragonius Clarus rode up, saluted and asked permission to signal the advance.

Macrianus surveyed the scene. A broad upland valley, the road from Serdica to Naissus running through it, almost due west, a small, unnamed stream alongside the road on its left. There was a low mist over the water and, about a mile away, the enemy. A large force, but no bigger than the army with Macrianus – about thirty thousand men. It was drawn up conventionally: heavy infantry several ranks deep in the centre, bowmen behind, some light infantry with slings and javelins in front, cavalry out on the wings. The standards made a brave show all along its front. The imperial standard was not there. Gallienus had not come himself. He was further west, preoccupied with getting revenge on Postumus for the death of his son. The army was commanded by Aureolus. The red Pegasus on white banner of Gallienus's Prefect of Cavalry flew on their right wing. It was said Aureolus was supported by several leading *protectores*: his near-namesake and fellow Danubian Aurelian, *Manu ad Ferrum*; Theodotus the Egyptian; Memor the African; the siege engineer Bonitus, and the Italian Domitianus, who implausibly claimed descent from the Flavian dynasty.

The army of the Macriani was virtually a reflection of its enemy. Stationed with the thousand troopers of the Equites Singulares just behind the centre of the infantry line, Macrianus the Elder had a good view from the vantage point of his horse. Everything seemed in order. His son was looking at him. He nodded. Macrianus the Younger told Ragonius Clarus to carry on. The latter gave the command to advance.

Centurions passed the order on, *bucinatores* sounded their instruments, standard bearers got ready to lift.

Ragonius Clarus was shouting something over the din: 'When the mist burns off, the sun will still be low, straight in the eyes of Aureolus's men.' Macrianus was finding it hard to listen: something was wrong with the unit directly in front. It was a *vexillatio* from Legio XI Claudia Pia Fidelis. The detachment, originally five hundred men, now considerably less, had been sent east from its base at Durostorum in Moesia Inferior for Valerian's Persian campaign. The standard bearer in charge of the *vexillum* had pulled the standard from the ground with no problem, but as he began to walk forward, the shaft tangled his legs and he lost his balance. The *vexillum* tottered and fell to the ground. The men of Legio XI halted.

Ragonius Clarus had seen what had happened. He stopped talking.

A terrible omen, thought Macrianus.

Ragonius Clarus spurred his horse forward. He was bellowing: '*Vexillarius*, pick the fucking thing up!' It was too late. Along the line, those unable to see what had caused the standard to go down drew the same conclusion: surrender. One after another, standards were lowered. Units halted. Legionaries, auxiliaries, barbarian allies put down their weapons. They stretched out their arms to the other side.

'Quick, this way.' Ragonius Clarus was tugging at the bridle of Macrianus's horse. 'The Pannonians are not surrendering. Quick, to the left.'

Macrianus looked around wildly to see that his son was safe. He was with them. They thundered across the ground.

'All is not lost,' Ragonius Clarus called over his shoulder. 'We can fall back on the camp.'

'All is not lost,' said Ragonius Clarus.

Outside, the setting sun was a huge orange ball. Long shadows stretched across the camp, played on the wall of the imperial tent. There was less than an hour to darkness.

Macrianus the Elder indicated that the Prefect of Cavalry should continue to address the much reduced *consilium*.

'We have nearly twelve thousand men: six thousand

Pannonian legionaries, five thousand of Sampsigeramus's bowmen from Emesa, about half mounted, and a thousand Equites Singulares. A sizable and useful force.'

All true, thought Macrianus, but our opponents now have nearly fifty thousand men under arms. He did not let these calculations affect the attentive and quietly confident set of his face. The officers were shaken. Macrianus the Younger looked scared. Macrianus smiled reassuringly at his son.

'We have plenty of supplies. The camp is well fortified. We could withstand a siege,' continued Ragonius Clarus.

Which would merely delay things for a time, thought Macrianus. There is no army that will come and raise the siege. We stripped the east bare to raise this force. We have no allies waiting in the wings. And it is not even as if Gallienus were leading the besieging army himself. In that case, almost anything might have happened – a stray arrow kills the emperor, or supplies fail, plague breaks out, the men get sick of hard labour and privations, from one motive or another Gallienus's own troops strike him down . . . Sieges are dangerous times for emperors. But none of that could happen. Gallienus was safe in the west.

Outside, a man was shouting, near the imperial tent.

'Alternatively,' said Ragonius Clarus, 'we can break out. A night march to Serdica, then east. Byzantium is one of the best-fortified cities in the world. It would hold up Aureolus while we regroup further east.'

Other voices had joined the man shouting.

Macrianus was no soldier, but he knew a night march was a desperate venture, one that might destroy an army all unaided.

One of the Equites Singulares burst into the tent. *'Dominus!'* Ignoring the young emperor, he spoke directly to the father. 'The Pannonians are mutinying. They are tearing the imperial portraits from the standards.'

Age cast aside, barely using his stick, Macrianus burst from the tent. The trooper was right: there was an ugly crowd around the standards of Legio II Adiutrix. The images of the young emperors were in the dust. Macrianus walked boldly up and halted a few paces from the mutineers. The noise dropped to a low, menacing muttering. Macrianus was pleased when, unbidden, his son came to stand at his shoulder. The boy was no coward. The show of unity might help. If ever they had needed help, it was now. Macrianus would have offered a brief prayer, but there was no time.

'Commilitiones.' Macrianus's voice carried well, betrayed no panic. *'Commilitiones,* this is not how the men of Legio II Adiutrix behave. Would the men who crushed the Batavians, ventured beyond the ocean to conquer Britain, drove the Dacian king from his throne, and sacked the Parthian capital of Ctesiphon have behaved like this? The legionaries of Legio II Adiutrix do not mutiny like a bunch of eastern auxiliaries or Arab tribesmen.'

Macrianus was not sure if he was winning them over. At least they had not offered any violence so far.

'You have taken the *sacramentum* to my sons. We have paid you the donative we promised. My son campaigns with you. He will lead you home to your base at Aquincum in triumph. Things look difficult today, but with the gods holding their hands over us, all will be well. *Commilitiones,* it is time to prove yourselves true to the title of your legio: *Pia fidelis.*' He repeated, 'Loyal and faithful,' and stopped. He had no more words.

A centurion stepped out of the crowd. He spoke deliberately, with an accent from the northern frontier. 'You are not our *commilitiones*. You are not soldiers at all. It is true, you have not treated us badly. But you betrayed our brothers in the legions when you betrayed the old emperor Valerian. Treachery turns on itself. The gods move slow, but in the end their power is shown.'

The echo of Euripides in the soldier's Latin, the invocation of the gods, silenced Macrianus. No, he wanted to say, that is all wrong, you do not understand, the gods approved of what happened to Valerian, the gods want Gallienus overthrown. Until today, they have given manifest signs of their favour. But it was all too complicated. He knew then it was hopeless.

Looking around, Macrianus saw that Ragonius Clarus had gone. Macrianus and his son were alone. It was hopeless.

But still he had to try. 'Do what you like with me, but have pity on my son. He is very young. None of this is his fault.'

'What can we do?' The centurion sounded genuinely apologetic. 'The camp is surrounded. It is not down to us. Censorinus brought word that Aureolus wants you dead. He has put a price on your heads.'

The treachery of Censorinus hardly made any impression on Macrianus. A price on their heads. It meant exactly that. Decapitation, their heads paraded before Gallienus, their bodies denied burial. Somehow he had to stop the mutilation of his beautiful son. He could not think of the boy's soul wandering hopeless for eternity.

The muttering was rising in volume. Macrianus had to act quickly.

'You said yourself we had done you no harm. Let us take our own lives, die like the Romans of old. There is money hidden under the floor of the tent. Try to prevent them mutilating my son's body.'

The centurion nodded. He rapped out some orders. Some of his men went inside, others formed a ring around the big purple tent. Close by, the noise of revolution swelled.

'I am afraid you must hurry,' the centurion said.

Macrianus turned to his son. There were tears on the boy's face. He was making no noise, trying to be brave. Macrianus folded him in his arms. He pressed his lips to his neck, breathing in the smell of clean, fresh sweat, the smell of his son. He kissed him on the eyes, the cheeks, the lips.

The noise was growing. Macrianus somehow forced himself to let go of his son and step back. He drew his son's eagle-headed ornamental sword.

'Use mine. It will be sharper.' The centurion handed it over.

Macrianus took it. He looked at his son, and he knew he could not do this thing.

'You want me to do it?'

Macrianus gave the sword back to the centurion.

'Who first?'

Macrianus thought of watching his son die. He imagined his son watching him die, the boy left alone, terrified, waiting. 'My son.'

Macrianus stepped forward. He and his son kissed for the last time. Macrianus stepped back.

* * *

In the imperial palace at Antioch, no one was sure if the *consilium* had started. Ballista was watching Quietus – not so as to attract attention – and so was everyone else. Titus Fulvius Iunius Quietus Augustus, *Pius Felix*, *Pater Patriae*, had ordered a large painting of Alexander the Great by Aetion hung in the audience hall. All his attention was on that.

Quietus's lips moved almost soundlessly. Everyone said he had been behaving oddly since the news had come about his father and brother. The following day Ballista had reached Antioch from Syria Palestina. When Ballista reported to Quietus, the emperor had given the impression that he was trying to look clean through him to see someone else. On their few meetings since, Quietus's gaze had slid off Ballista like water off a waxed cloak. Indeed, anyone remotely connected to the court had been acting strangely since the news from the west.

None had been acting more strangely than Julia. She had already shifted the *familia* out of the palace and back to the house in the Epiphania district before Ballista arrived. Her welcome had been reserved and, unexpectedly, physically reserved too. Afterwards she had made a comment about men marking their territory. She had said it on similar occasions before, as a joke, but this time it had a sharp edge. That side of things had improved a little since, but things generally were different, strained. Ballista wondered if someone had told her about the Persian girl Roxanne in Cilicia.

Quietus stopped muttering. He cocked his head to one side, eyes still on the painting. Allfather, thought Ballista, does he think Alexander is talking to him? It was a good moment to look away. It was a reduced *consilium*. Quietus's father and brother and their once-devoted supporter Piso were dead. Censorinus and Ragonius Clarus had deserted. The former had been appointed one of Gallienus's Praetorian Prefects, the latter told to retire into private life. But others from the east were missing. Trebellianus had withdrawn into the mountains of Cilicia Tracheia. Similarly, safe behind the deserts of Arabia, another governor, Virius Lupus, had not replied to the summons. Mussius Aemilianus, prefect of Egypt, had had himself declared emperor. As he was commander of quite sizeable forces and in control of the majority of the grain supply of Rome, his was not a hopeless revolt, but he would need allies. Obviously, Quietus would not be among them.

There were only two new faces on the dais. Quietus's nonentity of a cousin Cornelius Macer had been hurriedly appointed not only *Comes Sacrarum Largitionum et Praefectus Annonae* but *Princeps Peregrinorum* as well. Presumably the loyalty that blood might bring had outweighed any considerations of ability. Much more competent, standing near Ballista, was the tall red-haired figure of Rutilus, the new Prefect of Cavalry.

'Those who wear the likeness of Alexander in either gold or silver are aided in all they do,' Quietus said suddenly. 'My father often said that.' He pointed at the governor of Syria Phoenice. 'Cornicula, include that in your verse panegyric of them.'

Annius Cornicula bowed.

Now that Quietus seemed to be to some extent with them, unbidden, the senior Praetorian Prefect Maeonius Astyanax started talking. '*Dominus*, there are reports, completely credible, that Odenathus is assembling his forces in Palmyra. Supplies have been stockpiled on the road west to Emesa. He is getting ready to march against us.'

Quietus put his head in his hands. 'What can be done?' His tone suggested nothing.

'*Dominus*,' Maeonius Astyanax continued, 'it can be prevented. I have met Odenathus. The two of us got on well. It is true he is avaricious. We have money. Let me go as an ambassador. With adequate funds, I can stop the Lion of the Sun, turn his bellicose attention back to the Sassanids. It would be a good time to attack them. Not only did the Persians suffer defeats last year, but Shapur faces revolts from subjects to the east near the Caspian Sea. If Odenathus attacks now, he may get as far as the Sassanid capital of Ctesiphon almost unopposed.'

'Let it be so.' Quietus looked up, brighter. 'Should your mission fail, we will rout this decadent oriental anyway.' He jabbed a finger at one of the governors standing in front of him. 'Pomponius Bassus, you have four legions in Cappadocia, auxiliaries too. You will raise more men. Hire Albanians, Iberians, Cadusii, nomads, Alani or whatever, from beyond the Caucasus. Raise an army fifty thousand-strong. Lots of cavalry. Fast-moving. You will move with all speed down the Euphrates. You will make Arete your base, then strike at Palmyra from the east. Odenathus will have to scurry back to meet you. We will be hard on his heels. With Odenathus caught between our armies, we will win a famous victory in the desert. The so-called Lion of the Sun will grovel at our feet. It will do him no good. We will serve him as Aureolus served our family.'

Quietus again relapsed into a preoccupied silence.

His face very still, Pomponius Bassus intoned the ritual words. 'We will do what is ordered, and at every command we will be ready.'

No one else gave any indication of what they were thinking. There were just two legions in Cappadocia, both under strength; a handful of auxiliaries. As Ballista knew only too well, the king of Georgian Iberia had marched with Shapur to the capture of Valerian – would he ever forget the cell in Carrhae? The Alani crossing the Caucasus mountains had long been one of the keenest fears not only of the Roman *imperium* but of every people living to the south, even of the Sassanid Persians.

Ballista followed Quietus's gaze to Aetion's painting. Alexander was standing in a bedchamber. His new bride, Roxanne, half reclined on the bed. Small *erotes* prepared her, tugging her clothes off. Others – lots of them – cavorted everywhere. Wings beating, they flew up to the ceiling, clambered over the top of the bed. On the floor they were playing with Alexander's armour. Even in bed with a new, beautiful woman, Alexander kept his weapons to hand, thought Ballista. Allfather knew what Quietus was thinking.

'Antioch on the Orontes,' said Quietus. 'Metropolis of Syria. We will turn her into an impregnable fortress. Let Odenathus come. Or Aureolus, or Gallienus himself. They will break their armies on the defences of Antioch the invulnerable.' He seemed to have already forgotten the happy fantasy of victory over Odenathus at the gates of Palmyra.

'*Dominus*,' said Ballista, 'Antioch is almost indefensible. The walls up on Mount Silpius are overlooked by natural rock. The city is not safe. Antioch has fallen to the Persians twice in a few years.'

Quietus glowered at him. He started to say something then stopped. He looked away.

'*Dominus*' – the client king Sampsigeramus spoke good Latin, if with an effeminate lisp – 'my city of Emesa is devoted to your cause – no city more so. No place in the east has better walls or other defences. We have supplies, money. Move the court and the army there. When Pomponius Bassus strikes from Arete, you will be on hand to ride out and defeat the upstart Odenathus.'

Ballista had to admire the way Sampsigeramus both hid his own desperation and played up to Quietus's fantasies.

'Whatever, whatever.' Quietus had lapsed into miserable introspection. 'What does it matter? Why not Emesa? We will go there. We will go there straight away. Give the necessary orders.' He looked up at the huge cedar beams of the roof. 'They mutilated them, you know. Sent their heads to Gallienus. They can never know peace.'

XIX

Quietus's imperial court and army were moving down to Emesa. They were six days out of Antioch, strung out for miles along the road running through the Mere of Apamea. The scenery here was unusual for the east: lush water meadows and wild reed beds as far as the mountains on either side.

Ballista called Maximus to him, leant close, kept his voice low. When he had finished, Maximus asked him to say it all again in case he had somehow misunderstood.

'Yes, you are to desert, slip away through the wetlands to the east. There are only a couple of miles to cross, but take care. In a rare moment of clarity, Quietus has ordered a large number of mounted patrols to sweep the rear and both flanks for stragglers and deserters. There are villages in the hills, so there have to be reasonable paths across them. Apparently, the hills are only about fifteen miles wide here. On the other side, you will strike the Chalcis ad Bellum to Apamea road: take the turning south from a village called Telmenissos. This will bring you to the upland road, through places called Theleda and Occaraba, to Palmyra. When you get there, find Haddudad. It should not be difficult; by all accounts, the ex-mercenary has risen fast in his new *patria*.'

Ballista smiled. 'The two of us saved Haddudad's life at the fall of Arete: call in the debt. Get Haddudad to arrange a private audience with Odenathus. It has to be done in secret, otherwise news will get to Quietus, and that will be the end of me and the *familia*. When you see Odenathus, give him this sealed message.' Ballista passed over a small package. 'Hide it in your scabbard. It is well wrapped in oilcloth, so should not come to any harm, not even if it gets wet.'

Maximus made to interject. Ballista held his hand up. 'No, it is better if you do not know what it says. If you are captured, you can play the simple messenger. Quietus will still kill you, but possibly not torture you for quite as long first. Apart from handing over the letter, the vital thing that you have to do is to make absolutely certain Odenathus knows which of the towers of Emesa is the so-called Tower of Desolation. You remember it? It is the tall, thin one at the extreme south-east of the defences. If Odenathus does not already know it, Haddudad will.'

Maximus nodded, thinking it over. 'Sure, if I can get away, we all could.'

Ballista looked tempted but shook his head. 'No, Dernhelm is too young, and Julia is a woman. I have heard of too many would-be fugitives from the *imperium* who have been caught because they were slowed down by women or children. Anyway, there is still something I have to do.'

It was mid-afternoon when Maximus rode away. It was a good time to choose, in any army, no matter how disciplined – and this one was not particularly disciplined – there is always confusion when it comes to pitching camp. There was nothing furtive about him as he set off. He rode purposefully east, away from the army. The very set of his shoulders suggested a scout or suchlike on official duty.

When he had gone a short distance he reined in and dismounted. Having hobbled his horse, he went behind a low clump of marsh plants, pulled his trousers down and squatted. As he pretended to relieve himself, he scanned everything. No sign of pursuit, and no sign of men up ahead. After a time he set off again.

Not far along the way, it happened. A problem with travelling wet lowlands was always the finite number of paths passable to men on horseback. Those that existed were often elevated and exposed. No chance of slinking along; you had to go where the track took you. Maximus rode through one of the infrequent stands of trees and came out on to a raised, open grassy area. There, scattered, taking their ease, were the men and horses of a whole *turma* of cavalry.

Maximus wondered if he should try and talk his way through. He was good at talking. Back home, he had not been known as Muirtagh of the Long Road for his travelling. Maximus kicked his heels into his horse's flanks. He thundered across the clearing. A standing trooper tried to block his way. Of its own volition, the horse skittered around him. The thirty-man patrol was dismounted. Maximus was in the saddle. It gave him a few moments' headstart.

Maximus bent low over his mount's neck, urging it on. Great clods of mud cartwheeled up behind as they fled. The path ran straight; it had to be manmade. It was raised high above the marsh. The tall, tall reeds only reached to the horse's belly. They had to be visible for miles. Behind, the roar of the chase was loud. Maximus had thrown away his shield. Crooning into his animal's ears, he raced on.

At last the track dipped down almost to the surface of the fen. It turned gently, first right then left. The feathery heads of the reeds soared high above them. Maximus hauled the horse to a standstill. Leaping down, he feverishly untied his kit bag. He parted the reeds to the left with his arm, then threw the bag out of sight. Quickly, he fastened the reins over one of the front horns of the saddle. He drew his sword and brought the flat of the blade across the horse's rump. Startled, it squealed and leapt forward down the path. Again with the flat of the sword, he parted the reeds a pace or two from where the kit bag had disappeared. He took a step in. The ground gave a little under his boots. The reeds closed behind him. Another sweep of the sword and another step. The trick was not to break or flatten any more reeds than absolutely necessary.

Just four careful steps, and the thunder of pursuit was almost on him. He was still too close to the track, but there was no time to get away. Maximus sheathed his sword and dropped down full length in the mud. He rolled on to his back, then on to his front again. He checked that his now muddied cloak covered his armour, and pulled off his helmet and pushed it, crest down, into a pool of dark water. Smearing mud across his forehead, cheekbones and nose, he waited.

The noise built to a crescendo: the stamp and slop of the hooves in the mud, the high *ching* of the horse furniture, the deeper rattle of the men's equipment. The air was full of the smell of horse. The reeds swayed with their passing.

Lying in the cool mud, feeling his boots filling with water, Maximus tried to count the hoofbeats: ten, fifteen, twenty horses. It was impossible. The sounds faded. Maximus did not move.

A butterfly, pale yellow, almost white, flew in and out of the reeds in front of his face. The smell of rotting plants was strong in his nostrils. The noise of horsemen came again: fewer of them, travelling more slowly, again from the west. Maximus had guessed right. The majority had hared off after him while a few were following at a more leisurely pace in case he broke cover after the first lot had gone. Fuck you, he thought triumphantly. Fuck each and every one of you.

As soon as the horsemen passed, he got to his feet. Relying on their noise covering his, he plunged off to look for his kit bag. The leading group would overhaul his riderless horse all too soon. He splashed to where the bag lay, half submerged. Infernal gods, he had forgotten the helmet. Fuck it, no time. He turned to get deeper into the marsh.

The kit bag was heavy and incredibly awkward. If he held it upright, there was a danger it might show above the reeds. If he held it sideways, it would reveal his movement through them like a wave. Somehow trying to judge which tangles of vegetation would at least temporarily take his weight, he struggled along with the horrible thing jutting out in front of him.

Shouts, the noise of horses. They were coming back. Again Maximus dropped to the sodden ground. As soon as he had, he knew he had chosen a bad place. There was more water than soil or vegetation, and he was in mail armour. The liquid mud slowly but terrifyingly started to suck him down. Making a long arm, he dragged the kit bag to him and up under his chest. With his arms spread along it, his weight was more widely distributed. It was better, but it would not do for long.

'Come out, you cocksucker.' The voices were very close. 'Little Quietus will not kill you. He needs every one of us alive. Maybe he will just give you a stern talking to, send you back to duty with a sore arse and a nasty taste in your mouth – all the stuff you like.'

Shouts came from all along the path. They were walking their mounts back, probably in single file. Some called out. All would be watching the fen.

'Get your saggy arse out here, bumboy. If not now, when we catch you, we will all give you what a *cinaedus* like you wants.'

The sexual insults and obscenities amused them for some time. Eventually, though, they fell quiet. A lone voice, obviously that of their *decurion*, rang across the sedge. 'We will be back. If the mud has not swallowed you, we will get you. We will be back with dogs.'

After they had gone, Maximus levered himself up and sat on the mainly submerged trunk of a long-fallen oak. He had not been too worried about the threat of dogs. Most Romans used dogs that hunted by sight. Very few knew how to use dogs that hunted by scent. In any event, it would have to be an exceptionally fine hound that could track a man through this waterlogged wilderness. He would be long gone if they ever returned.

After a childhood and youth in Hibernia, marshes held few fears for Maximus. Certain, you had to treat them with respect. Many was the man who had thought the footfall solid and been sucked down to his death. Often at night their souls wandered, flickering lights, trying to lure others to their fate. Was it malice, or were they just after company? Maximus had never been sure.

He sat there regarding the kit bag. It was horribly heavy, more so now soaked, unwieldy too. Did he really need it? Was there anything precious in it? He had his weapons and armour, plenty of money in his belt, Ballista's letter. He wondered if it was good or bad to have so few possessions he cared anything about. If Demetrius had been there, certain he would have started to spout philosophy: the virtues of self-sufficiency, or some such shite. Philosophy was something Maximus was sure he did not need. He got up, rummaged in the kit bag for some air-dried beef and left the thing behind.

For most of the remaining daylight hours, he made his way, as far as he could tell, north-east; away from the track, but still towards the mountains. Every now and then he had a view of them: a darker line of blue below the pale blue of the cloudless sky. He remembered how Ballista had called them hills; made crossing them seem all the easier.

As the afternoon wore on, he came to a mere of open water. Its surface glittered beautifully in the sun. It lay north to south. It was between him and the dry land at the foot of the mountains, and it stretched as far as the reeds would let him see. It was only about a hundred paces across, but he had no intention of trying to wade or swim it. A mere like this might be bottomless mud, like the one at home they used to drown the buggers in. You could be sure this mere was full of vegetation waiting to tangle and trap your arms and legs. And what would he be doing with his armour? The path with the cavalry was to the south; he had set off north.

When the shadows began to lengthen, Maximus had scouted for a flat, dry place to lay his head.

He woke the next morning: caked in dried mud, flies all over him, only some dried meat to eat, and still stuck somewhere in the Mere of Apamea. The main road south from Antioch to Emesa could not be above half a mile away. Lying in the reed beds, Maximus could not see it. He was very still, listening, watching. The dry rustling of the tall reed beds moving was all he could hear.

Maximus filled in the shallow hole he had dug by the shore of the little lake and thought about the Persian boy Bagoas, years ago, telling him it was forbidden for Magi to foul running water. Would they relieve themselves in a non-flowing peat lake? Looking at the surface of the mere gently rippling in the breeze, it would be a shame. Better by far to bury your shit. And that way it was hard for your enemies to track you too.

After about half an hour, he came to a causeway. It ran straight as an arrow across the mere. On the far side, Maximus could see fields and a path grading the slopes, signs of terracing higher. On the nearer side, it connected to a well-made-up track. Over the track were fenced water meadows. He had reached one of the parts of the Mere of Apamea more tamed by the hand of man.

Yet as he lay in the reeds watching, there was not a person in sight. Actually, there were very few living things at all. At home, a fen like this would have been alive with wildfowl and all sorts. Out here in the east, you seldom saw many birds. Where had they gone? Had the luxury-loving locals eaten them all?

No point in waiting any longer, Maximus climbed up and set off.

When he was virtually at mid-point on the causeway, the two horsemen materialized at the mountain end like some unwelcome divine epiphany. They were trotting towards him, and they were in Roman uniforms.

Swearing quietly, Maximus looked behind him – too far to run – and to either side – just the glittering mere, the shining face of a dark fate. He stood still and waited for them. It was a shame, more than a shame it had to be this way.

The horsemen reined in some paces away. Their swords were drawn. They did not speak. The one on the right dismounted first, then the other.

'Drop your weapons.' The first to dismount spoke.

Maximus unclasped his cloak. As he dropped it off to his left, his eyes never faltered from the nearer soldier. No opportunity came – the soldier's gaze stayed on Maximus.

'Weapons.'

Maximus unbuckled his sword belt, shrugged the baldric off his shoulder and tossed them after the cloak. Again the soldier's gaze did not waver. This was not going to be easy. Maximus still had old Calgacus's trick in his boot. But he was running out of options and time.

The first soldier stepped forward, his blade at Maximus's throat.

'Not a good day for you, deserter.' The other one spoke.

You should keep quiet, like your friend, thought Maximus.

'Hands out. Wrists crossed.' The first was in charge.

Maximus did as he was told.

The first soldier glanced at his belt, going to free the leather strip to bind the prisoner.

Maximus took the edge of the sword on the right sleeve of his mail coat, pushed the point away. Stooping, with his left hand he drew the dagger from its sheath in his right boot. Staying low, he drove it into the soldier's right thigh, just below his armour.

The other one was on him, sword arcing down. Maximus only had the dagger to catch the long blade of the *spatha*. Most warriors, no matter what their training, shut their eyes at the moment of contact. Maximus forced himself to watch the blade. He blinked. The sound of steel on steel. The impact ran up his arm. Automatically, he rolled his wrist. He opened his eyes. The sword was being deflected wide.

The momentum of Maximus's opponent was carrying him past, slightly off balance. Maximus spun elegantly and kicked him hard behind the left knee. The man went down. Maximus pounced. He landed with all his weight on top of the soldier. Grabbing the man's helmet, Maximus forced his face down into the mud. The man thrashed about, the viscous black liquid pushing into his mouth, his nose. Maximus increased the pressure.

Maximus glanced at the first soldier. He was inching in agony towards the sword he had dropped. His thigh was running with blood. No immediate threat there.

The struggles of the man in the mud began to weaken. Maximus pushed down as hard as he could. A convulsive series of movements, and then nothing. Maximus did not ease up for several moments.

Finally, the other soldier was nearing his sword. When he got up, Maximus's legs were stiff. With a hobbling run, he crossed the track. He kicked the sword away from the desperate hand. Falling to his knees, he seized the man's chin, yanked it back. He wielded the dagger. There was a rasp of metal on metal as the edge of the blade slid down the nasal of the man's helmet. The tip of the blade entered the eye. The man jerked up rigid, went still.

Maximus got up, looked both ways. No one in sight. He felt an odd tiredness and lack of urgency. He forced himself to think quickly and get moving. Having cleaned the knife, he put it back in his boot. He went over and put his sword belt on again. At the side of the track, he washed the blood off his hands and arms in the mere. He picked up the leather thong that had been intended to bind him. Maximus had always been good with animals; the horses came to him, wary as they were of the smell of gore on the ground. He hobbled the first one with the piece of leather. Horses were herd animals, and it did not really matter if the other happened not to stay.

The man face down in the mud had a cloak of pale blue with a fancy gilded clasp. It appealed to Maximus, so he put it on. He tried the man's helmet, but it did not fit. He spread out his own muddied cloak and dropped the helmet in the middle of it. He went back to the dead man and searched him. The reasonable sum of coins he added to his own purse. He drew the man's sword and tossed that on to his cloak as well. Then he dragged the corpse to the edge of the causeway and rolled it into the water.

Maximus went over to the other man and – except for the cloak – repeated what he had done. When the water stilled, Maximus could see that this second corpse had settled partly on top, partly beside the other. They were not well hidden, but it was better than nothing.

The unhobbled horse had remained with its companion. The soldiers' shields, with their unit identification, Maximus unhitched from their saddles. They were added to the pile on his abandoned cloak. He tied the corners together and threw it as far as he could. In the water, it darkened, settled, then sank.

Maximus talked gently to the horses as he altered the hobble to a leading rein. Their breath was sweet on his face. He got into the saddle. He studied his work. The surface of the causeway was ploughed up and bloody. The mud would soon take care of that. The corpses were not deep enough to be invisible, but if you were not looking you might not notice them. It was a shame, more than a shame he had had to kill them. They had just been doing their duty. But then so was he. Turning the horses' heads, he trotted away towards the east and Palmyra.

It was eight days since Quietus's court and army had arrived in Emesa. Time for Ballista to rent a house, for the *familia* to begin to settle in. Time for Ballista to begin to hope that Maximus had got away, that things would work out.

The boots in the street woke Ballista. When they stopped, he slipped out of bed. It was very dark, probably well past midnight. His hand closed on the scabbard of his sword, hanging in its accustomed place.

The pounding on the main door boomed dully through the house.

Ballista pulled on a tunic and opened the door of the bedroom. Light came in from the corridor. Julia was sitting up in bed. She did not say anything, but her dark eyes looked frightened.

There was more pounding on the door, a muffled shout.

'It will be fine,' Ballista said.

Actually, he had no idea. There were troops outside. Roman soldiers walked differently to anyone else. But it could be anything. Emperors, especially erratic ones like Quietus, could summon men to their *consilium* at any time of night or day. There, by lamplight, while the rest of the world slept, they might be called on to discuss anything from war in the east to the best way to cook a fish. Even under Quietus a nocturnal *consilium* was not necessarily something to fear, and it would be most strange if, as one of the two serving Praetorian Prefects, Ballista was not summoned. But there again, no one in the *imperium* would feel completely safe when the soldiers hammered on the door gone midnight. It could mean something altogether different.

'It will be fine,' Ballista said again.

Julia did not reply. There was something wrong with her, had been since he came back from Palestine. In the old days, she would not have looked frightened, even if she had been terrified. In the old days, she would have spoken to him. Mostly, she was the same, but something had changed. He did not know what.

More pounding on the door. From the depths of the house came the wheezing voice of Calgacus in full peevish flow. 'Middle of the fucking night, fucking hold your fucking horses, you will have the fucking thing off its hinges.'

Ballista went out on to the balcony that ran all around the atrium at the first floor. He walked to the stairs that faced the entrance and waited. He found he was shivering. Maybe, even in Syria in high summer, there was more of a chill to the night than he thought.

Calgacus appeared, holding a lamp for a centurion. They were followed by about twenty Praetorians, who fanned out around the courtyard. Too many soldiers for anything but bad news. Ballista had known from the start but had failed to acknowledge it. He did not know what had caused this, but if Maximus had been caught, this was the end. Ballista battened down his fear.

Ballista was puzzled to see a centurion that he did not recognize. In the reduced numbers of the Praetorian Guard of Quietus, there were not that many of them. Yet the centurion looked familiar. If Demetrius had been there, he could have put a name to him.

'*Dominus*,' said Calgacus, 'this is Marcus Aurelius Jucundus.' The Caledonian's face was woeful.

Ballista did not recognize the name either.

'*Dominus*.' The centurion's tone was stiff, official. He read from a papyrus roll with a purple seal. 'The order of the most noble Caesar, Titus Fulvius Iunius Quietus, *Pius Felix*, *Pater Patriae*, *Restitutor Orbis*, *Invictus*. Marcus Clodius Ballista is relieved of his command as Praetorian Prefect. Furthermore, he is to be placed under arrest immediately and conveyed to the central gaol under the palace of the kings of Emesa.' The centurion paused. Very quietly, he said, 'I am sorry, *Dominus*.' Presumably that was not written on the papyrus. He took a breath and continued. 'The barbarian is to be confined there at our pleasure ... together with his wife and his sons.'

The centurion was most kind, consideration personified: they could have time to collect some things, as much as they needed, could take what they wished. They roused the children. At two, Dernhelm was too young to understand. He smiled at the lights glittering and moving in the Praetorians' armour then fell asleep on his mother's shoulder. With Isangrim, a thoughtful nine-year-old, things were different. Ballista spoke to him alone. Isangrim must be brave as an example to his younger brother, and to his mother. Isangrim and Ballista must be brave for each other. The boy nodded. He stood, straight-backed, a slight tremble to his chin. Father and son embraced. Ballista told his freedman Calgacus that he was in charge of the remaining *familia*; the *accensus* Hippothous would help him supervise the porters, cooks, maids owned or employed in the house. Ballista and Calgacus embraced.

As they walked through the darkened streets, Centurion Jucundus said he had been to see the gaoler before coming to Ballista's house. He had instructed the man that Ballista's family were to be allocated the outermost cell – it had a little natural light and ventilation. By now it should have been scrupulously cleaned and given furniture. The prefect and the *domina* could have their servants bring them any food or anything else they liked. Jucundus himself, or one of his men, would come every day to check that everything was as well as the circumstances permitted. It was notable that Jucundus still employed Ballista's title.

Reaching the palace, passing through its dark, squat walls, under its fantastic, soaring towers, all was as the centurion had said. Lamps were lit in the cell. There was a bed, a table, a few chairs. The bare walls and floor were clean. It had been scented, although nothing could quite mask the underlying prison stench.

Julia, her brisk, capable self again, was in constant motion, putting the children to bed, unpacking their hasty possessions, instilling order.

At the door, Ballista thanked Centurion Jucundus for his trouble.

'It is the least I could do, *Dominus*. The new prefect Rutilus – your replacement – promoted me into the Praetorians late yesterday. All my life, man and boy, I have been with Legio IIII Scythica. I served under you, in the ranks of Castricius's *vexillatio*, at Circesium. You never got the credit you deserved for that victory.'

Ballista smiled. 'I thought you looked familiar.'

Jucundus smiled ruefully. 'Castricius – a long time ago he was my *contubernalis* – has been appointed to replace Rutilus as Prefect of Cavalry. Not done badly, old Castricius, for a man who was once in the mines.'

Ballista also smiled. 'He is a resourceful man.'

'That is one word for him. I remember that night at Caeciliana – gods below, the two of you were drunk – when you burned that patrician officer's baggage. The boys and me could hardly stand for laughing. It was magnificent.'

Ballista dropped his voice. 'Jucundus, has my freedman Maximus been arrested?'

Jucundus shook his head. 'Not that I have heard.'

Ballista sighed. 'That is something at least.'

'I will see you tomorrow.' Jucundus snapped a salute, incongruous in the degraded surroundings.

Jucundus turned back. His eyes took in the small cell. 'Your wife and children too ... *Dominus*, I am so very sorry.'

The dead lived well in Palmyra. Maximus rode through the Valley of the Tombs; everywhere, the tall, well-built rectangular homes of the dead. Maximus had been this way before, six years previously, on his way to Arete. One of a company then, he had not really looked at the tombs. Alone now, he gazed at them. They spoke of wealth and power. And, to his mind, there was something more. Halfway up the steep slope on one side, three, four storeys tall, their masonry so well squared off, doors and windows so neatly cut, the ring of towers spoke of permanence. They were like a smoother version of the jagged rocks poking through the sand at the summit; grown out of nature, but shaped by man. Like the living rocks, they intended to be here for ever.

Looked at in a certain way, they seemed to be the walls, the natural rocks of the city; the dead men guarding the living rocks. Gods below, any more of this drivel and you would think I had been educated in Athens, thought Maximus. He had been out in the sun a long time. It had been a long, tough journey since the killings in the mere. Over the terrible hard mountains – Ballista's bloody *hills* – then monotonous days of dun-coloured, sun-blasted, rocky desert. But at last he was here: Palmyra, Tadmor to the locals, the oasis city of Odenathus, the Lion of the Sun.

There was a crowd at the gate jostling to get in. Most were farmers from the villages to the north-west, their donkeys, camels and wives laden with wheat, wine and fodder, olive oil, animal fat and pine cones. There were fewer traders from the west than there had been the last time Maximus had been here. But there were a couple. War or not, profits can drive a man from home. One of these hardy souls traded in Italian wool, the other in salt fish. It was very hot, and tempers were short. Men shouted and donkeys brayed; the camels spat.

Maximus sat on one of his two horses and looked at the city walls. He remembered his old drinking companion Mamurra sneering at them the last time they were here. The Hibernian checked the thought – as if that square-headed bastard Mamurra would ever be going anywhere again, buried as the poor bugger was in a collapsed siege tunnel under the walls of Arete. He was never the quickest man in the world, old Mamurra, but in time he had got things right. The low mud-brick walls of Palmyra would be as much use in a siege as a one-legged man in an arse-kicking competition. It was a good job the Palmyrenes were on the attack. They had better pray the tables were never turned.

Eventually, Maximus reached the customs post in the gate.

'What do you have to declare?' The *telones* spoke without looking up.

Maximus did not reply.

With a tut of irritation, the *telones* took his eyes from his

341

tally. He took in the mail coat; the worn leather grip of the sword; the missing tip of the nose; the two horses and the dust engrained thick in everything that told of a long journey at speed. 'Carry on,' he said. 'Next.'

Inside the gate, Maximus threw a street child a coin and said he wanted the house of Haddudad. He followed the lively bundle of rags and brown limbs up one fine, bustling colonnaded street, down another, through a monument of sixteen columns of swirling black and gold, passed a full *agora* and an empty theatre. The strong but not unpleasant smell of spices, horses and humanity, all with a slight edge of camel, was familiar. Maximus recognized the route to the palace of Odenathus. Three houses beyond it, his guide stopped, pointed at the marble entrance to a huge townhouse and jabbered excitedly in whatever language he or she spoke. Haddudad the mercenary had come up in the world.

Maximus showed the child – on balance, probably a girl – a quite high-denomination coin, mimed holding the horses and put the coin back in his wallet. Laughing, the child took the reins.

The porter created no fuss. It was as if armed, violent-looking men covered in dirt arrived at the door every day. Given that his *kyrios* was an ex-mercenary and his *kyria* the daughter of a caravan protector, quite possibly, they did. He showed Maximus to a small room and asked him to wait. He expressed no surprise when the visitor declined his offer to look after his weapons.

Maximus sat down and stretched out his legs. He assumed he was being watched. He looked around, unconcerned. The walls were painted and depicted some Greek myth. Large, near-naked and hairy men were running about on an improbable range of mountains. They were throwing huge boulders down at anchored warships. Most of the ships had been hit, and some were already beyond salvation. Their crews stretched their hands to the heavens in appeal or reproach. A shifty-looking man on the last vessel had the right idea. He was cutting the mooring rope. The galley was so far unscathed but, given the hairy boys' skills with a rock, Maximus did not fancy its chances.

Two armed men entered the room. Hands on their hilts, they hard-eyed Maximus. After them came a woman in eastern costume, fully veiled, only her eyes visible.

Maximus politely stood up. The guards tensed.

The woman passed the guards, came close. With her left hand, she reached up and across and undid her veil. Gods below, but Bathshiba was still attractive.

'It has been a long time,' she said in Greek. Her voice was as he remembered; the sort of thing that could take a man's wits.

'Five years.'

'I would kiss you, but you are filthy.' She smiled, stepped back.

Ballista, my old friend, thought Maximus, you were a fool not to fuck her when you had the chance. If it had been me she set her cap at in Arete, her bed would have been no place of solitude and quiet contemplation.

'As you can see, I am in my best demure-wife clothes. We are entertaining – just the one guest. You will join us; no need to bath or change.' She came close again, closer than before. He could smell her, beneath her perfume. *Ballista, you were such a fool.* She leant closer still and, her breath in his ear, whispered, 'Be very careful what you say in front of Nicostratus. No mention of coming from the army of Quietus. No mention of Ballista.'

The dining room was light and shady at the same time. For a Syrian afternoon in high summer, it was cool. A water feature played somewhere.

Haddudad rose from his couch. Prosperity suited him. His hair was longer, flat on top, curled at the sides, very artful. From behind his full, curled and perfumed beard, he grinned.

'Maximus,' Haddudad said. Although his clothes were yet more gorgeous and ornate than those of his wife, he hugged the Hibernian to him. They pounded each other on the back. Clouds of dun-coloured dust drifted up through the shafts of sunlight.

Haddudad gestured at the occupied couch. 'Maximus, this is the renowned historian Nicostratus of Trapezus.' Haddudad gestured back again. 'Nicostratus, this is an old *systratiotes* of mine from the siege of Arete, Marcus Aurelius Maximus.'

The man of letters got to his feet. There was no overt show of reluctance, but Maximus had the impression that Nicostratus of Trapezus did not often shake the hand of mercenaries, old companion of his host or not.

Servants brought in a third couch. Haddudad guided Maximus over to it. All three men reclined. Bathshiba sat on an upright chair behind and at the foot of her husband's couch. Maximus felt like laughing. He remembered the wild Amazonian girl from Arete: dressed like a man, fighting alongside her father's men, quite probably – much to his fury – saving Ballista's life.

First they brought him a bowl and ewer to wash his hands. Then a servant positioned a small table at Maximus's right hand. Another placed a selection of small dishes of pastries, olives and cheese and an empty wine cup on the table. A third poured the mixed wine. Maximus made a libation and drank the health of his host.

Haddudad and Nicostratus resumed a conversation they had obviously been having before Maximus arrived. It was about a historian called Herodian. Nicostratus tried to include Maximus. The Hibernian said he was usually paid to kill men not read books. Nicostratus did not try again.

Maximus drank his wine. He was impressed by Haddudad. The ex-mercenary had taken to this life as if born to it. His fine, embroidered tunic, trousers and boots – all dusty now – hung easily on him. He lounged elegantly and was more than holding his own in bookish discussion: 'So would you agree, my dear Nicostratus, that Herodian sacrifices certain trivial details in order to bring out more clearly what he regards as deeper and more profound levels of historical truth?' The false *nomen* he had given Maximus was clever. Since the emperor Caracalla – about fifty years earlier – had given Roman citizenship to all the free inhabitants of the *imperium* who did not already have it, almost every other person carried the Caracalla's *praenomen* and *nomen*: Marcus Aurelius.

A servant came and refilled Maximus's wine cup. That was another creditable thing about Haddudad – not just that he kept the drink flowing but that he had followed Bathshiba's father's way of employing fighting men at table. Much more use than some pretty boys or naked girls in the event of trouble.

Bathshiba leant forward and spoke to her husband. Hadd-dudad inclined his head, smiling. She got up. At her sign, a servant placed another upright chair by Maximus's couch.

'Historiography not your strong point?' Bathshiba's voice was pitched low, so as not to carry. She did not wait for an answer. 'Nicostratus is a pompous bore – failings not unknown among men of his calling. Zenobia summoned him here to Tadmor. She has commissioned him to write a history from the reign of Philip the Arab to the glorious victories of Odenathus. It will be ghastly – no chance of it standing the test of time.'

Maximus studied the reclining Greek historian. He had thin, pursed lips in a self-satisfied face. He did not appear a man much troubled by curiosity. Under his Greek *himation*, a pair of oriental embroidered trousers and finely tooled soft leather boots peeped out. This standard bearer of Hellenic culture had gone half native already. Not that Maximus cared.

'Odenathus's second wife is not the beautiful but submissive young girl we were all expecting. Zenobia is deeply ambitious. More ambitious even than Odenathus himself. And she is warlike.'

Maximus glanced sharply at Bathshiba, who ignored it.

'It frustrates her. Odenathus has a grown son, Haeranes, from his first marriage. The young man is a natural warrior. In Zabda and Zabbai, Odenathus has two generals he trusts. Now there is my husband. No need for a twenty-year-old girl in the councils of war of the Lion of the Sun.'

Bathshiba stopped as a servant replaced the empty dishes with ones of fruit, nuts and sweet things.

'So,' she continued, 'Zenobia has set herself up as the

great patroness of culture. From all over the east, philosophers and sophists, historians and poets, flock to the
court. These men of *paideia* infest the palace. Every one
of them is more greedy and ambitious than the last. But
every one of them owes his position to Zenobia. And that
is why Nicostratus is here, and why poor Haddudad is
putting himself out to be so charming.'

Bathshiba smiled charmingly as Nicostratus looked
around.

'Not that Zenobia does not get to ride with the army.'
Bathshiba's eyes sparkled with her old mischief. 'They say
she will not let Odenathus have what a husband needs
unless he lets her have her way.'

The last tack of her conversation sent Maximus's
thoughts wandering. Under all these eastern fabrics, was
Bathshiba still the nicely rounded armful she had been?
She had been one of the likeliest-looking bits of tumble
you could imagine. Lucky old Haddudad.

'Ow.' She had prodded him with a fruit knife. Maximus
quickly smiled blandly over at the others.

'That is better. My face is up here.' Bathshiba's teeth
were very white when she laughed. 'And I said, what are
you doing here?'

'Ballista wants Haddudad to arrange for me to see
Odenathus in secret.' There was no point in beating
around the bush.

'Why?'

'To give him a letter.'

'Saying what?'

'I have no idea.'

'Really?'

Maximus looked at Bathshiba. Surely she was not being so unsubtle as to push her shoulders back to accentuate her breasts. How shallow did she think he was? 'All I know is I have to make sure Odenathus knows which is the Tower of Desolation at Emesa.'

'The tall, thin one at the extreme south-east of the walls.' Bathshiba spoke, but her thoughts were elsewhere. 'Of course Haddudad will do it. But . . .' She paused. 'I am not sure what sort of a reception you will get. Your friend is a leading general of Odenathus's enemy. Obviously, much depends on the contents of the letter. But it is far easier to read Herodian's *History* than the Lord of Tadmor. He is unpredictable. It is part of what has made him so powerful. He is like a capricious elemental force. The Lion of the Sun may shower you with gold and make you his drinking companion – or he may kill you like a dog.'

Maximus shrugged. 'Sure, life would be terrible dull if we knew all the outcomes. Is there any chance of a bath?'

'Of course. Would you like some company?' At Maximus's grin, she quickly added, 'No, not me, you fool. One of the maids.'

'Well, that would be better than either your husband or the historian. I don't suppose there would be two of your maids at a loose end?'

Before she made the arrangements, Bathshiba spoke seriously one more time. 'It is lucky you have come now. You are nearly too late. The Lion of the Sun marches on Emesa in three days.'

It may have been the best cell to be found in the gaol under the palace of Emesa, but it was still dark, airless and insufferably hot. And familiarity did not stop the stink of it catching in Ballista's throat.

Ballista knew he had failed. Everything he had done during these years in the east had been to protect his family, and he had failed. He did not know why, but they were in gaol with him.

True to his word, Jucundus, or one of his men, had come every day to check that things were no worse than they had to be. This may have gone some way to explaining why the behaviour of the gaoler and his assistants had shifted from its customary and ingrained cruelty to a grudging near-politeness. The open-handedness of the prisoners with money and an unexpressed and incoherent fear of the mutability of fortune probably also came into play.

Under the supervision of Calgacus, servants delivered fresh food and drink. Every morning, maids dressed the hair and did the make-up of the *domina*. Other girls produced newly cut flowers. The women swept and cleaned, strategically arranged the flowers, lit scented lamps and liberally dispensed scented oils. Yet, no matter how many aromatics were deployed, still the prison stench seeped up from the lower cells, where those lacking in fortune and influence lay in their own filth, devoid of hope.

The children were doing surprisingly well. Admittedly, they had no fresh air, nowhere near enough space to run, and sometimes their own noise crashing back from the walls seemed momentarily to stun even them. But they had the rarity of near-undivided attention from their parents, all their favourite playthings, and were largely being fed things of their own choice. To all these benefactions, Isangrim added the absence of his schoolmaster.

If the boys were bearing up well, the same could not be said of Julia. Her usual disposition towards order had been elevated almost to the level of mania. She was always moving, tutting and complaining under her breath as she put things back in their right place after her husband or children had moved them. It was, thought Ballista, rather like being locked up with a better-looking version of Calgacus, but with his irony gone.

Ballista himself, as far as he could in the din of the confined space, retreated into reading. The second day, he had Calgacus bring him Arrian's *Discourses of Epictetus*. It was hard to think of a circumstance where some hard-line Stoic philosophy should not be more appropriate or sustaining. On the third morning, as instructed, the Caledonian arrived with a novel, *The Aithiopika* of Heliodorus of Emesa. Ballista wondered if he might learn some interesting things about the mentality of the town in which he was a prisoner. He did not. But it was a diverting enough series of picaresque stories within stories. After another day, he asked Calgacus to bring him some of Plutarch's *Parallel Lives*. They were far more like it – examples of men bearing changes in fortune set in exciting stories; philosophy in action for those like Ballista who could not quite stomach the unalloyed thing. He started with the lives of Demetrius and Antony:

Antony turned back to Rome. He disguised himself as a slave, made out he was carrying a letter to Fulvia from Antony and was admitted to her presence with his face all muffled. Fulvia was distracted and, before taking the letter, asked him whether Antony was alive. He handed it to her in silence, and no sooner had she opened it and begun to read it than he flung his arms around her and kissed her.

'*Dominus*.' Jucundus stood in the doorway. 'I am ordered to convey you to the sacred presence of our emperor. Your wife and sons are to remain here.'

There was only time for hurried farewells. Julia looked openly terrified, and her fear transferred itself to the boys – Isangrim cried, Dernhelm howled. An inauspicious way to leave.

Quietus was in the great temple of Elagabalus. As they marched through the streets, Jucundus, talking out of the corner of his mouth like a legionary on parade, said he had no idea what the summons portended.

When they had reached the sacred precinct and were rounding the altar, Ballista and his escort had to check their progress. A procession of members of the *Boule* of Emesa crossed their path. The councillors were clad in formal Roman togas, the majority with the narrow stripe of an equestrian, one or two with the broad purple denoting senatorial status. Each carried on his head a golden bowl of reeking intestines. Try as they might, the local worthies could not prevent the odd slop of blood landing on the snowy-white material of their robes.

Ballista took in his surroundings. The three fires on the altar hissed and spat, burning unnaturally bright colours: blue-green, yellow, red. Slaves were busy spreading clean sand on the ground. Mingled with the smell of incense were the stench of unwashed tripe and the powerful tang of urine. Flies buzzed thick in the air. The bowls on the head must be an Emesene particularity, but everything else could not be more normal: the aftermath of sacrifice, the *imperium*-wide mundanities of conventional piety.

A *silentarius* took charge of them at the foot of the stairs. After the bright sunlight, the interior of the temple was dark, cavernous. It stretched away, echoing into infinity.

In the gloom, a line of pinprick lights. As Ballista's eyes adjusted, these resolved themselves into a row of ornate candlesticks dividing the great room, dividing the sacred from the profane. In the middle of the row, on its small, portable altar, the imperial fire burned; beyond them, the golden statue of an eagle. It stood confident on its wide-spread legs. The many little lights slid over its mighty, outstretched wings, over the snake writhing in its cruel beak.

Beyond the eagle, seemingly hanging in the air, was the imperial throne. Quietus sat in it, as still as a statue. He was dressed all in purple and gold; a voluminous tunic and a tall tiara; innumerable jewels. His painted face was immobile.

And beyond Quietus, looming over everything, was the god himself. Elagabalus, the great black stone that had fallen from the heavens, towered up towards the shadowy ceiling. Impossibly dense, it drew what light there was into itself. Only the occasional little rill of light splashed across the god, animating the mysterious markings in the depths beneath his smooth, dark surface.

Neither emperor nor god took any notice of the newcomers. As Ballista and his escort rose from their *proskynesis*, the *silentarius* ushered them off to one side. There they waited.

There was a sudden clash of cymbals. From somewhere, the music of flutes and pipes: high, twisting, intricate.

Sampsigeramus, the priest-king of Emesa, danced into view. Apart from his necklaces and the many bangles on his wrists and ankles, he was naked. His body was thin, almost emaciated, the veins unnaturally prominent. Palms up, he danced before the emperor and the deity. To Ballista, there could not have been a more stomach-turning picture of eastern servility and effeminacy.

A high, shrill cry, and the act of worship was completed. Sampsigeramus went and sat on a low chair by Quietus. The emperor's non-entity cousin, Cornelius Macer – now the holder of three high government posts – was on the other side.

'Bring in the atheist,' said Quietus.

The Praetorian Prefect himself, Rutilus, brought in the prisoner. It was the tall, severe-looking senator Astyrius. They performed *proskynesis*. Quietus looked at the prisoner. The silence lengthened.

Astyrius was dressed in Greek *himation* and tunic, rather than his senatorial toga. He kept his hands clasped in front, eyes modestly downcast. Only a tiny tremor in his legs betrayed the doubts and terrors he must be feeling.

'Tell me' – Quietus's voice was light, conversational – 'have you been wondering where your pretty slave boy Epaphroditus has got to?'

Astyrius did not answer.

'No! Really, not at all?' Quietus raised his painted eyebrows. 'No concerns for his wellbeing? Not even considering the secrets the two of you share?'

Astyrius opened his mouth, but words failed him.

'Well, let me tell you anyway.' Quietus was enjoying this. 'At the moment, it must be said, he is probably none too comfortable. He is in one of the deepest dungeons under the palace. Although that is unlikely to be his main concern. Because your young friend, or should I say *brother*, is riding the *equuleus*. Have you ever seen the wooden horse in action? It is most ingenious. It must be agony for your pretty boy as the pulleys force his limbs apart.'

Astyrius made a small choking sound, then controlled himself.

'Not that he is all that pretty any more.' Quietus laughed. 'In fact, he is rather repulsive. You would hardly recognize him.'

The emperor stopped talking and peered closely at Astyrius.

'I am not sure what it is about your physiognomy, but I have never liked the look of you. Never trusted you. So I had the *frumentarii* lift your little boyfriend Epaphroditus from the baths. We hung him up – by one hand actually, much more painful – and while beating him – just the usual rods, thongs, whips – asked him some questions about you. Do you know, he would not say anything. You would have been very proud of him.'

Astyrius had mastered the trembling in his legs.

'And then the strangest thing happened,' Quietus continued. 'We got the claws to work on him. It really was terrible the way they were stripping the skin from his sides. But as he still refused to incriminate you, I suggested the torturers went to work on other bits of him: stomach and thighs, the soles of his feet, his pretty cheeks and forehead. And that was when he cried out: "*Even murderers are not treated like this, only us Christians.*"'

Quietus smiled at Astyrius. 'Well, you can imagine how

that encouraged us. We pressed on with a will. When I was at Ephesus, I discovered the pleasures of interrogating Christians. I even offered your little slave boy his freedom if he would admit you were a Christian. The impudent little *cinaedus* replied, "I have been freed by Christ." So once again you Christians, not content with denying the gods, stand convicted of attempting to undermine all property rights here on earth.'

'I am a Christian,' Astyrius said.

'Is it true you have sex with your sisters?'

'I adore Christ. I detest the daemons. Do what you will. I am a Christian.'

'And eat specially fattened babies?'

Astyrius squared his shoulders. 'I am a Christian. It is better to die than to worship stones.'

'You are about to find out if that is true.' Quietus signalled to the Praetorian Prefect.

Rutilus pushed Astyrius to his knees. The Christian did not struggle, but he called out, his voice powerful, 'You have condemned me, but God will condemn you. You will fall as the stars of heaven are swept down to earth by the dragon's tail.'

Rutilus drew his sword.

Astyrius leant forward, offering his neck for the blow. 'The devil goes about like a roaring lion, seeking whom he may devour.'

Rutilus raised the sword.

'It is for you, Christ, that I suffer this!'

The sword fell. It was a neat stroke.

Astyrius's head fell heavily, wetly, to the floor. It rolled an uneven two or three turns towards the row of lit candles.

For a time his trunk remained, four distinct jets of blood pumping out, splashing on the marble floor. The flow diminished, and the body collapsed sideways.

In the dark silence, Quietus spoke. 'With treachery all around me, only misfortune has remained faithful to me – misfortune, my doomed family and my Emesene friend Sampsigeramus.' He ruffled the priest-king's hair, and relapsed into silent introspection.

'*Dominus?*' Eventually it was Rutilus who dared try to break into the emperor's thoughts.

Quietus continued to stare at the decapitated corpse. 'Afterwards, one always regrets having been so benevolent.' He spoke more to himself than anyone else.

'*Dominus?*'

Quietus came back from his private world of sanguinary regrets. He snapped out orders. 'Get that thing out of here. We have news that Odenathus is marching against us. It matters little in the long run. Pomponius Bassus will soon appear at his rear. But until then we must take thought for our safety. I am advised I need officers experienced in siege works. The barbarian Ballista is reappointed as Praetorian co-prefect. His colleague Rutilus will command the west and north walls, the Prefect of Cavalry Castricius the east and south. Ballista's will be the overall plan for the defence of Emesa. The barbarian had better do a better job than at Arete. His wife and sons will remain in gaol. As the first Palmyrene is seen on the walls, they will die.'

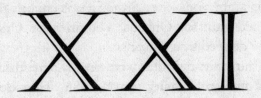

XXI

The Tower of Desolation of Emesa was more an observation post than a defensive work. Its circular battlements were only a few paces across. Its interior was entirely taken up with the twisting stone staircase. The tall tower looked out south-east: five miles of cultivated land, then the measureless high desert, stone-strewn, baked by the sun, infinitely harsh. That might account for its name.

Ballista leant on one of the crenellations and embraced the rare moment of solitude. Up here, the wind tugged at his cloak, made his long fair hair stream away. Out in the desert, he could see it raising tall, spinning dust devils. The wind was from the south. It was going to raise a fierce storm. Odenathus's main army was approaching through the desert from the east. When the storm reached them, they would hunker down, backs to the wind, cloths tied across the faces of men and animals – wait for it to blow itself out. It would delay them by a day or so.

Once, when the Persians sent an army across the Libyan desert to despoil the holy oracle of Zeus Ammon at the oasis of Siwah, a huge storm got up one night. As the soldiers slept, the sand buried them alive. The army was lost for ever. Ballista smiled – no chance of that here. This was a different desert: not enough sand, all too many rocks. Then again, the gods loved Siwah; it was unlikely they had a great affection for Quietus. The army of Odenathus would be delayed by a day or so.

The Palmyrene outriders were already here. Ballista had watched the light cavalry arrive. First, dense clouds of them, clothes flashing bright in the sun. They came in five groups. Each had ridden with purpose to its station. The four main roads – north to Apamea, south to Laodicea ad Libanum, east to Palmyra, and north-east to the distant Euphrates – were blocked. The fifth group spread out to westward, along the banks of the Orontes, watching for any attempt at intervention across the Libanus mountains from the old legionary base at Raphanaea.

The light horse in the second wave that encircled the town were in smaller units. Ballista had watched them swooping through the farmsteads and suburban villas. They were looting – when did soldiers not? – but there was no burning. Their discipline was good. Odenathus did not want to alienate the Emesenes. He wanted them to come over.

Not all the horsemen were Palmyrenes. Through the swirling dust, standards and shield patterns marked out regular Roman units. These *alae*, originally raised in distant Thrace, Dalmatia and Gaul, must have been provided by governors opposed to Quietus: Aurelius Dasius of Mesopotamia, Virius Lupus of Arabia, and maybe, if the rumours were true, Pomponius Bassus of Cappadocia. These Roman regular light horse came close to the walls, displaying themselves to the Roman defenders. Odenathus clearly wanted them to come over as well.

Ballista was impressed. It was like a hunting expedition on a huge scale. The fixed stakes were driven in, then the nets hung from one to the next, leaving no way out. Odenathus knew what he was about. No need for surprise there. No one harried Shapur out of northern Mesopotamia, retook cities like Carrhae and Nisibis from the Sassanids, unless he knew what he was about.

Numbers of light horsemen were always difficult to judge, but there looked to be about ten thousand of them ringing the town. The Palmyrene heavy cavalry and the infantry were still on the road. Ballista had no idea how many they were. Cornelius Macer – the cousin Quietus had made, among other things, head of the *frumentarii* – had produced no reliable figures whatsoever. The ineptitude was not enough to make Ballista wish Censorinus back as *Princeps Peregrinorum*. At a guess, it was unlikely the main body of Odenathus's army was smaller than the force already outside Emesa. So, the Lion of the Sun would have at least twenty thousand men, maybe more, maybe many more.

And to oppose him, Ballista had what? Quietus had a Praetorian Guard of a thousand. There was the core of Legio III Gallica, the main unit of the garrison of Syria Phoenice, some two thousand men. There were also *vexillationes* of five hundred men each from five other legions: IIII Scythica and XVI Flavia Firma from Syria Coele, X Fretensis and VI Ferrata from Syria Palestina, and III Felix from the outpost of Circesium. The five and a half thousand Praetorians and legionaries were augmented by about the same number of regular auxiliaries. Then Sampsigeramus claimed to have ten thousand Emesene bowmen, horse and foot.

It was a sizeable force: twenty-one thousand men, more than half of them Roman professionals. Unfortunately, it only existed in the mind of Quietus and, seemingly, those of his closest advisors, his cousin Macer and the king Sampsigeramus. In *consilium*, all the other officers – including Rutilus, Castricius and Ballista himself – paid lip service to it. But in the unobservable places of their hearts, they knew it was not true.

Ten years of wars, foreign and civil, since the coming of the time of troubles had worn the Roman units down. In a decade of confusion, detachments had been sent away and never returned, new recruits had not been levied. Death and injury, disease and desertion had left the units pale shadows of their former selves. Keeping old men with the standards far beyond their time for retirement had caused resentment but done little to maintain numbers. It was dubious if any unit, apart from the Praetorian Guard, had half the men it was said to have. And no one put any faith in the existence of the ten thousand Emesene warriors claimed by Sampsigeramus.

Numbers continued to fall. Desertions continued. Day by day, furtive figures slipped out of the postern gates or over the wall and away. Far from stemming the flow, the arrival of the enemy cavalry increased it. The Palmyrenes welcomed the deserters with open arms.

It was not just the rank and file who were abandoning the regime of Quietus. The sometime Praetorian Prefect Maeonius Astyanax had never returned from his embassy to Palmyra. Astyanax, the great *amicus* of Quietus's father, now was said to ride close to the right hand of the Lion of the Sun.

Then there was the governor of Cappadocia, Pomponius Bassus, the man who was meant to raise a great barbarian army of Iberians, Albanians, Alani to sweep down the Euphrates and save the day. For some time, no message had come from him. Now it was almost certain he had gone over to Gallienus.

It was surely a sign that even Theodorus, the elderly, hesitant governor of unarmed Cyprus, had sent messengers west openly repudiating Quietus.

A more visible proof yet was Fabius Labeo. Two nights earlier, the governor of Syria Coele had been apprehended inconspicuously leaving by the Apamea Gate. Few senators were much good at being inconspicuous. The two silver-mounted carriages and three wagons necessary to move his essentials and maintain the governor's *dignitas* had rather taken the clandestine edge off Labeo's movements. With tears running down his face, he had maintained he had been leaving to levy troops in his provincial capital of Antioch. Even Quietus had not believed it. Fabius Labeo now resided in a metal cage hanging over the Apamea Gate. No one was to give him food or water, on pain of joining him. It was generally agreed that the punishment, if novel and possibly unRoman, did show a certain poetic justice.

'Ready, *Dominus*?' The Praetorian's head popped up through the trapdoor.

Down below, Rutilus and Castricius were waiting. It was the appointed time to make their daily report to Quietus. Three senior centurions from the Praetorians, including Jucundus, fell in behind as they set off across town for the palace. Apart from occasional trips to the temple of Elagabalus, Quietus never left the palace now.

The officers did not talk as they marched. As soldiers did, Castricius twirled the end of his belt. The metal fitting at the tip thrummed through the air. It was good that he was here. Ballista would have liked to talk to him, but not in front of the centurions, any one of whom, even Jucundus, could be an informer. And there was Rutilus – a good officer, but he had never given any sign he was other than completely loyal to the house of Macrianus.

At the gates of the palace, the Roman officers were brought up short. There was not a single Praetorian to be seen. On duty instead was the royal guard of Sampsigeramus. They could not have formed a greater contrast to the Romans in their plain white un-dress tunics and dark trousers. The Emesenes owned a lack of uniformity that was magnificent and colourful – saffron, blinding white, delicate rose; embroidered with flowers, striped and hemmed. Some had put down their spiked helmets and inlaid shields. Most leant back against the walls, a few with their eyes shut against the glare. Off to the right, a couple had gone further. They sat, heads drooping, with their arms around their drawn-up knees.

Not all were so somnambulant. Their commander may have eased his feet out of his sandals, but his eyes were watchful. He admitted the Roman officers with pursed, contemptuous lips.

They went down one long, cool corridor after another. Now and then, windows opened on to well-watered, shady gardens where caged birds sang. It was hard to believe that the vanguard of the besieging army was not a mile from this profound peace.

A final corridor, and they were at the door of the women's rooms. The guards here had taken lethargy further. A scatter of slippers. Five pairs of naked feet. The warriors lay on a richly patterned carpet. The bottom step of a flight of three served as their pillow. At the top, their leader reclined against a doubled-over cushion. He spoke in Aramaic. One of his men got up and drifted through the door.

Awake, but supine, the guards regarded the Romans with insolent eyes. Behind the easterners, the door was opened. The Emesenes rose to their feet. Their gorgeous silks and languid movements suggested something of the inhabitants of the women's quarters. They followed the Romans up the steps and through the door.

The inside of the women's quarters of the palace of the king of Emesa would have confirmed every prejudice against the Orient of every stern Roman moralist of old. Cincinnatus would have fled back to his plough. Cato the Censor would have had apoplexy.

The room was bathed in a lurid red light. There was an almost overpowering smell of perfume and wine. The emperor Quietus lay on a couch. The priest-king reclined against his chest. Both men were half naked. Quietus absent-mindedly toyed with Sampsigeramus's hair. On another couch, the emperor's cousin Macer lay on his back unconscious. An equally comatose girl lay across him.

In the gloom at the rear of the room was an enormous bed. Girls moved in the shadows behind it. Four more slept on it. They were naked apart from the odd wisp of material, limbs sprawled in abandonment. Another girl had collapsed and lay with the crushed flowers and spilt wine on the floor.

Ballista started to make the daily report. It was a carefully worded thing, keeping to the official line and troop numbers. Even so, Quietus clearly was not interested. He quickly interrupted.

'It is written in the stars that this is a turning point for us. The gods turn their anger on the camel herder of Palmyra. The storm howls around Odenathus's impious ears.'

Ballista broke the ensuing silence. '*Dominus*, the storm is unlikely to delay the Palmyrenes for long, not more than a day.'

'They say Odenathus has a beautiful wife.' Quietus's voice was reflective. 'I will enjoy her when he is defeated.'

Sampsigeramus giggled knowingly.

Rutilus spoke. '*Dominus*, Odenathus will be here by dusk tomorrow.'

Quietus ignored him.

'We will form a new legion.' Suddenly the emperor sat up, full of manic energy. 'Legio XXXI Macriana Victrix. Its symbol will be the symbol of my family, the image of Alexander the Great. My father always said that those who wear the likeness of the Macedonian are aided in all they do. It will be the same with the legion. After its first victory, we will add the title "*Invictus*". Rutilus, conscript men from Emesa, and make up the numbers with drafts from the existing legions.'

'We will do what is ordered, and at every command we will be ready,' said Rutilus.

Quietus looked momentarily downcast. 'Treachery all around me. Maeonius Astyanax – my father trusted him. Now Pomponius Bassus – he will lead no army down the Euphrates.'

With no warning, the emperor brightened. 'But it is of no account, none at all. My *Princeps Peregrinorum* has arranged everything.' He looked over to where Macer lay, stunned by alcohol. The emperor laughed fondly. 'Before he took his deserved rest – *otium* must always follow *negotium*, it is the ancestral Roman way – my beloved cousin sent envoys bearing princely gifts to the leader of the Arab confederation of the deep desert. Jadhima of the Tanukh will ride at the head of his horde. The Arabs will fall on Odenathus, scatter his army like chaff on the threshing floor.'

The news was received in silence. The officers tried not to give away their feelings. The idea that any confederation of Arabs could ever come out of the desert and defeat a regular army in open battle was too ridiculous for words.

Rutilus tried again. '*Dominus*, our scouts say the storm will blow out quickly. Odenathus will be here by dusk tomorrow.'

'Tomorrow, the day after, it makes no difference.' Quietus waved a hand at Ballista. 'The night he arrives, you will lead a raid into the heart of his camp. If you cannot bring him to me alive, you will bring me his head. It will be finished.'

'We will do what is ordered, and at every command we will be ready.'

And Odenathus will be ready too, thought Ballista. Now a collection of Emesene guards and palace girls know of the plan. Odenathus knew what he was about. He would have spies in the palace.

'By the next dawn, the Lion of the Sun will be dead,' Quietus added softly, 'or others will suffer.'

*   *   *

Night and not enough darkness. The flames of the torches sawed in the wind. The orange glow illuminated the inside of the Palmyra Gate. Only at the very top of the tall arch night still held sway. Lower down, the sculptures of the eagle, altar and conical stone of Elagabalus were thrown into shifting heavy relief. Below them, the palimpsest of graffiti – thanks to the god for safe arrivals or pleas for help getting across the desert unharmed – was almost legible.

Night and far too much noise. The five hundred or so Praetorians gathering for the raid stamped their feet against the chill breeze, or just out of boredom. The unbound hobnails of their boots rang on the paving stones. There was a continual jingle and chink of equipment; several thousand metallic awards for valour, and good-luck charms hung on their harnesses. There was a low buzz of talk. One or two groups were passing around wine-skins.

Disciplina was not good in the army of Quietus. But there was a deeper reason for the men's behaviour. The Praetorians had been seconded from the eastern legions, and they had a reputation among officers for lack of *disciplina*. How could it be otherwise? Their camps were not in bleak frontier fastnesses like Caledonia or Germania but near comfortable towns. Sometimes they were even billeted in the towns themselves. And the towns were eastern. Most of the men had been recruited locally. At bottom, they were easterners, with all that implied about insolence and loose living.

No one had told the Praetorians to bind rags round their hobnails, to take off their charms. No one had ordered them to stop talking or drinking. There was no absolute certainty of being obeyed. Ask any legionary or auxiliary out on the frontier – the Praetorians were over-paid, arrogant and pampered; all plumes and sashes; parade-ground soldiers, useless in a fight.

Ignoring the commotion, Ballista leant against the wall. He pulled an old black cloak around himself and shut his eyes. The usual smell of Roman soldiers: unwashed men, with undernotes of garlic, cheap perfume and sour wine. Once – when the centurion and his men had come to the hall of his father – it had been alien and frightening. Now – twenty-three winters later – it was homely and reassuring. Like everything else we think innate, the evocations of smell are often shaped by circumstances outside our control.

Ballista found himself thinking about Turpio. His old friend had boasted of a particularly keen sense of smell. Ballista wondered what scents had come to Turpio five years earlier as he had waited under another gate to Palmyra, the one at Arete, to lead a mission with a different target but the same aim. Turpio had so nearly taken the Persian King of Kings unaware in his tent. But he had not. All he had taken was a golden bracelet. And years later, it had proved his death.

> *For mortals, mortal things. And all things leave us.*
> *Or if they do not, then we leave them.*

The lines ran through Ballista's mind. Turpio had been fond of modern poetry, but Ballista had no intention of letting this nocturnal raid be the death of him.

'Have a rest, you poor little thing.' Calgacus puffed up and put down the two lanterns he was carrying. 'After tonight, we may have all fucking eternity to rest.'

Somewhere in the town, dogs were barking. In Aeneas Tacticus's book on defending a town under siege, the general was advised that, to avoid noise and confusion, all dogs, strays and otherwise, should be rounded up and killed. Ballista had read the book at least twice. In this town, he had not acted on that piece of advice.

'Here comes Jucundus,' said Calgacus.

Ballista opened his eyes.

Jucundus marched up and saluted. The noise from the Praetorians had dropped appreciably with his arrival. Jucundus was solid dependability personified. He reported his men ready; a column five wide and a hundred deep to pass through the gate; once outside, they would redeploy ten wide.

Ballista thanked him. They waited for Castricius.

The sometime convict now Prefect of Cavalry came down the steps from the artillery platform two at a time. The stone-thrower and the two bolt-throwers were ready. Ballista thanked him.

The northerner drew Jucundus close to quietly explain the stratagem, for should Ballista fall, Jucundus must carry it out. The artillery pieces were drawn back but unloaded. At night you could seldom see the missiles fly. If the raid got into trouble, these two blue lanterns should be hoisted. Castricius would release the artillery – they sound the same whether they are loaded or not. With luck, Odenath-us's men would think they were being shot at – there is little more frightening than incoming missiles you cannot see – and retreat out of range. It had worked before with the Persians at the siege of Arete. The gods willing, it would work again now.

'We will do what is ordered, and at every command we will be ready.' The two officers went to withdraw. Ballista indicated Castricius to remain. The northerner talked so that only Castricius could hear. The latter listened intently, the flaring torches scouring deeper the many lines on his face, highlighting its points and sharp angles. The talk was obviously of serious matters, but in the flickering light Castricius never looked more like a playful creature from a backwoods myth.

It was time to see if the raid could go ahead at all. Castricius clattered back up the stone steps. Ballista asked one of the legionaries on the gate – they were from III Felix – to open the postern. Following Calgacus through, he noticed it was big enough for someone to lead a horse.

The postern shut behind them. The rectangle of orange light vanished. Ballista was left in profound darkness. He stood still, waiting for his night vision. Beside him, Calgacus hawked and spat.

The nearly full moon was somewhere over Ballista's right shoulder. He stood in the deep shadow of the town walls. Beyond was the moon-blanched landscape. He went out into it. Calgacus followed.

The road ran away, very light, smooth and straight. Near at hand, on either side, prominent and reassuring to Romans of rank with a clear conscience, stood the symbols of the divinely inspired power which upheld the stability of the *imperium*. The crosses were empty, but there was a dark stain at the base of the one to the left.

Ballista did not like to wonder what fluids were its cause. Maybe the local dogs pissed there.

The shadow of the right-hand cross pointed diagonally off down the road. The eastern necropolis of Emesa was like a reduced version of those outside Palmyra; the same tower, temple and house tombs, but most of them on a somewhat smaller scale. The houses of the dead were close-set. The ground between them was rough and stony. It would make it difficult to outflank the raiding party on the road. At least that was something good.

Little else was good. The necropolis ran for about two hundred yards. About the same distance further out were the picket fires of the Palmyrene army. They burned rose-red, were well made up, evenly spaced. Beyond them, yet another couple of hundred yards, were the bigger fires of another picket line around the main camp. These too looked well tended. There were Roman regulars among the blockading army. *Vexillationes* of at least three legions had been seen: III Cyrenaica from Arabia, XV Apollinaris from Cappadocia and, mirroring the detachment in Quietus's force, III Felix from Circesium. Yet Ballista considered that the Palmyrenes needed no guides in the craft of war – they knew what they were about.

As for Odenathus, he not only knew what he was about, nature was aiding him too. The moon, like some radical democrat in old Athens, wanted everything out in the open and treated all the same. It was bright as day but without the colours. The world was snow-blue or black. Anything that did not stay in the shadows was visible for miles.

As if the gods wanted to reiterate the point, a fox came

out from behind one of the furthermost tombs. Ballista watched it cross the road. Its high ears and low body were strangely one-dimensional; its shadow had an unreal depth. But tricks of the moonlight aside, it was easy to see.

A single fox at a couple of hundred yards – what price five hundred men at twice the distance? This was hopeless. If pressed home, suicidal.

Ballista walked back to the postern and kicked it to signal that the operation should get under way.

The Palmyra Gate had not been oiled. The shriek of its hinges rushed away across the plain. Not all the torches had been extinguished. The Praetorians were orange-tinged silhouettes as they emerged. The gate shrieked shut behind them. The soldiers jingled and thumped into their new formation.

As if Odenathus did not know we were coming anyway, Ballista thought. Calgacus at his side, he took his place with Jucundus at the head of the column. Ballista ordered the standard bearer Gratius to signal the advance. Best get it over.

In the forsaken, luminous light, their shadows went on far ahead. The shadows ran on as if the men's souls had already left and were flitting away, searching for some fissure to slide down to Hades.

Ballista could hear nothing over the heavy tramp of boots and the higher notes of harness and weapons, like ten thousand bone dice clinking together. He could see no movement from the nearer picket fires. Even if not forewarned, the Palmyrenes must have heard or seen them coming. He knew they were walking into an ambush.

They were clear of the last of the necropolis. The land opened up all around, flat and deadly. Two hundred yards to go. No movement by the fires. Come on, come on. Get on with it. One hundred and fifty. They were within bow-shot. In the darkness beyond the fires, the Palmyrene archers would be notching arrows, waiting for them to walk into a good, effective range – the range where the tip of an arrow can punch through the best steel armour and into the delicate flesh it covers.

Twang-slide-thump. From the wall behind them, loud in the night, the sound of an artillery piece. The lanterns were still shuttered in Calgacus's hands. Twang-slide-thump: the sound of another. Now there could be no question of surprise.

'Halt!' Even as Ballista's voice faded, a trumpet called from beyond the fires. Seconds later, no one in the column could help but duck as they heard the whoosh of arrows.

There was only one scream. The first flight had almost all fallen short.

'About turn. Quick march.' The Praetorians jostled to obey.

Again the horrible sound of unseen arrows. Again just a solitary yell of pain. The second volley had also been misjudged.

Ballista looked over his shoulder. He saw his own shadow, elongated into the distance. It was the moonlight. In the uncanny light, distances were hard to judge.

A terrible, huge, tearing sound. Screams behind them. Castricius had decided the time had come for his artillery to use missiles. All along the wall, from tower to tower, echoed the sounds of torsion artillery. They were shooting virtually blind into the night; aiming roughly at the picket fires. Yet it should be enough to deter any close pursuit.

'Run!' Ballista shouted.

The gate banged shut behind them. The orange torchlight could not have been more welcoming. They had not returned unscathed. The ever-efficient Jucundus reckoned ten men missing. It could have all been so very much worse.

XXII

The palace of Emesa, like that of Minos, was a maze. Of course, the Emesene priest-kings had had over three centuries to add architectural complexity. There had been a Sampsigeramus waiting all those years earlier when Pompey the Great had first led Roman arms into Syria.

Even if they had just been given instructions, it would be doubtful if Ballista, Castricius and Jucundus would have found their way to this secluded courtyard on their own. The morning after the failed raid, this had not been put to the test. Summoned in haste, they had arrived at the main gate and had been taken in charge by no less than sixteen of the Emesene royal guard. As Jucundus had muttered, the odds were worse than five to one.

Since the time of the first emperor, the Praetorians had been among the few who were allowed to be armed in the imperial presence. The more recent post of Prefect of Cavalry was one of the others. None of this held any longer at the court of Quietus. The Emesene guards had brusquely disarmed and thoroughly searched Ballista and the other two. Their weapons and armour were piled negligently against the wall. The easterners, uncaring of their wounded foreign *dignitas*, had hustled them like condemned prisoners through the myriad corridors of the palace.

Like the palace of Minos, at the heart of the maze was something unpleasant. Quietus at first completely ignored the new arrivals. The emperor was dressed in eastern fashion: long, flowing robes, a jewelled dagger in his sash. Arm in arm with Sampsigeramus, he wandered here and there across the courtyard. Quietus inspected things, issued commands and reproofs, even the occasional word of encouragement.

The open space was a hive of activity. At one end, slaves were laying out a huge array of precious things: paintings, sculptures, dinner services in gold, silver and electrum, intricate carpets and curtains, silken garments. Quietus studied them closely, head on one side, rearranging his hair with one finger. Sometimes he ordered an item removed and another brought out in its place. Opposite all this, other slaves were building an elaborate pyre, surely too close to the wall; with the amount of scented oils being poured, it would burn with an all-consuming ferocity.

Ballista had seen nothing like it before, but it was all oddly familiar.

There was an awning strung over the whole courtyard. It was torn near the centre and let in a column of clean light. The slaves walked tentatively around it, as if it were solid. The emperor and his friend avoided it as if it could hurt.

Despite the shade, it was hot. Soon Quietus and his delicate eastern priest-king needed a rest. At a word, work was suspended. A couch was brought out and they reclined between the mountain of luxuries and the half-built pyre. They sipped drinks chilled with the snow of Mount Libanus.

Ballista stood rigid. Castricius and Jucundus did the same. They were unarmed, ringed by guards, prey to justified fears. Quietus's words at their last meeting ran round and round in Ballista's thoughts: by dawn, the Lion of the Sun would be dead, or others would suffer. The northerner pictured the senator Astyrius in the gloom of the temple; his headless trunk in the pooling blood. Rather that happen to himself, here and now in this sweltering courtyard, than any harm come to his boys. Let this be over. It was the waiting that always threatened to unman you. Calm, calm. In a way, what was life but one long wait for the final, horrible thing?

At long last, Quietus waved a long-sleeved arm to summon them over. They got up from *proskynesis*. The sand of the yard had been watered to keep the dust down. It fell in crumbling lumps from the front of their tunics.

Quietus gestured, palm limply up, at a painting. Ballista recognized it as the one from the *consilium* in the palace at Antioch: *The Wedding of Alexander* by Aetion.

'What do you think it means?' Quietus asked.

The three officers may have had views, but they kept quiet.

'My dear Sampsigeramus thinks it shows how love and sex can make even the most warlike men, such as the great conqueror, forget the battlefield and soften their bellicose natures.'

Quietus gently ran his hand through Sampsigeramus's hair. 'My dear boy is too trusting. Look what those cupids are doing. Some of them distract Alexander by pulling the clothes off Roxanne. The others drag away his weapons out of reach. All the while, two men stand behind him, another peers around the door. Treachery – it is nothing but an allegory of treachery.'

The awning snapped in the silence.

'Nothing has been spared me,' Quietus complained. 'No disappointment, no treachery, no dishonour, no betrayal. Maeonius Astyanax, Pomponius Bassus, even that weak old fool Theodorus – all traitors. At least Fabius Labeo is discovering the ultimate wages of treachery.'

Quietus suddenly spread his hands wide, palms up. 'And where is the Lion of the Sun this morning? Is he grovelling in the dirt at my feet? Instead, the three of you stand here. Tell me, why did last night's raid end in ignominious failure? What was it if not yet more treachery?'

'No, *Dominus*.' Ballista was surprised how resolute his voice sounded. 'The Palmyrenes were vigilant. Our men were ill-disciplined. It was bad luck. No treachery.'

'That cannot be.' Quietus was adamant. 'Someone must be held accountable, or the world may think this failure reflects on our own majesty. Our *maiestas* must be sacrosanct.' His gaze flicked feverishly over the three officers. 'And one of you has already shown himself a traitor.'

The three men stood very still. More Emesene guards appeared from the corners of the yard. The officers were surrounded. There was nothing languid about these easterners. There was the slither of swords being drawn. The Romans stood empty-handed.

Ballista measured the distance to the imperial couch. Five, six paces. A ring of armed guards in the way. He had no weapon. Try to shoulder through, take the wounds. Get to the couch. Grab the ornamental dagger on the emperor's belt. Use it to kill Quietus. Hold the blade to Sampsigeramus's throat. The guards were his men. Bargain for a safe passage.

It was hopeless. Ballista knew he would not get two steps.

'Nothing spared . . . no betrayal,' Quietus said softly.

The three officers were rigid, waiting.

Quietus thrust out a finger at Jucundus. 'You' – his voice was low – 'you have been comforting my enemies. My enemy's friend is my enemy.'

The centurion knew his life hung on what he said. '*Dominus*, I have done no such thing. A malicious informer must have made a false accusation.'

Quietus, quiet as an owl, looked at him.

'*Dominus*.' The strain showed in Jucundus's voice. '*Dominus*, the *delator* must be in the pay of Odenathus – trying to remove your loyal officers.'

'Not at all,' said Quietus. 'What you did is widely known. You have not even made a secret of it.'

Jucundus was silent.

'You cannot deny taking all manner of comforts into the prison for Ballista.' Quietus smirked like a man who has made a winning throw at dice.

Ballista reacted first. 'But, *Dominus*,' he exclaimed, 'I am not your enemy. I am one of your Praetorian Prefects. You have entrusted me with the defence of the city.'

'All true now,' Quietus shouted, 'but not true then. Then I thought you were my enemy – that is enough. Jucundus openly succoured a traitor, threatened the gaoler

that he better treat the traitor well, betrayed all my trust.'
Quietus was almost screaming; flecks of spittle flew from
his lips. 'What price loyalty when my wishes are openly
mocked?'

Ballista persevered. 'You trust me to command Emesa.
Jucundus is one of my most trusted officers.'

'You boast of your loyalty? Well, prove it now. Take a
sword and execute the traitor Jucundus.'

A guard stood forward, reversed his sword, held the
hilt out towards the Romans.

Ballista did not move.

'Cut him down, or you will die with him.'

A rasp of steel. Quick as a snake, Jucundus had the
sword in hand. Its owner leapt back.

The Emesene guards crouched, ready to fight, just
waiting for a move or a word of command.

Jucundus changed his grip, thrust the tip of the blade
up under his breastbone.

'I will die like a man, not for your amusement.' Jucundus's eyes did not leave Quietus. 'You will die worse. I
pray to the gods to be avenged.'

Jucundus threw himself forward. The hilt hit the sand.
The blade tore up into his innards. He writhed sideways,
groaning in agony.

Ballista found himself on his knees by Jucundus. 'Finish it,' the dying man whispered. Ballista prised the hands
loose from the hilt. He twisted the blade, withdrew it,
thrust again. Jucundus sighed a great sigh and died.

Ballista got to his feet. The knees of his trousers were
soaked in blood. The reeking sword was still in his hand.

The guards hefted their weapons.

Ballista dropped the sword. It thudded on to the stained, fouled sand.

'For I too am dust . . . ,' Quietus mused. 'Life does not forgive weakness . . . You two return to your duties.'

They recovered their weapons and armour. They left Jucundus's where they lay. Outside, they shouldered the general guilt of the survivor and their own sharper, more specific, individual guilts. They walked. Briefly, they were alone. Ballista put his arm around Castricius's shoulder and talked low and fast into his ear.

Castricius turned off to his headquarters above the Palmyra Gate. Ballista walked on to the Tower of Desolation. He climbed the winding staircase. There were six Praetorians on lookout, about all the fighting top could comfortably hold. Ballista told one of them to go and get Calgacus; the freedman was to bring his *patronus* a papyrus roll, ink and stylus as well as his best, favourite black cloak. Ballista leant forward, settled his elbows on the low parapet and waited.

When Calgacus appeared, Ballista dismissed all the Praetorians.

'Quietus killed Jucundus.' There was no need for preamble.

'I heard.'

'Of the three of us, he was the innocent one. He was gone when I told Castricius to make sure one of the artillery pieces was released early.'

'I know it. But there is nothing to be done about it now.'

'Quietus is building a pyre in the palace.'

'Many men will kill themselves rather than be taken

alive – the Romans make a cult of it.' Calgacus shrugged. 'Sooner the fucker is on it the better.'

'It is not just himself he intends to kill,' said Ballista.

Calgacus pursed his lips.

'There was a king of Assyria called Sardanapallus,' said Ballista. 'He was besieged for two years in his capital, Nineveh. When there was no hope, he had every precious thing he owned and everything he had enjoyed collected together. The women and boys he had fucked, all the horses he had ridden – their throats were cut. The bodies and the treasures were burned with him.'

Still Calgacus said nothing.

'Quietus is heaping up his things by the pyre. I think he intends to play the Assyrian. He wants his passing to be marked by an orgy of destruction. He will take many others with him. Quietus is insane.'

'Aye, most likely,' said Calgacus. 'So you have to play the hero again.'

'I am going to fulfil a vow I made some time ago,' Ballista said seriously. Then he laughed. 'And you get to play the hero too.'

'Fucking wonderful,' Calgacus said, without expression.

'Get two quiet horses and some drab clothes. Keep an eye on this tower. When you see me wave this best black cloak from the battlements here, go to the prison. Kill the gaoler and any of his assistants – there is seldom more than one – they do not look like fighters. Ride with the boys and Julia to the Palmyra Gate. Castricius is expecting you. He will let you out through the postern gate. Take them to Haddudad and Odenathus.'

'And you?'

'I am going to play on Quietus's obsession with treachery to get him to come here.'

'And then?'

'Cheer up, sooner or later he will probably kill us all anyway.'

Ballista looked out from the Tower of Desolation at the desert and the sown. The strip of tilled land was full of Odenathus's army. In the desert was nothingness, desert absolute.

If you were dressed in just a tunic, with the breeze, it was almost cool up here. Calgacus had helped him strip off his equipment. Though they had done it before, it was hard saying goodbye to the old Caledonian, very hard. Nearly a lifetime of largely unspoken affection. Calgacus had asked him would he not go and see his boys. Ballista would not. He had not the courage for it. Tell them he loved them. Tell her too.

The old man had left without a word of complaint.

Up on the tower, Ballista had waited. Calgacus needed time to collect the horses and clothes. The sun had crawled across the sky. Eventually, Ballista had summoned a Praetorian to go to Quietus with a message.

Before he left, Calgacus had handed over the things. The best black cloak lay at Ballista's feet. The writing things were in his hands. He must write something. A letter to his boys and wife? Depending on how things fell out, it might be twisted and used against them. He wrote, 'Legio III Felix'. Then he tore from the roll the thin strip of papyrus with the words and twined it round his fingers.

Ballista, stylus in one hand, scrap of papyrus in the other, leant on the crenellations and tried to calm his thoughts. The Norns had spun his fate. The length of his life and the day of his death had been fated long ago. Nothing he could do would unpick it.

His mind was not stilled. Too many questions were running through it, treading hard on each other's heels. Would Quietus come? Most likely – he was baited with treachery, and he was mad for treachery. Had Maximus reached Palmyra? Had Haddudad taken him to Odenathus? Had the Lion of the Sun believed Ballista's letter? Was Maximus out there watching this very tower from somewhere in the camp now? There was no telling for any of it. Would Calgacus save his boys and Julia? About this, the most important question, he felt oddly calm. He had no doubt that Calgacus could deal with the gaoler and his assistants. Of course Castricius would see them safe through the postern gate. Haddudad owed Ballista's family every hospitality. He almost smiled at the thought of Julia and Bathshiba together. But then, what of himself – would he succeed or fail?

And when it was done or not, what then? Was there an afterlife? The Christians seemed certain. It buoyed them up in the face of the steel and fire. Ballista had seen the insane resolve it gave them. But it made no sense to him. The resurrection of the body – what a nonsense. Why would you want to come back old and infirm, wracked with the pain of the thing that killed you? And if you had a choice, how could it work? You wanted to be thirty. You wanted to be with the twenty-year-old woman you loved then. But your sons were not born then, and you wanted to be with them too. As for the woman, maybe she had a better time of it with someone else. It would be an accommodating god that would give each Christian their own heaven.

Ballista's ancestral Valhalla seemed a far better choice: the slick-palmed excitement of battle every day. You took the pain, but then wounds miraculously healed, there was a feast every night – food, drink, poetry, the friendship of men, and later, as the stars wheeled across the bottomless sky, the love of women. But even here, problems crept in, like the Evil One. In Ballista's childhood, there had been no mention of books in the hall of the Allfather. But now, without reading, it would be a barren existence for him. And his boys – there could be no certainty they would join him. And being without them would be far worse than losing all the books in the world. Twenty-three winters in the *imperium* had changed him. The boys had changed him.

Ballista felt hungry. He called down for a Praetorian to bring him some bread and cheese, some ham as well. After the soldier had gone, he realized ham might be difficult in a town where the natives appeared not to eat pork. Still, Roman soldiers had never been renowned for their sensitivities to other cultures.

No sooner had the food arrived, ham and all, than the cavalcade of Quietus appeared in the street below. The emperor was dressed in eastern costume and attended by twenty gorgeously caparisoned Emesene cavalrymen.

Ballista was eating when the Praetorian brought a couple of the local troopers up. The latter searched the northerner with as much impertinence as they could muster. They took away his food, fingered his cloak and writing materials suspiciously, and peered around the minuscule fighting area for anywhere a concealed weapon might lurk. When satisfied, one of them went back down the stairs. Neither the other nor the Praetorian took their eyes off Ballista.

It took some time for the emperor to climb to the top of the tower. When he emerged, he was out of breath, leaning on the arm of an easterner. Another Praetorian followed.

There was barely room for Ballista to perform *proskynesis*.

Quietus shook himself free of the trooper. The four armed men wedged themselves close together at the top of the steps. It gave just a little room to the emperor and his Praetorian Prefect.

'Get up.' Quietus's voice was peevish. 'This had better be true.'

As Ballista got to his feet, he picked up the scrap of papyrus and the stylus. 'It could not be more so, *Dominus*.' He handed over the curling papyrus.

Quietus unrolled it and read. 'Your messenger said this was shot over the wall tied to an arrow. It is the identity of the unit that wishes to come over to us.'

'The first unit that wishes to throw itself on your *clementia*. There will be others,' said Ballista. 'It makes sense that it is Legio III Felix. A *vexillatio* of the unit is already serving you.'

'And you arranged a signal to confirm this with the archer?'

'I am to wave a black cloak from this tower. If a similar cloak is waved from the siege lines below, Legio III will come into the city by the Palmyrene Gate tonight.'

'Well, what are you waiting for? Get on with it.'

Ballista reached down and gathered the cloak in his left hand. He lifted it high above his head. Making quite sure it could be seen from inside as well as outside the city, he waved it vigorously.

'From where in their lines will they answer?' Quietus was leaning on the parapet, gazing out.

'I do not know, *Dominus*.' Ballista put the cloak down. 'We must watch and wait.'

'There! There it is!' Quietus was pointing, all his attention on the enemy outside.

Do not think, just act.

Ballista stabbed the stylus into the emperor's neck. Quietus, howling, tried to turn, hands reaching up for the wound. Ballista withdrew the stylus, dropped it. He heard movement behind him. He grabbed the emperor, one hand clutching the embroidered front of Quietus's tunic, the other at his crotch. Blood was flowing down both of them. Ballista hauled him up the battlements, pushed him backwards. Quietus's hands clawed. One locked in Ballista's hair, the other scratched at his face. More violent movements at the stairhead, out of sight. Ballista pushed Quietus out over the crenellations. Only the emperor's legs were still in the tower.

Ballista let go.

Quietus's pouched little eyes were wide in realization and fear, filthy little mouth open in a despairing scream.

Ballista felt pain as a handful of his hair was torn out.

Quietus fell, arms and legs flailing hopelessly as he scraped down the sheer stone wall and on to the hard, unforgiving rocks below.

No noise behind Ballista. He had not been attacked. He turned slowly. He was unarmed. He had even dropped the stylus.

The two Praetorians faced him. Swords drawn.

A pool of blood flowed out from where one of the easterners lay. It began to drip and then run over the top step. The other Emesene was nowhere to be seen.

Ballista looked at the Praetorians. One of them had a distinctive angular face, a huge hooked nose.

The Praetorians looked at each other, then back at Ballista.

As one, they reversed swords, held the hilts out, and shouted.

'*Ave Caesar! Ave Imperator Marcus Clodius Ballista Augustus!*'

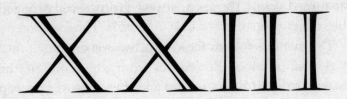

XXIII

An *imperium* of three men, one of them the emperor. There had been ten subjects, the whole *contubernium* stationed at the Tower of Desolation, but Ballista had sent one to each of the six legions, and one each to Castricius and Rutilus. None of them had come back. He was left standing at the base of the tower with Ahala and Malchus, the two Praetorians who had originally hailed him emperor.

Ballista laughed at the improbability of his elevation. An unarmed barbarian. He'd even left the stylus somewhere up on the battlements. A new Augustus with ten followers. Now down to two. It was good that the Emesene cavalrymen had run away when Quietus was killed. But this could still be a very short reign.

There came the sound of running feet. Hobnailed boots, jingling harness. Soldiers, coming fast, and not a few of them. It could be a very short reign indeed.

Ballista saw Ahala and Malchus look at each other. Any misgivings now were futile. Their fate was bound to his like a dog to a cart.

The soldiers came round the corner – from their shields, men of Legio XVI Flavia Firma. There were about forty of them, headed by a centurion. In the reduced circumstances of the army, it was what passed for a century. The legionaries had drawn swords. They were in no doubt where they were headed. They were running purposefully.

'Titus went to them,' said Malchus. 'He is bringing them to us.'

'I do not see him,' said Ahala.

Malchus looked beseechingly at Ahala. The latter shook his angular head. There was nothing to do. The two who first hailed a failed pretender had nowhere to run.

Sunlight flashed on the advancing blades.

The centurion flung up his right hand.

The legionaries halted. Five, six paces away. They were panting. They were tired, but they were ready to kill – they had that wildness about them.

'*Dominus.*' The centurion saluted. He was not young. The impressive array of awards on his armour rattled as his chest heaved. '*Dominus*, Sampsigeramus has declared himself emperor. He has ordered the palace fortified. He is leading troops to sieze the temple of Elagabalus.'

There had been no acclamation, no *proskynesis*, but the centurion had called Ballista *Dominus*. As emperor or as prefect? The thing hung in the balance. But clearly he would rather lead his men on the orders of Ballista than the priest-king of Emesa.

'Do you know how many men he has with him, Centurion?' Ballista's voice was calm, competent.

'No idea, *Dominus*. There has been fighting. Sampsigeramus's men attacked some of those who would not take the *sacramentum* to him.'

'Does he have Romans as well as Emesenes?'

'We saw some from Legio III Gallica, some auxiliaries as well.'

It was not a huge surprise. Legio III Gallica had been the local legion for a long time. It had supported other pretenders – Heliogabalus, Iotapianus, Uranius Antoninus – from the royal house of Emesa.

'Have any of the Emesene troops refused to acknowledge him?'

'Not that I know, *Dominus*.'

The Actium trick, thought Ballista, we will have to try that. Octavian, the first Augustus, had declared war not on Mark Antony but on Cleopatra. Turn a civil war into a foreign one. Any Romans on the other side have been so corrupted by decadent foreign ways, just like Antony, they have ceased to count as Romans.

'Men coming, *Dominus*,' said Ahala.

These soldiers were marching without undue haste. They were from a regular auxiliary unit, Dacian spearmen, about eighty of them. They stopped as one and saluted smartly. With the hope of a donative, they moved as if on a parade ground.

'*Ave* Imperator Caesar Marcus Clodius Ballista.'

Their centurion introduced himself and announced that imperial regalia must be found: the diadem and purple cloak, the sacred fire, the wreaths of oak and laurel. And *lictors*, there must be the right number of *lictors* carrying the *fasces*.

Ballista thanked him, but said finding him some arms and armour was more pressing. This went down well with all the *milites* present. Ballista sent a couple of legionaries to Hippothous at the rented house for his equipment, and another one to the Palmyra Gate to talk to Castricius. He had been going to send one to check the gaol when he remembered that Sampsigeramus had fortified the palace.

Now Ballista had about a hundred and twenty men with him. He knew more were prepared to fight Sampsigeramus, were already fighting him. Time for a speech while they got his armour, then off to try the luck of war at the temple of Elagabalus.

'*Commilitiones*' – Ballista's voice was used to reaching the rear ranks – 'The tryant is dead! I killed him with my bare hands – these hands.' He paused while they cheered. 'I had no thought except to free the army and the *Res Publica* from his foul actions, the filthy actions that degraded us all. When the soldiers hailed me emperor, I could not have been more surprised. I have no desire for the high office. I would walk away now, but the situation does not allow it. The *Res Publica* is in deadly danger again. The tyrant may be dead, but his teacher in tyranny – or should we say his husband? – is alive. Sampsigeramus, this *cinaedus*, this sniggering little easterner, is not only alive, but he has the audacity to claim the purple! These arrogant orientals never learn. We all know what happened to his kinsman Heliogabalus – dragged through the streets by a hook, then stuffed into a sewer.'

'The hook, the hook . . . drag him, drag him.'

Ballista waved his arm for silence. The chanting stopped as if performed by a well-trained chorus.

'And who supports him? A bunch of easterners like himself.'

The soldiers jeered – no matter where they came from, their primary identity was Roman soldier.

'Wait,' shouted Ballista. 'Do not get overconfident. We have a dangerous fight on our hands. These easterners are tough – they only ever wear the thinnest silks. And they have stamina – they must have to take it up the arse all night.'

The soldiers liked this stuff. Ballista knew it was all bollocks. But the soldiers liked this stuff.

'If you come across any from Legio III Gallica, do not worry. They have been out here so long, they have gone native. They are worse than the natives – taught the locals how to suck cock. Not one of them did not start his life abandoned on a dung heap in a back street of Raphanaea or some such Syrian shithole.'

'*Fuck them, fuck them . . .*'

'It is time to go and pull this effeminate off the throne. Sampsigeramus is hiding in the temple of Elagabalus. The god will not help him. We will drag him out and kill him.'

'Drag him, drag him . . . the hook, the hook.'

'Remember the temple is sacrosanct. Any soldier pillaging it will suffer the harshest penalty. But the palace is not. After we have dealt with Sampsigeramus, shall we see what we can find there?'

'*Dives miles, dives miles.*'

'After I have had a look at his treasury – all the wealth taken by the avarice of Quietus's father – a donative to the loyal troops will be announced.'

'Rich soldier, rich soldier.'

Hippothous and some other men had appeared with Ballista's weapons and armour, his original bird-crested helmet. They helped him into it. There was still no word from Castricius about his sons and Julia, but he had to put them from his mind.

The troops fell in, and they set off.

On the way across town, their force was augmented by a complete *ala* of Dalmatian cavalrymen. They had come straight from their barracks. They had left their horses behind as unsuitable for urban fighting. They were lightly armoured and there were only about two hundred and fifty of them but, to Ballista's tiny force, they were a hugely welcome addition.

The great temple of Elagabalus was set in a walled precinct, however, no attempt had been made to defend the outer walls. The main gates stood untended and open.

Perhaps Sampsigeramus did not have all that many men with him. He would have left a substantial number to hold his palace. Presumably more Emesene warriors would still be at their stations on the city walls. Ballista wondered just what Rutilus and Castricius were doing. This would be an opportune moment for Odenathus to attack.

While his men formed up in the street, Ballista peered in through the gates. The temple on its tall podium was in the region of a hundred paces away. Halfway between the gate and the temple was the great altar. Ballista noted that its three fires were still burning. There was no other cover. The sacred grove was off to the left, level with the temple. To the right there was nothing until some service buildings beyond the temple. Something like a hundred Emesene archers were drawn up at the foot of the steps in front of the temple. There were more of them up on the pediment and roof. It was quite possible yet more might be hidden among the conifers of the sacred grove.

Ballista had not yet seen any legionaries from III Gallica, or any Roman regulars at all, but this was going to be far from easy. One hundred paces across an open, arrow-swept yard. Ballista gave the order to attack anyway.

Ballista got ready to go in with the first rank from Legio XVI Flavia Firma. The days when an emperor could keep well to the rear – and keep the respect of his troops – were gone. His old enemy Maximinus Thrax had set the new precedent, charging in at the head of his men. Of course, apart from his strength and skill at arms, Maximinus Thrax had had little to recommend him as emperor. Like another barbarian very recently declared emperor, Ballista thought wryly.

The arrows came screaming at them as they went through the gate. They hunched forward like men advancing into hail. The noise was all-encompassing: arrowheads slicing into wood, metal, leather, flesh; men muttering, praying, shouting, howling. They kept going forward.

Ballista's shield felt as if it were being kicked as arrows slammed into it. Three of the warheads punched through, one only an inch or so from his face. He snapped them off, kept moving. He was sweating hard.

How far? Ballista peeped out around the edge of his shield. Allfather, they were only just coming up to the altar. The weird foreshortening as the arrows sped towards you. He ducked back, blocking out the screams, forcing his legs to keep moving.

A cheer from the men around him. Ballista looked out again. The arrow storm was still there, but less of it, and at a different angle. The archers at the foot of the steps had ceased shooting. They were fighting each other to get back through the doors of the temple. Those up on the pediment and roof still wielded their bows. There were not that many of them. Now Ballista was able to note there were no missiles coming from the sacred grove to his left.

Hefting their shields higher, the soldiers ran forward. The withdrawal of the enemy into the temple seemed to have struck shackles off their legs. They were at the foot of the steps in moments. They set off up them. Hobnails screeching, gouging the marble. The great dark-wood doors at the top slammed shut.

A whistling sound – above the noises of the men – unexplained, eerie. A terrible crash. The men stopped. A stunned silence, then the high screaming of men in agony.

Something made Ballista look up. Sometimes your eyes see something so unexpected your understanding lags behind. Figures falling through the air, turning slowly. Rigid, yet unresisting. Getting faster.

The next statue slammed into the steps a few paces away. Marble into marble. Vicious, jagged fragments flying. The white steps now veined red. Another crashed down. And another. Pandemonium.

Ballista was cowering down. His shield had a wide rent. There was blood on his right leg. The men were running. He looked up at the pediment. Another divinity was teetering on the edge. Ballista ran too.

Back safe behind the outer wall, Ballista called the officers to him and took stock. Not that many casualties. They had left twenty or so inside the precinct; the dead or those too hurt to crawl. About the same number had made it out but were incapacitated by injuries. Ballista ordered they be tended, as far as it was possible, where they were. He could not afford to be without the men needed to take them to doctors.

Ballista questioned those around him on the layout of the temple precinct. It was Ahala, now binding up the flesh wound in Ballista's right thigh, who proved extraordinarily informative. The wall was high all around the compound. There were two other gates. One at the far western end opened next to the service buildings. From there you could get into a low walled yard that butted up to the rear of the temple. There was a wicket gate to the yard and a small back door to the temple. They would almost certainly be defended, and it would be hard to force the narrow back door, but it was worth a look. The other gate was off to the left in the southern wall and led straight into the sacred grove. There was a forester's hut just by it.

'You know the layout well,' said Ballista.

Ahala looked embarrassed. 'When we first came here . . . some of the boys told me there were sacred prostitutes in the precinct – had to take you on for their god, no matter how low the coin.' He shrugged. 'I was stupid enough to believe them.'

'I would not worry,' replied Ballista, 'some years ago the same thing happened to a friend of mine.'

The laughter was cut short. A soldier running flat out down the street from the north. 'Men coming! Hundreds of them! Roman regulars.'

Ballista made what dispositions he could with his limited force: a few holding the gate from the temple at their rear, the rest blocking the street. There was no middle way here. It was either very good or very bad.

The noise built – it sounded like a lot of men. Soon such speculation was redundant. The soldiers turned the corner into full view, a solid phalanx of heavily armed men stretching as far as the eye could see. The sound of their coming bounced back off the walls. The shields at the front were those of Legio X Fretensis. Its station was the northern city wall, part of Rutilus's command. And there, bareheaded on horseback, was Rutilus himself. No one could mistake the flaming red hair of the Praetorian Prefect appointed by Quietus. Facing him, Ballista calculated quickly: counting the standards, multiplying the numbers in each rank by those in each file – must be about five hundred. Rutilus had brought the entire *vexillatio* with him. Further back, there were other standards – at least two auxiliary units.

Rutilus's force did not break stride at the sight of Ballista's men. Inexorably, the shields of Legio X bore down. One hundred paces. They had numbers and momentum on their side. Fifty paces. They would sweep the men facing them aside. Ballista knew being taken alive was not an option. No cell near the surface a second time. The deep dungeons and the claws.

Rutilus yelled a command. The *bucinatores* sounded their instruments. With a crash, the great phalanx halted.

In the succeeding quiet, Ballista heard a dove cooing from over in the conifer trees of the sacred grove.

The ranks of Legio X parted. Rutilus rode through and out into the space between the lines. All alone, and still bareheaded. He may have always been a faithful servant to the house of Macrianus, but he had never lacked courage.

Ballista stepped out from his meagre ranks.

The two men studied each other.

Rutilus got down from his horse. He untied something, a bag of sorts, from his saddle. He opened it and pulled out a human head. He held it by the hair then let it drop into the dust. His horse skittered sideways, away from the noisome thing. Rutilus prodded the head away with the toe of his boot.

'Death to all traitors,' he said.

The head was unrecognizable. Ballista waited, heart pounding.

'That was the tyrant's cousin and partner in vice – Cornelius Macer.'

Ballista exhaled silently.

Rutilus saluted. '*Ave* Imperator Caesar Marcus Clodius Ballista Augustus.'

Behind him, Rutilus's men took up the chant, with only the occasional '*Dives miles*' to remind their new Caesar of his obligations.

Rutilus had indeed brought with him all five hundred of Legio X Fretensis, as well as five hundred Armenian bowmen and five hundred dismounted Moorish cavalry-men armed with javelins.

Once Ballista was acquainted with the full force at his disposal, he outlined his plan quickly to Rutilus and the other officers. His original force was to guard the perimeter walls to the north and west and, without taking the risk of becoming too entangled, probe the gate near the service buildings, check the rear entrance. Ballista did not want to ask too much of them. It is always difficult to get men who have once escaped out of combat to go back into it the same day. The dismounted Moors and one hundred of the Armenian archers were to break in the southern gate, secure the sacred grove and prepare to shoot at the Emesenes on the roof of the temple. The men of Legio X would go in via the main east gate and assault the doors of the temple in two units formed in *testudo*. The remaining four hundred Armenians would follow them and attempt to discourage the men on the roof from intervening. To get them through the temple doors, a work party was to cut down two suitable conifers from the sacred grove as battering rams.

'Is it wise to chop down trees from a sacred grove?' A low muttering of concurrence greeted Rutilus's question. Soldiers were ever superstitious, especially when about to fight. This needed careful handling.

'The god will not hold it against us. It is our enemies – it is Sampsigeramus and his accomplices who have defiled the temple of Elagabalus. They have turned the god's house into a fortress. They have thrown down the sacred images from the roof.' Ballista raised his voice, made it ring. 'The great god Elagabalus offers us his sacred conifers. Elagabalus, *Sol Invictus*, calls on us to cleanse his house. Elagabalus, the unconquered sun, calls on us to drive out and punish the impious.'

Waiting frays the nerves. It seemed to take an eternity for the various bodies of men to get to their stations, for the huge tree trunks to be manhandled back, their branches lopped off and ends sharpened. Ballista's leg throbbed and stiffened. He felt slightly sick with hunger. His temper was getting short.

A messenger puffed into view. It took him a moment to spot the new emperor slumped against the wall.

'*Dominus*, the prefect Castricius sent me. Your wife and sons passed over to the lines of Odenathus some time ago, before ... before he heard that you had been acclaimed emperor.'

Ballista leapt up. His leg almost gave way as he lunged forward. He folded the messenger in a bearhug, slapping him hard on the back, kissing his cheeks. When released, the man reeled back, quite unsettled by all this imperial affection.

They were safe. Haddudad would make sure of it. Of course, Odenathus now had them, but they had survived – that was all that mattered.

'All ready, *Dominus*.'

Once more into the arrow storm. But it was different this time. The only Emesenes to be seen were on the roof of the temple. Being shot at by five hundred bowmen from two sides, they mainly kept their heads down.

Encased in their shields like overlapping tiles, the two bodies of legionaries lumbered towards the temple. Inside each *testudo*, soldiers grunted and swore at the ungainly weight of the improvised battering rams.

They passed the great altar – one of the fires had gone out – and struggled on. Overhead, the fletchings of hundreds of arrows snapped through the air. There was the occasional thump as an Emesene arrowhead hit a shield.

They were at the steps. Holding together, hauling the tree trunk, shuffling up the steps. Ballista fought down the urges to peer upwards, to cower down, to try to get free and run to safety.

A terrible crash. Thank the gods, off to the right. The statue had hit the other *testudo*. Poor bastards – but thank the gods it was them.

Sheltered under the jutting-out pediment, the legionaries

broke out of the *testudo*. No arrow or falling statue could get them here. They readied themselves. One, two, three ... now. Those with the ram swung it into the doors. A hollow boom. Plaster falling from the door frame. The doors shivered, but still stood.

The other *testudo* reached the shelter. Its legionaries shook themselves into order. Five of their *contubernales* lay twisted and broken on the steps.

One, two, three ... The two rams struck as one. The doors were massive. But their thickness was ornamental. If the god had foreseen this, the architect had not. A splintering, rending sound. The bolts and bars gave. The doors swung inward. The temple was open.

Arrows like disturbed hornets flew out at the faces of the legionaries. A man near Ballista staggered drunkenly, clawing at the shaft protruding from his neck.

Before the second volley, the legionaries charged into the cavernous gloom. They set about their grim work. Blades chopped and slashed. The air was close, thick with incense and the smell of blood.

A line of flickering candle-holders on the floor; beyond, the golden statue of an eagle, and beyond that again, dominating all, the great mass of the black stone loomed up. Huge, dense, pitiless, the top of it lost in the rafters. In front, light silks against the stone's gross negritude, Sampsigeramus.

As Ballista kicked one of the candle-holders out of the way, his right leg gave out. He crashed to the floor. A movement in the choking air. Ballista scrambled, crabwise, ungainly. The Emesene guardsman's blade sparked off the marble.

The easterner recovered his sword, raised it, came on again. On his arse, leather soles of his boots slipping, Ballista scrambled backwards. He raised his sword. His left hand was empty; somehow, his shield had gone. The Emesene struck. Ballista parried. The Emesene rolled their blades wide. With the advantages of height and weight, the easterner forced Ballista's out of his grip. The heavy *spatha* skittered away across the floor.

Ballista grabbed a big metal amphora. He swung it round to shield himself. The jar was unexpectedly heavy. It was full; liquid slopped out. The easterner chopped down. A clang of broken metal, the blade cut through the amphora, embedded itself. More liquid sloshed out – it was blood, the detritus of some sacrifice. Holding the handles tight, Ballista twisted the jar, twisted his body, put all his weight into it. They all went sideways – Ballista, the amphora, the sword, the Emesene. They landed hard in a tangle. Hands and feet skidding in the gore, Ballista scrabbled on top of his opponent. Grabbing his hair, he smashed the man's face down into the marble, again and again, in a frenzy. At first the Emesene struggled. Then he did not.

Ballista took the easterner's sword. He crawled over to a pillar and used it to pull himself to his feet. Blood slick on the marble, the dead Emesene, and, lolling out of the top of the ruined amphora, the dismembered arm of a child.

Ballista hobbled over to retrieve his own sword. He felt sick. Obviously, Sampsigeramus had stopped at nothing to try to ensure the support of his ancestral god. The sacrifice of a child had probably seemed a reasonable price to pay for his own survival.

The fighting boomed and swung through the monumental obscurity of the temple. The footfalls of the fighters echoed back as if from an age away.

Sampsigeramus still stood in front of his god. There were fewer guardsmen with him. One lunged at Ballista. The northerner took the blow on the sword in his left hand, severed the man's arm with the one in his right. The guard reeled away; Ballista limped forward.

Sampsigeramus saw him coming. He backed away. Nowhere to go. The stone was behind him. He was screaming incoherently.

The priest-king held his sword in front of him. With a savage blow, Ballista smashed it from his hand. It went spinning into the darkness.

Sampsigeramus turned. With hooked fingers and scrabbling toes, he tried to climb the side of the great black stone. There was no miracle. The smooth stone resisted his efforts.

Ballista dropped the alien sword from his left hand. He gripped the hilt of his own weapon in two hands, steadied himself and swung. The blade bit into flesh, sinew and bone. Sampsigeramus's head jerked sideways, almost severed. The killer of children, the would-be emperor, slid slowly down the side of his god. The blood that pumped so freely ran down the side of the dark stone. Deep in the shiny blackness of the god, the enigmatic markings rippled and moved.

XXIV

The sunshine was blinding after the shady corridors of the palace. Ballista stood blinking, letting his eyes grow accustomed to it. A grey horse was led out, its trappings purple and gold.

Time to go. As Ballista walked across, a groom hastened up with a mounting block. The northerner thanked him but waved him away. Even in armour, he swung up easily enough into the saddle. His leg was much better. He arranged the imperial cloak, settled the diadem on his head. Leaning forward, he patted Pale Horse's neck, murmured into his ears. *Who would have thought we would wear the purple? Enjoy it – like holding a wolf by the ears.*

There had been little time. With the death of Sampsigeramus, his supporters – the Emesene warriors, the men of the detachment of Legio III Gallica and the few Roman auxiliaries who had favoured him – had all put down their arms. Yet there had been much to do. Looting had broken out and had to be suppressed. A few high-profile beheadings, nothing too harsh – a dozen outside the palace and the temple, and a similar number in the *agora* – had taken care of that. Groups of individuals and whole units had left their stations on the city walls. They had been chivvied back into place. A large donative had to be promised to the soldiers and was then paid out of the treasures found in the palace. The family of Sampsigeramus was wealthy, and Quietus's father, Macrianus the Lame, had always been efficient in gathering money. Now, for a brief time until the bar and brothel owners took it, the *milites* were *dives* indeed. At a more exalted level, the army high command had been confirmed: Rutilus remained Praetorian Prefect and Castricius Prefect of Cavalry.

All the soldiers, from Rutilus as Praetorian Prefect to the lowest Emesene militiaman, had hurriedly taken the *sacramentum*. One from each unit had recited the oath: 'By Jupiter Optimus Maximus and all the gods, I swear to carry out the emperor's commands, never desert the standards or shirk death, to value the safety of the emperor above everything.' Then all the others had shouted, 'Me too!' It had always struck Ballista as slightly comic, but when addressed to himself, it came close to a ludicrous mime or farce.

Then there were the issues of familiarity and contempt. To how many emperors had these men given their oath? For a veteran nearing the end of his twenty years, there would have been a horde of *imperatores*: Gordian III, Philip the Arab, Decius, Gallus, Aemilianus, Valerian, Gallienus, Macrianus and Quietus. And that was if he had not followed any of the many ephemeral pretenders such as Iotapianus or Uranius Antoninus. And now there was Imperator Caesar Marcus Clodius Ballista Augustus.

So many oaths given. So many oaths broken. The new emperor knew all about that. *Gone is the trust to be placed in oaths; I cannot understand if the gods you swore by then no longer rule, or if men live by new standards of what is right?*

Ballista made a sign. Ahala rode up behind him and unfurled the northerner's white *draco*. The Equites Singulares fell in behind Ahala. Ballista waved, and they set off.

The streets were muted. Both soldiers and civilians acknowledged the cavalcade, yet the cheers were tentative, uncertain, and those he passed performed the lesser form of *proskynesis*. Of course, they knew the purpose of Ballista's ride – even if the outcome was in deepest doubt.

At the Palmyra Gate, the others were waiting on horseback. Ballista dismissed the cavalry guard, except for his new standard bearer. He spoke briefly with Castricius, who was to remain behind to ensure order in Emesa. Leaning far out of the saddle, they embraced and said farewell.

Ballista looked down the line at who would go with him. Ahala carried the *draco* directly behind him. Then, in columns of twos, were Rutilus and three senatorial governors. It had not only been the army Ballista had had to conciliate. Fabius Labeo, the noble and surprisingly resilient governor of Syria Coele, would probably have been grateful enough just to have been released from his iron cage over the northern gate. But he, like Cornicula of Syria Phoenice and Achaeus of Syria Palestina, had received substantial material inducements to join the new regime. It slightly rankled with Ballista. He had a healthy dislike of the religious bigot Achaeus but, ultimately, it was not his money. The avarice and ruthless efficiency of Macrianus the Lame had proved useful. For the moment at least, the three governors followed Ballista Augustus.

The gates squealed open. As he rode under the tall arch, Ballista saw the sculptures of the eagle, altar and black stone of Elagabalus and the innumerable scratched prayers for a safe journey. It was not his god, and it was not his way. *Allfather, Deep Hood, Death-blinder, keep your one eye on your descendant.*

The little column of six riders went on. Past the stark, stained crosses, the ornamented tombs of the necropolis. Across two hundred paces of no-man's land. Through the lines of the besieging Palmyrene army. Dark eyes, expressionless faces watched them. Up to the open space in front of the great tent, where the many standards flew.

The Lion of the Sun was seated on the ivory-trimmed *curule* throne of a high Roman magistrate. Odenathus was backed by his court. On one hand were his chief minister Verodes, two of his generals, Zabda and Haddudad, and the son by his first marriage, Haeranes – now grown into an active-looking young man. On the other stood the Romans: Pomponius Bassus, governor of Cappadocia; Virius Lupus, governor of Arabia; and Maeonius Astyanax, sometime Praetorian Prefect of the rebels Macrianus and Quietus – may their names everywhere suffer *damnatio memoriae*. In the background, but determined not to be left out, was his current wife. Zenobia was holding by the hand their infant son, Vaballathus, or Wahballat, as some called him. With her were a couple of earnest, hirsute men in Greek dress.

The entourage of the Lord of Tadmor was splendid in burnished steel, gilded armour and bright, nodding plumes. But the open space was dominated by someone else. More than half lifesize, the emperor Gallienus stood to one side. Brows furrowed, eyes hooded, the statue looked down on the scene. Ballista was reminded of a story that the successors of Alexander could only be brought to meet together if presided over by the empty chair of the great Macedonian.

Ballista dismounted. Those behind him did the same. Grooms took their horses away. Ballista took a couple of paces forward and stopped.

Odenathus rose from the *curule* chair. He was wearing a western-style corselet with big, buckled-down shoulder guards. On his arms and legs were cunningly embroidered eastern tunic and trousers. A golden brooch on his right shoulder secured a scarlet cloak; it was matched by a scarlet sash tied around his waist. His left hand was closed around the hilt of his long sword. The pommel was in the shape of a flower. The Lion of the Sun was magnificent, his painted face inscrutable.

The two principals regarded each other, in the background the unnatural silence of the crowd, the hiss and snap of the standards, the silica sounds of the breeze moving the sands – patterns fleeting across the surface.

Ballista walked to the statue of Gallienus. Under his long nose, Gallienus's beak-like mouth seemed set in disapproval. Ballista unclasped his purple cloak and set it at the feet of the statue. Then he took off his diadem and placed the strip of white material on top of the cloak.

Slowly, Ballista performed *proskynesis* in front of the statue. He got up and turned back to Odenathus.

In a confident, strong-voiced Latin, Ballista began: 'For the safety of the *Res Publica*, the soldiers demanded that I take power. Having killed the usurper, I now lay down all my power at the feet of my rightful emperor Publius Licinius Egnatius Gallienus Augustus. I give myself to his *clementia* in the person of his *Corrector totius Orientis*, Odenathus of Palmyra.'

At long last, the Lion of the Sun spoke. 'How slowly and painfully should I kill a man who has the arrogance to assume the trappings of imperial power?'

Ballista stood where he was.

'Or there again, no.' Odenathus smiled. 'By the *maius imperium* over the eastern provinces entrusted in me by Gallienus Augustus, I declare Marcus Clodius Ballista innocent of any and all charges of *maiestas*.'

The two men stepped forward, and formally embraced.

'Let them come out,' Odenathus called over his shoulder.

Isangrim, Dernhelm – his darling boys – Julia, and Maximus, Calgacus; all here, all safe.

'The throne of the Caesars is too high an eminence for weaklings like Quietus, or even for men like us,' said the Lion of the Sun.

Safe back in the arms of his *familia*, Ballista agreed.

And all unnoticed at the back, Zenobia scowled and whispered to Maeonius Astyanax.

Appendix

Historical Afterword

NB: Abbreviations mainly follow the standard forms of *The Oxford Classical Dictionary* (3rd edn, Oxford, 1996).

AD259–61

The events of AD259–61 are deeply obscure, because our sources are very poor. No two scholars agree on a narrative; neither the order in which events happened nor even in which years. Here is one example of this:

David Potter (*The Roman Empire at Bay AD180–395* (London & New York, 2004, pp. 256–7) holds that the revolts of Ingenuus and Regalianus happened in AD260 after the capture of Valerian; and that the raid by the Iuthungi and Semnones defeated in Raetia and known from an inscription (*AE* 1993, no. 1231) was part of the raid by the Alamanni which got as far as the outskirts of Rome and is known from literature (Zonaras 12.24; Zosimus 1.37.2, where they are part of an even larger 'Scythian' invasion, i.e. they act in concert with a Gothic invasion further east; cf. Eutropius 9.7, where they may be the 'Germans' who only get as far as Ravenna).

However, John Drinkwater (in *The Cambridge Ancient History* XII, A. K. Bowman, P. Garnsey & A. Cameron (eds.), 2nd cdn, 2005, pp. 43–4) holds the revolts took place a year earlier, in

AD259, before the capture of Valerian; and that the raids by the Iuthungi and Alamanni were distinct.

(NB: John Drinkwater, in his provocative recent work, *The Alamanni and Rome 213–496. Caracalla to Clovis* (Oxford, 2007), argues that the threat of the Alamanni was mainly an ideological fiction constructed by the Roman ruling class to serve its own interests. In this novel I see their threat as much more real and dangerous.)

Third-century Historiography

The third century is still understudied in English; probably because so few Anglophone undergraduate courses cover it. There is a new short, thematic introduction, with English translations of many key documents, by the Dutch scholar Olivier Hekster, *Rome and Its Empire AD193–284* (Edinburgh, 2008). Another useful work is by the Danish scholar Ragnar Hedlund, '. . . *achieved nothing worthy of memory*'. *Coinage and authority in the Roman empire c. AD260–95* (Uppsala, 2008).

Things are better on the Continent. There are several recent book-length studies: M. Christol, *L'Empire romain du IIIe Siècle: Histoire politique (de 192, mort de Commode, à 325 concile de Nicée)* (Paris, 1997); J.-M. Carrie & A. Roussel, *L'empire romain en mutation: des Sévères à Constantin, 192–337* (Paris, 1999); M. Sommer, *Die Soldatenkaiser* (Darmstadt, 2004); K.-P. Johne, *Die Zeit der Soldatenkaiser: Krise und Transformation des Römischen Reiches im 3. Jahrhundert n. Chr. (235–84)* (Berlin, 2008).

All the scholarly essays in M.-H. Quet (ed.), *La 'crise' de l'Empire romain de Marc Aurèle à Constantin. Mutations, continuités, ruptures* (Paris, 2006); and K.-P. Johne, T. Gerhardt & U. Hartmann (eds.), *Deleto paene imperio Romano: transformationsprozesse des Römischen Reiches im 3. Jahrhundert und ihre Rezeption in der Neuzeit* (Stuttgart, 2006) are relevant; as are most in O. Hekster, G. de Kleijn & D. Slootjes (eds.), *Crises and the Roman Empire* (Leiden & Boston, 2007).

Sassanid Persia

In addition to the works mentioned in *Fire in the East*, there are two excellent overviews of ancient Persia: J. Wiesehofer, *Ancient Persia from 550BC to 650AD* (London & New York, 1996); and M. Brosius, *The Persians: An Introduction* (London & New York, 2006).

Specifically on the Sassanid era are a new survey by T. Daryaee, *Sasanian Persia: The Rise and Fall of an Empire* (London & New York, 2009) and a French exhibition catalogue with wonderful pictures and useful text, *Les Perses sassanides: Fastes d'un empire oublié (224–642)* (Paris, 2006).

There is also much of interest in both P. Pourshariati, *Decline and Fall of the Sasanian Empire: The Sasanian–Parthian Confederacy and the Arab Conquest of Iran* (London & New York, 2008); and V. S. Curtis & S. Stewart (eds.), *The Idea of Iran, Volume III: The Sasanian Era* (London & New York, 2008).

The Augustan History

Also known as the *Historia Augusta* (and still sometimes as the *Scriptores Historiae Augustae*), it is a collection of Latin biographies of Roman emperors from Hadrian (reigned AD117–38) to Carinus (reigned AD283–5). They claim to be written by six men around the year AD300. They are an elaborate fraud, actually being written by one man around the year AD400. By the time the unknown author reached the mid-third century, he was writing free historical fiction. There is a complete translation in three *Loeb* volumes by D. Magie (Cambridge, Mass., 1921–32). The early lives, Hadrian to Heliogabalus, are translated by A. R. Birley, *Lives of the Later Caesars* (Harmondsworth, 1976), who also provides a clear and concise introduction to this endlessly fascinating text. For examples of the work's untrustworthiness see H. Sidebottom, 'Severan historiography: evidence, patterns, and arguments,' in S. Swain, S. Harrison & J. Elsner (eds.), *Severan Culture* (Cambridge, 2007), 52, n.2; 56–8.

People

Ballista

The meagre sources for the historical Ballista, or Callistus, as he is sometimes called, are late and unreliable. His biography in the *Augustan History* (see above) is as untrustworthy as any in that collection. Most of the sources are translated in M. H. Dodgeon & S. N. C. Lieu, *The Roman Eastern Frontier and the Persian Wars AD226–363: A Documentary History* (London & New York, 1991).

An officer under Valerian, Ballista served under the Macriani as either or both Prefect of Cavalry and Praetorian Prefect. He defeated the Persians at Soli, where he captured Shapur's harem, then at Sebaste and Corycus. He was with Quietus in

Emesa when Odenathus appeared before the walls. The *Augustan History* gives several different versions of what happened next. One of them is vaguely close to what happens in this novel.

Macrianus and His Sons

The short reign of Macrianus and Quietus can be dated roughly by papyri from Egypt. The earliest known reference to them as emperors is 17 September AD260 (*P.Oxy.* XLIX 3476), and the latest 30 October AD261 (*P.Strasb.* I 6.37–8). It all depends how long news of first their accession and then their overthrow took to reach and be accepted in Egypt.

As with Ballista, most of the literary sources are translated in Dodgeon & Lieu (*op. cit.*), and their biographies in the *Augustan History* are no more believable than his.

Their coins (whence the physical descriptions in the novel) can be found in R. Göbl, *Die Münzprägung der Kaiser Valerianus I. Gallienus/Saloninus (253/68), Regalianus (260) und Macrianus/Quietus (260/62)* (Wien, 2000).

In June 2008, Dr Nikolaos Gonis of University College London gave a fascinating paper in Oxford identifying a fragmentary papyrus from Egypt, [*P.Oxy.* inv]. 74/2, as a panegyric of the Macriani in hexameter verse. As he argued, the context does seem to be around the year AD260, but I am not yet convinced it is a work of praise of the Macriani. The poem twice mentions Mariades, the man from Antioch who became a bandit and then fled to Shapur. It is hard to see how his career or demise could have been spun to praise of the Macriani. No source says that they dealt with him.

Gallienus

Further reading on the emperor will be given in the next novel in the series, *The Caspian Gates*.

Hippothous

Calgacus is right in Ch. 14 to suspect that Hippothous's life story is from an ancient Greek novel. It is *An Ephesian Tale* by Xenophon of Ephesus. (Had Demetrius been at Corycus, he would have spotted it straight away.) For readers who want the whole story of Hippothous and much more of a similar sort, there is an enjoyable translation by Graham Anderson in B. P. Reardon (ed.), *Collected Greek Novels* (Berkeley, Los Angeles & London, 1989, pp. 125–69).

Odenathus

In addition to the works cited in *Fire in the East*, see now P. Southern, *Empress Zenobia: Palmyra's Rebel Queen* (London & New York, 2008), which is aimed at the general reader and gives good summaries of modern scholarship, if, at times, it is far too trusting of stories in the *Augustan History* (see above). The standard scholarly work remains U. Hartmann, *Das Palmyrenische Teilreich* (Stuttgart, 2001).

Places

Zeugma

The most accessible introduction in English to the twin cities of Zeugma–Apamea is N. Pollard, *Soldiers, Cities, and Civilians in Roman Syria* (Ann Arbor, 2000, pp. 257–61). The groundbreaking work of modern scholarship was J. Wagner, *Seleukeia am Euphrat/Zeugma* (Wiesbaden, 1976). Its findings are updated in D. Kennedy (ed.), *The Twin Towns of Zeugma on the Euphrates: Rescue Work and Historical Studies* (Portsmouth, RI, 1998). Since 2000, all of Apamea on the east bank of the Euphrates and a significant percentage of Zeugma on the west have been flooded by the Birecik Dam. Some details of the continuing work by the Zeugma Archaeological Project, especially its ambitious plan to turn the surviving remains into an archaeological park, can be found online.

Antioch

Sources for this city were given in *King of Kings*.

Cilicia

The essential modern works to begin to learn about Roman Cilicia, both the 'Rough' (*Tracheia*) and the 'Smooth' (*Pedias*) half, are A. H. M. Jones, *The Cities of the Eastern Roman Provinces*

(2nd edn, Oxford, 1971, Ch. 8, pp. 191–214); and D. Magie, *Roman Rule in Asia Minor to the End of the Third Century after Christ* (2 volumes, Princeton, 1950: for background, Chs. 11 & 12, pp. 259–301; and for this period, Chs. 28 & 29, pp. 659–723).

The key ancient text is Strabo, 14.3.1–5.19.

Demetrius's Cilician ethnography in Chapter 9 is constructed mainly from the First and Second Tarsic Orations of Dio Chrysostom (*Orr.* 33 & 34), and the *Lives of the Sophists*, and the *Life of Apollonius* by Philostratus.

The site of Sebaste, the modern village of Ayaş, is well worth a visit if you happen to be in the Turkish province of Mersin (although few non-Turks seem to holiday there). You can stand in the theatre where Ballista interviewed Trebellianus and, for the battle, follow his route from the south-western harbour to the north-east necropolis. Unfortunately, when I went there, the excellent little book *Elaiussa Sebaste: A Port City between East and West*, edited by E. E. Schneider (Istanbul, 2008), was not yet available. The map in this novel is adapted from there. Two things should be noted. First, the placement of the land walls is purely speculative (on the principle of excluding the *necropoleis* and including the civic buildings), the mainland part of the city actually may have been undefended. Second, the main, inner harbour was silted up by the sixth century AD; it is unclear how advanced this would have been in the third century AD.

The Barrington Atlas of the Greek and Roman Worlds, R. J. A. Talbert (ed.) (Princeton & Oxford, 2000), the standard work, does not show an island called Crambusa off Corycus. But Strabo (14.5.5) has one to the east of the Calycadnus river, which must be the islet with the castle which gives the mainland Turkish resort of Kizkalesi its name (Maiden Castle).

Caesarea Maritima

King Herod's Dream: Caesarea on the Sea, edited by K. G. Hollum et al (New York & London, 1988), is a great guide, splendidly illustrated.

Emesa

Sources for this city are given in *Fire in the East*.

Things

Valerian's Eastern Campaign of AD260

'Beyond Carrhae and Edessa we had a great battle with Valerian Caesar. With our own hands we took prisoner Valerian Caesar ...' So Shapur told it in the trilingual inscription he had put up celebrating his deeds, which is commonly known as the *Res Gestae Divi Saporis*. The sources from within the Roman empire have various stories of the capture, often involving treachery. Translations are to be found in Dodgeon & Lieu (*op. cit.*, pp. 57–66).

As Shapur placed the battle 'beyond Carrhae and Edessa', and the Anonymous Continuator of Dio (fr.3, *FGH* IV, p. 193) has Macrianus waiting in Samosata, it is likely that Valerian had crossed the Euphrates there and marched down from the north, rather than cross the river at Zeugma and advance from the west, as Crassus had done three centuries earlier.

The Ride to Zeugma

In a kind review of *King of Kings* in the *TLS*, Dr Gavin Kelly of the University of Edinburgh pointed to the material I use from Ammianus Marcellinus. The debt should be acknowledged. The last great Latin historian of antiquity was a wonderful story-teller, and is a constant source of inspiration. Never more so than here, where Ammianus's own ride to Amida was much in my mind. Ammianus is available in English translation in a three-volume *Loeb* edition by J. C. Rolfe (revised edn, Cambridge, Mass., 1950–52), and an accessible, but irritatingly abbreviated one volume by W. Hamilton in Penguin Classics (Harmondsworth, 1986).

A lot of the fieldcraft in these passages was learnt from Andy McNab's *Bravo Two Zero* (London, 1993) – which also helped with the effects of the cold in Chapter 16.

Shapur's Campaign into the Roman Empire in AD260

Every scholar who has studied it has produced a different reconstruction. The two most influential are E. Kettenhofen, *Die römische-perischen Krieg des 3. Jahrhunderts n. Chr.: nach der Inschrift Šahpuhrs I an der Ka'-be-ye Zartošt (ŠKZ)* (Wiesbaden, 1982), 106–22; and D. S. Potter, *Prophesy and History in the Crisis of the Roman Empire: A Historical Commentary on the Thirteenth Sibylline Oracle* (Oxford, 1990, pp. 337–41).

The reconstruction in this novel seems plausible to me, and I hope in the future to argue it in a scholarly article.

Bandits

Brigandage is a growth area of ancient scholarship, and will form the heart of a later novel in this series (provisional title, *The Sons of Aetna*). The social and economic background to banditry in Cilicia in *Lion of the Sun* is drawn from articles by the late Keith Hopwood; above all, 'Bandits, elites, and rural order', in A. Wallace-Hadrill (ed.), *Patronage in Ancient Society* (London, 1989, pp. 171–87); and 'Bandits between Grandees and the State: The structure of order in Roman Rough Cilicia', in K. Hopwood (ed.), *Organized Crime in Antiquity* (London, 1999, pp. 177–206).

Ballista in Palestine

The original inspirations for Ballista's operation against the Galilean bandits/rebels (Chapter 16) were a section in Ammianus (28.2.11–14) about a village of brigands in Syria (the Maratocupreni) and a story in Plutarch (24.6–8) about Alexander the Great in Phoenicia. The exact location was decided, and the caves and end stratagem added, after reading a passage in Josephus (*BJ* 1.304–14). Finally, rereading Benjamin Isaac, *The Limits of Empire: The Roman Army in the East* (Oxford, 1990, p. 63), I discovered that the Maratocupreni probably dwelt in caves all along.

In the novel (Chapter 17), the martyrdom of Marinus by Achaeus and his burial by Astyrius at Caesarea Maritima happen almost exactly as in Eusebius, *History of the Church*, 7.15–16, but, obviously, with the addition of a watching Calgacus.

Ghosts

The ghost stories Demetrius must have been reading in Chapter 2 are in *The Book of Marvels* by Phlegon of Tralles. There is a splendid translation, with good introduction and commentary, of this extraordinary book, by W. Hansen (Exeter, 1996).

Euripides

A good, short introduction is J. Morwood, *The Plays of Euripides* (London, 2002).

On the play that haunts Ballista in this novel, see W. Allan, *Euripides: Medea* (London, 2002).

Traditional thinking on the play has it that Jason had previously sworn an oath to Medea, so when he breaks it, in some senses he deserves his suffering as he brings death to his sons.

In a recent article, Arlene Allan has argued that Medea is a liar throughout the play, and that Jason had not sworn an oath to her ('Masters of Manipulation: Euripides' (and Medea's) use of oaths in *Medea*', in: A. H. Sommerstein & J. Fletcher (eds.), *Horkos: The Oath in Greek Society* (Exeter, 2007, pp. 113–24).

It should be noted that, while Jason in the play is not the brightest of men, he never denies he took an oath. The way Medea bounces first the chorus into a promise (252–70), then Aegeus into an oath (734–55), suggests she would have had few problems doing the same to Jason previously.

Other Historical Novels

As in every novel in this series, it is a joy to include homages to a couple of those novelists whose work has inspired me and given me great pleasure.

First, J. G. Farrell, *The Siege of Krishnapur* (London, 1973). Starting with comedy and cultural misunderstanding, then moving to violence and horror, this novel shows the literary excellence to which historical fiction can aspire.

Second, I don't think any extended series of novels has given me more pleasure than Patrick O'Brian's Jack Aubrey and Stephen Maturin books. They demonstrate how well-researched, well-written, thoughtful historical novels can break out of narrow, artificial genre boundaries and be ranked as literary works.

Various Quotes

The quotes and echoes of Euripides in this novel owe a lot to many different modern English translators; high among them John Davie and James Morwood.

The *Iliad* of Homer is quoted from the Penguin Classics translation of Robert Fagles (New York, 1990).

The poem – an anonymous Greek epigram – that comes into Ballista's thoughts in Chapter 4 can be found translated by Peter Porter in *The Greek Anthology* edited by Peter Jay (Harmondsworth, 1981), Number 775. The one that occurs to him in Chapter 21 is by Lucian, and is translated by Edwin Morgan in the same volume, Number 627.

When Ballista reads Plutarch, *Life of Antony* 10, in Chapter 20, it is in the translation of I. Scott Kilvert (Harmondsworth, 1965).

The Persian songs in the first chapter are from Edward Fitzgerald, *The Rubaiyat of Omar Khayyam* (1st edn, 1859) – anachronistic, but wonderful.

Thanks

As always, it is a pleasure to thank lots of people who have helped me in different ways.

First, the professionals: Alex Clarke, Anthea Townsend, Jen Doyle, Katya Shipster, Tom Chicken, Ana Maria Rivera at Penguin; Sarah Day, for copy-editing; and James Gill at United Agents.

Next, colleagues and friends at Oxford: Louise Durning and Maria Stamatopoulou at Lincoln College; John Eidinow at St Benet's Hall; and Ewen Bowie at Corpus Christi College. Various students who had a lot of Ballista in their tutorials: Laura Holloway, Harry Lancaster, Ollie Stephen and Nicky Wingfield-Digby.

Then, friends: Peter Cosgrove for Cyprus, Mersin and other stuff. Steve Billington for the website. Adi Nell for the animals. Jeremy Tinton for all sorts of odd ideas. Jeremy Habberley for lending Rutilus his looks, and Katie-girl for providing the most inventive obscenity in the book.

Last, family, for their love and support. In Suffolk, my mother Frances, and aunts Terry and Sheila. In Oxfordshire, my wife Lisa, and sons Tom and Jack.

Harry Sidebottom
Woodstock

Glossary

The definitions given here are geared to *Lion of the Sun*. If a word or phrase has several meanings, only that or those relevant to this novel are given.

Ab Admissionibus: Official who controlled admission into the presence of the Roman emperor.

Accensus: Secretary of a Roman governor or official.

A Cubiculo: Official in charge of the emperor's bedchamber.

Aelia Capitolina: Latin name given to Jerusalem by the emperor Hadrian.

Agora: Greek term for a marketplace and civic centre.

Ahriman: The Evil One, the 'Lie', in the Zoroastrian religion of the Persians.

Ala: Unit of Roman auxiliary cavalry; usually around 500-, sometimes 1,000-strong; literally, a 'wing'.

Alamanni: Confederation of German tribes. The name probably means 'all men', either in the sense of men from various tribes or 'all real men'.

Alani: A nomadic people north of the Caucasus mountains.

A Memoria: Official responsible for reminding high-status Romans, and especially the emperor, of the names of the people they meet.

Amicus: Latin, friend.

Ancillariolus: Latin, literally, a maid-chaser; a flagrantly unfaithful husband.

Angles: North-German tribe living in the area of modern Denmark.

A Rationibus: In the principate, the official in charge of the emperor's finances; later overshadowed by the *Comes Sacrarum Largitionum*.

Aquincum: City and military base; modern Budapest.

Armillae: Metal armlets awarded for valour in the Roman army.

Artagatis: The Syrian Goddess. One important cult centre was Hierapolis.

A Studiis: Official who aided the literary and intellectual studies of the Roman emperor.

Ataraxia: Freedom from disturbance of the mind/soul; the key aim of Epicurean philosophy.

Atrebates: Northern Gallic tribe famous throughout the Roman period for its woollens, especially cloaks.

Atrium: Open court in a Roman house.

Augustus: Name given to the first Roman emperor and taken by all his successors.

Auxilliary: Roman regular soldier serving in a unit other than a legion.

Ballista, plural *ballistae*: Torsion-powered artillery piece; some shot bolts, others stones.

Ballistarius, plural *ballistarii*: Roman artilleryman.

Barritus: German war cry adopted by the Roman army.

Batavia: Roman name for present-day Netherlands; roughly, the area around Nijmegen.

Bavares: German tribe; part of the confederation of the Franks.

Borani (also *Boranoi*): German tribe, one of the tribes that made up the confederation of the Goths, notorious for their piratical raids into the Aegean.

Boule: Council of a Greek city, in the Roman period made up of local men of wealth and influence.

Bucinator: Roman military musician.

Bucinobantes: German tribe; one of those making up the confederation of the *Alamanni*.

Cadusii: People living to the south-west of the Caspian Sea.

Caesar: *Nomen* of Julius Caesar; a title of the emperors; in this period often used to designate imperial princes.

Caledonia: Area of Britain north of Roman provinces; roughly modern Scotland.

Capax Imperii: Expression used by Tacitus to designate those men 'capable of being emperor'.

Cappadocia: Roman province north of the Euphrates.

Carrhae: City in Mesopotamia, in 53BC the scene of the defeat of the Roman general Crassus by the Parthians.

Cinaedus, plural *cinaedi*: Derogatory Latin term (taken from Greek – Romans liked to pretend all such habits came from the Greeks) for the passive one in male–male sex.

Circesium: Town on the Euphrates.

Circus: Latin, course for chariot-racing. The one in Rome was known as the Circus Maximus.

Clementia: Latin, the virtue of mercy.

Clibanarius, plural *clibanarii*: heavily armed cavalryman, possibly derived from 'baking oven'.

Codex: A bound book (rather than a papyrus roll).

Cognomen: Second family name of a Roman; see below, *Nomen*.

Cohors: Unit of Roman soldiers, usually about 500-men strong.

Colonia Agrippinensis: Important Roman city on the Rhine; modern Cologne.

Comes Augusti, plural *comites*: Companion of Augustus; name given to members of the imperial *consilium* when the emperor was on campaign or a journey.

Comes Sacrarum Largitionum: Count of the Sacred Largess, very important official in the late empire; controlled mints, mines, monetary taxation, pay and clothing of soldiers and officials.

Comitatus: Latin, literally, a following; name first given to barbarian war-bands and then to the mobile, mainly cavalry forces set up by Gallienus to accompany the emperor.

Commilitiones: Latin, fellow-soldiers (in Greek, *Systratiotes*), often used by commanders wishing to emphasize their closeness to their troops.

Conservator Pietatis: 'Preserver of Piety'; a slogan used on the coins of Gallienus.

Consilium: Council, body of advisors, of a Roman emperor, official or elite private person.

Contubernium: Group of ten (or maybe eight) soldiers (*contubernales*) who share a tent; by extension, comradeship.

Corona Muralis: The mural crown; an award given to the first man over the walls of an enemy position. In the principate, only officers were eligible.

Corrector totius Orientis: Overseer of all the Orient; a title applied to Odenathus of Palmyra.

Cronos: In myth, the reluctant father of the gods; as each was born, he swallowed it. Thus the expression, 'to have the eye of Cronos on you' meaning that something bad is about to happen.

Cubiculum: Latin, bedroom.

Cularo: Roman town; modern Grenoble.

Cura: Latin, literally, care; among many meanings, the care for or running of a household, which a husband might delegate to his wife.

Curule Chair: Chair adorned with ivory; the 'throne' which was one of the symbols of high Roman office.

Custos: Latin, literally, a guardian; one would accompany an upper-class woman, in addition to her maids, when she went out in public.

Daemon: Supernatural being; the term may be applied to many different types: good/bad, individual/collective, internal/external, and ghosts.

Dalmatian: Person from Dalmatia; used in the third century AD to label a type of light cavalry from the Balkans.

Daphne: Suburb of Antioch, famous for sacred sites and notorious for luxury.

Decurion: Officer who commanded a troop in a cavalry unit.

Delator: Legal accusers/informers; hated and feared but, in an empire without public prosecutors, indispensable. Their motives were often held to be mercenary; if they got a conviction, they received a financial reward taken from the assets of the convicted.

Deus ex machina: Expression from the theatre, when an actor playing a god appears via a crane over the stage buildings and sorts everything out/brings the play to a close.

Devotio: Roman ritual of devoting oneself to the gods of the underworld (to become *devotus*); a sub-Faustian pact: the gods give you what you want but take your life.

Devs: Persian *daemons*/evil spirits.

Dibir: Persian, secretary; one recorded what was said when the Persian king was drinking and read it back to him the next day – an alarming practice, probably leading to enhanced self-control.

Dignitas: Important Roman concept, which covers our idea of *dignity* but goes much further; famously, Julius Caesar claimed that his *dignitas* meant more to him than life itself.

Diogmitai: Constables in Greek cities; commanded by an *eirenarch*.

Disciplina: Latin, discipline; Romans considered that they had this quality and non-Romans did not.

Dominus: Latin, Lord, Master, Sir; a title of respect; the feminine is *domina*.

Draco: Latin, literally, a snake or dragon; name given to a wind-sock-style military standard shaped like a dragon.

Dracontarius: Roman standard bearer who carried a *draco*.

Drafsh-i-Kavyan: Battle standard of the Sassanid royal house.

Drug: In Zoroastrian religion, falsehood; see above, *Ahriman*.

Durostorum: Port city on the southern bank of the Danube; in modern-day Bulgaria.

Eirenarch: Greek, title of chief of police/the watch in many Greek cities, including those of Cilicia.

Elagabalus: Patron god of the town of Emesa in Syria, a sun god; also, name often given (sometimes in the form of Heli-ogabalus) to one of his priests, who became the Roman emperor formally known as Marcus Aurelius Antoninus (AD218–22).

Empusa: Shape-shifting creature from Greek myth; possibly more frightening to Demetrius in this novel than to most in antiquity, where it appears mainly in comic contexts, in Aristophanes, and Philostratus, *Life of Apollonius*.

Epiphania: District of Antioch.

Equestrian: Second rank down in the Roman social pyramid; the elite order just below the senators.

Equites Singulares: Cavalry bodyguards; in Rome, one of the permanent units protecting the emperors; in the provinces, ad hoc units set up by military commanders.

Equuleus: The 'Little Horse' or 'Wooden Horse'; a Roman instrument of torture, which involved the stretching of the limbs.

Erotes: Plural of Eros, the god of love; both the emotion and the god could multiply; often found in art and poetry.

Eupatrid: From the Greek, meaning well-born, an aristocrat.

Exemplum, plural *exempla*: Latin, an example to be imitated or avoided; very important concept in Roman culture.

Exploratores: Scouts; in the Roman army, these were initially temporary groups of men seconded from other units. In the second and third centuries AD, some of these become permanent formations, and other specialized units of *exploratores* were created.

Familia: Latin, family; by extension, the entire household, including slaves.

Fasces: Bundles of wooden rods tied around a single-bladed axe; the symbol of power of Roman magistrates; carried by *lictors*; origin of the modern term 'fascism'.

Felix: Latin, lucky; an attribute of emperors and some legions.

Fides: Latin, faith, as in 'in good faith', keeping one's word to men and the gods.

Floralia: Roman festival to the goddess Flora, held between 28 April and 3 May, featuring obscene mimes.

Framadar: Persian military officer.

Franks: Confederation of German tribes.

Frumentarius, plural *frumentarii*: Military unit based on the Caelian Hill in Rome; the emperor's secret police; messengers, spies and assassins.

Galli: Eastern eunuch priests.

Germania: The lands where the German tribes lived.

Gladius: Roman military short sword; generally superseded by the longer *spatha* by the mid-third century AD; also, slang for 'penis'.

Gloria: Latin, glory.

Goths: Confederation of Germanic tribes.

Gravitas: Latin concept of seriousness, importance and authority.

Harii: German tribe, renowned night-fighters.

Hecate: Sinister three-headed underworld goddess of magic, the night, crossroads and doorways.

Hel: In Norse paganism, the citadel of *Niflheim*, the world of the dead; also the name of the female monster who ruled there.

Hermanduri: German tribe; one of the confederation of the *Alamanni*.

Hibernia: Modern Ireland.

Himation: Greek cloak.

Hippodamian: Adjective applied to a planned street grid; after Hippodamus of Miletus, the famous fifth-century BC town-planner.

Hostis: Latin, an enemy, especially of the *Res Publica*.

Humanitas: Latin, humanity or civilization, the opposite of *barbaritas*. Romans thought that they, the Greeks (at least upper-class ones), and, on occasion, other peoples (usually very remote) had it, while the majority of mankind did not.

Ides: The thirteenth day of the month in short months; the fifteenth in long months.

Illyricum: Roman name for the Balkans beyond the Adriatic; vaguely applied.

Imperium: The power to issue orders and exact obedience; official military command.

Imperium Romanum: The power of the Romans, i.e. the Roman empire, often referred to simply as the *imperium*.

Impluvium: Square basin used to collect rainwater in the centre of an atrium.

Invictus: Latin, unconquered; an attribute of Roman emperors.

Iuthungi: German tribe.

Kalends: The first day of the month.

Kyrios: Greek, Lord, Master, Sir; a title of respect; the feminine is *kyria*.

Latrones: Latin, robbers/bandits.

Legio: Legion, a unit of heavy infantry, usually about 5,000-men strong; from mythical times, the backbone of the Roman army. The numbers in a legion, and the legions' dominance in the army, declined during the third century AD as more and more detachments, *vexillationes*, served away from the parent unit and became more or less independent units.

Legio I Adiutrix: The First Legion, the Help-Giver; based at Brigetio in Pannonia Superior (Szony in modern Hungary).

Legio II Adiutrix Pia Fidelis: The Second Legion, the Help-Giver, Loyal and Faithful; based at Aquincum in Pannonia Inferior (Budapest in Hungary).

Legio III Cyrenaica: The Third Cyrenean Legion; legionary garrison of Arabia, stationed at Bostra (Busra esh-Slam in Syria).

Legio III Felix: The Lucky Third Legion; mentioned only in the *Historia Augusta* (Aur. 11.4), and thus most likely fictional. In this novel, it is a unit formed of detachments from the historical Legio III Gallicana and Legio IV Flavia Felix, and stationed at Circesium (al-Busaira in Syria).

Legio III Gallica: The Third Gaulish Legion; raised by Julius Caesar; at the period of this novel, stationed either at Raphanaea (Rafniye in Syria) or Danaba (near Damascus).

Legio IIII Scythica: The Fourth Scythian Legion; from the second half of the first century AD based at Zeugma in Syria Coele (Kavunlu, formerly Belkis, in Turkey).

Legio VI Ferrata: The Sixth Iron-Clad Legion; based at Caporcotani in Syria Palestina (el-Qanawat in Syria).

Legio X Fretensis: The Tenth Legion of the Sea Straits; one of the two legions of Syria Palestina, stationed at Aelia Capitolina (Jerusalem). It took its name from battle honours won at the battle of Naulochos, near the Straits of Messina.

Legio XI Claudia Pia Fidelis: The Eleventh Legion, Claudian, Loyal and Faithful; based at Durostorum in Moesia Inferior (Silistra in Bulgaria).

Legio XV Apollonaris: The Fifteenth Apollonarian Legion; stationed at Satala in Cappadocia (Sadak in Turkey).

Legio XVI Flavia Firma: The Sixteenth Legion, Flavian and Steadfast; based at Samosata in Syria Coele (Samsat in Turkey).

Legio XXX Ulpia Victrix: The Thirtieth Legion, Ulpian and Victorious; stationed at Vetera in Lower Germany (modern Xanten).

Legio XXXI Macriani Victrix: The Thirty-first Legion, Macrianan and Victorious; a figment of Quietus's imagination; invented for this novel.

Lemuria: The days (9, 11 and 13 May) when dangerous ghosts were said to walk, necessitating propitiation.

Libertas: Latin, liberty or freedom; its meaning is contingent on when it is said and who by.

Liburnian: Name given at the time of the Roman empire to a small warship, possibly rowed on two levels; from 'Liburnia', an area of modern-day Croatia.

Lictors: Ceremonial attendants of a Roman magistrate.

Lykas (or *Polites*): Ghost; see *Temesa.*

Magi: Name given by Greeks and Romans to Persian priests, often thought of as sorcerers; see *Mobad.*

Maiestas: Latin, majesty; offences against the majesty of the Roman people were treason; being charged with *maiestas* was a grave fear among the elite of the *imperium.*

Maiuma: May festival held in many cities of the eastern empire, including Antioch and Edessa; it was nocturnal and orgiastic.

Maius Imperium: Supreme military authority; one of the two legal bases of the emperor's power (the other being *tribunicia potestas,* the power of a Tribune of the Plebs). Occasionally, others could be granted this authority, but usually only over a designated area of the empire; often, such men were imperial princes marked out and trained for the succession.

Mandata: Instructions issued by the emperors to their governors and officials.

Mardi: A people living to the south-west of the Caspian Sea.

Mattiaci: German tribe; one of the *Alamanni* confederation.

Mazda (also *Ahuramazda*): The Wise Lord, the supreme god of Zoroastrianism.

Mediolanum: Roman city in northern Italy; modern Milan.

Mesopotamia: The land between the rivers Euphrates and Tigris; the name of a Roman province (sometimes called Osrhoene).

Miles, plural *milites*: Latin, soldier.

Mobad: Persian Zoroastrian priests; see *Magi.*

Moors: In Latin, *Mauri*; indigenous people of western North Africa; much employed as light cavalry by Roman armies in the third century AD.

Mos Maiorum: Important Roman concept: traditional customs, the way of the ancestors.

Mursa: Roman town in Pannonia; modern Osijek in Croatia.

Naissus: Roman town in Moesia; modern Niš in Serbia.

Nasu: Persian; *daemon* of death.

Negotium: Latin, business time, time devoted to the service of the *Res Publica*; the opposite of *otium*.

Nobilis, plural *nobiles*: Latin, nobleman; a man from a patrician family or a plebeian family, one of whose ancestors had been consul.

Nomen: Main family name of a Roman. The Romans were distinctive in the ancient world in having at least three names each; e.g. Gaius (*praenomen*) Julius (*nomen*) Caesar (*cognomen*).

Nones: The ninth day of a month before the *ides*, i.e. the fifth day of a short month, the seventh of a long month.

Norns: In Norse myth, the three fates that weave the destinies of men, gods and all living things.

Numerus, plural *numeri*: Latin name given to a Roman army unit, especially to ad hoc units outside the regular army structure; often units raised from semi- or non-Romanized peoples which retained their indigenous fighting techniques.

Optio: Junior officer in the Roman army, ranked below a centurion.

Osrhoene: Roman province in northern Mesopotamia.

Otium: Latin, leisure time, the opposite of *negotium*; it was thought important to strike the right balance between the two to lead a civilized life.

Paideia: Culture and/or education. Greeks considered that it marked them off from the rest of the world; the Greek elite considered that it marked them off from the rest of the Greeks. Some knowledge of it was thought necessary to be deemed a member of the Roman elite.

Pater Patriae: Latin, Father of the Fatherland; a title of the emperors.

Patria: Latin, Fatherland.

Patronus: Latin, patron. Once a slave had been manumitted and become a freedman, his former owner became his *patronus*; there were duties and obligations on both sides, although unequally balanced.

Pax Deorum: Very important Roman concept of the peace between the Roman *Res Publica* and the gods.

Pax Romana: The Roman Peace; a mission statement and justification for the Roman empire; at times, such as the mid-third century AD, more an ideology than an objective reality.

Pepaideumenos, plural *pepaideumenoi*: Greek term for the highly educated or cultured.

Periplous: Greek, a list and/or diagram of ports along a coast.

Peroz: Persian, victory.

Phalerae: Metal military decorations worn on the chest.

Pharos: Greek, lighthouse; the most famous was at Alexandria.

Phoenicia: Where the Phoenicians lived; an area of the coast of Levant. 'To play the Phoenician' was a slang expression meaning to perform cunnilingus.

Pietas: Latin, piety; the human side of the *Pax Deorum*.

Pilus Prior: Most senior centurion in a unit.

Pius: Latin, god-fearing, pious; a quality of the Roman emperor.

Polis, plural *Poleis*: Greek, a city state; living in one was a key marker in being considered Greek and/or civilized.

Praefectus: Prefect, a flexible Latin title for many officials and officers; typically, the commander of an auxiliary unit.

Praefectus Annonae: Prefect of the Provisions, title of official in charge of the grain supply of Rome and of imperial expeditions.

Praenomen: Roman's first name; see *Nomen*.

Praetorian Prefect: Commander of the Praetorian Guard, an

equestrian; one of the most prestigious and powerful positions in the empire.

Prefect of Cavalry: Senior military post introduced in the mid-third century AD.

Princeps: Latin, leading man; thus a polite way to refer to the emperor (see *Principatus*). In the plural, *principes*, often denoted senators or great men of the *imperium*.

Princeps Peregrinorum: Commander of the *frumentarii*.

Principatus: Rule of the *Princeps*, the rule of the Roman *imperium* by the emperors. In English, the principate.

Proskynesis: Greek, adoration; given to the gods and, in some periods, to some rulers, including emperors in the third century AD. There were two types: full prostration on the ground, or bowing and blowing a kiss with the fingertips.

Protector, plural *protectores*: a group of military officers singled out by the emperor Gallienus.

Providentia: Latin, foresight; a quality of the Roman emperor.

Raetia: Roman province; roughly equivalent to modern Switzerland.

Ragnarok: In Norse paganism, the death of gods and men, the end of time.

Res Publica: Latin, the Roman republic; under the emperors, it continued to mean the Roman empire.

Restitutor: Latin, restorer; emperors were often hailed as restorers of the world or at least of a part of it.

Rhodion: Greek, literally, the rose garden, a district of Antioch.

Roxolani: Sarmatian tribe.

Sacramentum: Roman military oath, taken extremely seriously.

Sarmatians: Nomadic barbarian peoples living north of the Danube.

Sassanids: Persian dynasty which overthrew the Parthians in the

220s AD and was Rome's great eastern rival until the seventh century AD.

Saturnalia: Roman festival which started on 17 December and, in the period of the novel, lasted for seven days. It was a time of license and the inversion of the norms of society.

Scaenicus Legionis: Actor-soldier in a legion; many legions had troupes of such men.

Scythians: Greek and Latin name for various northern and often nomadic barbarian peoples.

Sea of Tiberias: The biblical Sea of Gallilee; large inland body of water, now called Lake Kinneret.

Semnones: German tribe.

Senate: The council of Rome. Under the emperors, it was composed of about 600 men, the vast majority ex-magistrates with some imperial favourites. The senatorial order was the richest and most prestigious group in the empire, but suspicious emperors were beginning to exclude its members from military commands in the mid-third century AD.

Serdica: Roman town; modern Sofia in Bulgaria.

Silentarius: Roman official; as his title indicates, he was charged with keeping silence and decorum at the imperial court.

Silvanus: Patron god of quarrymen.

Sinistus: High-priest of a German tribe.

Skoll: In Norse paganism, the wolf who chases, and at the end of time catches, the sun.

Sol Invictus: Latin, the Unconquered Sun; widely worshipped at this period as a god.

Spatha: Long Roman sword, the usual type of sword carried by all troops by the mid-third century AD.

Stationarii: Roman soldiers on detached duty from their main units.

Stola: Roman matron's gown.

Superbia: Latin, pride; a vice often thought inherent in barbarians and tyrants.

Symposium: Greek drinking party, adopted as social gathering of choice by the Roman elite.

Syria Coele: Hollow Syria, Roman province; often referred to as Coele Syria.

Syria Palestina: Palestinian Syria, Roman province.

Syria Phoenice: Phoenician Syria, Roman province.

Systratiotes: Greek, fellow-soldiers; *commilitiones* in Latin.

Tadmor: Locals' name for the city of Palmyra.

Tanukh: Group of Arab tribes.

Telones: Greek name for a customs official.

Temesa: Greek city in Italy; scene of a famous ghost story. Polites, one of Odysseus's crewmen, was stoned to death by its citizens after raping a local girl. He returned from the dead as a murderous *daemon*. The Delphic Oracle told the local inhabitants to propitiate him by building him a temple and every year offering him the most beautiful virgin in the town. This continued until an Olympic boxing champion called Euthymos one year fell in love with the girl chosen and beat the *daemon* in a fight. The story is in Pausanias (6.6.7–11), who had seen a painting of the story in which the revenant is called Lykas.

Testudo: Literally, Latin for tortoise; by analogy, both a Roman infantry formation with overlapping shields, similar to a northern shieldburg, and a mobile shed protecting a siege engine.

Thessaly: Area of northern Greece.

Theta: Eighth letter in the Greek alphabet; written next to the name of a deceased soldier on a military roster; in soldiers' slang, 'to be *theta*ed' was to be killed (from *Thanatos*, death).

Thrace: Roman province to the north-east of Greece.

Time of Troubles, The: Name given to Persian invasions of AD252–3.

Trierarch: Commander of a *trireme*; in the Roman forces, equivalent to a centurion.

Trireme: Ancient warship, a galley rowed by about 200 men on three levels.

Turma, plural *turmae*: Small sub-unit of Roman cavalry, usually about thirty-strong.

Tutor: Guardian legally necessary for a child, imbecile or woman.

Tyche: Greek, the goddess Fortune; each *polis* was thought to have its own *Tyche*; e.g. the Tyche of Antioch.

Valhalla: In Norse paganism, the hall in which selected heroes who had fallen in battle would feast until *Ragnarok*.

Vexillatio: Sub-unit of Roman troops detached from its parent unit.

Vexillum: Roman military standard.

Vir Clarissimus: Title of a Roman senator.

Vir Egregius: Knight of Rome, a man of the equestrian order.

Vir Ementissimus: The highest rank an equestrian could attain; e.g. Praetorian Prefect.

Vir Perfectissimus: Equestrian rank above *Vir Egregius* but below *Vir Ementissimus*.

Virtus: Latin, literally, man-ness; courage, manliness, virtue; sense far stronger and more active than English 'virtue'.

List of Emperors in the First Half of the Third Century AD

AD193–211	Septimius Severus
AD198–217	Caracalla
AD210–211	Geta
AD217–18	Macrinus
AD218–22	Elagabalus
AD222–35	Alexander Severus
AD235–8	Maximinus Thrax
AD238	Gordian I
AD238	Gordian II
AD238	Pupienus
AD238	Balbinus
AD238–44	Gordian III
AD244–9	Philip the Arab
AD249–51	Decius
AD251–3	Trebonianus Gallus
AD253	Aemilianus
AD253–60	Valerian
AD253–	Gallienus

List of Characters

To avoid giving away any of the plot, characters usually are only described as first encountered in *Lion of the Sun*.

Accius: Tribune commanding third cohort of Celts; captured by the Persians with Valerian.

Achaeus: Governor of Palestine/Syria Palaestina.

Achilleus: Gallienus's *a Memoria*.

Acilius Glabrio: Gaius Acilius Glabrio, a young patrician, one of Gallienus's *comites* at Mediolanum in AD260.

Aemilianus: Mussius Aemilianus, Prefect of Egypt (the most prestigious post held by an equestrian).

Aeneas Tacticus: Greek writer on military tactics of the fourth century BC. His *How to Defend a City under Siege* survives.

Aetion: Greek painter of the fourth century BC.

Ahala: Legionary of Legio IIII Scythica.

Albinus: Decimus Clodius Septimius Albinus, contender for the imperial throne AD193–7.

Alexander Severus: Marcus Aurelius Severus Alexander, Roman emperor AD222–35.

Antigonus: One of Ballista's Equites Singulares, who died at Arete.

Antiochus: A lost child, the son of Barlaha, a member of the *Boule* of Zeugma.

Anthia: Maid of Julia's.

Apollonius of Tyana: A philosopher/wonder-worker of the first century AD.

Appian: Son of Aristides, a Christian martyred at Ephesus.

Archelaos: King of Cappadocia towards the end of the first century BC, built a palace on the promontory at Sebaste.

Arellius Fuscus: 'Father of the Senate', i.e. most senior ex-consul, in AD260.

Arrian: Lucius Flavius Arrianus, Greek author and Roman consul, *c.* AD86–160. Several of his works survive, including *Anabasis of Alexander.*

Astyrius: Roman senator and *nobilis.*

Attalus: King of the Marcomanni, father of Pippa.

Aurelian (1): Lucius Domitius Aurelian, a Roman officer from the Danube, known as *Manu ad Ferrum* ('Hand to steel').

Aurelian (2): Tribune of the Equites Singulares, known as 'The Italian' or 'The Other Aurelian'; captured by the Persians with Valerian.

Aurelius Dasius: Roman governor of the province of Mesopotamia (or Osrhoene, as it was sometimes also called).

Aureolus: Once a Getan shepherd near the Danube, now Gallienus's Prefect of Cavalry, one of the *protectores.*

Bagoas: See Hormizd.

Ballista: Marcus Clodius Ballista, originally named Dernhelm, son of Isangrim the *Dux,* war-leader, of the Angles. A diplomatic hostage in the Roman empire, he has been granted Roman citizenship and Equestrian status, having served in the Roman army in Africa, the far west and on the Danube and Euphrates. When the novel starts, he is a prisoner of the Persians.

Barlaha: Member of the *Boule* of Zeugma.

Bathshiba: Daughter of the late Iarhai, a *synodiarch* (caravan protector) of Arete, now married to Haddudad.

Bonitus: Roman siege engineer; one of the *protectores.*

Calgacus: Marcus Clodius Calgacus, freedman of Ballista. Originally a Caledonian slave owned by Isangrim; sent by him to serve as a body servant to his son in the Roman empire.

Caligula: Gaius Julius, Roman emperor AD37–41; as a child nicknamed 'Little Boots'/Caligula, because his father had him dressed in miniature soldier's uniform.

Callistratus: Friend of Demetrius in Hierapolis.

Camillus: Tribune commanding Legio VI Gallicana; captured by the Persians with Valerian.

Camsisoleus: Egyptian officer of Gallienus; brother of Theodotus; one of the *protectores*.

Caracalla: Marcus Aurelius Antoninus, known as Caracalla, Roman emperor AD193–217.

Castricius: Centurion in Legio IIII Scythica.

Cato: Marcus Porcius Cato, known as 'Cato the Elder' or 'Cato the Censor' (234–149BC), stern moralist of the Republican age.

Celer Venerianus: Italian officer of Gallienus, one of the *protectores*.

Celsus: Pretender to the throne from Africa.

Censorinus: Lucius Calpurnius Piso Censorinus, *Princeps Peregrinorum*, commander of the *frumentarii*.

Cicero: Marcus Tullius Cicero (106–43BC), the great orator of the late republic.

Cincinnatus: Lucius Quinctius Cincinnatus, supposedly summoned from his plough to be dictator in 458BC; his duty done, he returned to his fields. An *exemplum* of old-style virtue for the Romans.

Claudius: Marcus Aurelius Claudius, a Danubian officer of Gallienus, one of the *protectores*.

Cledonius: *Ab Admissionibus* to Valerian; captured by the Persians with the emperor.

Commodus: Lucius Aurelius Commodus, Roman emperor AD180–92.

Cornelius Macer: Cousin of Quietus.

Cornelius Octavianus: Marcus Cornelius Octavianus, governor of Mauretania.

Cornicula: Annius Cornicula, governor of Syria Phoenice.

Crocus: War-leader of the Alamanni; in his own language, Hroc or Wolfhroc.

Decianus: Governor of Numidia in Africa.

Demetrius: Marcus Clodius Demetrius, the 'Greek Boy'; secretary to Ballista; originally a slave purchased by Julia to serve her husband.

Demosthenes: Officer serving under Ballista in Cilicia.

Dernhelm (1): Original name of Ballista.

Dernhelm (2): Lucius Clodius Dernhelm, second son of Ballista and Julia.

Deucalion: In Greek myth, the survivor of a world flood; a Greek Noah.

Dio of Prusa: Dio Chrysostom, the 'Golden-Mouthed'; a Greek philosopher of the first to second centuries AD.

Dolon: In the *Iliad*, a Trojan who goes on an ill-advised night-time reconnaissance.

Domitian: Titus Flavius Domitian, Roman emperor AD81–96.

Domitianus: Italian officer of Gallienus, one of the *protectores*; claims descent from the emperor Domitian.

Epaphroditus: Slave of Astyrius.

Epicurus: Greek philosopher, 341–270BC, founder of Epicurean philosophy.

Exiguus: Governor of Cappadocia under Valerian.

Fabius Cunctator: Quintus Fabius Maximus Verrucosus Cunctator, appointed Dictator (for the second time) to defend

Rome from Hannibal in 217BC. Avoiding pitched battle, and thus defeat, he earned the name Cunctator, 'the delayer'.

Fabius Labeo: Ex-consul, supporter of Macrianus.

Fabius Pomponianus: *Dux* of Libyan frontier.

Felix: Elderly senator; defended Byzantium from the Goths in AD257.

Gaius Julius Aquilius Aspasius Paternus: Elderly senator, ex-consul.

Gaius Julius Volcatius Gallicanus: Roman senator of Gallic extraction; Julia's late father.

Galliena: Female cousin of Gallienus.

Gallienus: Publius Licinius Egnatius Gallienus, declared joint Roman emperor by his father, the emperor Valerian, in AD253.

Gallus: Gaius Vibius Trebonianus Gallus, a successful general on the Danube, he defended Novae from the Goths in AD250; emperor AD251–3.

Garshasp the Lion: A Sassanid warrior who commanded the Persian forces at Circesium.

Genialis: Simplicinius Genialis, acting governor of Raetia.

Gratius: *Miles* of Legio IIII Scythica.

Haddudad: Mercenary captain who served Iarhai, Bathshiba's father; now an officer in the service of Odenathus of Palmyra.

Haeranes: Eldest son of Odenathus and first wife; thus stepson of Zenobia.

Hamazasp: King of Georgian Iberia.

Heliodorus of Emesa: Greek novelist, author of the extant *Aethiopica*; scholarly opinion is divided if he is to be dated to the third or fourth century AD.

Heliogabalus: Derogatory nickname for the emperor Marcus Aurelius Antoninus, AD218–22; he was also known after the name of his god, Elagabalus.

Heraclian: Once a Danubian peasant, now commander of the Equites Singulares of Gallienus; one of the *protectores*.

Hermianus: *Ab Admissionibus* of Gallienus.

Herod the Great: King of Judea 40–44BC; founder of Caesarea Maritima.

Herodian: Greek historian of the third century AD; his *History of the Empire after Marcus* survives.

Herodotus: The 'Father of History'; fifth century BC Greek historian of the Persian Wars.

Hippothous: Rough Cilician, claims to be from Perinthus originally.

Hormizd: A member of the Persian priestly caste; one-time slave to Ballista (then known as Bagoas).

Iarhai: A caravan protector who was killed in the fall of Arete; father of Bathshiba.

Ingenuus: Governor of Pannonia Superior; one of the *protectores*.

Isangrim (1): *Dux*, war-leader, of the Angles, father of Dernhelm/Ballista.

Isangrim (2): Marcus Clodius Isangrim, first son of Ballista and Julia.

Jadhima: Leader of the Tanukh Arabs.

Josephus: Flavius Josephus, a general of the Jewish rebellion against Rome, went over to Vespasian; his *Jewish Antiquities* and *Jewish War* survive.

Jucundus: Marcus Aurelius Jucundus, centurion of Legio IIII Scythica.

Julia: Daughter of the senator Gaius Julius Volcatius Gallicanus; wife of Ballista.

Kirder the Mobad: Zoroastrian high priest, *Herbed*, of Shapur.

Licinius: Gallienus's brother.

Lucretia: Wife of Lucius Tarquinius Collatinus; raped by Sextus, the son of Tarquinius Superbus, the last king of Rome. She became an *exemplum* of a Roman *matrona*.

Lydius: Rough Cilician, follower of Trebellianus.

Macrianus (1): Marcus Fulvius Macrianus 'the Elder'; *Comes Sacrarum Largitionum et Praefectus Annonae* of Valerian.

Macrianus (2): Titus Fulvius Junius Macrianus 'the Younger'; son of Macrianus (1).

Maeonius Astyanax: Senator, supporter of Macrianus.

Malchus: Praetorian guardsman.

Mamurra: Ballista's *Praefectus Fabrum* and friend; was entombed in a siege tunnel at Arete.

Marcus Aurelius: Roman emperor AD161–80; author of philosophical reflections in Greek, *To Himself* (often known as *The Meditations*).

Mariades: Member of the elite of Antioch who turned bandit before going over to the Sassanids.

Marinianus: Third son of Gallienus.

Marinus: Marcus Aurelius Marinus, an *optio* in Legio X Fretensis.

Maximillianus: Governor of the province of Asia.

Maximinus Thrax: Gaius Iulius Verus Maximinus, Roman emperor AD235–8, known as 'Thrax' ('the Thracian') because of his lowly origins.

Maximus: Marcus Clodius Maximus, freedman bodyguard to Ballista. Originally a Hibernian warrior known as Muirtagh of the Long Road, he was sold to slave traders and trained as a boxer, then gladiator, before being purchased by Ballista.

Memor: African officer of Gallienus; one of the *protectores*.

Messalina: Valeria Messalina, wife of the emperor Claudius; notorious for immorality.

Minos: Mythical King of Crete; had the labyrinth built to contain the minotaur.

Morcar: Son of Isangrim; elder half-brother of Ballista.

Nero: Nero Claudius Caesar, Roman emperor AD54–68.

Nicostratus of Trapezus: Greek historian; his history from Philip the Arab to Odenathus does not survive.

Odenathus: Septimius Odenathus, Lord of Palmyra/Tadmor, a client ruler of the Roman empire.

Palfuerius: Rough Cilician, follower of Trebellianus.

Palfurius Sura: *Ab Epistulis* of Gallienus.

Perilaus: *Eirenarch* (chief of police) in Soli.

Pippa (or Pipa): Daughter of Attalus of the Marcomanni; known as Pippara to Gallienus.

Piso: Gaius Calpurnius Piso Frugi, a senator and *nobilis*, supporter of Macrianus.

Plotinus: Neo-platonist philosopher, AD205–69/70.

Plutarch: Mestrius Plutarchus, Greek philosopher and biographer of the first to second centuries AD.

Polykritos of Aitolia: The subject of one of the most bizarre ghost stories from antiquity; *see* Afterword: Ghosts.

Pompey the Great: Gnaeus Pompeius Magnus, 106–48BC; Roman general.

Pomponius Bassus: Marcus Pomponius Bassus, elderly patrician.

Postumus: Marcus Cassianus Latinius Postumus, governor of Lower Germany.

Priscus: *Trierarch* of the galley *Concordia*.

Quietus: Titus Fulvius Iunius Quietus, son of Macrianus the Elder.

Quirinius: Gallienus's *a Rationibus*.

Ragonius Clarus: Gaius Ragonius Clarus, senator, supporter of Macrianus, Ballista's legate in Cilicia.

Rebecca: Jewish slave woman bought by Ballista.

Regalianus: Governor of Pannonia Inferior; claimed descent from the Kings of Dacia before the Roman conquest.

Romulus: Standard bearer to Ballista, died outside Arete.

Rufinus: Gallienus's *Princeps Peregrinorum*, spymaster, commander of the *frumentarii*.

Rutilus: Marcus Aurelius Rutilus, prefect of a cohort of Thracian auxiliaries.

Saecularis: Senator, Prefect of the City of Rome.

Salonina: Egnatia Salonina, wife of Gallienus.

Saloninus: Publius Cornelius Licinius Saloninus Valerianus, second son of Gallienus, made Caesar in AD258 on the death of his elder brother, Valerian II.

Sampsigeramus: Priest-king of Emesa.

Sardanapallus: In Greek myth, a decadent oriental Assyrian king.

Sasan: Founder of the Sassanid house.

Selurus: A bandit leader active in Sicily in the late 30s BC; known as the 'Son of Etna'.

Seneca: Lucius Annaeus Seneca, philosopher and politician of the first century AD.

Septimius Severus: Lucius Septimius Severus, Roman emperor AD193–211.

Servius: Syrian prefect of an *Ala* of auxiliary cavalry.

Shapur I (or Sapor): Second Sassanid King of Kings, son of Ardashir I.

Silvanus: *Dux* of the Rhine.

Simon: Simon-bar-Joshua, a young Jewish boy rescued by Ballista and taken into his household.

Successianus: Praetorian Prefect under Valerian.

Suren: Parthian nobleman, the head of the house of Suren, vassal of Shapur.

Tacitus (1): Cornelius Tacitus, *c.* AD56–*c.*118, the greatest Latin historian.

Tacitus (2): Marcus Claudius Tacitus, Roman senator of third century AD (most likely) of Danubian origins. He may have claimed kinship with or even descent from the famous historian, but this is unlikely to be true. One of the *protectores*.

Theodorus: Senatorial governor of Cyprus.

Theodotus: Egyptian officer of Gallienus; brother of Camsisoleus; one of the *protectores*.

Theotecnus: Bishop of Caesarea Maritima.

Tillorobus: Bandit active in Asia Minor; Arrian wrote his biography, which does not survive.

Titus Esuvius: Once a Roman soldier.

Trebellianus: Gaius Terentius Trebellianus: a man of influence in Rough Cilicia.

Turpio: Titus Flavius Turpio, army officer and friend of Ballista; executed by the Sassanids.

Valash: Persian Prince, 'the joy of Shapur', a son of Shapur.

Valens: Senator; governor of Syria Coele.

Valentinus: Governor of both the provinces of Moesia Superior and Inferior.

Valerian (1): Publius Licinius Valerianus, an elderly Italian senator elevated to Roman emperor in AD253; captured by Shapur I in AD260.

Valerian (2): Publius Cornelius Licinius Valerianus, eldest son of Gallienus, grandson of Valerian, made Caesar in AD256; died in AD258.

Vardan: Captain serving under the Lord Suren.

Verodes: Chief minister to Odenathus.

Vibius Passienus: Senator; governor of Africa.

Virius Lupus: Governor of Arabia.

Volusianus: Lucius Petronius Taurus Volusianus, Gallienus's Praetorian Prefect, an Italian risen from the ranks; one of the *protectores*.

Wahballat (or Vaballathus): Son of Odenathus and Zenobia.

Zabbai: Palmyrene general serving Odenathus.

Zabda: Palmyrene general serving Odenathus.

Zeno: Aulus Voconius Zeno, equestrian governor of Cilicia.

Zenobia: Wife of Odenathus of Palmyra.

Zik Zabrigan: Persian commander, *framadar*, at Corycus.

Warrior of Rome

PART IV

The Caspian Gates

Read on for a taster of the next instalment
in the *Warrior of Rome* series

Prologue

(The Caucasus, Autumn AD259)

*A family formed by crime must be broken
by more crime.*

Seneca, *Medea* 55

The man was wounded and unhorsed, but he was alive. At the top of the slope was a stand of mountain pines. In cover, back against a tree, the man tried to listen for the pursuit. He could hear nothing over his own agonised breathing.

The shaft of the arrow had snapped when he crashed from his mount. The arrowhead was embedded in his left bicep. The blood still ran hot down his arm. The pain came in sickening surges.

He was a fool to have agreed to hunt bear. Lonely wooded glens, many armed men; it was all too easy to get isolated, then all too easy for an *accident* to happen. He was a fool to have trusted his brother. There had always been something not right about the youngest of them. The presence of their sister and her retinue had lulled him. If only he had remained close to her. His brother and his followers would have attempted nothing then. The man knew he had been a fool, and now he would die. He despaired.

This was not right, not for a descendent of Prometheus. The man tried to control his sobbing. On the peaks above, Prometheus had been persecuted. Spiteful Zeus had hung him in chains. Every day, with the sun, the eagle had come. Its cruel, sharp beak lunging into the soft flesh, tearing, slicing, gobbling down chunks of Prometheus' delicate, dark liver. With the night, the eagle left. As the cold winds blew and the snow flurried, miraculously the liver was healed. And then, with the dawn, the eagle returned. Thirty years of torment until Heracles had shot the eagle and freed the man's ancestor.

Prometheus was a lesson in endurance, in suffering overcome, of ultimate redemption. Who should learn it better than his distant offspring? The man drew a slower, deeper breath; still ragged, but more in control. He forced the pain away and kept very still. He listened. All was quiet, so quiet you could follow a mosquito by its hum.

The hunters were out of earshot, at least temporarily off the trail. After the ambush, he had ridden some distance before the pain-induced inattention and the low branch that had swept him off his horse. The horse had bolted. He was alone.

The man looked around. The copse was shot through with shafts of weak sunlight. It was quite considerable, and not of pine alone. Here and there blazed the autumnal reds and golds of beech, maple and birch. There was no undergrowth, but the trunks and low branches, the odd fallen tree, all gave some cover.

The man turned his attention to the arrow. Thinking of it brought back the pain. He forced it down again. His left arm was almost useless. Using his teeth and the dagger in his right hand, he cut the sleeves of his sheepskin coat and linen tunic away from the wound. He had to bite his lip hard when the material pulled clear. The blood started to flow fast again.

The man unstoppered his wine flask. Not pausing to dwell on it, not giving cowardice an opportunity to undermine his resolve, he poured the alcohol over the wound. The pain was searing. He drummed his heels, clenched the discarded sheepskin in his teeth. Not crying out, he cleaned the wound.

The pain, the stench of greasy sheepskin, its revolting lanolin taste; the man spat and then retched. The convulsive movement made the pain worse. He fought for control. He used the mental tools at his disposal. Imagine the pain as a red hot ember, his arm as a fennel stalk. Force the ember down inside the stalk. Let it glow there in the dark, smoulder, do its worst; you can carry it for miles, the surface of the fennel barely warm to the touch.

The pain somewhat mastered, the man sniffed the wound. Nothing, just blood and wine; the homely waft of sacrifice. Relief ran through him. They had not used the most potent of local poisons, not the one whose mere scent could injure or blind. If they had employed another, it probably mattered little. Every morning, like all his family, he had climbed the ladder to the top room of the tower. There his father had unlocked the big, bound chest, had measured out the portions. Every morning the seven of them – father, mother, the four boys and their sister – had drunk down a little draft of every poison except one known in the region. It took a time, there were many poisons known in Suania. Endless innocent mornings vitiated by nausea and pain, but all worth it on a dreadful afternoon like this one.

There was an inch or so of splintered shaft protruding. It was inscribed with strange markings. The arrowhead was barbed. It could not be pulled out. He could cut it out. But he would scream, and bring the hunters down on him. He sat and thought.

He unbuckled his bow case and quiver. They are useless to a one armed man. He took two straps from them. One he tied tight above the wound. The flow of blood slowed almost instantly. The other he fashioned into a sling. He regarded the bow case for a time. He considered his weapons. On his belt a sword and dagger, another two daggers, one hidden in a boot, the other in the lining of his coat. He pulled a bowstring from the case, and, gripping one end in his teeth, made it into a lariat.

Somewhere in the distance a hound gave voice and a man called. The main body of the hunt or the assassins? There was no way to tell. It was time to move, time to decide what to do.

Leaving the bow case and quiver, the torn scraps of clothing, the bloodied ground, the man moved off through the trees, away from the direction in which he had come. He tracked up the slope until he came to a small glade. Through the break in the foliage he could see the sky; a hard, distant blue. Darkness would fall within two hours. He looked north to the mountains. The Croucasis lived up to their Scythian name, in the cold sunshine their flanks were still 'gleaming white with snow'. But the mountains were smoking. Wisps of vapour curled up towards the peaks, coalesced into a dark cloud at the very summit. The first snows would fall here in the upland valleys in an hour or so. Darkness would come early. Not long to stay alive.

The man felt sick again; sick and weak. He thought for a moment, then, taking a slightly different angle, stepped back into the trees the way he had come. He cast about for a place to lie up. A great fallen beech, its dying branches fanned up, abutted a standing evergreen. He settled himself into the space between the screen of dying deciduous leaves and the grey lichened trunk of the pine.

The man was shaking slightly. He did not know if it was cold, or fear and the shock of betrayal. Fumbling, he fed himself some cold pheasant and a little flat bread from the pouch on his belt. He had never trusted his youngest brother, not since childhood. Somehow he had always known things would not go well for him if he fell into his hands. From the wine flask he poured libations to Prometheus, Heracles and Hecate, and prayed; especially to the dark goddess of revenge.

It was still dead calm in the wood. The storm would not get here very soon. He had to decide what to do. Hiding here did not seem good. He would get colder and weaker. He would get discovered and killed. He needed to be on the move. But where?

Listening hard, he shut his eyes and thought. He could try to get back to the main body of the hunt. Among his own retainers and his sister's men he would be safe. He would have to avoid the assassins. His brother would have them spread out searching, maybe they were already following his trail. He did not know how many there were; he had seen only two. Had there been several more, unwounded the man would have put money on ghosting past them. He had always been good on the hill and in the forest. But he was wounded; slowed down and in pain.

There were sledge tracks off to the left. The first snows next to never closed the nearest pass. Despite the lateness of the season, there would be Scythian nomads, Alani or more likely men from their subject tribes, still driving their herds back north over what they called the Croucasis.

If the man could fall in with a group of the Scythians, he would be safe. Obviously they were aware of his father. Last spring they would have handed over to his father's men fleeces, hides and slaves to be allowed to make the passage south. It might be that his own name was not unknown among the Scythians. The nomads would protect him. Of course he would have to cross the mountains with them, spend the winter out on the plains. And come next spring, they would not need fleeces or slaves. His safe return would open their way. But the man cared nothing for that. He would be alive to be ransomed; alive to take revenge on his youngest brother.

A strange languor was creeping over him. The Scythians would be in a good mood. The bellies of their animals full of the sweet, meadow grasses of Suania, their own saddlebags stuffed with apples and pears. They were going home. A winter with the Scythians would not be so bad. Drifting after the flocks across the wide plains of the nomad sea. Their tents would be snug; braziers lit, a pleasant fug of conversation, food and drink. The women of the Alani were said to be tall, beautiful and wanton. Their men were complacent. All you had to do was hang your quiver outside her tent and the husband would go off and leave you in peace until you had finished enjoying his wife.

The sharp ring of metal on metal snapped the man's eyes open. He held his breath, listening. Nothing. Slowly he turned his head side to side; eyes wide. Nothing. He knew he had not imagined it. Up above the top branches were stirring with sluggish menace. The storm would get here soon.

His arm hurt like a Christian on the pyre. He tried to push the red hot ember back into the fennel stalk. Careful not to make a sound, he wriggled his toes, with his good hand massaged his thighs, tried to get feeling back into his legs.

Another sound. Off to his right, a careless footfall. In the gloom, the man grinned. He had always been good on the hill. Another sound. There was his brother's creature, not above twenty paces away. Alternately the hunter bent to peer at the ground, following the trail, and stood scanning ahead. He had a bow in his hands, arrow notched, half drawn. His jerky movements betrayed his nerves.

You are right to be nervous, thought the man. If I had two good arms and a bow, you would already be dead, shot as easily as a sitting pheasant. Even with one arm, I have marked out for Hecate.

The hunter stopped at the edge of the glade; just as the man had hoped a pursuer would. It was an obvious place for an ambush. Anyone would fear that as you stepped into the clearing an arrow might whistle out from the tree line ahead. Only the deepest thinking would suspect anything from behind.

The man eased himself to his feet. Oddly his left arm, though still incapacitated, had ceased to hurt. He studied the way first he, then the hunter, had come. The wind hissed through the branches. Nothing else; no human movement or sound.

The man glided forward, feet placed carefully, the lariat in his right hand. The gathering storm covered his approach.

The hunter still hesitated. The man closed behind him. An innate warning of danger; the hunter began to turn. Too late. With fluid movements, the man slipped the noose of bowstring over the hunter's head, yanked the slip knot tight around his neck, pulled as hard as he could.

Instinctively the hunter's fingers scrabbled at where the cord bit deep into his throat. There was no purchase to be had. Blood ran down his neck.

The man, left shoulder braced between the hunter's shoulder blades, exerted all his strength. Boots slipped and stamped on the forest floor. The man's breath came in harsh, animal pants. The hunter's was a death rattle. Convulsions, then a heavy stillness. A foul smell of voided bladder and bowels. The man continued to choke the life out of the corpse.

'Impressive, brother, you have killed him five times over.'

The man's youngest brother emerged from the shadows of the wood. Above him branches whipped this way and that. The tails of his long native coat were thrown back, the sleeves hung empty. In his unencumbered hands was a drawn bow.

The man turned, dragging the body round to act as a sort of shield. 'This will not look like an accident.' He spoke to buy time, to distract. Slipping his injured arm from the sling, despite the pain, he took the weight of the dead man with it. Out of sight, his right hand drew the dagger from his belt.

'Indeed not, brother. It is no accident. You were waylaid by a band of Alani. A tragedy.'

Fifteen or so paces on either side of the speaker two more hunters materialized up the hill out of the darkening wood. Hoods up, menacing, like creatures from Hades. The three bowmen were well spaced, grudgingly the man recognized good tactics.

'Who can say what happened,' his brother continued. 'Everyone knows those nomadic barbarians are irrational, bloodthirsty – eaters of flesh. Robbery, ransom, who knows what they were after? Perhaps you resisted – you always were the brave warrior, our father's favourite. Whatever happened, they killed you. Shot you down like a deer.' He smiled, gloating. 'Have you noticed the arrow in your arm was made by the Alani?'

The man did not answer the rhetorical question. While his body was perfectly still, his eyes flicked this way and that, measuring, estimating. He did not intend to die here, not at the hands of his brother.

'We have more than enough Alanic arrows. Do you not admire my foresight? You were always the brave one. I was always the one with foresight. Do you remember how our old tutor always admired my disquisitions on the quality of *Pronoia*. Odd how the old Greek's philosophical idea seems so much more real here than it ever did in the classroom.'

The first snowflakes were falling, twisting and turning in the gusting wind.

The man grimaced through the pain in his arm. 'And did the philosopher's lessons in ethics not do you any good? Who should you love if not your brother?'

'Oh, but I do, brother, I do. Both love and admire.' The voice was unctuous. 'Because I admire you, I think it certain you will follow the heroes to the Islands of the Blessed. And because I love you, I will send you there forthwith.'

'My death will do you no good.' The man's thoughts were racing. The dialogue had to continue, had to win him time. 'Our father will not name you his heir. If I am dead, he will turn to one of our brothers. Failing that old Hamazasp of Iberia or whoever our sister marries. The council of three hundred would be happier with any of them than you. The members of the *synedrion* will never willingly accept you.'

The darkness was gathering. Straight ahead, thought the man.

Throw the dagger; kill or wound my brother. Run straight ahead. The bowmen on either side should be reluctant to shoot and risk hitting my brother or each other. Prometheus, Hecate, hold your hands over me.

'Enough talk.' A new voice; a female voice. Out of the gathering storm walked their sister. Her face was very pale, her lips a deep red in the half light. She too held a drawn bow.

The man knew then it was all over.

'Enough philosophizing.' She addressed herself to the younger brother. 'You are not now the least of four boys sat at a teacher's feet. Stop your ears to clever words and remorse. Show yourself a man.'

It was all over with him, but the man was not going to go quiet, not like a sacrificial animal. In one move, he let go of the corpse, threw the dagger, and launched forwards. The dagger spun through the falling snow. The younger brother twisted his head. The dagger caught him in the face; opened up his cheek. He dropped his weapon, reeled away, howling.

The man had made three steps when the first arrow hit in the thigh. He managed another two steps before his leg gave way. The late autumn grass rising up, bruising his face. The thump and searing pain as another arrow found its mark in his back. Fingers clawing in the turf, pulling him forward. Prometheus, Hecate . . . The pain of another arrow, and another, and another. The fingers stopped working. The darkness surged up.

The snow was falling heavily in the glade. It was settling in the sightless eyes of the corpse. The living siblings of the dead man stood close together, right hands clasped. One of the two hunters had tied their thumbs together. The brother had a knife in his left hand. Deftly he cut their bound thumbs.

'Neither with steel nor poison,' he said. Leaning forward, he licked the blood from his thumb then that of his sister. 'Sealed and countersealed in blood.'

The girl repeated the words. She dipped her head, and her red lips parted and her tongue curled around his thumb.